APPRENTICE TO THE VILLAIN

APPRENTICE TO THE VILLAIN

#1 *NEW YORK TIMES* BESTSELLING AUTHOR

HANNAH NICOLE MAEHRER

Preview of *The Games Gods Play* copyright © 2024 by Abigail Owen.

Entangled Publishing, LLC
644 Shrewsbury Commons Ave., STE 181
Shrewsbury, PA 17361
rights@entangledpublishing.com

Red Tower Books is an imprint of Entangled Publishing, LLC.

Visit our website at www.entangledpublishing.com.

Edited by Stacy Abrams
Cover illustration and design by Elizabeth Turner Stokes
Interior map art by Elizabeth Turner Stokes
Interior design by Britt Marczak

TP ISBN 978-1-64937-717-3
B&N Edition ISBN 978-1-64937-760-9
Ebook ISBN 978-1-64937-553-7

Printed in the United States of America

First Edition August 2024

10 9 8 7 6 5 4 3 2 1

RED TOWER BOOKS™

To my brothers, Avery, Jake, and Ben, for every time you made my heart lighter even at its heaviest and for every time you told me I smell (I know that was code for I love you).

And for all of you, this is what I think it would be like to be the morally gray fantasy villain's apprentice.

Apprentice to the Villain is a laugh-out-loud fantasy romance with severed fingers rolling across the office floor and a murder incident board that hasn't left 0 this quarter. As such, the story features elements that might not be suitable for all readers, including familial estrangement, perilous situations, graphic language, battle, violence, blood, death, torture, injury, imprisonment, illness, burning, drowning, accidental intoxication, and alcohol use. Readers who may be sensitive to these elements, please take note.

RENNEDAWN
EVIL 4EVA
SAVE THE VILLAIN!
THE GLEAMING CITY
EVIL TO-DO LIST:
☐ ENACT REVENGE
☐ BE DASTARDLY
☐ CHAOS
☐ CONFUSION

NOT HIM-
SAVE ME!
KISSING CAVES
HICKORY FOREST
HEART VILLAGE
LANDS
EATER
/5★
EVIL RULES
LILAC SEA

PROLOGUE

Once upon a time…

It was an ordinary day for The Villain, aside from his body being on fire.

Evie Sage's first week on the job was terrible—at least for Trystan Maverine. Wax dripped from one of the candles before him onto the parchment he was reviewing, just missing the tiny rim of its holder. He sneered at it. Its defiance mimicked the woman he'd hired when he'd been bleeding out and losing all sense of himself in Hickory Forest.

An excellent time to make life-altering decisions about new hires.

In his defense, he'd been certain she would quit almost immediately. But the woman was unbreakable. He'd tried everything, and not short of murder— he'd done that, too. But even a body on her desk didn't make her or her wretched smile falter. No matter what tasks he threw her way, no matter the danger or the disgust they should've evoked, she smiled. And worse yet, she *stayed*. Her persistent presence inspired a feeling that he couldn't figure out for the life of him.

He could sense her standing off to his side, practically glowing with heat, like an array of flickering light. Light he had to fight to stop himself from looking at, like it was physically tugging at his attention, his mind. But he wouldn't let her distract him. Instead, he stared intently at the deep onyx of his desk, where another drop of wax fell. He was near the tipping point—he could feel it like lighter fluid tipping near a powder keg.

The correspondence in his hands wasn't helping. *Blasted nobles.* Another invitation from Lord Fowler, the only noble in the land willing to do business with The Villain. It would have been a mark in his favor, if the lord didn't consistently send him dinner party invites. May as well send him dynamite.

Fortunately, friendliness over mail correspondence was easy to ignore. It was decidedly less so when the source of friendliness was a mere five feet away, smiling and…dear gods, was she *humming*?

No one should be this cheery. It was unnatural.

He wondered if the assistant he'd hired was, in fact, not human—perhaps she was some sort of manic sun sprite that had never seen darkness. And unfortunately, that unnatural disposition didn't end with her. Her contagious energy was spreading through the office faster than the Mystic Illness, which had been brutally claiming victims through Rennedawn for the last decade. He seemed to be the last one unscathed by her. His workers seemed happier, the murderous depictions on the stained-glass windows brighter; even his guards seemed more amiable, less bloodthirsty.

He'd seen an intern skip through the office that morning. That had been his final straw.

Sage let out a second hum from across the room. He wanted to grab her shoulders and demand to know where it came from, this endless well of pleasant emotion. She hummed again, and his eye twitched. He was wrong. *That* was his final straw.

He turned from his correspondence, his mouth open to chastise her, but stopped when he took in the dreamlike state of her expression. She was leaning into the wide-open office window, her profile illuminated by the moon and stars. The night air caressed her dark hair, creating the illusion she was flying. He stared at the slope of her nose, almost…charmed?

Something had to be done.

He tore his gaze away from her before growling, "This paperwork won't sort itself, Sage." He glowered, his calluses sliding over the smooth parchment as he pretended to sort the pages. A corpse on her desk might not be the thing that broke her, but late-night paperwork had an honest chance.

Her face danced into view as she neared his desk, nose scrunched as she angled her head toward him, black curls falling over her shoulder. "But wouldn't that be convenient!" she responded brightly.

He was going to be sick.

Coughing, disgusted by the warmth spreading through him, he looked back toward his desk, at Kingsley—one of his oldest friends and his near-constant companion for the past decade. The once-human prince was the reason Trystan was in this mess in the first place. Kingsley's wayward walks had led the amphibian right into the arms of the king's magical guard. Which had led Evie Sage right into the arms of Trystan, literally. He could still feel her warm body pressed against him; her hair had smelled of roses.

The troublemaking frog's crown currently was slipping precariously to the side as he held up one of his signs. It read: PRETTY.

"You think I'm unaware of that?" Trystan grumbled, taking the sign from the precocious frog's tiny, webbed foot, then slamming it face down on the desk before Sage could see it.

"Unaware of what, sir?" she asked. *Shit.*

"How your daydreaming is interfering with getting this done in a timely manner," he grumbled, glaring when Kingsley shook his tiny head at him. *I won't be commanded by a damned frog.*

Sage practically floated back to his desk, her light eyes a meld of mischief and sincerity. "I wasn't daydreaming. I was making a wish." Her bright-green skirts covered in little flowers swirled around her as she cast the full force of her joy at him.

He almost ducked.

But he distracted himself with her comment instead. "A wish?"

She sat down in the new chair across from him, pushing her curls away from her face, grabbing a stack of papers to sort. "Didn't anyone ever teach you that stars listen for wishes?" she asked, perplexed, as if *he* was the absurd one.

"I was never afforded that particular lesson in school," he replied dryly and turned his attention back to a report from the head of his Malevolent Guard, Keely.

Her brow furrowed. "Oh, no, I didn't learn about stars in school. I learned from my mother and her family. Uncle Vale was an expert on them. My cousin Helena and I used to spend our summers learning of them—we'd lay in the grass at night just talking to the sky. It was fun." Her joyful eyes were suddenly far away, the smile faltering just for a second. But he tracked it. Odd.

She kept speaking regardless—on instinct, it seemed.

"My school lessons were never so interesting, but I missed them after I left."

He trained his eyes on the candlewax on his desk. "Your education was not listed on your résumé."

She was too casual in her response. "I had to leave after my mother disappeared. My father had his business, and someone needed to stay home with my little sister."

Don't press. It matters not.

"How old were you?" he asked. *Damn it.*

He heard the papers in her hands rustle. She must have been gripping them firmly. "Thirteen."

His chest went tight.

Kingsley had another sign up now, clearly meant for him. The frog swung it in front of his face. Ass.

"Sage, I—" He halted his words. An apology tipped against his tongue. *An apology?* The Villain didn't *apologize*. The mere urge to do so stunned him so much, he closed his lips.

Her surname hung awkwardly in the air between them. He crumpled up a letter and threw it in the waste bin so he wouldn't look at her, but of course he ended up looking anyway.

A horrified mien had overtaken her cheery facade. Her horror turned sheepish when she caught his uncomfortable stare. "Oh— Oh, I'm sorry. I don't usually talk this much."

Well, that certainly wasn't true. In the last seven days alone, he'd heard the little liability speak more than any other human being of his acquaintance… and he alarmingly could recall every word.

"I think you are lying." He said it gruffly, not kindly.

"Oh, I am," she deadpanned and then promptly giggled. "About the talking, anyway, but I *am* sorry."

There was that sunny ease she possessed. So quick to apologize. She made it look so simple. "It's fine," he grunted.

She brightened, and he blinked. Did he do that?

"I must be growing comfortable with you," she observed. My gods, the woman was like the sun. He needed tinted glasses just to look at her.

He squinted and frowned. "Well, comfort is unacceptable in this office. Perhaps now you *should* apologize."

She bit her lip, but the curve upward came through anyway. Her head turned back toward the window, toward the brightest star gleaming through it. Wistful.

Too much to bear. He needed her out of here. Now.

Before he could scare her off, though, she looked back to him, her cheeks blushing a rosy hue. Her small fingers loosened on the papers in her hands as she said with the most open sincerity, "I'm sorry. But it's true. This is the best job I've ever had."

He muttered a curse under his breath. It had felt like a blow, so harsh he was almost knocked backward. He pulled at his collar so he wouldn't choke.

The mystery feeling that appeared after every test he'd given her, after she smiled through them, finally revealed itself. Relief.

His heart pounded, signaling the danger in the emotion, but he sucked in a breath anyway and replied, "I'm…pleased to hear it." He stood, taking the papers from her hands. She released them readily. "You're dismissed for the day, Sage. I think I've tortured you enough."

Her eyes flashed to his office doors as she stood, too, placing a hand against her hip and lifting a brow. "I don't think the men downstairs in the dungeons would agree, sir."

He choked and hit his chest to smother the laugh, the urge shocking him. Instead, he flattened his lips into a firm line. "Unless you'd like to join them, I suggest you take your leave."

She scrunched her nose once more before making her way toward the door, but she stopped again to look out the window, something drawing her to the pearly gleams up in the sky reflected in her eyes.

He couldn't help it; he didn't know why. But he had to know.

"What did you wish for?" His words came out in a raspy whisper.

She faced him fully as she slowly backed all the way to the door, reaching behind her and gripping the handle. There was a soft look on her face that made his bones feel like jelly. "I'll let you know when it comes true."

The door closed gently behind her, and the stars glimmered once more in the corner of his eye. He scoffed at them and moved swiftly to his desk, digging in the top drawer for a caller's ruby. Wishes. Ridiculous.

The caller's ruby, like many other gems in his possession, was used to communicate with the members of his guard. Different sectors had different magically enchanted jewels depending on status, but this situation called for the Ruby Sector. The most lethal. His favorite.

He swiftly called an order for someone qualified to follow Sage into the darkness, to make sure she arrived home in one piece. There were many dangers in Hickory Forest, waiting to sink their claws into someone precisely like that young woman, and he'd already invested a week of his time into her. He wouldn't let that go to waste.

I won't let her *go to waste.*

After all, what good was having an assistant…if they were dead?

CHAPTER I

THE KNIGHT

"Evie Sage is dead."

The knight's words echoed through the airy entryway of the king's study, rebounding off the opulent walls like a cry of mourning.

King Benedict's face was tipped down, his unblemished hands flat against the pages of an open book. The sunlight from the large window spilled over the silver-lined pages, its heat making the room stifled and cloying. The knight fidgeted beneath his tight armor, but when the king's head tilted up, he went deathly still.

This was a mistake.

King Benedict shut the book, and the light from the sun dimmed a little, like it was disappointed. He stood slowly, a sympathetic smile tipping at his lips.

"A pity," he said, rubbing a hand through his sandy-colored hair. There were only a few small streaks of gray in it, which was surprising for a man of the king's advanced years. "The poor girl was corrupted by The Villain. I suppose, though, in its own way, it was a merciful death. There's no saving someone who has tread so close to the darkness. Now she can be at peace." It was self-satisfied, the king's smile.

I hate you.

The knight's fist tightened at his side, but he released it before the king could notice. He nodded. "You are ever merciful, my king." The words burned on his tongue.

Benedict's eyes narrowed as he gestured to a cushioned chair. "Please have a seat. The journey back to the palace must have been strenuous. How does Sir Ethan fare? He remained with you to see the job done, did he not?"

The knight moved carefully toward the red velvet chair; the cushion gave as he lowered to sit. Only his green eyes were visible beneath his helmet as he gently corrected, "Sir *Nathan*, Your Majesty."

"Ah yes! Sir Nathan." The king chuckled.

The knight said bluntly, "Dead."

"Oh?" The king's brows shot up.

The knight said the words exactly as he'd practiced. "Otto Warsen, I'm afraid, became a bit lustful for blood. I dispatched him myself after he turned on Sir Nathan and me." He was proud he kept the shaking from his voice at the lie.

The king did not appear saddened, a shock to no one—well, at least no one in the room. "Very well. The fewer loose ends, the better. I trust that you took care of Warsen's corpse?"

The knight's lips twitched beneath his helmet, remembering exactly how Mr. Warsen's head had been...*taken care of.* "Yes, my king."

More sweat began to build at the back of the knight's neck. He knew what the king was about to ask him.

"And Evie Sage's body? May I see it?"

Stray light from the window slid against the back of the knight's hands, now covered by a fresh set of gloves. No blood splatters. The light gave him a sense of peace as he said, "I'm afraid the healers need time to repair her wounds and make her presentable, as you requested. They ask your benevolence in not being disturbed while they work."

Silence followed. The knight held his breath lest the king notice his rapidly moving chest. *Keep it together*, he ordered himself, sure his heart was pounding so loudly the king could easily hear it.

The king smiled; it did not reach his eyes. It never did. "I suppose I can oblige them. Just be certain she's prepared for the unmasking at the end of the week."

The knight nodded, slowly exhaling. "Yes, my king." He didn't need to ask about what this "unmasking" was. The king was rather good at boasting about his achievements.

I give it three, two, one—

"Come the week's end, we are to unmask The Villain in front of every notable noble in the land." *Huh, I thought he'd only make it to two.* But His Majesty *was* eager. Something manic shone in his eyes as he boomed the news.

"A true accomplishment, my king." The knight squinted to fake a smile.

"Congratulations."

The king stood with a flourish, his fur-lined cape flying behind him as he tossed a book from his desk onto the small tea table in front of the knight. It jarred the wood, rattling the silver chalices with mere drops of wine left inside. He could use a cup. Or several.

"It is only the beginning of a new era for Rennedawn."

The knight's brows shot to his hairline. That sounded...ominous.

The king kept speaking. "Presenting Evie Sage as the perfect victim will solidify the kingdom's hatred for The Villain. Finally, proof of all his wrongdoings—" He gestured to the book, the cover an opulent array of shimmering colors. *"Rennedawn's Story."*

The children's fable? *Rennedawn's Story* was the epic tale of how Rennedawn came to be and the enchanted rhyme that would save its fading magic, supposedly handed down by the gods themselves—though more often heard from the mouths of parents chastising children. Each of the magical kingdoms on the continent of Myrtalia held its own origin story, many equally outlandish or nonsensical. The knight had never seen a published version of Rennedawn's before today, but the colorful cover did little to proclaim the text's legitimacy. Was the king having trouble differentiating between fiction and truth?

Perhaps his crown is a little too tight.

Though there were whispers, rumors, that Rennedawn had truly begun to fade into the earth. If the story were true...

Could there be merit to those rumors?

The king sighed. "I'm afraid that to ensure we remain the strongest of the magical kingdoms, I need you to do me a great favor."

The king had asked the knight for *many* great favors, and every time, without fail, his reply was, "Yes, my king."

"I need you to go to the Sage family home and retrieve Nura Sage's letters. Return them promptly by the day's end."

The knight proceeded cautiously. "Whatever His Majesty commands. But might I ask what need you have of them?"

"I'd been hopeful that the older Sage girl might possess the same powers as her mother, but despite Griffin's best efforts, the girl was useless." Benedict tapped his chin and gave a mock frown. "Well, useless *alive*." The knight remained impassive. "In any event, the letters will help us find Nura's location. She hasn't been seen in years."

The knight's voice barely leveled above a whisper. "And the younger Sage girl?"

The king waved a hand. "As good as dead. Taken by The Villain's horde."

The cloying heat had become so suffocating, the knight felt dizzy. "And what of the guvres, sire? The venom of one of their lets? I was of the understanding you need them, too. Starlight and Fate, or something to that effect?"

A vein pulsed in the king's forehead, but his face remained blank. He reached down, retrieved the book, and placed it gently in a crystal-paneled case by the windows. His clear, almost melodic baritone rattled the walls with his disdain.

"Fortunately, I have in my possession just the man to help with that."

The knight knew who he meant, but a shiver still cooled the heat in his blood.

The Villain.

CHAPTER 2

THE VILLAIN

The Villain didn't miss light. He missed color.

Trystan's eyes drew upward, head ringing against the wails of the other prisoners trapped with him in the dark. The stone beneath his palms was rough against his clammy skin, the only thing grounding him through the unending blackness. It was like death, the dark. Death without peace, a dark without light—the pain in his limbs was the only indicator that he was alive.

His heart rate climbed; he couldn't breathe. There were no bars to hold on to. No power to summon, like his mist had been walled in, trapped like him. But he could feel it twisting and curling inside him. It begged for freedom— that made two of them.

"Enough." He stumbled, and his shoulder landed blessedly against a bumpy, uneven surface. Brick. Thank the gods. There was a wall, its sturdy weight comforting against his greatest fear: the dark. His blistered hands followed its curve around and around, but there was no end in sight. Where was the godsdamn door?

He halted to take a deep inhale. *Breathe, Trystan.* He had to get out of there, had to find Sage. Evie—Otto had Evie, was hurting—

No. He couldn't focus on that now. Not yet.

He kept following the wall, feeling from top to bottom. Moving himself in an endless mind-altering loop. For minutes? Hours? He didn't know.

Fatigue forced his eyes to close for a moment. What difference did it make? There was no way in the deadlands he'd be able to break out of here— not with his magic out of commission. This wasn't his cell in the king's summer home: it was a chamber meant specifically for his imprisonment, his torture.

The irony was not lost on him.

Hopelessness was a horrid feeling, not to mention a useless one. But he felt hope leech away as he dropped to his knees for the second time that day.

He groaned, missing indifference, missing smothering his feelings like banking a fire. It was preferable to the burning eating at his insides. But he'd been powerless against indifference with Sage. He knew that now, just as he knew—prickling awareness raised the hairs on his neck—he knew he wasn't alone in this room.

"You look just terrible, my boy."

Rage pulsed behind his aching eyes, his vision futilely straining to see Benedict before him. The king had devices for hunting in the dark, had used them during Trystan's first stay in order to torment him. In another life, he might have admired the showmanship, but in this one, he merely wanted to kick the king's teeth in.

Pushing himself to stand on shaking legs, he struggled to speak evenly. "Ah, well, I'm sure that's a comfort to you, Benedict. Like looking in a mirror."

Benedict chuckled. "Now, now. No need for hostilities. I've merely come to talk to you."

"The torture's starting already?"

Trystan knew the blow was coming, waited to gauge its direction. The fist landed in his gut so hard, the air knocked from his lungs and his knees gave out. Did the guard have steel knuckles on? By the gods, that hurt.

Benedict chuckled again. A sharp, disorienting pain stabbed at Trystan's middle as he inhaled. It was no matter; he knew pain, knew agony deeper than the waves of the Lilac Sea. He'd learned long ago to lean in to the hurt instead of away from it.

Rough hands closed a tight metal cuff around each of his wrists, rubbing the skin there raw as he railed against the chains, pulling them taut against the wall. The feeling of immobility was worse, somehow, than the pain had been.

The king's voice was mocking. "How disappointing. I'd hoped for a civil conversation."

"I've never been very good at social niceties." The splintering pain was throbbing in his side now. Wonderful. He'd bruised a rib.

The king hummed. "Then I'll get to the point. I need the mated guvres—promptly."

It was Trystan's turn to laugh. "And why in the deadlands would I give you anything?"

"Shall I shed some light on the issue?" A sound rustled, and then the room was flooded with dim torchlight. Tears burned in Trystan's sensitive eyes, and he blinked harshly. "There. Now you can see me more clearly."

"The horror. Put it out."

Another blow to the gut, but he was able to see the fist this time and brace for it. *Small miracles.*

He could see Benedict now, too, in the light of the torch he was holding: hair perfectly groomed, in well-tailored clothing, making Trystan's now visibly torn shirt look like rags. "I'm giving you the opportunity to redeem yourself, Villain. The guvres are essential to the future of this kingdom and all its people. This is your final opportunity to redeem all the harm you've wrought."

Trystan sneered. "And what about the harm you've wrought?" He disdainfully scanned Benedict from head to toe, knowing the ire it would invoke. "I suppose you think your crimes are excusable, so long as you commit them in the dark."

The king swallowed, his shoulders going tense, as if he was physically restraining himself from striking out. "You don't know what is at stake, you damned fool."

There was a precipice that Benedict was teetering on, and Trystan could sense the bubble of truth building behind Benedict's snide lips. Pride would be the king's downfall—he knew it like the moon knew the stars and the grass knew the sun. All Trystan had to do was press at the right wound.

"All your failures finally catching up to you, Benedict?" Trystan smiled.

A vein bulged in Benedict's forehead as he moved closer, just out of reach. "I haven't failed. I've been failed, first by you, then by the female guvre." Benedict paused, eyes alight in dangerous satisfaction. "Fortunately for me, mistakes can be rectified. Beginning with Evie Sage's poor, deluded mother."

It was a call to war, mentioning her name. A quick flash of white-hot anger seared across his skin, distracting him from the words, from the truth Benedict shouldn't have revealed.

What did the king want with Sage's mother?

Trystan tried his hardest to keep his face blank, but he'd flinched in time with her name. Benedict smirked at the reaction, likely knowing now what that name did to him, after how he'd begged for her. How odious, to have your failings displayed outright; how wickedly painful.

Trystan steeled himself against it, raising his shoulders back an inch, playing the game. "Keeping a newborn guvre in captivity could hardly keep you in Fate's good favor, Benedict. You kept the female trapped for nearly a decade—that couldn't have been without consequence."

The king smiled. "Who said it wasn't?"

Trystan gritted his teeth, resolved not to give the king a damned thing. But curiosity bit at him like a rabid hound.

The king's mask of gentility cracked when Trystan kept his mouth shut. "You are a selfish wastrel." Benedict's lip curled in distaste. "I made you my apprentice. I taught you everything I know; I molded you in *my* image. Not only that, I trusted you to do what's best for this kingdom, watched as you endeavored to help me save it...and as you tragically failed."

The sting in Trystan's chest, behind his eyes, it wasn't real. He didn't need to feel it if he didn't want to; he was in control. He sniffed and blinked away the liquid beginning to blur his already straining eyes, his torso protesting as he stood up straight. "Terrorizing the kingdom is so much more fulfilling than noble heroics. I'm glad I outgrew them."

I won't be shaken.

"Besides." Trystan sneered, a surge of anger energizing him. "I helped you in my own way. I became The Villain of the tale—and isn't that what you *really* needed?"

The king smiled and nodded toward the doors, signaling the guards to leave. He didn't want them to hear what came next. He waited until they were gone to speak again. "I don't know what you could possibly mean."

"I helped you scour the kingdom for starlight magic, if you recall. I helped you catch the female guvre. I watched as you identified my magic just to use it against me. I'm not a fool, Benedict. I knew those things were connected—my spies have heard the rumors of *Rennedawn's Story*. There's no need to pretend any longer."

Benedict raised a hand to strike, but he caught himself, swallowed, and lowered it. "You're so like your mother. Then again, I suppose Arthur wasn't around enough to give you much of his temperament."

The king spoke like he knew his parents well, but Trystan would have to mull on that later. For now, he was too distracted thinking of Arthur, his father, who had been captured by the king's men and—he felt a stone sink in his gut—falsely accused of being The Villain. "Surely now that you have me, you'll release Arthur."

"All in good time, my boy." Benedict turned, torch still in hand, making his way to a sliding-open wall, all the light fading away with him. "I *will* have the guvres, no matter the cost."

As the darkness crept back in, Trystan lurched forward, suddenly desperate. "Benedict." The king halted, his back turned. "My assistant is of great value to my business. If anything has befallen her, if she's been harmed in any capacity…I will ruin you. And I will be sure to do it in broad daylight for all to see." His gravelly voice was low, calm despite the jitteriness in his body.

The king turned, sensing the threat. Evie's face appeared in Trystan's mind; he couldn't keep it at bay any longer. Her tears, her screams as Otto Warsen wrapped his disgusting hand around her mouth. Trystan's physical wounds were nothing compared to the piercing ache pressing against his heart. He hadn't felt so defenseless in more than a decade. His body couldn't handle the strain of it all, the raw urge to protect her while being completely helpless to do so.

The king tilted his head, furrowing his brow in mock sympathy. "Did I forget to tell you? My apologies—"

Trystan could almost feel the words coming before the king said them. The foreboding suddenly made the darkness look like home. How fitting.

"She's dead."

CHAPTER 3

THE VILLAIN

Seven days later

Sage is not dead.

The sun had disappeared beyond the horizon, but the night sky seemed to almost be mocking him with its brightness, teeming as it was with stars.

The guards had dragged him from the dungeon, his limbs like sandbags thanks to the magical cuffs sapping his strength. He'd maintained his will thanks to one irrefutable truth, repeated like a mantra these last few days.

Sage is not dead.

The king had to be lying to torment him—a valiant effort, Trystan had to admit. But Benedict hadn't factored in that he and Sage were irrevocably linked by a gold ink bargain: an employment tool that was originally supposed to ensure loyalty from his new assistant but had instead become a way to monitor her safety. Though Sage was still under the impression the inked gold band around her pinkie finger would kill her if she betrayed him, he quietly vowed to tell her the truth when he saw her again.

And he *would* see her again.

It would be a disaster, of course. The way he would take perverse delight in her face flushing with anger and her nose scrunching. How she'd yell at him, and then the flush would go all the way down her chest, dipping below her bodice, at which time, naturally, he'd be distracted by it and stop listening. She'd notice and yell at him some more.

He couldn't wait.

The chains at his wrists were long enough that they dragged to the floor, which was appallingly filthy and sticky with grime—even his dungeons weren't this vile. But there were windows, and he could see, and at least the chains no longer bound him to the wall, so all in all, lovely upgraded accommodations.

"Could I get a corner cell?" he asked the guards through the bars. He'd barely spoken in the last however many days had passed, and one could hear it when the words croaked out, like sandpaper against stone.

"Shut it, you lout! I hope the king guts and hangs you after the unmasking." The guard on his left pulled on one of his chains, and he stumbled.

"Will you be unmasking as well?" Trystan asked gruffly.

The guard lifted his helmet to expose his gaunt face and what Trystan assumed was an eternally scowling expression. Did Trystan look like that when he scowled?

"I'm not wearing a mask," the guard said.

He sighed. "Pity."

The guard's face twisted with rage as he raised a fist. "You godsdamn—"

But the man was stopped by the guard to Trystan's right. "Stay your hand, Sir Seymore, and worry not. I will be the one to bring him into the ballroom for the unmasking." This new guard's deep voice sounded oddly familiar, but his face was covered, only his green eyes visible.

Had he seen those eyes before?

While Trystan was contemplating that possibility, his own eyes drifted toward the end of the hall. His vision was still blurry and strained from so long without light, but he could make out the brown door, slightly ajar. His tongue pressed to the roof of his mouth—*an escape route*. Was he to be taken to the unmasking immediately? The open door should've looked like doom, but all he saw was freedom. He simply needed a good enough distraction and a way to remove the magically suppressing cuffs cutting off the blood supply to his wrists...

His gaze roamed over a larger window beyond the bars, and the night sky blinked back at him. Of course, he knew it was irrational to wish, but as the star out the window twinkled, daring him to—as it had once before—he found himself doing it anyway.

He wished to find Sage.

He wished to tell her he was sorry.

He wished to be better about revealing how he felt, bit by bit.

And perhaps, most importantly—he wished to have a godsforsaken tea party with her little sister, Lyssa.

It felt ridiculous, but it was that thought that somehow energized his languid limbs as he heard the green-eyed guard unlocking his cage.

Not yet. Not yet. NOW.

He sprinted through the open door, the chains dragging behind him, the metal biting into his hands as he gripped it. The muscles in his legs burned as he ran, but he couldn't stop—the exit was so close. His breaths were coming in uneven pants, his sock-clad feet making him slide against the stone. Gods knew where his boots had disappeared to.

Mildly mortifying, he thought through breathless gasps, *how hard I fought to keep them.* They'd been a gift from Sage.

Nearly to the door, he could hear the guards yelling behind him. The loudest voice belonged to the green-eyed knight, who was begging him to halt. The pure desperation—and was that a hint of fear?—in his voice made Trystan pause as he put a hand on the door.

"Don't go in there, Mr. Maverine. You'll regret it, I swear." *Ah,* Benedict had finally revealed Trystan's true name to the Valiant Guards. It would no doubt spread to the kingdom next, the Maverine name damned, his family ruined.

Intolerable.

Not that they would be affected—but that he *cared.*

He pushed on the door and heard Benedict's satisfied voice from behind him. He should've paused, should have listened to the warning bells in his head, but his mind and body had gone haywire; he couldn't trust his instincts any longer. They were as good as a broken compass.

This was why he could ignore the malicious subtext in Benedict's order. "No, men. Let. Him. Go. Let him *see.*"

Trystan didn't wait, just exited the hall and sprinted to what was hopefully a stairwell but—no. It wasn't a stairwell; it was a small room.

And what he saw inside proved once and for all that wishes were not made for people like him.

Only horror.

CHAPTER 4

THE VILLAIN

Trystan had never believed death to be beautiful.

It was logical in his mind, necessary—even enjoyable, if the person very much deserved it. But never beautiful, never so achingly difficult to look at that his entire body froze, his muscles tightening so hard that they pulsed beneath his flushed skin. Never so painful that his brain could not connect the pieces of what he was looking at.

For on the marbled white table before him, in the small room with stone walls and dim, flickering light, lay his assistant, Evie Sage.

Dead.

Shock settled in the marrow of his bones, in the startled stiffness of his legs. His eyes were burning again, but not from the light. From the *pain. Move*, his mind ordered Sage, but she lay still, unnaturally so. More still than he'd ever seen her. A woman who had always been buzzing with erratic energy, her mouth never tiring of the words that spilled out—and now he waited for them to say something, anything.

But her red-painted lips were closed in a flat line, unexpressive. So unlike her, it was startling. *Impossible.*

He took a shaky step forward, ignoring the creak of the wooden door behind him and the clanking of armor that followed.

"I'd hoped to spare you this, as a final kindness." So at odds with the merciful words, Benedict's voice was dripping with disdain. But Trystan wouldn't turn, couldn't give Benedict his attention.

His eyes were on Sage, on the way her black hair was artfully spread around her, like an ethereal halo of curls, with small, colorful flowers placed throughout it. A lump formed in his throat as he stepped forward, his emotions hidden behind a wall of disbelief. Until he saw them.

Black-and-purple fingerprints around her throat.

He shut his eyes tightly. His fists clenched so hard at his sides that his nails broke through the blisters in his palms.

Benedict spoke again, closer this time. "Worry not, my dear boy."

Trystan sucked in a deep inhale.

"She didn't suffer...*much*."

His eyes flew open. His fists unclenched. An eerie calm settled over his face, and for just a moment, the world was still.

And then that moment was over.

"You *bastard*!" His voice was guttural as he dove for Benedict, the chains on his wrists suppressing the magic raging beneath the surface, though it was no matter—he had his anger. It was primal, it was white-hot, it was *enough*. Flames licked at his skin, his heart pounding as he surged forward.

Benedict slammed against the wall, his crown toppling off his head and clattering at Trystan's feet. The king's eyes flared with fear. *Good.* Trystan knew fear far better than the turbulent emotions ravaging his insides. The guards gripped each of his arms, desperately trying to pull him back, but he was stronger.

He had nothing to lose now.

He closed both hands around Benedict's throat, squeezing as hard as he could manage with his wrists chained and two guards furiously pulling against his tensed biceps. Benedict's eyes widened as he choked, struggling to breathe.

Squeezing harder still, Trystan felt his conscience—small as it was—reemerge. Suddenly, it was no longer King Benedict looking at him; it was Evie. Her sweet eyes brimming with tears, terrified. She was choking, dying. *Oh gods.*

His hands had never felt more like a danger as he released them, the guards finally managing to yank him backward. Back toward Sage, back toward where she rested. His head angled to the side, taking her in, ignoring the backdrop of Benedict's cursing gasps as Trystan stumbled toward her.

It didn't matter. Nothing did. All he saw was her.

Swallowing hard, he moved until he was right there, dropping to his knees beside her.

"Sage," Trystan said on a whisper. "Sage, wake up." He scanned her face. Her eyes were closed, dark lashes laying gently against the tops of her cheeks—cheeks that were pale without their usual rosy hue. "I command you as your employer to wake up."

He could feel his blood pumping harder through his body, felt it accelerate further still when his mind finally connected the truth to this reality. Sage, Evie, the woman who owned the entirety of his blackened, tattered heart, was well and truly gone.

A hot rush of liquid burned behind his eyes. "That's an order, Sage." He rasped out the command with none of his usual authority. "Open your eyes."

He looked to her hands, both wrapped around a small bouquet of white roses, and he took hold of one. It was like ice, the inked gold employment ring on her smallest finger faded against her skin, all the magic gone. He didn't feel it, couldn't help her. He'd thought the inked bond hadn't glowed against his biceps because of the magic-suppressing cuffs, but that wasn't it at all. It hadn't glowed because there was no life left in it, no life left in *her*.

As he tried to blink back the hot liquid, a single tear escaped down his cheek. He brought her hand up and laid his lips like a whisper against her knuckles, so light that he knew it would barely be felt, should she still be with him. "I failed you. I'm sorry. Come back."

She didn't answer, wouldn't, and it occurred to Trystan then that he would never hear her voice again. Her excited yells, her infectious laugh, her melodic humming, her jokes, her candor. It was a piece of his world he'd taken for granted, and now it was gone forever.

Just as everyone he encountered, everything he touched, was left ruined.

He'd been so selfish. Since the day he hired her, he'd made her a target. He'd foolishly believed that if he ruined with purpose, it could never happen by accident again. That being The Villain would save him.

Instead, he'd destroyed the one person who'd looked past it all, who'd not only truly seen him but who didn't flinch when she did.

Gods, he would never forgive himself for this. *Never.*

Sir Seymore took his arm in a viselike grip, but he barely felt it. Two more guards joined in, and then another two. It took that many people to drag him away from her. He yelled until his voice was raw, bucked and flailed against their hold, but he wasn't strong enough. Not anymore.

Still, he kept fighting anyway, fighting until he couldn't, until his weakened limbs gave and his vision went spotty, until all he saw as he was dragged through the doorway back toward his open cell was the last remaining knight, the one with the familiar eyes.

And he was mouthing something.

Something that looked suspiciously like the word *"hope."*

It was so strange that it distracted Trystan from his despair. He furrowed his brow as the knight disappeared behind the closing door.

Hope? Why would a Valiant Guard want The Villain to have hope?

It didn't matter. Hope would do nothing. Evie Sage was dead.

CHAPTER 5

BECKY

This plan was dangerous.

These people were pompous.

And worst of all, *she* was out of her mind for agreeing to go along with this walking HR violation in the first place.

"You're stepping on my foot," Becky growled at Blade, who stood beside her dressed in the finery of a nobleman, the pristine fabric stretching awkwardly over his large arms. Whatever aristocrats Tatianna had nicked their disguises from, Blade's was obviously from a gentleman who didn't ever engage in the sorts of physical activities the dragon trainer met with on a day-to-day basis. Like wrestling with a reptile twice the size of a house.

Still, he looked handsome, which sent a ripple of annoyance through her.

"My apologies, lovely Rebecka." The low timbre of his voice raised the fine hairs on her arms, as did the way he smiled at her. Her stomach flipped at the half curl of his lips, teasing and warm all at once. A rather lethal combination.

A rather horrific one, actually. Intra-office relations are highly discouraged, Becky, remember?

With a furrow in her brow, The Villain's HR manager looked to the rest of the party. The ballroom was the largest she'd seen, and in another lifetime, she'd seen her share. The vaulted ceilings gave the illusion that the room was wide and endless, the crystal chandelier glinting with hundreds of candles. Nobles wanted only the best, and this world was built to readily give it to them. It was unfair to the rest, and oh how she despised when things were not fair.

Her most recent example? Being stuck with Blade.

"I wish you'd pay more attention." She skewered him with a look of censure, her most intimidating look—her best, really.

His amber eyes, so often filled with mirth, grew intense as he replied, "I promise you: I do." And then, without warning, he reached out and gently pushed her glasses back up her nose. She hadn't even noticed they'd slipped.

But he had.

Her heart fluttered, and she railed against it. *Knock it off, you little traitor.*

"Thank you," she said, surprised and alarmed by the softness of her voice. Where in the deadlands did that come from?

Blade was surprised, too, judging by the way he gaped and the slight crack in his voice that he tried to disguise with a cough. "You're, uh, you're welcome."

The unsureness she experienced in their interactions was growing entirely unpleasant. She'd agreed to work for The Villain to *escape* her chaotic life, to have order. Instead, she had been handed a healer who dressed in frilly pinks, a boss's assistant who was the human version of a cannonball, and a filthy dragon trainer who smiled so brightly at her it burned her corneas.

But now that he was not smiling…she felt oddly bereft.

This is what I get for agreeing to a social gathering. Work-related or not, it compromises one's principles.

When she left her family, she'd vowed to live by solitude and organization as the only ways to find even a semblance of comfort in this mixed-up world. Which made her decision to join in on this mission even more confounding, considering she could barely stand the lot of them on a good day. Nonetheless, she found she couldn't allow them to do this without her. Besides, it was simply another opportunity to tell everyone where to go and what to do.

She happened to be quite excellent at that.

She was also excellent at keeping to a schedule, a skill the king clearly lacked. How long had they been standing here, waiting for the unmasking to begin?

Blade lifted a brow, following her eyes to the large, gilded clock that hovered between the ornate windows. He cupped a hand around his mouth as he leaned in, his breath tickling her ear. "Wasn't it supposed to start at nine o'clock?"

"Yes!" she cried, mildly embarrassed by the outburst.

He somehow managed to look incensed on her behalf. "Unacceptable. Do you want Fluffy to singe them into ash for you?"

She arched a brow and folded her arms. "Would the dragon do that on my behalf?" Becky angled her head back to him, startled by the seriousness on his face.

"I have it on good authority the dragon would do anything on your behalf." He blinked, almost as if coming out of a trance, before returning to his cheery demeanor. "If he ever manages to light more than a birthday candle, that is."

There was a spell on this room—it was the only explanation for the disappointment she felt when he returned to the sunshine expression he gave to everyone. The intense one had oddly felt…like it was meant just for her.

A subject change was needed, and quickly. "Do you think they managed to—"

But she cut off on a gasp as Blade gripped her by the hips, nearly shoving her until her back landed hard against the wall, his arms caging her in the alcove.

Her heart raced, and a wild excitement heated her blood as she gawked behind the lenses of her large glasses. "Mr. Gushiken, unhand me at once!" She was too close, so close she could smell the cedar on his skin. It was disarming.

He winced, looking apologetic, but he didn't move his hands. He kept them almost protectively around her head. "It appears my father has decided to attend his first celebration at the Gleaming Palace. I never imagined he'd come. He's not usually one for social mingling." Ah, she'd forgotten that Blade had grown up here, his father a political advisor to the king.

She licked her lips, and his eyes dipped along with her stomach. "I suppose it won't do if you're recognized."

"No." The rasp in his voice made her shiver.

Three loud thuds echoed throughout the vast space, calling the attention of the entire party. It caused Blade to remove one hand so they could both see King Benedict standing atop the grand staircase.

"Welcome! Welcome, my honored guests, to The Villain's unmasking!"

The crowd bowed before cheering as several Valiant Guards came through the open doors behind the king, dragging a figure with them: a man dressed impeccably in black, from the mask around his eyes to the shiny boots at his feet. The cheers turned to boos.

"Boss," Blade whispered, his voice laced with concern.

The Villain was dragged down the marble steps, stumbling as he went, wrists chained, mouth set in a firm, harsh line. He never flinched, not even when a Valiant Guard chained him to the pole jutting out from the middle of the raised dais on the back wall. There was already another man chained beside him—one with long red hair and a red beard.

"Arnold," Blade whispered.

Becky turned to look at him, pausing her tumultuous thoughts. "The Core Healer's name is Arthur."

Blade frowned. "Are you sure?"

"Yes! And we hardly have time for this!" she chastised.

A ragged breath escaped the dragon trainer, but he kept his body angled over hers, like he was shielding her from the rest of the room as the king continued.

"Tonight, we finally end The Villain's decade-long tyranny, and we mourn those we've lost by his violent hands." The king bowed his head in solemn salute, but Becky swore she saw the tiniest of smirks flash across his mouth. "Behold The Villain's final victim!" he announced as he raised his head. "A light forever extinguished by darkness. The daughter of a beloved knight. Our own Evangelina Sage."

Becky felt her eyes bug out of her head as a large, adorned glass coffin was dragged through the side doors to the center of the room. The crowd hovered around it, making it difficult to see.

"This is unacceptable," she bit out when the clock struck ten minutes past.

"Rebecka!" Blade yelled as she pushed her way through the crowd, but she stopped when her path to the gilded coffin was finally clear.

Evangelina lay within, still as death. *No, this is wrong. Something went wrong.* This was never the plan…

The king's voice boomed through the room once more as Blade gripped her shoulders from behind, cursing when he saw Ms. Sage.

"Together, on this night, we enter a new era for Rennedawn, as my Valiant Guards and I begin our quest to complete the prophecy of *Rennedawn's Story.* For if we fail…"

Another hint of a smirk dusted the king's lips before it disappeared, though not before Becky committed the small movement to memory.

"Our kingdom will cease to exist."

The crowd erupted.

CHAPTER 6

THE VILLAIN

"Look at me!"

Arthur Maverine was calling to Trystan, but he pretended not to hear. The blur of his black mask obstructed his peripheral vision, leaving him only the view of the audience throwing food at his feet. Everything felt slower, duller, like time had faded the world into something he no longer recognized.

"You swine!" a member of the gentry yelled, lobbing what appeared to be a cream puff at his feet.

He frowned at it. "What a horrible waste of pastry. I'd rather they throw rocks." He said the words, emotionless, in an attempt to ward off Arthur's insistent prodding.

"Trystan, we must get you out of here before you are unmasked." There was pleading in his father's voice, but it did not touch him—nothing would. He'd numbed his emotions so completely at this point, he wasn't sure he could feel anything anymore.

Sage is gone. What does any of this matter?

He sniffed, frowning again at the desserts discarded around his shiny-booted feet. Benedict had had him dressed for the occasion, likely wanting him to look formidable instead of tattered and weak. It wouldn't do for The Villain to have the audience's sympathies.

"It is fruitless to worry for the Maverine name, Arthur. I've already quite readily destroyed it."

Arthur sputtered beside him. "Th-That is hardly my concern at present, son! Nor should it be yours."

Trystan lifted a brow beneath his mask and finally looked at his father.

"My concern is for the poor cream puffs, actually."

Arthur glared at him, all the while fighting against his own chains. "Be serious, Trystan. Your future is at stake."

Trystan scoffed, fists clenching behind him. "What future?"

Arthur must have followed as Trystan's eyes were drawn to the coffin; he couldn't look away, wouldn't. "Oh, my son," Arthur said sadly. "She'd want you to—"

"Do not *dare* tell me what she would want. Do not speak of her at all." The few nobles still throwing things at him halted at the venom in his words, smartly lowering their hands and backing away a few steps. The rest of the crowd was already parting, leaving room for Benedict as the king, in his jewel-encrusted crown and expensive fur cape, made his way to the dais.

Trystan stiffened when Benedict passed Sage's coffin, running a hand over it with feigned sympathy. Trystan's chains rattled as he pulled against them, a snarl behind his lips, and all his mind knew then was anger.

"For too long, I have failed in bringing The Villain to justice, in stopping the horrors he's committed against my people!" the king bellowed out. "He is a danger to us all, his magic made to hurt, to *kill*." All eyes were on the king, even those of the guards inching away from their posts to get a better view. "He's terrorized noble families, stolen goods, and made Hickory Forest—a once beloved place—too fearsome for travel."

In a different time, a different place, the flattery might have gone to his head.

"And the worst of his offenses—one I've endeavored to spare you all from." The king sighed, like the words were painful, and Trystan had a strong desire to lob a tomato at him; his acting was that bad. "An atrocity committed ten years ago."

Trystan's head snapped up, his shoulders straightening at the hint of a reveal…but of what?

What is your game, man?

"Because of The Villain capturing and keeping Fate's precious guvre for the last decade, the citizens of Rennedawn were made to suffer in nature's act of revenge."

Trystan's subconscious cleared his despair-driven haze as he realized with shock what Benedict was accusing him of.

"The Villain is the cause of the Mystic Illness."

Fucking damnation.

The crowd cried in outrage, yelling vulgar insults—nothing he wasn't used to; in all honesty, some of them were quite creatively colorful—but his verbal lashings were usually for atrocities he'd *committed*.

This has nothing to do with me and you know it, you wretch.

Benedict stepped closer. "And now I will reveal the horrible traitor to you all!" Benedict got right up next to him, murmuring low. "Ready, my boy?"

Trystan nodded in deference, keeping his voice low, too. "I must say this role suits you, Benedict."

The king narrowed his eyes. "What role?"

He curled his lip, knowing the effect his words would have. "Why, that of the villain."

Benedict's nostrils flared, his eyes wide and furious. He reached out, gripping Trystan's shirt, but before he could fully raise his hand to strike, an ear-piercing scream wrenched through the room.

"Sh-She's *gone*!" yelled a noblewoman.

Everyone, including Trystan, looked to where she was pointing—to the coffin that had been ignored for the last few moments.

He didn't have a clear view any longer. The crowd had pushed forward, hiding his nightmare from view. All he saw was a glint of glass beyond the writhing mass of noble heads as more screams arose from the onlookers.

His heart raced as prickles shot up the back of his neck, a roar echoing in his ears. The chains clanked and rattled behind him as he strained against them, angling his head up, desperately waiting for the crowd to part.

"Move, you godsforsaken peacocks!" he boomed, and miraculously, they heeded his command, the nobles diving to either side of the room, revealing what was beyond.

And he saw.

The glass coffin, previously filled with the fruition of his greatest fear, was empty.

"What in the deadlands is this? Who is responsible?" the king shouted, pounding down the stairs of the dais. But there was no time for speculation… as a light and familiar whistle danced through the air.

Time stopped.

The room rapidly fell silent—silent enough to hear the nervous shuffles, the jittery clanking of the guards going to grip their swords. It sounded like fear.

And fear it was, as every set of eyes in the room followed the whistling sound to the top of the grand staircase.

There, with flowers falling from the length of her hair and a wicked smile on her red-painted lips, stood Evie Sage.

Alive.

Her smile widened as the crowd gasped and screamed in terror at the dead risen. An answering smile impossibly pulled at the corners of his own mouth, overriding the muscle-tensing shock freezing his limbs. That shock thawed slowly as his eyes drank in every inch of her. He'd never be able to look away again.

"What a lovely party," she said, her smooth voice like a beacon cutting through the fog of his earth-shattering bewilderment. He was unsure if what he was seeing was real.

But with the next words out of her mouth, he knew it was truly her. Sage was alive.

His knees buckled as her blue eyes caught his, and her smile pushed even wider still.

"I am perhaps a little hurt that you neglected to send me an invitation."

CHAPTER 7

EVIE

There was quite a bit more screaming after that.

Evie would've been amused by it if she wasn't so out of sorts. It hadn't been her intention to make an entrance of this caliber—in fact, it hadn't been her intention to make an entrance *at all*. The cure to the sleeping-death fruit—the rare magical fruit Becky had procured to make her appear as if she'd lost her life—was supposed to take effect *before* she was displayed like a macabre painting to a room full of nobles.

The coffin, morbid as it was, had thankfully been propped open by a stack of thick parchment for her escape. An escape that had been rather…less than graceful—akin to an enormous slug trying to cram through a drainpipe. She'd flopped to the ground with a humbling *thud* and made a beeline for the stairs, hoping to escape to the shadows while the guards were otherwise distracted. It was safer there. It was where she was meant to be while her plan unfolded.

But she'd made the mistake of turning back, of searching the room, of looking right at *him*.

The Villain. *Trystan.*

Seven days was nothing in the grand scheme of time, but it may as well have been an eternity for the way she'd lurched toward him, like there was an invisible cord pulling them together. She'd frozen, hovering on the brink, teetering between the safety she'd known and falling headfirst into an uncertain future. Two choices lay before her, two paths to take. But then the king had moved to unveil The Villain, and there was no choice any longer.

Her choice would always be him.

So instead of keeping to the shadows to hide away from the scrutiny, the censure, she moved into the light. She unveiled herself—for him.

And the response was less than welcoming, to put it mildly.

"Necromancy! Dark magic! She's a witch!" The cries came from a noblewoman in a feathered gown who was swooning against her escort, gripping his arm.

The pride Evie felt at the words was disconcerting, but she let herself relish it anyway. When one spent their entire life feeling weak, it was quite thrilling to be viewed as a threat.

She scrunched her nose and resisted the urge to respond with something entirely inappropriate, like *"Boo!"*

The swooning woman fainted dead away, hitting the ground with a hard *plop.*

Oh—I did say it. Oops.

Biting her lips to keep from smiling, she turned her attention back to the room, back to the king, as she descended the stairs. If she was damned anyway, she may as well take her amusements where she could get them. "My apologies for my delayed arrival, Your Majesty. It appears I was…indisposed."

A chorus of gasps sounded, in tune with the crudeness of her comment, but they sounded like a bluebird chirping in her ear. Lovely.

A low, gruff voice echoed in the awkward quiet, but she knew who it belonged to. "Sage." The sound of Trystan's voice was lovely, too. *The loveliest.*

She looked for him again across the room. The black mask covered a wide portion of his face, making him appear dangerous and cold. But his eyes—his incredulous eyes were molten as they bore into hers. He straightened slowly when he caught her smile, the black depths of his gaze never leaving her person as his posture went fully straight.

He nodded gently at her.

Her pulse fluttered in her neck, the splendor of the ballroom no match for the magnificent relief she felt looking at his face, the comfort that they were once again in the same place.

"King Benedict." Evie projected her voice, though the room had quickly grown quiet. "Isn't it proper etiquette to greet your guests as they arrive?" She quirked a brow, gesturing to herself, gripping her surge of boldness with both hands.

The king stalked toward her, flanked by two guards. She backed away slowly but halted when she realized she was blocked on every side by more Valiant Guards filing in. It was no matter. She set her chin in a hard, defiant line. Being surrounded by men who wanted to hurt her was nothing new. A low, dangerous sound came from the stage—the clinking of chains. Trystan was fighting, thank the gods. He'd looked defeated in the moments before she appeared, but no longer. The candles around them flickered like they could feel the shift, and that growing strength made her wonder. Was it hope for escape that had caused this change in Trystan?

Or was it…her?

She didn't have time to turn this over in her brain before Benedict took her arm in a bruising grip, holding her close enough for her to see a vein pulsing just beneath where his crown met his glistening forehead. He hissed, "What have you done, you foolish girl? How is it you live? Tell me at once!"

She didn't cower the way instinct told her to—instead, she held the king's wild eyes, and she smirked.

He was nearly shaking with barely contained rage. "Good people of Rennedawn, it appears we've been deceived! This is a trick! A last-ditch effort by The Villain to escape. He manipulated this young woman into faking her death and coming to his aid." Benedict squeezed her arm so tightly, it felt like it would break in his grip, his handsome face ruined by the scowl forming between his thick sand-colored brows. "All for naught. Take pity and behold The Villain's true final victim."

A beat, a breath, and then fury—fury so righteous, her trepidation mattered no longer. She was aflame. In a flash, she angled herself down, unsheathing the dagger from the strap hidden beneath her dress. It was up against Benedict's throat before he could blink.

Her loose curls brushed her bare arms with the movement, and her words dripped with burning poison. "I. Am. Not. A. *Victim*."

The guards advanced, but the king stayed them with his hand. Training his gaze on her blade with bored condescension, he said, "You are only offended because I speak true. Think, Ms. Sage—do you honestly believe that saving this man is a just choice? A good one?"

Her heart beat faster, her voice lightening as her eyes shone with unshed tears. "No, you're right." She allowed her face to change into amused malevolence. "I suppose…it's an *evil* one."

She lifted the dagger and slashed it across Benedict's cheek before jumping back out of reach. The king screamed, holding a hand against the shallow wound, howling like it went all the way to the bone. *Why do men take pain as well as ice takes heat?* "You wicked bitch!"

She took a bow. "At your service."

"Seize her! Now!"

The guards advanced on her, and she felt a flare of panic from the top of her head all the way to her toes. She'd dillydallied too long; it had to be now.

Clearing her throat, she held the dagger out. "Before you attempt an arrest, gentlemen, I'd like to make a proposal." The silver-clad men looked at one another in stark confusion at the casualness in her voice; thankfully, it hid the shakiness. "Release The Villain and Arthur Maverine, and I'll allow everyone in this room to leave with their lives."

The king, his guards, and even a few nobles had the gall to laugh, finding humiliating amusement in her ultimatum. The king swiped an imaginary tear of laughter away from his emerald-green eyes. "A magicless young woman with a dagger is as threatening as a rabbit with a letter opener," he said, speaking to her as if she were a child—not an unfamiliar feeling for her. "You are weak and surrounded by enemies, you thoughtless girl."

She *was* afraid, but she knew now: fear usually meant you were standing on the edge of something new, something self-altering, something potentially *good*. Fear was not something she would shy away from ever again.

Nodding demurely, she responded, "Too true, Your Majesty. I am nothing compared to the men you have in your service, nor the noblemen at your command." She made a show of scanning the crowd and tapping her chin twice. "I find it impressive that you should know so very many people, that you should facilitate such devotion. It makes me wonder, however, if you might know my favorite distinction between your Valiant Guards and The Villain's Malevolent."

The king noticed her slowly inching backward with a satisfied gleam in his eye. "You're stalling, Ms. Sage. But I'll humor you before I send you to the gallows. *My* guards fight for the good of the kingdom. The Villain's guards fight for its destruction."

"An important distinction, to be sure!" She leaned in and whispered her next words for only the king to hear. "But I was referring to the fact that a majority of those who make up the Malevolent Guard are *women*." She watched the king slowly piece together her words but didn't allow him to finish before lighting her final match.

"Are you certain you know *everyone* in this room?"

Satisfaction sang through her blood as the king's wide eyes darted around in dawning horror.

Evie rocked back, another flower slipping from her hair as she spun toward the onlookers. Tatianna appeared from the throngs like a vision, the pink sash around her green gown marking her as real in a sea of falsity. Winking at Evie, Tati pulled a pocket light from within the folds of her dress, shaking the cannister before releasing the bursting firework into the open air.

The signal was received like ripples in the Lilac Sea. One by one across the vast room, women stepped forward out of the crowd, discarding shirts, hats, or dresses to reveal their Malevolent Guard uniform beneath. They'd been there all along, hidden behind the misplaced idea that women did not need to be watched so closely, that they couldn't be any sort of true risk. The words The Villain had spoken to her in his brother's dilapidated tavern became a melody in her mind.

"I would never make the mistake of underestimating a woman like you. It would be a fatal one."

The king wouldn't make that mistake again, she predicted. His gaze on her had changed—to one of fear.

Finally.

"I hope you remember that whatever happens next—"

She tilted her head, grinning through her final damning words.

"I did so try to warn you."

CHAPTER 8

THE VILLAIN

The Malevolent Guard attacked without reservation, without restraint, and entirely without honor—exactly as Trystan had trained them.

Women all over the room were felling knights one by one, leveraging their surprise attack against the king's meager numbers. Keely, the head of his guard, was seamlessly handling three knights at once, while another guard, Min, had backed two into a corner and was pelting them with...cream puffs?

She's getting a raise.

As was whoever had organized this: a feat of genius. *Surely Becky was involved*, he thought with some satisfaction. *And Sage...* The ballroom had descended almost instantly into beautiful chaos. Screaming nobles scattered as bodies and weapons littered the floor, food trays and wine spilled or abandoned in the servants' efforts to get away.

He had to break free of his binds, had to get to her. *Alive.* Sage was alive.

She appeared then, stumbling through a litter of bodies, tripping on the hem of her dress. A wave of tenderness came over him through the fierceness igniting his bloodstream, his battling emotions of rage and relief making him feel wild as his starving eyes took her in. Rosy cheeks, bloodred lips, wild black curls.

Mine.

He'd do battle with that unruly thought later, but for now his brain would not be trifled with—he wouldn't even try.

"What a remarkable young woman," he heard Arthur say breathlessly.

He didn't look away from her, just stared ahead before coolly replying, "An understatement, I assure you."

Arthur must have heard the hitch in his voice. "Trystan, could it be that

Evie is—"

A waiflike woman with a hood obscuring her face pushed onto the platform. "I don't mean to interrupt—pixies know, you two should really have it out—but perhaps later?"

Arthur's brows lowered as the woman pulled back her hood—part in anger and part in fatherly protectiveness. "Clarissa! You should not be here."

Trystan's little sister, the youngest of the Maverine siblings, was before them, dressed in Malevolent Guard armor. A sight he never thought he'd see, since, for all intents and purposes, his sister fucking hated him.

"Relax, Father. I'm hardly here to fight. I'm the locksmith of this operation." She reached a slender hand into a pouch tied to her waist and pulled out a small vial of liquid. "Orange ink does wonders as a solvent."

Trystan flinched away when she got close. "I've seen you dissolve an entire sofa with that. Are you certain it's safe to use so close to someone's skin?"

Clare grinned, looking a bit evil herself, in the way that little sisters do. "I'm not certain at all, actually, but you'll be a lovely test subject."

Clanking metal echoed as two Valiant Guards edged toward the dais, aiming arrows right at Clare's chest. "Stop where you are, wench, or we'll shoot you through the heart!"

Trystan heard a delicate snort and then the sound of a familiar voice. "Good luck finding it."

He grinned. "Tatianna."

"Mother hen." The healer winked at him, standing behind the knights with a hand propped on her hip. Her dark braids were adorned with pink bows, matching the deep fuchsia rouge on her lips and the blush on the apples of her dark-brown cheeks.

The guards whirled on her. "Back away!"

Tatianna's eyes flickered to Clare's, and she relaxed slightly before looking back to the men now aiming their weapons at her. The healer gave the knights a mock pout before lifting her glowing right hand. "I'm afraid there are only two options, gentlemen—and I do use that term *loosely.*" Her amused expression turned lethal. "Get the deadlands away from my family or I'll liquify your bones."

They looked at each other, wary, but didn't move.

Tatianna clicked her tongue. "Suit yourself!" Her left hand joined the right, but it was too late. Both men yelped, scattering into the wild mob of fighting as quickly as their legs would carry them.

"Well done," Trystan said gruffly, flinching as Clare made quick work of pouring the orange ink onto Arthur's binds. The metal melted into shimmering rivulets on the ground, and thankfully, his bones stayed intact.

Clare turned to Trystan, looking more than a little evil now. "Your turn."

"Oh, good," he said dryly, wincing as she disappeared behind him.

As she worked, Clare asked a question, trying a tad too hard to seem disinterested. "Can you really melt someone's bones, Tati?"

Tatianna shrugged. "No. But *they* didn't have to know that."

Trystan lifted a brow, but the woman's utter hubris was forgotten when his chains finally fell away. It wasn't just the freedom—his wrists unshackled for the first time in what felt like ages—it was his magic. *Free. Awake.*

It came to life in startling waves, in righteous anger, in uncontrollable spirals as his mist moved to every corner of the room, only visible to *his* eye. His magic fell out more powerfully than usual after so long contained. Every body in the room had glowing weak points for him to hit, for him to kill. Injuries, fatalities, alight with vibrant color. His magic found every living soul in the room.

But he only wanted one.

"Where is—" Trystan didn't need to finish; Tatianna knew what he was about to ask.

The healer searched the room. "She's... Oh dear." Her lips pulled back in a grimace.

And when Trystan looked, he saw why.

Sage was at the wall, closer than before, but this time she had a rope in her hands. A rope they all followed up the wall, across the ceiling, all the way to...*the godsdamn crystal chandelier.*

Clare clapped a hand over her mouth. "By the gods, she wouldn't, would she?"

He stalked to the end of the dais, his mist twisting and curling, the magical mark across his upper arm awakening and proving Sage was well and truly alive. He could see the breath pulling through her body, the rise and fall of her chest, the freckle on her collarbone, the curl of her grin.

She was looking right at him, boldly, unabashedly, as she lifted her pinkie, glowing with gold ink, and gave him a polite mock salute.

He shook his head, grinning as he answered his sister's question. "Evie Sage? She absolutely would."

And she did.

CHAPTER 9

EVIE

The crystal shattered in every direction.

Unfortunate, since one of those directions was right at Evie's head.

Her stomach hit the floor as a large shard embedded itself in the wall directly above her, so close she could feel a whoosh of air brush her hair back as she dove.

More unfortunate still, since the candles from the chandelier had scattered and were currently catching on the drapes.

Don't be an arsonist, Evie!

She frowned. That was a new one.

But she was snapped from her inattentive musings when the boss's voice boomed out, closer than she would have expected. "Sage! Where in the deadlands would you get such a dangerous idea?"

She blinked up at his obscured face. "A book."

A Valiant Guard entered his path, but it didn't slow him a wink. With both hands, The Villain tossed the knight away like a piece of furniture, not breaking stride until he was right in front of her.

He was breathing heavily, not from the strain but from anger. "It is fiction for a reason, you menace. By the gods, what if you carried out every impossible act you read about?"

It was a rhetorical question, but she couldn't resist the urge to slip into the normal ease of their cadence, like no time had passed. "Oh, I suppose that I would need to become very, um—*flexible.*"

An inarticulate sound left his throat, his eyes on the ceiling as he likely prayed for patience before responding, "I beg you not to elaborate."

But when his eyes came back down, there was nothing but intensity in them. He scanned every inch of her face, and she scanned what she could of his. Suddenly, she hated the scrap of fabric of his mask; it was merely a means to keep him from her. She reached up a hand but halted—there were still guards in the room, even a few stray nobles, some watching them from their hiding places.

She couldn't reveal him here; they'd have to wait until they were—

"Do it."

His words were so resolute, her eyes widened in shock, her mouth gaping open like a fish.

"You think I would allow you to reveal yourself to the public in such a way and not do the same for you?" he asked.

Her chest rose and fell in rapid succession as she desperately tried not to read into the words. "Sir, really. There's no need to feel guilty—I'm a nobody; my name means nothing. Come, we must leave at—"

His words were angrier this time. "Do it. Or I will."

She knew his threats well enough to know when they were sincere. Which meant there was no point in arguing any further.

He urged, "Unmask me, Evangelina."

It was impossible to not be moved by the low caress of his voice, like fingers gliding up her bare back. She was human, she had a pulse, and it beat in the worst way for someone it very much was not supposed to.

Slowly, she reached up, fingers nearly stilling when she felt his body tense at the brush of her touch. But instead of stilling, she was spurred to move faster. She removed the mask, letting it slip through her fingers until it landed soundlessly on the floor, his face bare.

Familiar and beautiful.

Relief and comfort eased the tightness in her chest. A warm tear tracked down her cheek as she smiled shakily and said, "Hello, evil overlord."

The Villain did not cry; she knew this. But she also knew that for the rest of her life, if she got to grow old, wasting away in a bed, recounting her adventures of working for the darkest figure in the land, she would swear to herself, even then, that she saw The Villain's black eyes glisten.

His words finally came on the turn of his lips that, if stretched up any further, she knew would reveal…one singular dimple.

"Hello, little tornado."

More screams cut through the space. Fighting and destruction surrounded them. The room was on fire, literally.

She made to step away from him, not noticing the large shard of glass until her foot was nearly upon it. With a gasp, she was swept up atop The Villain's shiny boots. His large hand splayed against her midsection, and the mere sight of it caused a jolt of excitement that made her cheeks flame. His other hand fell to the curve of her hip.

She angled her head back toward him, and he took her wide, panicked eyes as a sign of confusion, which was preferable to explaining that his hand felt as if it was burning through her clothes.

He spoke gruffly. "I did not think you wished to be impaled."

She couldn't help it—she snorted, clamping her lips shut to keep the inappropriate response in. But he saw, shaking his head and sounding annoyed.

"You are unbelievable."

But his hand tightened on her waist.

And for a moment, it was only them.

Until Blade appeared in front of them, cheery and joyful amid the chaos. The sleeves of his fine shirt were torn, revealing his large, muscled arms. Evie pulled away from The Villain, and then Blade was gripping her by both shoulders and planting a kiss on her cheek. "Thank the gods you're all right, Evie! We thought—" Blade suddenly cried out in pain, leaning down to grip his shin, then turned accusatory eyes on The Villain. "Nice to see you, too, boss. Might I ask why you just kicked me?"

He continued to stare, expressionless. "My foot slipped."

Becky appeared behind Evie's shoulder, causing her to jump so hard, she almost gripped the woman for balance.

"Hello," Becky said flatly before glaring at Blade. "We're off schedule, Mr. Gushiken."

Blade saluted her, already disappearing into the crowd. "Can't have that, lovely Rebecka! I'm on it!"

The Villain furrowed a brow. "On what?"

"We need to leave, sir—there are more Valiant Guards coming." Becky did a double take when she looked at Evie. "I am…glad you are not truly dead."

Evie put her hand to her chest, absurdly touched. "Oh, Rebecka, I didn't realize you were so sentimental."

"I take it back," she said with a huff before following Blade into the crowd.

The screams were dying, the room was sufficiently destroyed, and the boss had a weary, shadowed look that made her heart twinge. There was no telling what nightmares he'd endured. There were no words sufficient to express how she was feeling right then, so she simply clasped their fingers lightly together. The jolt of electricity at the contact was like a shock to her heart. He looked at her, startled.

She softened as she said, "Let's go home."

His throat bobbed, his eyes darkening as his hand relaxed in hers. "Sage, I—"

"Leaving without saying goodbye, my boy? And without your companion? I thought I taught you better than that." The voice chilled her as The Villain dropped her hand, the gentle look on his face replaced by a scowl.

Companion? What companion?

King Benedict stood there, a far cry from the glorious picture he'd made at the beginning of the night. His crown was gone, along with his fur-lined cape. A furious vein pulsed at the top of his forehead, which matched the fevered look in his beady eyes. But what made them both pause was the small green animal Benedict had gripped in his fist.

Kingsley.

CHAPTER 10

THE VILLAIN

The stupid godsdamn frog.

Trystan resisted lunging for Benedict and snatching the amphibian from his harsh grip. The magic living beneath his skin begged to be unleashed, to hurt, to *punish*, but it would only take the king a second to squeeze the life from Kingsley's body. He couldn't risk it.

"Sage, why is Kingsley here?" Trystan asked, attempting leveled calm.

"He likes cream puffs."

And the calm was gone.

"*Sage,*" he bit out, furious beyond belief that he had been seconds away from leaving here, from being free of this wretched castle and returning to the one place he felt less broken.

"*Let's go home,*" she'd said.

When he'd stumbled across the manor a decade prior, he'd thought it a good place to rest his head, to plot, perhaps even to disappear for a good long while. Nature had taken control of the crumbling structure hidden deep in the trees of Hickory Forest, its vines and overgrowth practically part of its architecture, holding it captive. It was easy for him to belong there. From the beginning, he'd worked to make the manor a place of coldness and bone-chilling fear. He'd replaced all the original, cheery stained-glass art in the windows with depictions of sinister acts—save for his favorite one in the manor kitchen. Every inch was made to keep people away.

It shouldn't have surprised him that none of that had fazed her, that it had utterly failed against her impenetrable ability to spin the ugly into something not only amusing, but worth loving.

She'd found something worth loving even about a place called Massacre Manor.

And he would resort to whatever dark evil necessary to get her back there.

Sweeping Sage behind him, ignoring her yelped protests, he summoned his power. The dark-gray mist twisted and curled around Benedict, causing the king to freeze. A black spot pulsing by his jugular signaled the perfect place to strike, to rid the world of Trystan's greatest foe for good—

Until Sage asked a question that slammed him back to earth. "Sir, wh-what is that?"

His brows knit together, his power halting in midair. "You are referring to…?"

She whispered, "The gray fog circling the king like a weird-looking storm cloud?"

There's no conceivable way…

His lips parted, but nothing emerged at first. Then, finally: "Y-You can see my magic?"

She squeaked. "Is that what that is?" Her fingers left his shoulder, her head tilting as she took in the violent power with a charmed curiosity. "How interesting. I didn't think it would look like that."

"What are you two conspiring about?" Benedict asked, clearly unable to see the mist yet stopped in his tracks anyway. A prickling began at the back of Trystan's neck, climbing to the sides of his head before settling into a steady pounding at the top of his skull.

It was only Sage who could see his magic.

How unreasonably terrifying.

Trystan decided he was better suited to ferocity than the new emotion fighting its way to the surface. He did not *experience* fear. He merely caused it. "We're just having a chat about all the different ways I could kill you, Benedict. I'd be happy to share."

Without warning, Sage's hand slipped around Trystan's middle, nudging him aside. "Kingsley! Remember what I taught you."

He watched Sage with horrified amusement as she opened her mouth and then clamped her teeth down. The tiny amphibian blinked in awareness, then opened his mouth and closed it…right around Benedict's hand.

"*Uck!*" Benedict bellowed, releasing Kingsley to the floor, the green of the frog's skin camouflaging him some as he scrambled across the tile toward them. "The little monster *bit* me!"

While the guards' attention was focused squarely on the king, Trystan scooped up his friend. They needed to leave—*now*. As he started slowly nudging Sage toward the back terrace doors, he turned the frog over, inspecting him for injuries. He arched a brow and murmured so only Sage could hear, "You taught him to bite?"

"Frogs have weak jaws. He required practice."

Satisfied his friend was without injury, he allowed Kingsley to hop onto his shoulder. "How in the deadlands did you determine that?"

"He had difficulty when I was feeding him pie."

Trystan sighed. "Naturally."

The guards had noticed their movements by now and drew their swords, advancing on Trystan. He tried to push Sage behind him, but she stubbornly remained by his side.

Trystan waved a stiff hand in Benedict's direction. "It's been a painful experience as always, Benedict, but I'm afraid we must take our leave."

"Go ahead and try," the king called roughly from behind his guards, still shaking his hand. "But be warned that I will spend the rest of my days ensuring that you never know peace for the way you've humiliated me. The entire kingdom will know your name before this night is through—and all of them will want you dead."

Trystan shrugged. "That isn't so very different from every other day of my life."

Benedict raised a cruel brow. "I wasn't talking to *you*."

Trystan's entire body clenched at the words, relaxing only slightly when Sage gripped one of his tightened fists in her hand and subtly unfurled his fingers.

"Fear not, Ms. Sage. Despite your betrayal, I will take kind care of your mother when my knights bring her into my custody."

Her hand tightened on Trystan's, and her light eyes narrowed into slits.

The king didn't heed the warning in her stare; vitriol continued to spill from his lips. "When a parent abandons a child, it always makes me wonder: Was it the parent's shortcoming"—the king grinned—"or the child's?"

Bastard.

But Sage put her chin up. "When a knight is willing to betray his king, it always makes me wonder: Was it the knight's shortcoming"—now her brows raised in satisfaction—"or the king's?"

Benedict's face paled, and Trystan's heart skipped a beat. The knight who had mouthed to him about hope.

Is she so charming that she could convince even a Valiant Guard to do her bidding?

He looked to the curve of her cheeks, the slyness in her expression, the quiet wheels of her mind working and shifting even now to make a new plan.

Yes. This woman could convince someone to defy the hands of time if it suited her.

She missed the longing in his gaze as she leaned in to whisper, "Be ready to run."

Before he could react, Sage reached behind her back, gripping something tucked away in the back sash of her gown, hidden from view. He trained his gaze on it, astonishment washing over him when he realized what it was. A stack of papers—letters, all signed and dated by one swooping signature barely visible at the bottom.

Nura Sage.

"You're wrong about my mother, and you'll come to find—if you haven't already—that you are very wrong about *me*."

Trystan hauled Sage by the arm, dragging her toward the back terrace doors before she revealed anything more, before Benedict saw the letters, before she pushed any further than she already had, knowing the danger she'd just brought upon herself. And the hungry gleam in Benedict's eye only confirmed it.

Still, he found it extraordinarily difficult not to grin as she smiled and waved behind her, eyes shining as she called, "Happy hunting, King Benedict."

And to the sound of their ruler's outraged screams, they ran for their lives.

CHAPTER II

EVIE

The threat of death followed them down the terrace steps, through the palace gardens, and right to the edge of Hickory Forest, as did the familiar sounds of arrows cutting through the air. Evie moved briskly in the dark, creeping around the tree line and through hedges, and The Villain followed closely behind her the entire way.

She might have found that sweet, even intriguing, but he wasn't moving the way she was used to, like the world would bend and mold around him. Rather, it seemed like he was dragging himself through it, as if his time in the king's custody had beaten him down so thoroughly, the only way out was to throw himself into the open air and hope for the best.

The realization caused a surge of protective anger, so strong she nearly turned around just so she could take a metal rod to their esteemed ruler's head.

I could dent his stupid little crown, she thought maniacally.

"Cease whatever trickery you're planning. You're terrifying the shrubbery with that look on your face." He huffed, straightening, Kingsley clinging to his shoulder for dear life. They kept moving at the forest's edge, their steps quiet and voices low so as to not alert the guards to where they were hiding in the shadows. "It was unwise to taunt the king like that, Sage. You've put a target on your back."

"Do you think that's what the archers were aiming at?"

It was meant to be lighthearted, to relieve the line of tension pulsing in his neck, but it was a very large, very dangerous mistake.

She could make out little of his eyes, but she could see them flare as he took two strides toward her, towering over her as he hissed sharply, "Threats to your life are not something to jest about. *Ever*."

Her lips parted, and all she could do was blink, wariness and confusion swarming around her like killer bees. Their buzzing rang in her ears as she asked, "Why?"

The intensity in his wild gaze was shuttered out, so quickly morphing into a neutral indifference it made her head spin, and—just like those killer bees—it stung.

She shook her head. "Never mind. Forget I asked. That was silly." Her strides became longer, more determined. She'd wasted too much time.

"Sage," he whispered. "Where are you going? The manor is that way."

"I'm going to the ravine."

He stood right next to her, his face impossible to read. "Has working for me become that bad?" he deadpanned.

She snorted, shouldering past him, stumbling over her skirts for what felt like the millionth time. She glared at the hem and then stared at him. He arched a brow in question as she lifted it with a frank grin.

"Rip it off."

The Villain's and Kingsley's mouths opened in tandem, so comedic a view that she bit her lip to keep from chortling. Composing herself—poorly—she said, "I cannot continue back to the manor with the hem tangling about my feet."

He choked out, "Could you try?"

She folded her arms, arching a brow. "What are you so afraid of, evil overlord?"

"Afraid?" His low voice was like two stones rubbing together.

Kingsley hopped from Trystan's shoulder, sensing the danger—or perhaps just the awkwardness. In the dim light of the moon, she could just barely make out the lock of his heavily shadowed jaw as her boss dropped to his knees in front of her. The sight of his dark head made her stomach pool with warmth.

With a grim, businesslike determination, he took the thin fabric and wrenched it in two so the hem brushed the tops of her knees. She gasped as cool night air kissed her skin, wishing a little that he would do the same.

Don't wish for the boss to kiss your skin, Evie!

Even if that sounds…entirely too pleasant.

His large hand was warm against the bare skin of her legs, his fingers resting around her thigh a little longer than could be reasonably explained away. "There." His breathing was labored—she could hear it. It matched hers.

She backed away before she did something completely mad like grab his hand and return it to her thigh. He'd probably reel back, appalled. Whether their attraction was mutual or not, the boss was clearly too weighed down by professionalism to act on any lurid thoughts, and she'd just have to live with that.

The way one lived with a fork through a lung.

"Right, um—thank you." She continued toward her destination, moving easier when he came up beside her, scoping out the area for threats.

"Here's a good spot to head into the trees." He nodded toward the forest. "I can get us home from there."

"As I said, sir, I'm going to the ravine." She kept walking, stiffening her back. "I have a plan. Trust me."

He sighed, pinching the bridge of his nose. "A terrifying prospect. Sage, I must insist that—" But he stopped, obscenities leaving his mouth in rapid succession as he shoved her ahead, scooping up Kingsley. "Run! *Now!*"

"There they are!" The guards burst from the trees, but she was already moving, quicker without the threat of her hem tangling about her feet.

She kept going, sprinting faster, her hair whipping around her, some pieces sticking to her face as grass stuck to the bottom of her thin slippers. The ravine's edge appeared on the horizon. So close. Blood pumped hard through her veins as she pounded against the soft grass, surprised when she turned to find the boss doing the same beside her. His legs were longer, his body lither; he could move faster if he wanted to.

But just like the first time they met, he slowed to keep pace with her.

She swallowed the lump in her throat, grabbing his hand as they inched closer and closer to the edge. There was only the merest hint of hesitation in his voice as he said, "Are we going over, then?"

He would follow her off a cliff without question.

And Evie knew she was in love with him. Right then, right there.

She could only hope the final piece of her plan was still in place...

They reached the edge, not stopping as she screamed, "Don't let go of my hand!"

His only response was the tightening of his fingers, and then they were airborne together, for just a moment, her heart bottoming out as she swallowed a scream. She felt the loom of death as wind brushed her cheeks, suspended until—

They both landed on the back of something scaly and purple.

"Fluffy!" He was here.

They'd done it.

Evie laughed as they soared out of the ravine and into the skies. Blade was at the helm, all the others safe and sound on Fluffy's back. He steered the animal over the guards as the group of them waved to the confused faces below.

"So long!" Tatianna said, fluttering a pink handkerchief at the knights shouting beneath them.

"Gentlemen!" Blade saluted.

Becky didn't say anything, just quirked a brow and dropped a large rock over the side. Blade and Arthur both chuckled, the latter being fussed over by Clare.

The echoes of the guards' shouts faded as they soared through the night sky, every star twinkling brightly around them.

It almost didn't seem real, as if nothing was between the large expanse of night and them. Her relief was so palpable—*we're all here; everything's all right*—she couldn't help but laugh again as the wind whipped through her hair, tugging pleasantly on her scalp.

She breathed, "It's so beautiful."

Her boss had been silent beside her, but now he replied hoarsely, still gripping her hand, "Yes, it is." And when she turned, he was looking at her.

Her wide smile faded into something softer, her once fragile heart now strong and bursting at the fact that they were all together, that they were all safe. A separate exit strategy had been in place for the Malevolent Guard— one involving tunnels, disguises, and maybe some fireworks—and she could only hope they had made it out without casualties as well.

Blade yawned and stretched. "I think after that, we all deserve a well-earned holiday." He waggled his brows at the boss. "A paid one."

The Villain released her hand, and she frowned at him.

"There will be no holidays," he said grimly. "Not until we figure out what we are to do about the guvres."

Becky straightened, her glasses wobbling on the tip of her nose. "What do you mean? They are happily contained."

The Villain shook his head. "That's precisely the problem. We don't know what natural consequences will occur should we keep them that way for much longer. The Mystic Illness could only be the beginning."

Gods, it wasn't a dream. That was real. Evie had heard the king's speech when she'd awoken in the coffin, had hoped her recovering poisoned mind had conjured the terrible lie. *Mystic Illness,* Rennedawn's Story, *fading magic, cease to exist.* It made her head spin so hard her stomach lurched.

"At the very least, we need to separate them again." The boss kept speaking, not realizing the apprehension creeping into her soft smile. "If they are together too long, nature could take its course, and we can't risk the consequences of imprisoning one of their hatchlings should the female fall pregnant."

Blade's shoulders stiffened.

Tatianna shifted, patting The Villain's arm. "Oh, mother hen. Do we have bad news for you."

CHAPTER 12

THE VILLAIN

Trystan's tentative to-do list early the next morning was as follows:

1. Bathe.
2. Get a report on all he'd missed while he was gone.
3. Avoid thinking about Sage's thighs.
4. Murder Gushiken.

He'd been successful with the first two, failed at the third, and was about to check the last off his list.

"This is hardly my fault," Blade grumbled, tossing several slabs of beef in to the mated guvres. The male, resplendent with his iridescent skin, eyed the meat but paused, motioning for the brown-gray female to have her fill first. *Rather gallant*, Trystan supposed with an eye roll, *since she is eating for two.*

His fists were clenched at his sides. The dark cellar was making him agitated and jittery. The sight of the bars sent him back, back to the cell he'd sat in for days with no hope. It was likely why his patience was so frayed— well, that and the worst night's sleep of his life. He'd ordered everyone to bed upon their return, despite Sage's protests. She'd laid a hand against his arm, an indecipherable look in her eyes, and asked if he wanted to talk. He'd had to leave before he did something drastic, like drag her to bed with him to do much more than talk. In the morning, he'd figured, his head would be clear and he'd see reason again.

But morning had come swiftly, and not only was he still exhausted, he was also spitting mad.

"I don't care if it's your fault or the fault of a celestial god. If the female gives birth to her baby trapped in our cell, we're doomed," he yelled.

"A baby guvre is called a let," Gushiken instructed, then his amber eyes went round, and he stopped with another piece of raw meat in hand. "You think keeping the let will start another Mystic Illness?"

Trystan shook his head darkly. "No. I think whatever vengeance Fate would reap on behalf of its young…would be something far worse."

The firelight from the torches crackled in time with Blade's wince as he tossed another beef slab in between the bars. "I sure missed your foreboding speeches, sir; my nightmares didn't have nearly as much fodder while you were away."

Trystan rolled his eyes again. "Very amusing."

"We should just let them go if you're so worried."

Trystan had considered the option, but it couldn't be risked. Not when the Valiant Guards were likely tearing through Hickory Forest, searching high and low for Massacre Manor, for the guvres, for Sage. The manor at least was cloaked in an impenetrable ward, but if they set the guvres free, they'd be sitting ducks.

"That would be handing Benedict exactly what he wants, and I would rather rip my own heart out." Running a hand through his hair, he nearly tugged out the strands. "How long is a guvre's gestational period?"

Gushiken chuckled nervously. "Um…"

Trystan's head felt like it was going to pop off. "You don't know?" he growled.

"*Yet,*" Blade corrected with an easygoing grin that made it difficult for Trystan to keep hold of his anger.

Kingsley appeared as if summoned, crown reaffixed to his head as he leaped in front of Blade like an amphibious shield. Trystan lifted a brow at his old friend's blank gold stare, then sighed. "Figure it out, Gushiken. Or I'm finding another 'expert.'"

Kingsley held up a sign. MEAN.

Trystan nodded at the frog. "Thank you. I needed that." The small animal shook his head hopelessly.

Blade chuckled, scooping up Kingsley, placing him on his shoulder, and leaning them both back against the wall with his arms folded. "So, once we have a timeline for this detonating bomb"—he nodded toward the female—"then what?"

A shiver ran down Trystan's spine. "Then I'll know how much time I have to destroy any hope of Benedict fulfilling Rennedawn's little storybook prophecy."

Blade's brows shot toward the ceiling. "So that wasn't just for show? The king was being serious? I thought *Rennedawn's Story* was just a tale to keep kids from misbehaving. My father used it as a threat to stop me from stealing cookies after dinner. Told me that Rennedawn's storybook would steal all the magic in the land if I kept being so greedy. I always considered it a bit dark for a children's story, but I never thought it was actually real."

Rennedawn's Story was an extremely rare text that had been mythologized for years, so long fizzled out and warped that much of the public had never even heard of it. Those who had chalked the tale up to a benign way of keeping children in line, like Gushiken's father.

It seemed the darkest tales held the harshest truths.

He himself had thought it false, too, until he was trapped in the dark these past days and recounting his time with Benedict, how obsessive the king had become with the inner workings of magic. How he'd had Trystan out searching for people and animals with unnamed purpose, back when he was Benedict's apprentice. How his guards had recently recounted to him whispers of the fable spreading throughout the kingdom, though he hadn't given it any merit then. How the guvres were a piece of Fate—and then Evie's mother's erratic power had all along been…starlight magic. The king had told him a decade ago about finally having a user of starlight magic in the kingdom and how much it would help his cause. Trystan hadn't known then that it was Evie's mother. If he had, perhaps he could've stopped it… Perhaps he could've saved Sage the pain of losing everything in one fell swoop.

He heaved a world-weary sigh before answering Blade's lingering question. "It's real. Or at least real enough that Benedict is dangerously obsessed with it. And though the loss of magic isn't ideal, Benedict enacting the *Rennedawn's Story* prophecy isn't ideal, either."

Blade rubbed at his chin. "Why? We don't want the magic to die. Why not just let him do it?"

"Well, for one thing, it would require him to use Sage's mother in some way, and for another, we don't know what kind of power Benedict would gain from reaping from Fate and fulfilling a tale supposedly crafted by the gods."

Blade *tsk*ed. "So we're damned if we do and damned if we don't, then?"

Trystan frowned at the guvres' meat-munching forms. "I never should've removed that fucking wall."

Blade gave the creatures a crooked smile. "Oh, come now, sir. There are some beings you simply cannot keep apart; they'll always find their way back to each other." The dragon trainer's eyes landed on him meaningfully. "You should know this better than anyone."

The statement triggered panic—panic that Blade or anyone else might have caught on to the affection plaguing him for the past six months. Not only was it inconvenient, it was dangerous—his magic hadn't felt normal since Sage laid eyes upon it last night, and he could hardly afford unruly magic. Not when he was so close to destroying Benedict, and especially not now that Trystan suspected Benedict's plans were far more nefarious than the king would have Rennedawn believe.

Curling his lip in disgust, Trystan replied, "I don't know what you're referring to. Sage and I are hardly comparable to a mated pair, Mr. Gushiken. She is my assistant; we *must* spend an inordinate amount of time together. Further, I am not trying to procreate with Sage."

Blade looked at him skeptically. "Are you sure?" He stumbled back when Trystan took a menacing step toward him.

Kingsley held up a sign that read: HA!

"Do you both want to keep your heads?" he sneered, jaw clenching so hard his teeth ground together.

Blade opened his mouth to answer while Kingsley hid in his hair, but they were saved by Tatianna, who glided down the cellar stairs, looking fresh and well rested in a swirl of vibrant pink. "Good morning! Isn't it a lovely day?"

Trystan merely grunted.

Tatianna grinned, every subtle move of her face visible with her dark braids pulled back high by a large, gauzy bow. "Ah, sir, always so eloquent."

His mouth set in a grim line as he straightened the cuffs of his billowing black shirt. "What do you want, Tati?"

She arched a thick brow as she handed him a crisp envelope. "From Arthur. He departed early this morning for home. He didn't want to wake anyone."

The crinkled parchment was merfolk made; he could tell by the shimmer in the firelight. The envelope read: *To my son.*

Trystan crumpled it and put it in his pocket, ignoring Tatianna's look of censure. "And Clare?"

"Is insisting on staying, but I'd be happy to arrange for the guards to throw her from the premises should you wish it, sir."

Trystan moved closer to the stairs, feeling in better spirits now that his emotions weren't the ones being exposed. "If you can't handle being around her, then by all means." He said it airily, like it didn't matter to him either way.

Tatianna stomped a foot, her lovely face twisting in fury. "I can handle it fine. I am not affected by her at all," she ground out.

"Of course not," he replied with just a touch of condescension.

In the cage, the mated guvres had finished their meal and were curling up together, looking almost like... Were they *cuddling*? He saw himself wrapped that way around Sage, and the image was so startling he nearly fell headfirst into the bars.

He looked up to see Tatianna smiling at him in that way that always sent his interns running for the hills. "Speaking of which. I also thought you'd like to know that word of your return has gotten out to the workers, and the office is in an uproar. There's a mob forming on the main floor."

A mob? How delightful.

"Oh, but worry not," she continued, a gleam in her eye that he did not care for at all. "The Malevolent Guard have nearly returned, and I'm sure they'll make it there in time to assist Evie with the crowd."

At the mention of his assistant, Trystan groaned, turning immediately to head for her as his employees snickered behind him.

His frantic magic stirred underneath his skin. It was different, somehow, in the most unsettling of ways; this couldn't be a coincidence. It had to be Evie.

The wall between the guvres may have been toppled, but Trystan needed to reestablish the wall between him and his assistant. Before it destroyed them both.

Before it destroyed them all.

CHAPTER 13

EVIE

"**R**eturn to your posts at once!" Evie called as she was jostled and shoved through the absolute upheaval of workers. The cobwebbed chandelier was swinging precariously above them with the stampede of movement, as was the ceramic chalice of cauldron brew in her hand. She called to the group, trying to reason with them. "I understand it has been a perilous week without him, and I understand the discontent about the pixies using the cauldron brew as bathwater, but it was just the one batch and we really must—" She was shoved into her desk so hard, she almost toppled over completely.

Okay—that's it!

"Hey! Vultures!" she screeched as hard as her lungs would allow. All at once, the workers halted. "Clear the floor this instant or we'll have an impromptu Scatter Day and I'll be sure to include *everyone*!"

Scatter Day, like many things in The Villain's office, was equal parts horror and comfortable familiarity. At least, it was for Evie. She wasn't sure the interns would concur, considering the event consisted of them being chased across the courtyard by whatever dreadful creature the boss deemed acceptable that day. He'd finally promised Evie before he was taken that he would cut it back to once a month, but given the fury on his face as he stared at the chaotic crowd, she had a strong inclination that the promise would not hold for very long.

"Did you not hear Ms. Sage?" The Villain roared. "Scatter!"

And they finally did, the wide-eyed humans, the pixies—even ravens fluttered out some of the open windows. People were practically breaking their necks as they moved away, so intent were they on staring at the boss. Not that she could blame them. He looked strikingly handsome this morning—though the dark circles under his eyes seemed more pronounced. They matched hers.

She'd barely slept a wink before finally giving up and making the awful mistake of searching through her mother's stack of letters, which were practically *ruined*. The scraps were barely legible, save for a few innocuous words. It was a wonder the king had wanted the letters in the first place—they would hardly be a help in locating her mother or her magic. But the letters were not the only thing stashed among the parchment she'd made off with the night before.

Gripping her journal tight, she pulled the papers from inside, then dropped the book onto her desk. "Sir, may I talk to you in private?"

The boss looked at her like she'd asked him to strip naked. "I suppose if you must." Grimacing, he gestured to his office doors.

She scrunched her nose at the coldness but walked in, skidding to an immediate halt when she saw who was inside. "Lyssa!" Evie hissed. "What on earth are you doing here?"

Her little sister, who Evie had ensured was confined to their large rooms in the manor's west wing for the past seven days, sat in the boss's large black chair, twisting the end of her dark braid around her finger. She blinked innocently at Evie, but her brown eyes hinted at mischief. "I'm working. From what I've seen, you all don't do very much of it." Lyssa tried to push the chair out to stand, but it didn't budge. "What are you doing?"

Evie gave a panicked side glance to The Villain, who was staring at his desk and the person in his chair with resigned acceptance.

"I've been replaced."

Kingsley, well timed as always, hopped up onto the desk, holding up two different signs. More and Competent.

"I should've let the king turn you into soup." The Villain rolled his eyes at the animal.

Lyssa burst from the chair and ran toward them, Kingsley following near her like a guard frog. "Lord Trystan!" To Evie's horror, Lyssa threw her arms around her boss, looking up at him with an elated expression. "I'm so happy to see you!"

"Are you certain?" he asked dryly.

When Lyssa stepped back, Trystan very studiously took her sister's hand and bowed deeply over it. "How are you finding the manor, Lady Lyssa?" There was no teasing or malice to the question, simply earnest inquiry.

Evie would have to be dead to not swoon over that just a little—it was the law.

Her sister answered bluntly: "I'm very bored." Evie winced.

A bemused look overtook The Villain's forbidding aura, blooming into full warmth when Edwin, the manor's ogre-turned-chef, barreled into the room, a tray of sweets in each hand. "Trystan!"

The Villain's lips curved up at the ogre's entrance. "Hello, Edwin." But the smile dwindled when Edwin dropped the trays and hoisted The Villain into his large arms. "Edwin," he rasped. "You'll break my spine."

Edwin dropped him, then used his white apron to wipe the tears fogging up the too-small spectacles perched on the tip of his nose. Ogres were notorious for their deep wells of emotion. "I missed you a great deal, Mr. Trystan." Edwin noticed Evie off to the corner and nodded politely at her. She smiled in response.

The Villain cleared his throat uncomfortably. "I suppose, uh, I…missed… Um, thank you." His black eyes were looking anywhere but at the ogre, falling to Lyssa, who was watching the interaction with interest while slowly sneaking a pastry from the dropped tray. The boss grinned at the sight. "Edwin, while I appreciate the sweets delivery, I wonder whether you might show Lady Lyssa how to make those lemon tarts you're so famous for. I fear she is suffering from a case of boredom."

Lyssa beamed, jumping up and gripping Edwin's large hand in her own, practically dragging him toward the door. "Yes, please! Can I wear an apron?" Edwin gave the boss a knowing look as he followed Lyssa with a soft smile on his face, shutting the door behind them.

Evie gaped. "You busied her in less than two minutes. What kind of wizard are you?"

The Villain let out a noise that sounded suspiciously like a snort as he walked across the room, lightly bumping into her usual chair on the way, causing it to tilt slightly toward the window. "Have a seat, Sage," he said, rounding his desk and lowering slowly into his chair.

She smiled lightly, realizing how much she had missed their morning briefings. "Your cauldron brew, sir," she said, placing the ceramic chalice in front of him, frowning slightly. "I had intended to give it to you earlier—I even tried to make a skull with the milk—but I fear it's gone cold. Your first day back, maybe I should just—"

She reached to pick it up, but The Villain had already snatched it from the desk and taken a hearty sip. "I shall enjoy it just like this, thank you," he said gruffly, staring at her rather strangely while she seated herself. The sunlight was pouring in, brushing her cheeks, and it felt lovely.

"What did you want to talk about?"

She got right to the point. "My mother's letters are mostly ruined." She stood again, leaning over slightly, and placed the papers on his sleek black desk, sliding the parchment closer as loose curls fell in her face. His eyes moved in three different directions: first to the pants hugging her thighs, then to her red lips, then back to the papers. He made no expression, but his hand was gripping the desk so tight, his knuckles went white.

Don't read into it, Evie.

Tucking the wayward strands of hair behind her ear, she kept speaking in hopes it would calm her fast-beating heart. "The only words I could truly make out are 'hasibsi,' 'love,' 'starlight,' and this dirty little rhyme that makes absolutely no sense."

The boss looked at her, suddenly alert, but she continued on.

"Oh! And there was something else stashed between the pages. My, um, *informant* also slipped in this." She dropped the glowing, silver-edged page on the table. "I think... I think it's a page from *Rennedawn's Story*. It details tools to enact the prophecy, to save the kingdom and its magic."

His eyes widened as he scooped up the single sheet of parchment with an alarmed swiftness. Scanning furiously, he breathed out, "The seal." He ran his hand down the inked marking toward the top—the one glowing from ancient magic. "By the gods, it appears you beguiling a Valiant Guard was an advantage indeed."

Her brow furrowed in indignation as she tugged at the top of her green floral corset; it was much tighter suddenly. "I didn't beguile anyone, sir."

His eyes followed her hand and shot away fast as he grumbled, "Of course you didn't."

She had every intention of telling the boss of her plans, of exactly who she had colluded with, of how she'd done it. But it was that little twinge of anger, that fleeting sign of discontent in his voice, that made her stop. He was bothered that he'd been shut out of what she'd done, and Evie found that she enjoyed that very much.

"It's occurring to me, sir, that if you want to prevent Benedict from fulfilling this little plan, you might consider gathering the tools necessary and simply enacting the prophecy yourself."

He gripped the page tight in his fist, giving her a cynical expression as he read the words aloud, the bitterness in his voice giving the whimsical magic a biting sound. *"The person who saves the magical lands will take Fate's youngling well in hand; when Fate and starlight magic fall together, the land will belong to you forever. But beware the unmasked Villain and their malevolent dark, for nothing is more dangerous than a blackened good heart…"* He stopped, eyes widening. "I'm in this?"

Evie nodded. "You are."

The Villain flipped the paper over and made a twisted expression when he realized that was all that was there. "Your informant couldn't have given us the whole book?"

"No."

"Why in the deadlands not?"

She shrugged before saying cheekily, "It wouldn't have fit in my dress."

The Villain groaned, collapsing back in his chair, holding the paper before him like it was about to detonate. "Fulfill the prophecy ourselves and then… what? The land will be mine?"

She took her seat and folded her arms. "That's what it says. It's why he wanted to unmask you, I think, so that the beginnings of the prophecy would take hold. Assuming this is all real, that is."

"Oh, it's real," he said grimly. "Trust me." Shaking his head, he pushed away from his desk and walked toward the windows. The sunlight shone a little brighter, like it was eager to kiss the skin of his cheeks. Evie understood the feeling all too well. "I never wanted the land. I merely wanted to terrorize it—and Benedict—until one of us succeeded in destroying the other. I'm the one meant to ensure all hope is *lost*, not that hope still endures." There was a vulnerability in his voice, which cracked at her heart like an ice pick against a glacier.

She came up behind him, wrapping her arms tentatively around his middle and laying her head gently against his back. He jumped at the touch but didn't pull away. It gave her the courage to say, "There is nothing written in any text, gods-created or not, that says we cannot be more than one thing. You've been told for a very long time that you are made for destruction, but there is nothing that says you cannot be more. You can be capable of bad and do good. You can do good things and still be bad. Nothing is set in stone, and if it helps, I'll stand by you no matter who you choose to be."

A ragged, self-deprecating laugh left his lips. "Why?"

She couldn't reveal the real reason without throwing them both completely off their axes, so she merely said, "Because I like who you *are*, not what you're capable of."

He ripped himself from her hands and fell back against the wall, looking astonished, looking...revolted? "Sage, are you of the delusion that everything can be fixed with a hug?"

The lack of composure he was exhibiting in their interactions was growing addictive. "No," she said sweetly. "But don't they help?"

"No."

Kingsley held up a sign: Yes.

The boss narrowed his eyes at the frog before sighing in resignation. "So, we are enacting the prophecy. We are saving the magic."

Evie grinned, clapping gleefully. "What better way to torment the kingdom than for you to take it over? We have the guvres, we have you, and according to the story, all that's left is..." She swallowed. The thought had not fully registered until just then.

"Your mother and her starlight magic. We must find your mother," he finished for her, picking up the ruined letters. "Sage—will you be okay? I know that your mother..."

"I'll be fine, sir," she assured him, though whether she could assure herself of the same was another question entirely. It had been many years since her mother abandoned her family—would Evie ever truly be able to face her again? Clearing the lump from her throat and trying to hold back her sense of foreboding, she said curiously, "But without the letters, we don't really have a place to begin."

The Villain seemed to assess her as if he were not sure she could truly be believed. *That makes two of us, sir.* "Read the dirty rhyme she left behind, Sage. Aloud, if you will." He handed her the stack of letters.

Licking her lips, she looked down at the discolored paper and to the suggestive words at the top. "Where the oaks begin to kiss—" She paused, hoping the blood would leave her cheeks. "The caves below are where the gods once lived. Retrieve the dust that makes wishes come real—"

"Or you shall become the monster's next meal," The Villain completed and then immediately angled his head at her, looking very disgruntled.

Her heart was beginning to beat at a race hummingbirds would find disagreeable. "You know this rhyme?"

He gaped. "Yes. Why on earth did you think it was dirty?"

Marvelous. Now all the blood in her body was racing upward. Her face was on fire. "I, um…I suppose the kissing and the…caves might have given that impression."

There was no emotion in his voice when he said, "Does your mind live in the gutter?"

She shook her head, tapping a finger against her lips. "No, but it rents there on occasion."

The smile that stretched across his cheeks was sudden, with just a peek of a dimple before it disappeared. *Come back!* "The real estate of your thoughts aside," he said, "this rhyme is exactly how we'll begin our search. The kissing oaks aren't terribly far away."

"Wait, what? It's a real place?"

He took the paper back from her and rescanned the words. "Indeed. It's a short journey there. Pack your things, Sage; we'll leave first thing tomorrow." His eyes stayed down, and she hoped they remained off her inflamed cheeks. "If we don't find your mother there, at the very least we'll be able to retrieve a piece of magic that helps uncover lost things." He raised one dark brow, eyes catching now on the anxiety she thought she'd been hiding so well. He watched her closely as he finished. "Stardust."

She only managed to nod stiffly, could barely process that such magic existed—she was too busy remembering her mother's face, hearing her final screams on the last day she'd seen her.

The Villain's voice was muddled as he called her name. A blurry hand reached for her. "Sage? Evie?"

The use of her first name snapped her away from the terrible memories. Pasting on a smile so wide it almost split her lip, she jumped away from his touch. It would cause her to crumble, she knew. "I'll prepare promptly! Let me know if you need anything else, sir!"

She was out the doors before he could say another word, her body reacting violently to the thought of seeing her mother again after so many years. Her chest was heaving against her constricting corset, and she had a wild urge to rip the thing off so she could take in a full breath of air. Stumbling to her desk, she reached for her journal to write it all down, to calm herself.

But it was gone.

CHAPTER 14

EVIE

The boss had requested that Evie meet him in the entryway of the manor the next morning.

So it was no doubt curious to Rebecka Erring why Evie was instead standing in front of the HR manager's desk with her hands folded together, pleading.

"Please, Becky, I have to be downstairs in five minutes, and I don't know who else to ask." Her voice was practically at a whine pitch, which certainly wouldn't get her very far in endearing Rebecka to her cause.

The woman looked up, her light-brown eyes made larger by the round lenses perched atop her pert nose. "I am not helping you look for your ridiculous journal—if you've lost it, buy a new one." Becky paused, pointing a finger at Evie. "With your own money. It's not an approved business expense."

There was hardly anyone in the office to hear Becky's censure; it was far too early for most employees to be in yet. But Rebecka Erring wasn't "most employees." She was dedicated, organized, studious, and wildly observant. There couldn't be a woman more opposite to Evie in the entirety of the continent, and Evie was coming to find that was a very, *very* good thing.

"I know I can be forgetful, but I'm telling you it was on my desk! Someone must have taken it. I looked everywhere! Becky, if you could just please keep a look out for it while I'm gone with the boss today, I will do *anything*."

Becky's eyes drew slowly upward before she leaned back in her seat, gripping her cauldron brew with one hand, the forefinger of her other hand tapping her chin. There was a look of realization on her face that made Evie's skin crawl. "All right, spit it out. What's in it?"

Evie pretended not to know what she meant. "It's a work journal...so, you know, just work things."

Becky raised a brow, contemplating Evie before replying flatly, "It's a bawdy sketch, isn't it?"

Evie's eyes darted around, checking to see if anyone had heard the mortifying question, but the office was still quiet, the first rays of sun just beginning to shine through the windows. "It is not!" She chewed her lip, contemplating how much embarrassment she could take in one conversation. Admittedly, her threshold was higher than most. Which was why she had the confidence to admit, "...Not a *bawdy* sketch per se."

The HR woman gave her a once-over before picking up her empty ceramic chalice, motioning for Evie to follow her all the way to the kitchens. She hadn't been in there for more than a minute in the last week. The first time she tried, the boss's chalice had still been sitting on the counter, and it was just too painful to see.

But now, the boss had returned, Lyssa and Edwin looked hard at work on a chocolate batter, and her favorite window welcomed her—the one pleasant stained-glass depiction in the entire office. A sun shining down on an old book. She smiled at it like she was greeting an old friend.

Becky refilled her chalice from the cauldron before motioning for Evie to continue. She looked far too interested now. "The bawdy sketch? What is it?" She was quiet enough that Edwin wouldn't hear, but Lyssa looked like she had one hand in the baking and one ear on their conversation.

"It's a, um, drawing of me—and also the boss, and we are...uh..."

Becky's face twisted so fast that she almost dropped her cup, and Evie realized immediately what she had assumed.

"Kissing! Just kissing! That's it!" Evie hoped the ground would open so she and her big mouth could fall right into it.

Edwin turned this time, forehead wrinkling, before he turned Lyssa gently around to add chocolate chips to the bowl.

Becky motioned her closer, close enough for Evie to notice the flecks of gold in her brown eyes. "All right, you ninny, I'll help you, but you needn't worry. I've seen you doodle before, and you're so terrible I doubt anyone would even be able to make out what you were trying to draw."

It wasn't an insult; it was honesty—blunt honesty. And it was oddly very comforting. She sighed in relief, her arms coming up out of instinct as she moved forward toward Becky. "Thank you."

Becky held up a hand to stop her. They both blinked at each other, shocked. "Were you about to hug me?" Becky asked warily.

Evie just stared before replying, "Uh, I, uh—"

"Get away from me," Becky said flatly.

"Okay!" Evie squeaked, ready to leave. But right then, Keely, the head of the Malevolent Guard, entered the room in red leather garb. "Keely? How are you?"

By some miracle, Evie's exit strategy for the Malevolent Guard had been a success. There had been minor injuries, but nothing Tatianna and Clare couldn't fix.

Thank the gods.

Keely pulled her thick, honey-colored braid behind her head before grinning. "I am well. But I suggest you make your way downstairs, Ms. Sage. The boss has just noticed your little add-on to the entryway, and he seems... less than pleased."

The Villain hadn't seen it before now: the newest hanging head.

Mr. Warsen.

Uh-oh.

CHAPTER 15

THE VILLAIN

Trystan stared at Otto Warsen's head with a dumbfounded expression. "She scared the wits out of me when she first brought the thing in, sir. But she made a nice, clean cut, just the way you do. A quick study, our Evie." The front-gate guard, Marv, nodded beside Trystan, his spiky light-brown hair going in all sorts of different directions. It was a constant state for the man, always looking a bit frazzled, like he had just been electrocuted.

Fitting, as Trystan felt like he'd just been painfully shocked as well.

"Sage—she—his head was…?" Never had he had more difficulty stringing words together, and on top of that, he felt humiliated to be so tongue-tied in front of the Malevolent Guard sparring around him in the entryway. Their training room was undergoing an intense round of cleaning after one of the new, more obstinate interns had taken it upon themselves to feed a messenger raven prunes and set it loose upon the sparring space as a prank. After all his guard had done for him, he was more than willing to allow them to train anywhere they liked, but a bit less so when they were bearing witness to his pathetic display.

He should've departed already, anyway. Blade was in the back courtyard, saddling the dragon with Tatianna and Clare. Gods knew why his sister was coming, but he wouldn't begrudge another magic user on a journey so fraught with peril. And the clock was ticking—they had to be there before nightfall, or the danger of their destination would increase tenfold. He didn't have time to ruminate on Sage and her shocking act of violence.

But he would anyway, because there was no one he liked to torture quite as much as himself.

"Keely! Where. Is. Sage?" He bit out the words, his patience at a minimum. He wanted his focus only on Benedict, only on vengeance, only on taking over this kingdom and destroying all the good inside it. But he couldn't with this discomfort lodged where his heart should be.

Keely ran in, already out of breath. "She's right behind me!"

Sage stumbled down the stairs, wearing another pair of thigh-hugging pants that made him want to do bodily harm to anyone whose gaze lingered on them for too long.

"Are we ready to go?" she asked happily, gliding toward the back doors, giving Otto Warsen's head only a cursory glance before practically sprinting to the courtyard, her pulled-back curls bouncing behind her.

He followed her with a purposeful gait, saying with a low growl, "Oh, you can run, little tornado, but you cannot hide."

Blade waved to them as he tied a leather strap under Fluffy's belly. The dragon shifted nervously. Sage did, too.

He hauled her by the arm into the arched stone alcove beside the back entrance and nudged her into one of the pillars. She looked sheepish as he loomed over her, like a dog that had chewed up some fancy shoes. Except in this case, the pair of shoes in question was a man's severed head hung from the wall. "What exactly were you up to while I was gone, Sage? Anything interesting occur?"

"I knit some mittens," Sage said pleasantly.

"Delightful. Anything else?" he pressed. She was deliberately keeping things from him, he realized. The thought made him panic.

"I learned how to use a paperweight as a weapon."

He followed her lead, realizing that forcing it out of her would be fruitless. "Fascinating. How?"

She placed both hands on the curve of her hips. "You throw it, um...really hard."

Unamused, he replied coolly, "Perhaps I'll test the theory."

Office pixies floated past them, murmuring about the commute as one of them pulled at the ends of Sage's hair. "Ow!" They darted away, cackling. "Don't you all have copies to make? Expense reports to file?" she yelled and then sighed as they fluttered away. Looking directly at him, she completely disarmed him as she asked, "Are you angry, sir? I'd hoped you'd be impressed."

In fact, he was feeling a plethora of different emotions in that moment. Frustration, confusion, and yes, seething anger—but only because he'd realized her pulled-back hair perfectly showcased the fading bruises of fingerprints around her neck. Impressed? He supposed he was impressed as well—even though he shouldn't be, even though it was alarming that she wanted his praise in the first place.

"What occurred after they took me? What happened to Warsen?"

"I…I cut off his head," she said bluntly, clapping a hand over her mouth like she couldn't believe she'd said it. He couldn't quite believe it, either.

"Yes, I gathered that. My question is more pertaining to when and why."

She swallowed, and the nervous motion of it made every muscle in his body stiffen. "After you were taken, h-he tried to kill me."

Trystan's power came out in curling waves around his feet, looking for a place to land, looking for someone to hurt. Sage eyed it, then gave his death magic a little wave like it was a blasted newborn. It curled around her hand in greeting, and she squealed in delight.

"Oh, it's so sweet!"

Sweet? The woman had no sense of self preservation. "Come back to me, you deviant!" Trystan growled, calling the magic back, and it came…very slowly.

Sage must have mistaken the murderous look in his eyes for disappointment, because she fumbled out, "I'm sorry if I overstepped by, you know…having it, uh, hung up with the other heads. I was trying to prove myself capable. I didn't think you'd mind."

Mind? I want to take the head down just so I can kick it and then pass it along to the rest of my employees so they can kick it, too.

Likely not what Ms. Erring had in mind when she'd suggested more office morale–building activities, but he could feel his own enthusiasm boosting at the prospect.

He shook his head, refocusing on the crinkle at the top of Sage's nose. "I mind that the man hurt you and I wasn't there to prevent it."

Something dark glittered in her light eyes. "But he didn't hurt me, sir." Her lip twitched. "I hurt him."

Goose bumps rose on his arms, and he was grateful his long sleeves covered them. He shouldn't be proud of the wickedness emanating off her like a dark aura, should be trying to distance her from him lest he taint her good nature any further. And he would—he had to.

But right now, he'd allow her this victory. As he leaned down toward her, their faces mere inches apart, he murmured, "Good."

Blade called out then, breaking the spell between them. "Time to go, everyone! Fluffy's getting restless, and we can't risk another bunny rabbit frightening him."

Tatianna was gently patting the animal's side. "He eats goats. How can he be scared by a tiny fluffball?"

Trystan cleared his throat, gently taking Sage's arm and guiding them back out in the open, toward the waiting group. "So let me see if I have this correct," Trystan said, watching her pop a vanilla candy into her mouth. "You killed Otto Warsen, crafted and executed a plan to smuggle every woman in my Malevolent Guard into the king's castle, faked your own death, *and* rescued me with a nearly flawless escape. Did I leave anything out?"

She nodded earnestly. "The knitting."

He turned her around and hoisted her atop the large saddle, hoping she didn't see the wide grin on his face. It wouldn't last anyhow.

As soon as this pride faded, he would be back to worrying. Evie was being corrupted by him.

This was unacceptable.

CHAPTER 16

THE VILLAIN

They flew in silence for more than two hours, then landed just before the border of the northern kingdom, Roselia. The air was cooler this far north, refreshing like crisp water as opposed to the sometimes-damp heat of Rennedawn. Hickory Forest's trees thinned, making the area a more difficult place to hide. Odd, considering this part of the land was one of the few in Rennedawn that was thought to be brushed by the gods. The creators of their world had laid their hands all over Rennedawn, painting a once-gray earth in vibrant shades of color, but there were points rumored to have larger drops of magic, places where gods spilled extra, places they had once even lived. This was one of those places.

Upon landing, Trystan was given four separate questioning looks—five if you counted the dragon. "We'll take the rest of the journey on foot," he explained, dismounting. "It's just up that path, and I don't want to risk being spotted by Roselia's men. Our welcome would be less than warm."

Clare slid off after him, fiddling with the flowered headband pushing the dark hair from her face. "Because it's cold there." When everyone stared, she clarified, "That was a joke."

Tatianna gave a saccharine smile. "We know. It just wasn't funny."

Clare lifted a single finger at the healer, but there was a gentle playfulness between them that hadn't been there before Trystan was taken. By the gods, his assistant was severing heads, his sister and her ex-betrothed were flirting; what was next?

"Where did Evie go?" Blade questioned as he led Fluffy to a nearby stream for a drink.

"What?" Trystan raged, a vein pulsing in his neck as he caught her dark head nearly disappearing through the thin smattering of trees. "Gushiken, wait here. Tatianna and Clare, you're with us."

"Wonderful," Clare said with a roll of her eyes, then stumbled over Tatianna's outstretched foot. "You are a child!"

Trystan ignored them, coursing forward after Sage. She'd become entirely unpredictable, which, granted, wasn't so wildly different from before, but the lack of openness she usually displayed so readily was distracting him from his plans, his revenge. She was making him *wonder*.

Curiosity is so obscenely annoying.

But not as annoying as the needle of protectiveness when he found her standing in front of one of the most dangerous beings in all of Rennedawn—in all of the magical continent.

A sentry. Immortal beings that appeared human and guarded some of the most magical points of the land. And not "immortal" like the people who stand on the side streets selling false love potions—"immortal" like *get Sage away from there before we all become puddles of blood.*

"Sage!" Trystan thundered, coming up next to her as she waved a hand in front of the purple-uniformed sentry's vacant look. "Stop it, you urchin. Do you have a death wish?"

She began making faces at the being, trying to get some sort of a reaction out of it, then growled in frustration when it did not cooperate. Gripping her hips, he hauled her back, ignoring the warmth of her skin and the sensations tingling up his arms as he held her. She struggled in his grip. "Let me go!"

He released her immediately. What was this feeling festering in his chest? Was it…hurt? Disgusting. This woman was unraveling him like a bloody ball of yarn. Tatianna and Clare halted beside them, gaping at the grandiose sight before them.

The clearing of trees opened onto large swaths of the brightest green grass—brighter than even Clare's home in the Rosewood Meadow, where the healing plants grew—where the gods had spilled pigment. They must have dumped a bucketload here. At the other side of the clearing, two large oaks grew separately, their trunks meeting just above the entrance of a cave, fashioned like a kiss. The whole of the clearing was lit up like firelight, like a rainbow…like Sage.

Bloody yarn.

"You cannot simply approach a sentry," he chastised her, desperately trying to ignore the endearing notch that had appeared between her brows. "I tried once, and it nearly killed me."

It had been years ago, not at the Kissing Tree Caves but farther south, toward his old home, when he'd still had hope of changing Kingsley back into a human. He double-checked his pockets now to make sure the animal hadn't stowed away again.

"You've been here before?" Her tone was accusatory, but he was too distracted by the way her hair shined in the sunlight, the way her white tunic moved across her dewy skin, her light blue corset fitted tight against her waist and bust.

Clearing his throat and looking away, he said, "No, but I've seen sentry-guarded land before. They may appear harmless, but they are ruthless, magic-made killers with zero emotions, and they cannot be destroyed."

"He looks like a man," Tatianna argued.

Evie nodded to herself, twirling a loose lock of hair. "That makes sense."

Tatianna waved a hand in front of the stoic man's face as Evie had done. "Is he actually…alive? He's not even blinking."

"Sentries appear human, but they are not. They are merely vessels made to keep people away from priceless god-made objects." Trystan demonstrated, attempting to walk forward, and he was promptly blocked by the sentry's wooden spear, even though its face still did not turn or react. "See?"

"Well, how in the deadlands do we get past him, then?" Sage turned back to the sentry, flailing her arms and making a ridiculous face, unnaturally obsessed with trying to get it to blink. It would've been amusing if— No, damn it, it *was* amusing. Grating.

Tatianna attempted to pass the sentry and was pushed back by the blunt end of its spear. Clare dove forward with her arms out to catch her. "All right, Trystan," Tati grumbled, sliding away from Clare and shaking out her shirt. "How do you propose we get through? Your magic?"

"My magic cannot be used against a sentry—none can. Passing one requires careful trickery, a mastery of the mind, an intellect that is unmatched by even the gods that made our world—"

Without warning, Sage clicked her tongue and shouldered past Trystan. "I would like to enter," she said, then smiled politely at the being. *"Please."*

The sentry lifted its spear and took a wide step to the side.

What in the deadlands…?

Sage began toward the cave, walking backward to face them with her palms up, as if to say, *"Well, look at that!"* But she slowed, frowning, when she saw him hesitating. Small torches lined the beginning of the cave, but the rest was banked in shadow. So much darkness, it made his hands shake at his sides. He tried to clench his fists, but Sage saw.

"I could go on my own if you'd prefer?" she asked gently. The wall—he needed the wall up between them, needed it now.

"I wouldn't trust you to do this by yourself." She flinched. Good. *Hate me*, his mind begged. It would make it all easier. But he couldn't resist lightening his barb by adding, "Whatever beasts lay inside would come crawling out, begging to be saved from your prattling."

She giggled, taking another step back. "Well, then you best come and save them from—"

On a ringing scream, Sage fell.

A drop-off into the darkness. Her shrieks shattered the air as she disappeared. The sentry surged forward, shoving Tatianna and Clare back.

A trick. It was a trap.

He didn't hesitate anymore.

He dove forward after her, around the immortal sentry, and into the darkness, following the echo of her screams into the nothingness.

And then it was silent.

CHAPTER 17

BECKY

Meanwhile, at the manor…

Rebecka Erring did not like children, and children, she found, did not much like her. Her little brother was the only exception, but most children were not like her little brother. This child in particular must have been malfunctioning. Lyssa Sage had pulled a chair up to her desk, insisting upon helping her organize, and then the little nuisance had learned of her greatest weakness.

Alphabetizing.

"This goes in that pile, Ms. Sage," Becky said, pointing to the neighboring stack of papers before smoothing out her tight bun.

"Sorry!" Lyssa jumped around as she straightened the stack she was holding and placed them in the opposite pile. "Shall I put them in your desk drawer?" The little girl yanked open the top drawer, and Becky's set of keys came tumbling out. "Oh, oops!"

She picked them up, handing them over to Becky before waving at the workers passing by. One intern tucked his shirt in when Becky glared at him.

"Why do you have so many keys, Ms. Erring?"

She didn't have so very many; it was just a matter of organization and safety. "One of the keys is to my cottage, this one is to the cartography closet, this bronze one is to the weapons room, this one to lock the office windows, and this silver one is to the dungeons belowstairs." She took the key ring from Lyssa's grip, but the little girl's eyes caught on the largest one, plated with gold and etched with a small *F*.

"What about this one?" Lyssa blinked, pointing to it while shoving another lemon tart into her mouth.

Becky didn't talk about that one. "It's to a place I no longer go."

Lyssa pulled the key off the ring. "Then should we get rid of it?"

Her pulse sounded in her ears as she ripped the key from Lyssa's hand. "No!" When she saw the hurt look on the child's face, the panic was quickly— and irritatingly—replaced by guilt. "I apologize. I do not like when people take liberties with my things."

Lyssa leaned in, her orange dress swishing about her tiny feet as she whispered, "Evie doesn't, either. Whenever I touch her stuff, her face gets all red and she looks like an angry tomato."

Becky resisted the pull of a grin at her lips, biting her tongue to keep from laughing. "I would like to see that."

The lunch bell tolled, and Becky stood, calling to the workers walking and flying from the room. "Anyone not back at their posts in sixty minutes on the dot will be docked in pay for the week!"

Those who were walking began to run, and Becky felt a hum of satisfaction when she saw a gleam of wonder in Lyssa's eyes. Seeking validation from a child was not something she wanted to make a habit of; regardless, it made her feel three inches taller.

"Well then, now that that's cleared up…" She pushed away from her chair and motioned for Lyssa to join her. "Shall we look for your sister's silly journal?"

Lyssa shook her head, an unreadable emotion passing over the young girl's face. "Oh, it's not silly. Our papa gave it to her! She's probably very worried it's gone forever." Her shoe bumped against Becky's desk. "Sometimes I worry my papa is, too."

Oh no. No. She was not equipped to deal with a child's hurt feelings. She could wring Evie's neck for putting her in this position. "Your father's not gone, he's just…uh…"

"In jail."

Deadlands take her. "I wouldn't call the dungeons jail." She straightened her glasses and frowned when she saw Lyssa pull a knit dragon from her dress pocket. "Where did you get that?"

"Blade gave it to me!" Lyssa had an almost dreamy look on her face—the girl had a crush. Well, that made two of them, tragically.

If Blade would just be less charming, if he wouldn't smile so much in Becky's direction, if he would just be less *everything*, she might be able to stand it. Though she supposed she could do without his petty theft.

"That wasn't his to give—it's mine. I thought I'd lost it."

Lyssa handed it over readily, and Becky considered the toy from her childhood. It had been a gift from her father, who had fully fueled her obsession with the winged beasts when she was herself a little girl. She swallowed the memory, lest she begin to weep; she detested weeping.

Handing it back to Lyssa, she smiled lightly. "Keep it, actually. I don't have much need for it now."

Lyssa stared at her, that wistful expression back. "You have a beautiful smile, Ms. Erring! You should do it all the time."

She had smiled often...*before.* But Becky had learned a lesson in the past few years that she would carry with her until the day she laid down for her eternal rest. Bending to meet Lyssa at the little girl's height, she said, "I do not smile when I don't feel like it."

Lyssa blinked, surprised. "Why not?"

"Because we are always expected to plaster a grin on our faces even when we don't wish to. I used to do it so often, I stopped being able to tell when I was smiling for me or for someone else. So now, I don't smile unless I'm one hundred percent sure it's something *I* want to do, not something someone else wants me to do." She smoothed a lock of hair away from Lyssa Sage's face. "And you shouldn't, either."

She could almost see the words sinking into Lyssa's spongelike mind, the girl appearing a little sad as they registered. "I think... I think Evie smiles when she doesn't want to. I think she does it all the time."

And there it was—that was it. The reason Becky could barely stand the woman: she was in a constant state of fulfilling the needs of others, and it reminded Becky just a smidge too much of a person she no longer knew.

"Ms. Erring! Ms. Erring!" Marvin burst through the now empty office, interrupting them, sweaty and out of breath. "I'm." He wheezed. "Sorry—the stairs, they..." He wheezed again. Lyssa handed him her canteen, and the front guard smiled at her. Lyssa paused for a second, contemplating, then smiled back.

Good girl.

"What is it, Marvin?" Becky gathered her stacks of paper and straightened them neatly.

Marvin gripped his middle, and Becky's blood turned to ice when she realized he wasn't just out of shape—he was out of his mind with terror. "The ward," he started. "The ward over the manor. It's broken!"

"What?" Becky dropped the papers, time dilating around her so they fell almost in slow motion. "What do you mean *broken*?"

"Massacre Manor," Marvin said gravely. "It's visible."

CHAPTER 18

EVIE

Dead. I must be dead.

Evie hadn't stopped screaming. Her throat had grown raw as she fell, waiting for the impact of the ground, but instead, she'd landed against something soft and dewy. Then the darkness had faded, and when she finally brought herself to open her eyes, she was surrounded by a sea of bright, pale-blue light and countless little clouds.

The sky. She was in the sky, but she had fallen downward. How could that be possible?

Another body landed beside her, causing her to bounce again, and this time she couldn't help it—she laughed. She was on a godsforsaken *cloud*—there was clearly no other appropriate reaction.

"Sage, are you hurt?" The graveled rasp of his voice made her breathe a sigh of relief, and a warm sliver of comfort eased into her heart that at least if she was dead, they were dead together. When she looked at him, she laughed again: his hair was sticking up in every direction. She'd never seen it so mussed.

"I'm well, but your hair has seen better days," she responded casually, biting her lip when he started shuffling frantically to smooth it. Leaning over the side of the cloud to see what was below, she felt her face prickle with trepidation.

A field of dandelions.

She swallowed and shook the memories away. Memories of her brother Gideon's screams, of her mother's disappearance, of the day her childhood ended—abruptly, traumatically, tragically. These were the small moments of life, when one's innocent view of the world was corrupted, when the magic curtain was ripped away to reveal something sinister or ugly. A moment when one stopped believing and viewed the world with different, weary eyes.

It was a natural part of life, one of the rules of growing older, but she'd never been very good at adhering to rules. Yes, she'd grown older, but she still had faith in goodness, in people, in *magic*.

The soft grass below looked even greener than the patch of land outside the cave—like a mossy cushion. Standing on shaky legs, she walked toward the edge of the cloud, mesmerized, ignoring the boss's warnings. "Sage, don't you dare—"

She jumped.

The distance to the ground was farther than she'd anticipated. She let out a panicked cry as she angled herself to roll, but the impact was soft, like the only thing below the grass was more grass, no hard earth beneath. She let out a very unladylike *"oof."*

The boss landed gracefully a few feet away from her—*because of course he did*, she thought with a roll of her eyes. He did everything seamlessly. It was why she liked to see him so ruffled. And truly, he was a mess. Shirt untucked, hair out of place, pants wrinkled, and a bitter frown marring his features as he stared at her in disbelief.

"I have to wonder," he bit out, stalking over to her and pulling her up to stand, "do you have absolutely no care for your own well-being? Or are you simply so naive to the world that you believe it will never harm you?"

She flinched, and he let go, his dark eyes softening with regret—but it was too late. He'd called her naive, and it couldn't have enflamed her more if he'd set her on fire.

The words tumbled out of her mouth before she could halt them. "I've been hurt plenty by the world, by people, by *men*. Just because you bury your bad experiences behind revenge schemes and scorn doesn't mean that I must join you in your misery. Being a cynic doesn't make you wise. It makes you *a coward*."

She put her hands out and shoved him away from her, and he stumbled, gobsmacked for a moment.

And then his eyes darkened, his fury matching her own.

Oh, now you've done it.

Don't find his murderous rage so entrancing, Evie!

He prowled forward like a predator, and she stumbled back with every step until she bumped into a wall of blue sky. It was a barrier, smooth beneath her touch. She didn't have time to study it further, as he was already looming over her.

"It's not cynicism, you natural disaster," he snarled. "It's realism. It's knowing people, and the elements, well enough to realize that they are always against you. I don't want you hurt! I don't want you to die! Which is very fucking frustrating when you act in ways that could easily accomplish both!"

Oh. This isn't condescension… This is…protectiveness? That's a little dramatic; I jumped from a cloud, for goodness' sake. She'd be in more danger having a snowball fight with tissues.

The whole disagreement was beginning to feel silly. "That's a lovely thing for you to say. Thank you for caring." She awkwardly reached up to pat his shoulder, shrinking when he angled closer. Not to mention getting a little excited by it, if she was being completely honest. And completely pathetic.

"You are the most frustrating person I've ever met, and I work with *hardened criminals.*" He shuddered. "And *interns!*"

She didn't think those two groups were necessarily equivalent, but judging by the flare of his nostrils, it was likely not the safest time to point that out.

Still, it felt a little like a compliment. She licked her lips as she said candidly, "Well, I wouldn't be so frustrating if you didn't incense me so."

His chest was moving rapidly, his pupils dark and large. His words came from low in his throat. "I've incensed *you*? What do you think you've done to *me*?"

Her lips parted on a gasp at the heavy tension suddenly between them. It felt like the air was too thick—hard to breathe it in; hard to breathe at all. "I annoy you," she said, attempting to divert this pressure, desperate to.

Thick hair fell over his eyes as he shook his head, hand raising slowly, too slowly, to caress the skin of her cheek with his knuckles, light, like a whisper of a touch. It triggered a memory, vague and blurry through her poisoned state after she'd eaten the sleeping-death fruit. There had been a warm voice through the blurriness and another whisper-light touch against her own knuckles.

"I command you as your employer to wake up."

He shook his head again, his hand curling around the back of her neck, lightly pulling her closer. Their lips were scant inches apart; she could practically taste the sugar from his cauldron brew on his breath.

She should move away, or he should.

But neither of them did.

"I incense you," she breathed, then nearly buckled when she heard a low sound in the back of his throat, almost like a groan.

"Completely." His lips were nearly on her—

When the blue skylike barrier around them began to shake.

And move.

They jumped apart. Breathing heavily and red-faced, she held fast to his tensed arm as they stumbled backward. "What is that?"

The blue sky around them began to move as something that had been camouflaged slowly revealed itself. A creature so tall, the clouds floated near its mouth, which was now visible, displaying two rows of razor-sharp teeth.

"The end of the rhyme. The monster's next meal," The Villain said beside her, his chest still heaving. The beast from the story had revealed itself at the most inopportune moment.

Evie gulped before saying, "Do you think it's married to that ending?"

CHAPTER 19

THE VILLAIN

As far as interruptions went, it was well timed. If the monster coming out of the blue sky had revealed itself even a moment later, Trystan would've lost control…and there was no telling what atrocity he would've committed next.

Part of him *still* wanted to find out.

BOOM!

The beast fully formed before them. A shrieking howl came from its large mouth, so loud it made them both stumble back. Its skin seemed to be made up of cloud and marble in equal parts, its face grotesque yet *almost* human, save for the horns growing from its giant head. Misted clouds surrounded its temples, almost like a crown, and they stayed perfectly in place, the way Kingsley's crown often did.

When it slammed its fist against the ground, the entire hidden oasis shook.

"Who disturbs me?" the monster howled.

Good—this was good, actually.

Dealing with mortal danger was far preferable to ruminating on what he'd almost done.

He would instead remain fixated on the monster's horns, its deathlike stare. Not on the gasp that had sounded out of Sage's lips mere moments ago, a sound that would surely haunt him in his dreams, his nightmares—should he escape the current situation, of course. He'd gone far too long without bedding a woman; it was the only reasonable explanation for losing control of himself so thoroughly. It had been six excruciating months of abstaining.

Abstaining for no particular reason, it seemed in this moment.

The monster slammed its fist into the ground once more, snapping Trystan back to reality, back to all that truly mattered to him. Revenge, villainy, murder—staying alive.

He sucked in a breath, feeling focused. *That's better.*

"I said who!" the monster cried.

It was a rhetorical question—surely they both knew this—and yet that didn't stop his assistant from cupping her hands around her mouth and screeching like she was speaking to an elderly grandparent: "EVIE SAGE!"

Trystan gawked at her before rubbing at his cheek. "You forgot to curtsy," he said incredulously. She shrugged and started to dip but halted when he gripped her waist. "Are you having an episode?" He needed migraine potion and a very long, very cold bath.

The creature was still reeling from Sage's response, furrowing its— Well, it didn't have *eyebrows*, but Trystan imagined they would be furrowed should they have been present.

"Back away," he warned it, praying the monster wouldn't see the emptiness in the threat. He could feel from its stillness inside him that his magic wouldn't work here; he had no means of protecting them, no means of protecting her. But he'd hardly have need to, because instead of remaining safely hidden behind him, Sage circled around and presented herself to the monster, dropping into a deep curtsy, smiling wide before yelling loudly, "Hello!"

…Was she attempting to make a polite introduction to a creature that would likely try to eat them? "Sage!" he hissed. "What in the gods' names are you doing?"

"What's your name?" She smiled at it.

Yes, of course she did.

But instead of eating her whole, the creature dropped to its large knees, knocking dandelion bristles through the air like party confetti and extending one of its long, gray hands covered in purple markings that looked like vines. Trystan lurched forward, ready to do battle, but instead he stopped in frozen awe.

One large finger was slowly extended. It was enormous compared to the size of Sage's hand, but it was extended nonetheless. She jumped, delighted, as she wrapped both hands around its finger and shook.

"I have no name," the creature said, slowly pulling its finger back, anger fading from its tone. "I am a part of this world, and by natural law, I can take none."

Sage frowned. "Well, that's a silly rule! Who came up with that?"

The monster frowned back at her, and then it...chortled.

"Sage," Trystan whispered. "Do you remember that time I confiscated those mushrooms from the interns? This is beginning to resemble that."

She scrunched her nose and scratched the side of her head when she looked at him. "Those made you hallucinate."

"Precisely."

The creature's voice boomed again. "The rules were made by the architects of this world, the creators—gods, you call them," it said; Sage gave it her rapt attention. "They made every corner of this world what it is. Every person, every living thing exists because of their sacrifices."

"Oh. They did a very good job!" Sage nodded encouragingly; he could practically see the thoughts spinning behind her eyes. "I'm a big fan of, um—oh, the trees!" She seemed calm, but she was nervous. He could tell by the way she wrung her hands.

She had no need to be, because after the compliment, the creature looked...*bashful*?

"I think I *am* hallucinating," Trystan whispered.

Sage knocked him in the shoulder. "Hush!"

"They were my idea, actually." One of its large fingers began to draw circles in the grass, its attention glued to his assistant. She was charming the thing into a stupor.

He could sympathize with its plight.

She brightened. "And what a grand idea it was!" She did another curtsy, her head bowed in respect. "We owe you our utmost thanks." She elbowed Trystan, hard.

He rubbed the spot before frowning, then said, "Oh yes...thank you." He didn't sound thankful. He sounded befuddled and irritated.

The creature's attention went back to him, and it turned cold. "I don't like him."

Sage waved her hand and patted its finger. "That's all right." She stage-whispered behind her hand, "Lots of people don't."

"That's enough small talk." Trystan wouldn't stand here idle while Sage conspired with a monster of legend. He was The Villain, for gods' sake. "We are here for a vial of stardust. We need it to find someone who's lost. Someone who can help us fulfill *Rennedawn's Story*."

The creature's large eyes rounded on him. "You want to fulfill *Rennedawn's*

Story, Trystan Maverine?"

His stomach dropped into his shoes at his name on the creature's lips.

Before he could inquire as to how the creature knew who he was, it grinned, marbled teeth shining as it said words that rattled him down to his misplaced soul.

"It took you long enough."

CHAPTER 20

EVIE

Evie looked between her boss and her new, very large friend. "Do you two know each other?"

Her boss deadpanned, "Yes, we have tea every other Thursday."

"Really?" she asked, her brow furrowed.

He pinched the bridge of his nose. "No, Sage."

Rocking back on her heels, she clasped her hands behind her, not missing a beat. "How do you know my boss's name?"

The creature shifted, flurrying more dandelion heads about. The wisps of them danced in the air and tickled her nose. "I know all names. I know all things, as nature does."

She blurted without thought, "Do you know my mother, then? Nura Sage? Where she is?" It was a dangerous question for many reasons. The first being she wasn't entirely certain she was ready to face the woman who had abandoned her in a place not unlike this one. A field of wishes. A field of forgotten hope. The second being that this godlike creature could probably crush her for her impertinence...and the third was that her judgment was still incredibly clouded from the haze of passion she'd been trying to clear out of her mind for the last couple of minutes.

Completely, he'd said.

No one could be expected to be of sound mind with the tingling sensations his voice had spread throughout her body. Never had angering someone felt so sensual, so wanting, so—

This needed to stop, or she was going to pin him to his desk when they returned and do something they'd regret. Well...something *he'd* likely regret.

She didn't have the will or the self-control when it came down to the things she wanted, the things she loved.

Because she loved him. So much so, it made her brainless enough to ask questions she still wasn't sure she wanted the answers to.

It was fruitless anyhow. The creature frowned, looking at her with a sympathetic mien. "I am sorry, Evangelina Sage. I cannot interfere in human affairs." The creature scoffed, brushing its large hand through its cloud crown, which immediately formed again in place. "As much as they may need the intervention, it's forbidden."

The Villain's eyes were on her when her face fell. He looked at the creature and said angrily, "That's unicorn shit."

The creature shrugged. "On this, we agree, but I cannot risk the already waning magic, even if I wished to. This cave is no enchantment, but a piece of the world and sky that I've stolen and hoarded as my own. The rest of the creators have moved on to paint another realm, but I remain here."

The boss frowned. "The waning magic. You feel it here?"

The creature was forlorn. "The shift has already begun. You, Trystan Maverine, with all your great power, should feel it, too. Your magic is slipping, isn't it? Beginning to fade? Becoming defiant? There is something happening to Rennedawn. As predicted long ago, the humans have become greedy, wielding the magic like it is a thing to manipulate instead of a partner."

The creature then pointed to a rift in the sky of its lair; it appeared as if a large piece of it was missing, with a dark void beyond.

"Oh no. What happened?" Evie asked, a sick sensation in her gut as she looked at it.

"Greed. Humans desire to take; they rarely seek to give. The magic of this world knows this and is beginning to hide to protect itself. The book was written to save it when that time comes."

She shifted her gaze to her boss's hands, knowing his magic lurked beneath their surface. But his magic was no longer hiding—not from her. What could that mean?

The Villain read her thoughts and grimaced as he tucked his hands into his pockets, turning his attention back to the creature. "You could've left with the rest of the gods, so why did you stay?"

Clouds shook above their heads, almost sentient as they rolled toward the creature, surrounding it. "I cannot abandon my piece of world, my piece of sky. My cave of stars when the night turns dark. I cannot leave it to hands that will hurt or destroy it. Precious things must be protected."

Evie knew that better than most. "I understand."

The creature looked right at her. Its eyes were a swirl of lilac color, round and large, making it look almost innocent. "I know you do, Evangelina Sage." It pulled a vial from the air, then tossed the glittery substance to the ground in front of them. "A token, for the kindness man so often lacks. A rare gift. Harvested from the stars themselves."

Evie picked it up and saw a glistening powder within. Her heart soared at the sight.

"Stardust, to help guide your way to what you seek. For the daughter of wishing stars."

Her eyes widened. "The daughter of…"

The creature gave no explanation, just summoned a cloud from above, then blew a gust of wind the way one might blow a kiss. The force of it caused Evie's stomach to flip until her heeled boots touched down on the surprisingly firm cloud's surface. "I wish you luck, Evie Sage. This cave is a wonder of stars at night. I hope you will return to see them."

She gripped the vial tight in her damp palm, using her other arm to hold on to her boss, who spoke to the creature with stark confusion.

"Why does the nursery rhyme paint you as a carnivorous monster when you are merely protecting this cave? Why do you allow the legends to spin you in such a light?"

The cloud began to soar upward, so high they were face-to-face with the creature. Then it started to fade back into the sky, its skin melding into the blue. "You know as well as I, Trystan Maverine, that humans demonize what they cannot understand. It isn't our job to educate them, just to live the way we're meant to with the knowledge that being called a monster does not make you one."

The Villain nodded, sniffing back emotion she knew he didn't want either of them to see. "For what it's worth…I do not think you a monster."

The creature was nearly faded back into the hidden sky, the cloud shooting them upward faster and faster, but Evie still heard the echo of the words left behind. "From you, Trystan Maverine, that means a great deal."

• • •

"It's been too long. They're not coming out!"

"You are so negative all the time! Isn't it exhausting? Aren't you tired?"

"I'm preparing for the worst! They have clearly fallen to their deaths!"

"Clare, shut up! They are *not* dead!"

As the cloud launched Evie and her boss out of the opening, she wondered if they were about to be. But then they were flailing in open air. She let out a very unladylike curse as she hit the ground. "We're okay!" she rasped, pushing up, feeling Tatianna's hands on her cheeks as the healer examined her face.

"What happened?" Tatianna said, eyes moving over to The Villain, who was already on his feet, brushing the grass from his person.

The sentry was back in front of the cave, but Evie no longer viewed him as an adversary—she was just grateful that the creature below had someone, immortal or not, looking out for its well-being. Everyone should have someone like that.

"I met the inventor of trees." She sounded as mystified as she felt.

Tatianna rolled her lips, looking at her pityingly. "Of course you did, dear. Come, let me examine your head."

A low yell sounded from the trees. Blade.

"Another mouse?" Clare guessed, crossing her arms. But Evie saw a flash of silver.

Her heart quickened, her palms dampening. "No. Blade!" she screamed as she stood, running for the path, footsteps sounding behind her as the rest of them followed.

And when she cleared the path through the trees to the stream beyond, she saw her dearest friend pinned to the ground with a sword at his throat.

The Valiant Guard had found them.

CHAPTER 21

EVIE

"If you plan to drive me through with that, could you get it over with?" Evie called to the knight holding a blade at her back.

"Sage, do not move!" The Villain ordered, hands raised, ready to use his magic.

"I don't need to move, sir. Can you see how much he's shaking?" She angled her head to look at the sword pressed to her back. It shook along with its wielder. "At this rate, he'll run me through by accident."

The sword slipped, nicking her. She winced, and the guard's eyes widened with panic.

"First day?" she asked sympathetically.

"Sage," The Villain bit out.

"It is, actually," the knight mumbled.

The Villain groaned. "Oh for the love of—"

Evie waved a hand. "Ignore him. You're doing fine."

"Thank you, milady," the knight replied earnestly. He almost lowered the sword but was reprimanded by his captain—the one holding Blade at knifepoint while Fluffy howled beneath a weighted net. The poor animal was blowing gusts of smoke in feeble attempts to produce flame.

"Simon!" the captain yelled. "Stop flirting with the enemy and retrieve the stardust."

"Yes, sir," Simon said nervously, tucking his chin against his chest.

She held fast to the vial in her pocket, hoping they wouldn't search her first, though as usual, her fears were for naught. Dark shadows pooled at her feet—the boss's magic. This was the power that was rumored to be strong enough to rip apart homes, rip apart *bodies*. She swallowed, watching it…play with the laces of her boots like a cat.

Oh dear. "Sir?" she asked, trying to shake it away by wiggling her foot, but it merely clung tighter.

The Villain's face twisted with anger as he tried to pull the mist closer. "Obey!" he yelled, but it was too late.

A helmeted knight had stepped out of the throng with an outstretched hand—the same knight who had subdued The Villain's power before he was taken from her last time.

She wouldn't let it happen again.

The mist about her feet vanished as The Villain dropped to the ground, screaming in agony.

The sword at her back slipped again. "Ow!" she wailed overdramatically.

"I'm sorry, miss!" Simon yelped from behind her, sword moving away for a second, but it was enough. She turned, kicking him hard in the shin before pulling her dagger from her side and banging the blunt end against his unguarded head. He dropped immediately.

"No, *I'm* sorry!" She winced, stepping over him, then charged for Trystan. Another knight ran at her but skidded to a halt when Evie's dagger took on a life of its own. The scar on her shoulder pulsed as her hand parried and the dagger thrust itself through the man's chest. Her eyes widened. That hadn't been her. Not really. Right?

"How did you do that?" Tatianna asked, her hands beginning to glow as she gripped one of the knights by the arm. Whatever she did, it caused the man to collapse on the spot.

"I don't really know, but I—I don't think that was me." She exhaled hard, coming face-to-face with Clare in front of The Villain, guarding him. Clare nodded at Evie before pulling a well of orange ink from her pocket. She tossed the glowing liquid out of the well, then wielded and bent the ink through the air like a weapon before splashing it toward the three knights charging them.

They dropped, screaming as it burned their skin. The smell of charred flesh permeated the air. "Ew." Evie pinched her nose.

Three knights remained, one holding magical cuffs as he charged for The Villain, but he was stopped—by a large green blur that flew out of nowhere, covering the front of the knight's helmet. "Get it off!" he shrieked. "What is it?"

They all grinned. "Kingsley, you are a shameless stowaway!" Evie cried, but she smiled, too, as the frog held on for dear life and the knight flailed, trying to see around the amphibian, until he tripped, hit his head on a nearby log, and lay still.

The knight holding Blade let go, realizing he was sorely outnumbered, and the dragon trainer didn't waste the opportunity. He sprinted for Fluffy, cutting through the netting with gentle purpose and murmuring soothing words to the frightened animal.

They were winning, but the boss was still subdued on the ground, the knight with the outstretched hand moving forward.

"Finish The Villain!" the injured captain ordered from where he lay against a tree, seething with anger. He had removed his helmet to reveal a drawn face and furious eyes. "Do it now!"

"No," the remaining knight said. "I don't think that I will."

The knight dropped his hands, releasing The Villain from his painful vise grip, and spun on the captain, running him through with his sword. The captain's face was frozen in outrage, blood dripping from the corner of his mouth, before he fell to the red-soaked grass, dead.

The treacherous remaining knight removed his helmet, revealing a pair of green eyes so familiar, she almost wept to look at them.

The knight smiled, small and hesitant. "Well, that was a bit messy, wasn't it?"

Her informant had come at last.

CHAPTER 22

THE VILLAIN

"Wait. I know you," Trystan uttered in absolute astonishment at the man before him. He rarely forgot faces, and though this one had lost the final dregs of adolescence and now angled out into that of a man in his mid-twenties, he was still recognizable.

"I'm honored you remember! It was my first week as a knight when we met in that corridor. Right before you were, uh…"

"Imprisoned?" Trystan offered sardonically.

"I wasn't going to say that part," the knight muttered quietly. The man had been a recruit when Trystan was apprenticing for the king ten years ago—they'd chatted for a bit, all small talk; he'd never even gotten the youth's name. But it had been the first time in weeks that someone didn't skitter away from him, frightened for reasons he didn't then understand. He'd liked the boy.

The knight's eyes fell to Sage, soft and grinning.

Not anymore.

"And who are you?" Tatianna asked, narrowing her gaze on the newcomer. The knight's expression turned to one of interest when his green eyes found the office healer.

"Someone who'd like to know you," he said.

Tatianna scoffed, rolling her eyes and shaking her head. "I could break you in two."

The knight gave her a crooked grin. "Do you promise?"

Trystan watched Clare's eyebrow twitch before he noticed her reaching for the leftover orange ink in her pocket. He gripped her wrist. "Don't," he warned.

That was, until Sage nearly knocked Trystan out of the way, throwing her arms around the knight and burying her head in his neck.

"Okay, Clare, go ahead," Trystan said, waving her on.

Tatianna grabbed Clare's hand when it moved to her belt. The healer looked a little like she was herding two rabid racoons. "Stop it, you two! Good grief."

Kingsley landed on Trystan's boot, eyeing the hugging pair.

Trystan looked at his frog friend. His frog friend looked at him.

A sign slowly crept upward that read: Uh-Oh.

"That's helpful," Trystan hissed, rolling his eyes before scooping up his little nuisance and placing him on his shoulder.

Sage separated from the man—*finally*. But Trystan's pulsing anger worsened when she began fussing over him, putting all her caring attention into brushing back his golden-brown locks, wiping a dirt smudge from his cheek.

This was what Trystan wanted. He wanted her to develop affection for someone else; it would be easier to not care for her, easier to not think of her as his. But there was a rather primitive part of his mind—and magic—that did not care about any of those things. Just wanted to take the knight's discarded helmet and beat him over the head with it till it dented.

The comforting thought calmed his heart rate.

"You were supposed to meet us right after the unmasking! What happened?" Sage cried, shoving the knight's shoulder. Trystan's head spun. She'd done it; she'd flipped a hero to their side. Next she was going to ask the sun and the moon to host a dinner party together...and she'd likely be successful.

"I was waiting for the right moment to slip away without arousing suspicion. Then, when I heard the king order the men here to steal the stardust from you, I saw the perfect opportunity for a grand entrance." The knight held his hands out in a flourish.

Sage rolled her eyes, but there was affection in it. "You and your theatrics."

The vein in Trystan's forehead was about to break skin when she dragged the knight toward him—unwise of her, but Trystan kept his face impassive. She wouldn't know he was planning the man's death, that he hated him with the fire of a thousand suns, that he thought the knight a reckless ingrate who needed to be put down and—

Sage presented the knight proudly. "Sir, I'd like you to meet my older brother, Gideon Sage."

What? Oh.

The impassive mask cracked into stupefied shock. "Th-That isn't possible. Your brother is dead." But then he saw them—the similarities between the two: the same tick in Gideon's lip, the same high cheekbones, the same mischief in the eyes. Her godsdamn *brother*.

I am pathetic.

CHAPTER 23

EVIE

Two weeks earlier…

It had been a mere handful of hours since Trystan was taken. Lyssa was happily settled into a suite in the west wing of the manor, a place Evie couldn't bring herself to linger—not without him. She watched Otto Warsen's head sway gently with the draft coming in from the front door with a morbid satisfaction. She didn't know how long she'd been staring. She should've been disgusted with what she'd done. She should've been appalled and frightened by her brutal actions. But instead—

She smiled.

A plan was brewing in her mind, like chemicals melding together to create something lethal, a poison so toxic and pungent it could kill in seconds. But the malevolence was burying something, and as soon as she glanced to the gilded ink ring around her pinkie finger, she choked on it.

Loss.

Trystan lived in every inch of the walls, in the kitchens, in the offices, in the decaying heads above, in everything. The manor was him. But he was gone, and she couldn't breathe. Stumbling out the front door, she ran past the manor's barriers, past the safety and protection, past any reminders of him, and dropped to her knees on a keening cry. Fisting wet grass in her palms, she stared at a flower she wanted to tear from the ground. She pinched her eyes shut instead.

Too much loss, too much heartache, too much pain.

"Please no, please no," she chanted. The scar on her back no longer stung, but it tingled as if sensing her distress. The dagger at her thigh warmed in answer. "I'll get him back. I will."

"I'd like to assist with that, if I could?"

The unknown voice mixed with the wounded ache in her heart, and the combination proved lethal when her eyes darted upward and saw the glinting silver. Saw the king's insignia. Whatever was left of her reason snapped like a rotting branch.

"Aaaaah!" She screamed, dagger unsheathed, and ran for the knight, swiping through the air like she was chopping flying vegetables.

"Hold on!" the knight shouted, stumbling back. "Just let me explain."

But Evie didn't. She kept coming, and when she finally got close enough, she brought her booted foot up between his legs as hard as she could manage. The knight went down with a howl, his helmet rolling off his head into a puddle of mud. Evie blinked.

Because she knew that mop of hair. She knew that chin, the nose, the green eyes. So like her father's...

The knight before her was Gideon.

Her older brother, who she'd believed dead for the past decade, was laying before her, clutching his groin and moaning into the grass. "I deserved that, I suppose," he rasped, breathing deeply through his mouth. His skin was red and tanned and...not corpse-like at all.

She blinked. "You are dead."

"Eve," Gideon said, climbing to his feet—because he had feet. They moved and everything—they weren't decayed or rotting; they moved quite efficiently as he slowly edged closer.

"No!" She held up the dagger. "Stay there."

Gideon halted, his throat bobbing as he rolled his lips and rocked back on his heels. "I, um. I know this is probably very confusing, but if you'd just give me a moment?"

"Are you a demon?" she blurted, then almost covered her mouth to hold the embarrassment in. But what in the deadlands did she have to be embarrassed about? She was not the one who had come back from the dead. Although...her plans weren't veering so far away from that.

Irony was funny sometimes, and other times it was like someone had slapped you with an umbrella.

"I am a Valiant Guard, so...you're close!" Gideon said with a smile, and a beat of recognition ran through her as the shock began to wear off. She stepped closer, her hand drifting up toward his face, brushing over a faded white scar on his cheek. He'd gotten it from a fall he took while climbing a tree to retrieve her favorite kite. Her fingertips brushed over it, and tears burned her eyes.

"Gideon?"

He nodded, tears brimming, too, and Evie brought her other hand up.

And knocked him square in the jaw.

"What. In. The. Deadlands!" she screamed, pulling her fist back to hit him again, but he was already on his feet.

Her brother stumbled away, deeper into the trees, and she ridiculously followed him.

"We thought you were dead for ten years! *Ten years!*"

He kept stumbling, trying to keep his eyes on her as he moved back and away from her swinging hands. "I know, Eve, I know! Please let me explain! Did you just throw a rock? Villainous work has really hardened you, huh?"

She picked up another rock.

"I'm sorry!" he cried. "I practiced this a million times, and I'm already mucking it up. Just let me say my piece, and then you can hit me with whatever you want."

"How about an anvil?" she grumbled. The sun was sinking through the trees in a display of muted greens and golds, nearing its descent beyond the horizon. Like it didn't want to stick around for this horrendous display.

"Years ago, in the field, when the light hit me. It didn't actually...hit me."

Her brows shot up, and she was ready to protest, but he kept talking— likely knowing his time to do so was limited. "Remember that fever I got at school? When I was in bed for a week?"

She remembered. She'd had to console her mother and play nursemaid at his bedside, but she hadn't complained. They needed her, and she'd needed that. "I remember."

"The trauma of the sickness woke up my magic. Father didn't want to alarm any of you until we knew what sort of magic it was, so he called for a specialist while you were at school. It's a magic that sort of, um...suppresses other kinds of magic."

Dots were connecting in a very ugly way. "You're the knight who messed with his magic, aren't you?" They both knew who she was talking about.

"I had to, Eve. I was following orders. Several of those knights have magic of their own. Should I have fought back, even if I'd wanted to, we would've been outnumbered. He would've been taken anyway." Gideon cleared his throat and pulled at his silver armor, which was caked in blood. Blood from the knight he'd felled to save her after she killed Otto. "I was always going to step in, I swear it. I knew Mr. Warsen was a creep—by the gods, I would've liked a shot at murdering him myself, but you beat me to it."

It wasn't that her knees were weak; it was just that her body was tired of holding the weight of all the realizations. The whiplash of her father's betrayal, her boss's capture, and her brother's revival, all within a twenty-four-hour period. She knew she was chaotic, but this was a bit much, even for her.

She sank to her knees in the grass, then sighed when Gideon sat beside her, maintaining a careful distance. "I want to help you. I didn't know about Father, or I would've—"

"Don't." She cut him a look so mired in hatred that he flinched.

"I'm sorry. I'm so sorry. Regardless, the crux of it all is that I was able to save myself that day in the fields, but Mother's magic was unstable and strong. I was knocked practically into another dimension—like actually another dimension, for a second—but then I landed somewhere in the vicinity of the Gleaming Palace with practically burned-off clothing and no memory of who I was or what I was doing there. Someone pointed me toward Valiant Guard recruiters, and it all sort of spiraled after that."

"Memory loss? You expect me to believe nobody in the Valiant Guard barracks recognized you? When Father worked so closely with the king?"

"The king did."

This caused her to go silent.

"He called me Gideon the first time he met me. My memory started coming back around five years later, in jagged bits. Even when it had all returned, I never revealed that it had—and the king didn't reveal anything about my past to me, either."

She glared at him, trying to kick her sympathies away. He didn't deserve them. "Am I supposed to feel sorry for you?" she asked while pulling soft pieces of grass between her fingers. "You never came back! We mourned you! This is the most heinous act I've ever seen anyone pull, and I've watched my boss cut someone's tongue out for eating all the vanilla candies."

Her boss. *Trystan.*

"He's gone because of you," she whispered. A tear slid down her cheek.

Gideon nodded, eyes getting red as he rubbed at them. "I know. But I've come to make it right. I've come to help you get him back."

She sneered. "Why should I trust anything you say? You've been working for the king for *ten years.*"

"I killed one of my own to save you. You think I would not betray the man who stole so many years of my life without a care for the one I had before?" He looked so sincere, so serious. So unlike the Gideon she remembered. "All I ask is sanctuary when we get him out. When the deed is done, all I ask is a safe place to go."

She shook her head and pulled a hand through her hair before looking at him, more tears falling. "Why should I give you a safe place, when you stole mine from me?"

And like that, Evie watched her brother's heart break.

She wanted to lock him away with her father, wanted him to suffer alongside him. The two men in her life destroying her trust and discarding her feelings like they were flimsy, inconsequential things. But there was a difference between Gideon's eyes and her father's, and it wasn't the color. It was the hope.

Pure and honest and pleading. It grounded her; it pulled at her and rooted her like a tree.

And despite all her anger and hurt, she felt a little grateful for the brother who had abandoned them reappearing now. She needed a way into the Gleaming Palace—someone on the inside—and if he said he could do it... she'd allow him to help. With the knowledge that at any moment, she could have the Malevolent Guard tear him apart.

Gideon was slumped back against a tree trunk, his shoulders bunched. "I suppose there's nothing I can say to make this right. But I hope to show you—"

"Can you get me into the Gleaming Palace undetected?"

The hope in his eyes had gone from a torch to a catching bonfire. "I can. I'll do whatever you need me to do. But I will tell you that the king instructed me to retrieve Mother's letters and your, uh...dead body."

She smiled. *Perfect.*

Gideon frowned. "I don't remember you being this scary... Why is that making you smile?"

"Because I plan to give the king exactly that. And so much more."

CHAPTER 24

EVIE

Two weeks and a very awkward conversation later…

The ride back to the manor had been tense and uncomfortable. Which was generally how the vast majority of Evie's interactions went, but it was a little more difficult to bear when so many people she cared for were in one place.

And they all *hated* each other.

Not only had Trystan been opposed to Gideon returning to the manor with them, he'd still wanted to kill her brother for how he'd gotten Trystan captured and kept his powers repressed while he was held in captivity. Evie had spent most of the flight on Fluffy tersely whispering to him about all her reasons for trusting Gideon and how those reasons were justified.

"I don't understand what would prompt you to align yourself with *my* enemies."

Her face had reddened in anger, and a flash of intrigue won over her boss's expression before it leveled back to rage. "I wanted to lock him up!" she'd hissed. "I wanted to never see his face again for how he betrayed our family. For how he betrayed me! But I put my personal feelings aside—for you!"

The Villain's mouth closed, and he'd stared blankly at her before uttering one infuriating word. "Oh."

"Oh?" She'd seethed, clenching her fists.

"Do they always fight like this?" Gideon had whispered loud enough for all of them to hear.

"Always." Tatianna had nodded gravely.

"Not true!" Evie had yelled at the same time Trystan objected, "Hardly!"

Gideon had nodded as well. "Excellent. You've convinced me." They clearly had not.

"Might I remind you," Evie had continued whispering to The Villain, "he helped me save *your* life! And besides, if he steps out of line, you can just kill him." She had almost done so herself, after all, not so very long ago.

"*He* is sitting right here," Gideon had said dryly.

Both The Villain's and Evie's eyes had darted for Gideon, who held his hands up in surrender.

"Look, for what it's worth, I didn't make this decision lightly. I've been planning on leaving the guard for years." Gideon had grinned at her, keeping his hands up. "And I would never hurt my sister."

Her boss had narrowed his eyes at her brother. "By my measure, you already have."

So now, back at the manor, Evie left Gideon in a guarded room to change out of his Valiant Guard armor before any more of the Malevolent Guards saw him. It was a wonder Keely didn't string him up by his toenails in the courtyard, but the captain instead had offered to stand outside his door with another guard, Nesma, who had whispered to Evie that she'd keep Keely from killing him.

Evie's grateful smile carried her all the way back up to the office space, where Malevolent Guards and workers flurried about in a tizzy. "What's going on?" Evie asked Becky as a pixie dove through her hair and three interns flew past her with stacks of paper and old-looking books. It was near the end of the workday, and the setting sun cast an orange glow over the room. This was usually when the office was at its calmest.

Becky sighed, crossing her arms over her chest. "We're taking care of it," she started. "But it's the manor's barrier. It's become a little…faulty."

Evie chewed nervously on her lip. That certainly didn't sound good. "Shall I call maintenance?" Although maintenance was still repairing one of the walls the boss had tossed an intern through a few weeks ago—a not-irregular occurrence—and besides, if she was understanding Becky right, this likely wasn't something the magical fixers could repair.

"Right now, it's only a single door that's visible," Becky clarified. "Nothing to be overly concerned about, I'm sure, but I sent for an enchantress just in case. We'll see if any of the ravens are successful in finding one." Becky sighed again when Lyssa appeared, gripping the woman's drab brown skirt. "Lyssa Sage, must you skulk about? I thought you were looking for your sister's journal," Becky scolded, but there was more warmth in that interaction than Evie had ever seen her display. It made her a little giddy.

"I can't find it, Ms. Erring. I searched everywhere!"

Becky looked toward the ceiling. "I find it incredibly hard to believe you swept every nook and cranny of this office in such a short amount of time."

Lyssa pulled some pastries from her pocket, handing one to Evie and then one to Becky—who held the powdered dough sphere like it was a dirty sock. Lyssa giggled at her expression, and Evie did, too. She'd let Lyssa stay innocent just a little bit longer before unleashing Gideon on her. Her little sister had been merely an infant when Gideon died—well, *left*—so Evie wasn't sure exactly how she'd react, for one. But for another, she so rarely got to experience unfettered joy, and Evie so badly wanted to give Lyssa that—and so much more.

"There was one place I didn't check, Ms. Erring," Lyssa admitted as the three women walked farther into the office space, toward the boss's closed black doors.

"Where?" Becky asked, lifting a brow.

The black doors were no longer closed. They slammed open, rattling the walls, rattling the workers, rattling Evie as The Villain walked out with her gold-foiled journal in hand. Opened right to the page she least wanted him to see.

The drawing. The sketch. The kissing. *THE HORROR.*

"Sage?" The Villain held up the notebook with a white-knuckle grip. "What in the deadlands is this? And why was it on my desk?"

Both hands flew over her mouth, one then coming down to grip Becky by the arm for balance. "He's holding it."

Becky said nothing, just stared at the journal with round, unblinking eyes, her usually stern mouth in the shape of an *O*.

"Becky, he's holding it!" Evie hissed again.

Becky shook off Evie's hand. "I have eyes, ninny!"

The boss pointed to the poorly drawn depiction of her, the doodled spiral curls giving her identity away. "This is supposed to be you, correct?"

Divert! Divert! "Um, sir, I have the stardust vial in my pocket—shall we get to work on using it to find my mother? The clock's ticking, and the baby guvre is, um…growing."

Becky brightened, which should've made Evie immediately suspicious. "An excellent point, Evangelina! I'll go gather your mother's letters at once! Come, Lyssa. I left them in the kitchens." The HR manager turned to go, guiding Lyssa along with her—but not before throwing Evie a shrewd smile.

Evie almost fell on her ass trying to dive after them. "Rebecka, don't leave me alone with—" She turned, and the boss was right in front of her, molten eyes boring into hers. The shadow along his jaw was darker and fuller than it usually was, and there were no subtle shifts in his face. Just an accusatory intensity as he pointed at the drawing.

"This is you?"

She paused and then nodded. It was hopeless, anyway; may as well cut her losses.

"Then who is this you're kissing?" The boss raised a brow.

She almost fainted dead away. Did he not know? By the gods, it was so obvious! Either the sketch was truly abominable or her boss was incredibly obtuse. Or both. She *should* just admit it, throw the truth of her feelings out in the open, and see where they landed. But instead, the only thing that fell out was, "You wouldn't…know him."

She wanted to smack her palm against her forehead.

It looked rather like he was about to bend the book in half, but his face was deathly calm. "Oh, no? Let's see. Tell me his name."

She had a strange feeling that whoever she named would suffer a mysterious disappearance by the day's end. Which shouldn't have thrilled her, but it did. There were a few screws loose in her skull, and they all fell out when she realized the boss was jealous.

Don't make the boss jealous, Evie!

Even if it's really fun!

"No, thank you," she said, rolling the vial of stardust in her palms before dropping it in her pocket.

"I think that looks like Terrence McChalice." She jumped out of her skin when Gideon appeared over her shoulder.

"Gideon!" she gasped. "How did you get out of your room?" Her brother had changed into a nondescript green tunic that brought out the green in his eyes, and he wore mischief like it was the latest fashion.

Gideon shrugged. He no doubt had observed the boss's pulsing vein. "Don't fret, Mr. Villain. Terrence is the object of affection of every woman in our village. Though if I recall, he only ever had eyes for Evie."

It was a foolish thing to say, considering there was no Terrence McChalice.

The boss handed the journal back to her with a gentleness she knew he didn't feel. He had his torture face on, and she had caused it with her ridiculous little drawings. How thrilling. "Sir? Are you all right?"

He was contemplating his next move; she could tell by the way he swallowed, by the way he tilted up his chin. "Yes, I suppose there is no time to waste. The guvres have us on a ticking clock."

She nodded, ready to make for the kitchens to reprimand the two traitors who had fed her to the wolves, but one of the Malevolent Guard barreled in—a new recruit. A brutal and cruel one. Damien.

"Oy! King-kisser! Get back to the cushy rooms they set up for you, or your next lodgings are gonna be belowground in the dungeons with your rutting father!" Damien gripped Gideon by the arm, and Evie felt herself freeze at the mention of Griffin Sage.

She'd been avoiding the topic of her father for a reason. She hadn't even uttered his name since that night. It hurt too much to say it, to think of him at all. It felt like her chest had been cracked open and all the pain was spilling out onto the floor in front of everyone. She took in a deep inhale, then another, willing herself to calm, willing the burning tears in her eyes to dissipate, but they didn't. They pooled in the corners of her eyes and then slid down her face.

Workers passed by, gawking at her. She felt naked as tears rolled down her cheeks.

Gods, at this rate, there should be an incident board for her tears.

It's been zero days since Evie's last sob.

"Eve?" Gideon said, stepping closer, face pinched with concern, but his path was blocked. Trystan loomed in front of her, shielding her from the rest of the room before passing her a light-blue handkerchief from his pocket.

The Villain's loud voice echoed on the walls, and though she was looking down, she could feel his eyes like a finger gliding along her cheek. "Everyone get out!"

The workers froze, and so did she. Nobody moved…until the boss boomed again, "NOW!"

The room was emptied in seconds. Gods knew where they went. The only remaining bodies in the space were her, Trystan, Gideon, and Damien, who looked furious.

Her lip wobbled, and she closed her eyes as she took the scrap of cloth from Trystan's hand. The brush of her fingers against his skin calmed her. "Sir, why did you do that?"

"Edwin's nearly finished with a batch of cookies, and I did not want to share."

She blinked up at him. His dark eyes weren't angry, and they weren't full of censure; they were full of mirth. He was trying to make her laugh, to lighten her heart. The way she always tried to do for him, the way she tried to do for everyone. Nobody had ever done that, had ever tried to lighten things for *her*.

She didn't think. Placing a hand on either side of Trystan's head, as she did that first time, that first day, she pressed a gentle kiss to his warm cheek. Stubble pricked beneath her lips, and her eyes watered again. Falling back down on her heels, still holding his face, she said, "Thank you."

His eyes were dark, his brow stuck in a furrow, like he couldn't believe what she'd just done. Excellent—that made two of them. She waited for him to chastise her for such an unprofessional display.

But he didn't chastise her, and he didn't look away from her face.

"Here," she said, carefully handing back the blue scrap of cloth.

"Keep it," he said gruffly.

Gideon winced as Keely came in and practically dragged him away. To his credit, he went willingly.

"I'm going, Captain! I'm going!" Gideon called, trailing miserably behind her. Her brother—despite his deceptions—was someone she would always love, and if he was someone she loved, he was someone she protected.

"Damien?" Evie's tone wasn't playful or teasing or malicious. She delivered her next sentence evenly, calmly. "If you ever threaten my brother again, I will take the dagger at my side and use it to carve out your heart, small as it may be."

Damien was already halfway to the door when he muttered under his breath, *"Two-faced bitch."* She flinched but kept her eyes on the handkerchief in her hands.

When she looked up to her boss again, he was glaring after the retreating guard. "Sage, if you don't want to continue—"

She interrupted his dismissal. She needed anything but to be coddled. "What I want is to do my job, sir."

There was a strange gleam in his eyes as he gazed at her for just a second. "Very well," he said, still looking like he might follow after Damien. It seemed like he was physically rooting himself to the spot beside her to fight the impulse.

"Follow me, Sage. I have an idea."

CHAPTER 25

EVIE

Someone was dripping water on her face.

It was cold and ran down her cheek, curling along the base of her scalp and the back collar of her shirt. She woke with a start, remembering she had stumbled into the guest room she and Lyssa occupied in the west wing, intending to only lay down for a moment after an exhausting brainstorming session with the boss, where they laid out their plan to use a bit of the stardust on her mother's letters. They were meant to do it right then and there, but after her head had nearly hit the kitchen's wood table in exhaustion, the boss had insisted she rest, promising he wouldn't use the stardust without her. He even sent it along with her, safely in her pocket.

She scanned the room, noting the darkness. She supposed she'd rested far more than a moment.

"Oops." She winced, rubbing a hand down her face, then noticed Lyssa standing over her with a damp cloth.

"You say funny things when you're asleep."

Evie tilted her head, massaging her neck. "How rude of you." She tapped Lyssa on the nose. "I say funny things when I'm awake as well." Lyssa crawled into the bed next to her as Evie scanned the room, whistling low. "This room really is absurdly large. Who needs a bedchamber this size?"

"Is it so the nobles have room to do cartwheels?" Lyssa asked.

Evie scoffed. "Obviously."

Lyssa cracked first, giggling, and moved to sit up against the pillows next to Evie. "You slept for a while." Her sister had changed into a nightgown, and the clock that stood sentry in the corner read that it was half past ten o'clock.

"I'm sorry I slept so long, Lyss." She moved to put her arm around her sister, who cuddled in closer. "Did you have fun with Ms. Erring today? That woman's sharp as a sewing needle. I know you're missing school, but I was thinking I could hire someone just like Rebecka to be your instructor. They can come to the manor, and you can select whatever subjects you want to learn about! Doesn't that sound exciting?"

"Evie, was Papa really sick?"

The words washed over Evie like ice water, but her cheeks burned. "Why would you ask me that?" She tried to keep her tone light. "Did someone say something to you?"

The blue corset that had felt movable and comfortable that morning was now pinching into her ribs, making it hard to take a full breath. She stood and grabbed her nightgown, needing a second's break from her sister's probing stare.

Lyssa picked at the edge of the sheet, eyes downcast to it. "No. But he did do something bad, right? That night we left home. He tried to hurt you... didn't he?"

How should Evie answer? How could she tarnish the sweet image her sister still had of the man who had been a constant in her life since the day she was born?

Behind the changing screen, Evie dropped her expression. *What can I even say that won't break her heart? How can I be enough for her? For anyone?* She nearly jumped when she saw herself in the floor-length mirror. The girl who looked back was so sad, with eyes that looked like they were crying for help. She glanced away.

But her sister had asked a very honest and direct question, and Evie knew she would rather gently guide her through the truths of the world than have her thrown in the deep end to learn on her own, as Evie had.

So she changed quickly, emptying her pockets and brushing her hair, then returned to sit gently at the edge of the bed, placing a hand over Lyssa's. "Yes, he did. And no." She paused when Lyssa looked up with red-rimmed eyes. "No, he wasn't sick."

Lyssa bit her lip, looking distraught. "I knew it. I should've told you."

"Told me what?"

"He used to leave all the time when you were at work. He didn't think I'd notice, but I did. He would get better when you weren't home, coughing one minute and stopping almost the second you were out the door. He had white powder."

"White powder?"

"I saw him put it on, to look paler." *To look sicker* was what Lyssa meant, but she was too young to understand the lengths Griffin Sage had gone to in order to deceive the ones he swore he loved. "I should've told you. He wouldn't have been able to hurt you if I had!" Lyssa cried.

Evie's chest was in a knot when she placed both hands on her sister's cheeks, angling her face so she could look right into her eyes.

"Lyssa, no. What happened with Papa was not your fault. He is a grown-up; he knew better. You are a little girl. Your only job is to be just that, a little girl, and let me take care of you." Lyssa dove into her arms, and Evie cradled her hands around her sister's head, gently combing her fingers through her hair.

"But—" Lyssa sniffed, dampening Evie's nightgown with her tears. "Who is going to take care of *you*?"

Oh, Lyssa, myself. I've always taken care of myself with a false smile and brittle strength.

Her burdens would not be Lyssa's. She vowed it. "Don't you worry about me, love. There are lots of people here who look after me. Why, it's like a little family!"

Her sister pulled back, her young face sticky with tears. "But we aren't related to anyone here."

Evie had to bite her tongue to keep from blurting out, *Well, Gideon is locked in a bedroom two doors down, and Father is also here, but he's belowstairs in the dungeon, hopefully being fed stale bread and dodging spiders like they're cannonballs.*

She coughed into her hand. Probably not the best way to break the news.

Fiddling with the tie around Evie's nightgown, Lyssa watched her. Evie started, "Sometimes family isn't a thing we are born into but a choice we make. Sometimes"—Evie smiled—"the people who love you most in your life are the ones who choose you."

It was saying it out loud that made Evie realize how fiercely she believed it. The family she had been born into was fractured, jagged, broken in ways she could not repair. It would never be what it once was, but it was not fully gone. And even if it were, she was not alone. She had a family. It was filled with villainy and mischief, but it was honest, and it was the one truth she could hold on to. One truth she could pass down to her sister.

They laid down then, side by side, and talked for hours. About the manor, about Evie's job—excluding some of the finer, more violent details about The Villain, about Trystan.

"It wasn't difficult to figure it out, you know. Everyone keeps calling him The Villain, Evie," her sister said, resting her head against her hands and giggling.

"And that doesn't bother you?" she asked hesitantly.

Lyssa shrugged. "He's nice to me."

Evie internally groaned. She was passing her warped logic down to the next generation, and everyone should run for the hills.

Lyssa's lids seemed to grow heavy as her eyes drifted shut. "Evie?"

Evie's lids had begun to grow heavy as well. The single candle on the bedside table was fizzling out. "Hmm?" she murmured, settling farther into the silken sheets, the crackle from the fireplace lulling her.

"I'm nervous for you to find Mama." Lyssa's voice was small, like she was almost too ashamed to admit the truth to her. "I'm afraid to meet her."

Evie's eyes opened, startled. "Why, love?"

Lyssa's little face looked fierce, even seconds from sleep. "Because you're the only mother I've ever had." Soft, even breaths followed the statement. Her sister had fallen into a deep sleep.

Evie leaned over and kissed her on the forehead, brushing the stray hairs away. Lyssa's admission had repaired a fissure that had cracked within her—one she hadn't realized was there. She still had so much to protect, so much to care about. Losing someone didn't mean the end; it merely meant the beginning of the life you'd lead without them, the beginning of letting in the people you'd gain in their stead.

She'd protect those people by any means necessary.

That wicked, malevolent thought—the thought that there was no cost too great for the people she loved—settled in. It made her feel safe, powerful. The scar on her shoulder hummed, a warmth seeping into her limbs.

It chased her toward sleep.

But she remained that way for only a moment before her eyes shot open and she stumbled up, gripping her discarded pants as she searched frantically through every pocket, then did the same with the contents she'd left on the counter by the changing screen. It wasn't there.

The vial of stardust.

She'd lost it.

CHAPTER 26

EVIE

E vie's mind spun through endless disastrous scenarios, then played them all the way through, beginning to end. Between the catastrophizing and the yawning ache in her stomach from sleeping through dinner, when the clock softly chimed midnight, she knew she'd hit her breaking point.

I can't spiral through my anxieties without proper nourishment!

She softly padded out of bed, using the guiding light of the stars peering through the window, then found the latch of the door and swung it open. The hallway was considerably colder than the warmth of the bedroom, though it was well lit by the torches hung on the walls. Lyssa's quiet snores resounded behind her as she latched the door shut and tiptoed across the long corridor, rubbing her chilled arms. A clang farther down the long, winding hall made her startle and stumble, stubbing her toe on a raised stone in the floor. "Damn it!" she cursed quietly, gripping her foot in her hand and hopping on the other for balance.

Another low curse echoed through the hallway — so like hers, she thought her voice had somehow reverberated off the walls. Until another series of crashes sounded, followed by more cursing and a low growl.

The vial of stardust, nearly glowing, rolled down the hall until it landed right at her feet, almost greeting her. "Uh…" was the only noise she could make as she realized the vial was essentially moving of its own accord and was leading the person behind it on some sort of goose chase.

"Where are you going, you demonic reprobate?" The Villain seethed from a doorway down the hall, head knocking back in surprise when he saw her. "Sage?" His eyes scanned from her messy hair all the way down to her thin wisp of a nightgown before coming up and fixating on her face. He seemed quite determined to have them stay there.

"I was going to look for a snack," she said bluntly.

The boss pinched the bridge of his nose. "I wasn't referring to you."

The vial kept rolling, like it knew it was the topic of interest, until it was atop her foot. She bent low to pick it up, her mass of curls spilling forward, covering her front. Rolling it in her palm, she watched as the contents of the vial almost danced.

"Well, I am very glad to see you." She scrunched her nose in delight. "Aren't you a curious bit of magic?"

The boss's next words rumbled out of him as he plucked the vial from her hands. "It's not curious—it's cursed. It rolled into my room earlier like it had an appointment. Then the blasted thing began to glow so bright, I could barely see. And then it burst from the room like an escaped criminal."

Evie felt happiness, true happiness, for the first time in a while at the image of this intimidating, fearsome man traipsing up and down the halls, chasing stardust like a dog off its leash. His nostrils flared at her amusement. His black shirt was untucked, exposing most of his chest in a loose V—it was clear he had either been lying in bed or preparing to do so.

Don't think about the boss in bed, Evie! But that ship had sailed so far beyond the horizon, it practically lifted its middle finger in farewell.

He cleared his throat, and she realized she had been staring at a patch of skin on his chest, imagining laying her lips to it. Her cheeks burned in embarrassment as blood rushed to her face.

Trying to redirect the conversation, she blurted, "I missed dinner." Well, that and she'd thought she lost the dust. How had it ended up in the boss's room?

"Oh, of course." He licked his lips, releasing his tightened fist. "Wait here. I'll return." He dropped the vial back into her palms, and the magic inside vibrated like it was about to explode. She clapped both hands on it, watching the boss disappear down the torch-lined hallway. A few anxious moments passed as she shifted from one foot to the other, trying to keep the thing in place.

"I understand better than most not wanting to be still, but if you could just give it your best attempt? My fingers are tiring," she told the vial politely, and miraculously, it stopped. That was, until the boss appeared back down the corridor, surprisingly fast, holding a covered plate and looking at her with tired accusation.

"Are you talking to inanimate objects again?"

She threw her eyes skyward, gripping the vial, but it jumped out of her hands. "Does this look inanimate to you?"

The warm covered dish was thrust into her hands as the boss dove to catch the vial, banging his head on the wall as he clasped it in his fingers. She clapped a hand over her mouth at his bark of pain. "Did that hurt?" she asked, cringing.

"No, it felt as good as my torture rack," he said dryly, rubbing his head and holding tight to the vial. "This dust wants to be used, and I cannot spend the night trying to keep it contained. I'll go mad."

Whatever was beneath the cover of the dish smelled divine. Her mouth watered, and she darted her tongue out to lick her lips. "Perhaps we should just use it on the letters now instead of waiting until morning. Get it out of the way." She contemplated the idea, grimacing. "Though I think Becky has the letters, and I would hesitate to go through her desk without asking her first."

He stiffened. "She handed them off to me earlier. They're…in my bedchamber."

Oh. Oh dear.

The best course of action would be to wait there in the hall while he grabbed them and then they could head to a more neutral location. Her tangled thoughts didn't much care, however, as jumbled words spilled out of her lips like an overflowing dam she was about to drown beneath. "Then we'll go to your bed!"

He stared at her, expressionless, but she saw his mouth tighten. Never a good sign. She kept speaking, unfortunately. "I meant to your bed*room*. Your bed*chambers*. Not your bed. I would *never* go to your bed, sir. I assure you!" She laughed, trying to clear the awkwardness, but she failed miserably. It was in the air like noxious smoke.

His brow twitched, but other than that, his face didn't move. "Prefer to share a bed with Terrence McChalice, do you?" The low words prickled along the top of her scalp like someone was running their nails over it.

"Oh, um—no?" That didn't sound convincing, so she tried again. "That is, I don't really have an interest in sharing a bed with anyone again for the foreseeable future. Every time I was with Rick…" She paused. "You remember him? We used to court?"

"I do." She wasn't sure what expression he was giving her—she was too busy staring at her fingers. But his tone sounded serious. Hard.

"Well, he was always so... I don't know, every time we were intimate, I just always felt so lonely and unsatisfied after. I think I don't want to be with someone like that again until I'm sure they can give me everything I want." There! She'd waded through the embarrassment rather eloquently, if she did say so herself.

But her opinion on that changed when she saw her boss standing so rigidly before her, she thought he might crack in two. "Sir?"

He turned down the corridor. "Just come," he barked. "And bring your plate."

She scurried after him until she was right beside him, holding tight to the food. "Sir, did I make things very awkward?"

His whole body remained rigid as he moved, like he was made of tin. "No."

"Then why do you look like you might weep?"

They reached a black door at the end of the hall, surrounded by several torches. It was the brightest point of the corridor. He yanked it open and gestured her forward with one hand. "In," he ordered.

She didn't hesitate, just poked her head through first before entering.

The Villain's bedchambers.

Oh, cruel world.

CHAPTER 27

THE VILLAIN

*F*UCK. FUCK. FUCK.

"So, this is your room?" Sage's voice glided over his tidy, secluded sanctuary. Her hair moved as she did, teased from sleep and looking so soft in the low-burning candlelight that his hand twitched at his side.

This was ill-advised—and frankly foolhardy.

Her eyes scanned every inch of the space, and it felt like an invasion. But not an unwelcome one. The room was large but sparse. There was one oversize four-poster bed adorned with black curtains and his collection of throw pillows. He had a small desk off to the corner with one comfortable chair, an armoire against the wall, and a fireplace with a log that never burned out... That, along with his—

"Nightlight!" Sage squealed, rushing over to the corner and finding the tiny lantern that made the space glow. "You really do have one!" She turned it over, and he rolled his shoulders to relieve the tension. "But what is this shape? It's almost like a cone?"

Trystan rushed to make up an excuse, but Kingsley had awoken from his slumber in the small, gilded bed on the table beside his own. *Don't*, he mouthed at the frog threateningly.

But of course, he didn't listen. Just held up a sign that read: TORNADO.

Edwin would serve frog legs tomorrow.

Sage squinted at the sign and then back at the nightlight before giving him a thousand-watt smile. "Is this a little tornado, sir?"

He ripped it out of her hands. "It was the only one left at the shop," he grumbled, returning it gently to its place.

Trystan had finally been steering himself back into line, back to his one true purpose: revenge. Stealing the kingdom from Benedict was a far cry from what he'd set out to do a decade ago. It was better; it was worse. It was perfect, and they were getting close. All he needed was Nura Sage, and then he could enact the prophecy. He'd find a tiny patch of land with butterflies and sunshine and send Sage where she belonged—away from him.

He only needed to muddle through the next few steps, the ones that would lead him to Nura. All he needed to do was remain indifferent, as he'd always been.

Indifference, while Evangelina Sage was in his bedchamber.

It was like keeping a blank face during an avalanche.

He straightened his shirt and smoothed his breeches, then grabbed the chair to tug it next to the desk. "The letters are on my table, just there. We'll only need a touch, hopefully, to reveal some of the hidden words, and then we can save the rest for—" He released the chair, blinking at the woman in front of him. Did he say avalanche? He meant inferno.

Sage placed her plate gently on the desk before searching the small table for the letters, then laying them gently out around the wooden surface. Her back was to the fire, the light illuminating her from behind.

And turning her entire nightgown sheer.

"Um, Sage?" He attempted to steady his voice, but the words came out garbled. The stardust vial jumped in his hand, apparently sensing his distress as it leaped around. He hardly noticed, fixated on the plain view of gently curved hips, of soft lines of stomach, of ample thighs that looked made for grabbing.

Mantras began in his mind, steadying him, grounding him. *I am malicious. I am evil. I am feared!*

She turned, and he caught the side of her breast.

I am going to die.

A strangled sound left his lips as he flew to the armoire across the room, yanking out a blanket so hard that the rest of the contents nearly tumbled out as well. The blanket was draped around her shoulders before he released another breath.

She gripped both ends of it, looking up from the letters and her plate of food with a smile. "Thank you, sir. That was… Are you all right?"

"I'm thinking about death."

Her eyebrows shot to her forehead. "Oh my."

"Move aside, Sage, and eat your food." He paused, thinking through his next words. "Edwin made that plate especially for you." He bumped her with his hip, and she sank into the armchair. The vanilla smell lingered where she'd stood. The woman ate so many of those blasted candies, they were coming out of her pores. Uncapping the vial, which was now moving furiously, he tapped several drops of dust onto the pages.

The stardust glowed over the letters, slowly covering the entire surface with shimmering white light. They both watched, waiting. A few seconds passed before Sage reached down, took a spoonful of mashed potatoes and thick brown gravy, and brought it to her mouth with a gentle moan. "So good."

His knees almost buckled.

He'd never reacted this way to any woman, to any person. There must be a logical explanation. "Sage, do you have any enchantress or siren lineage in your family?"

She trained an unamused look at him. "I'm not certain I want to know what prompted that question."

He pinched the bridge of his nose again. "You definitely don't."

The stardust was nearly gone now, and the table began to shake, as did the rest of the room, including his chair. Sage popped up and gripped his arm. "What's happening?"

Alarm bells were blaring in his head, something telling him to duck for cover. "Get down!" They both dove for the floor, Trystan holding Sage's head and angling his body over hers. A large spark and a small boom took the legs of the table out entirely. It collapsed in front of them, revealing what Trystan assumed was going to be destroyed and scorched letters, but instead—

"A map. The dust turned the letters into a glass map?" Sage reached out and brushed her hand over the shimmering surface of the depiction of Rennedawn. Peaks, valleys, villages, and Hickory Forest were all displayed on the slab. Places Trystan hadn't even known existed were highlighted by the celestial glow, but only one area of the map was marked by a five-pointed star.

"Here. What we seek must be here," he said, running a finger over it, the light flickering under his touch. Sage was breathing heavily, her eyes drooping against the light, wearing a confused and frightened frown.

Suddenly, the door to his chambers was thrown open. Blade stumbled in, clutching his knees and taking heaving breaths. "Boss! You okay? I was up with one of the guvres and I heard a crash." Blade halted when he saw Evie, his eyes taking in the condition of the room: the table broken on the floor, a blanket discarded on the ground, both of them in a state of undress.

He grinned.

"Evie!" Blade put a hand up and leaned against the doorjamb, taunting Trystan like he had a death wish. "Did the boss need *assistance* with something in his bedchamber?"

Trystan picked up a pencil from the ground and gripped it tight in his fist. "What are you doing coming into my room in the first place? There is no possible excuse you could have for such an overstep. I don't care if you thought a murderer was in here," Trystan said in a low voice.

Blade clicked his tongue. "You mean besides you?"

"Get out," Trystan growled.

"So you can continue?" Blade asked cheekily before ducking away from the pencil Trystan chucked. Sage ripped a second pencil from his hand before he could toss it, and he scowled at her.

"Blade, dear, what are you doing up?" Sage asked gently.

"I was checking on the female guvre, but it's difficult for me to get close without the male freaking out and getting violent." The dragon trainer hesitated, smirking at Trystan before saying, "You know what that's like, don't you, boss?"

Trystan started forward, and Sage grabbed the back of his shirt, digging in her heels. "Don't," she warned. "Are you any closer on a timeline for when we can expect her to give birth?" she asked Blade.

The dragon trainer sobered almost immediately. "Judging by her already distended stomach and how attentive the male is being—seriously, he won't let her leave his sight for even a second; it's quite adorable—it could be anywhere from two weeks to six months before their let arrives."

Trystan rubbed at his temples. "That hardly helps at all."

Blade nodded, looking chastised. "I'm sorry, sir. Truly. I'll keep looking. You can count on me."

Trystan wet his lips and sighed. He was developing an irritating level of sympathy for those around him, and Blade was no exception. He took pity on the man, sensing the dragon trainer's sincerity. He used to hate sincerity—it never seemed real—but Blade always came across as very determined to prove himself, to please. It reminded Trystan a little of himself, long ago, and the spike of sympathy turned into a spear.

"Don't fret, Gushiken. I hardly have time to hire someone in your stead. Just continue searching and come to me as soon as you find something useful."

Blade looked at him suspiciously and then glanced around like he was checking for an ambush. "Oh, thank you, sir. I will do that." He spun on his heel, waving. "Good night! You two have fun."

The boss picked up another pencil, but Sage had dashed in front of him. "Knock it off."

Trystan sighed, placing it her waiting palm. "He's impertinent."

"So am I," she said gravely.

"Well, that I know," Trystan said, grinning despite himself. He watched as Sage's eyes flickered right to his dimple. "The Heart Village is accessible by horseback. We'll leave at the week's end."

"Why not tomorrow?" She frowned. "Isn't time of the essence?"

He spun her toward the door, holding it open for her. "I have things I need to look into tomorrow."

She huffed. "Like why you feel the need to have a thousand pillows on your bed?"

"Out!"

She hurried out of his bedchamber, but he could hear her giggle echo down the corridor. A hall he'd walked many times, once lonely and cold. Shutting the door against the chill, he walked over to the armoire to return the blanket, but as soon as he opened it, another scrap of fabric fell into his hands. A scarf. Wool that had been gently cleaned of any remnants of blood and kept safely tucked away.

"For the blood, Your Evilness."

Gripping it hard in his fist, he shoved away the memory of his first meeting with Sage, along with any other feelings that came with it. His only goal now was to destroy Benedict—and he'd take down anyone or anything that got in his way.

CHAPTER 28

GIDEON

Gideon Sage had made several observations in his short time in Massacre Manor. The first was that The Villain's office was run entirely different from the Valiant Guard's. The Villain himself seemed to know everyone by name, what their job function was—almost like he *cared*. And unlike Benedict, the man didn't walk around with a politician's grin; instead, his face seemed stuck in a permanent scowl.

Unless, of course, Gideon's sister was anywhere within his vicinity. That was Gideon's second observation.

Gideon turned to address the two Malevolent Guards trailing behind him. "Might I wander the office without you two tailing me?"

"No, sir knight." Keely had golden skin that matched her honey-blond hair. She looked like the sun…that had descended to fry him to a crisp. She and Min had been his near-constant companions since his arrival, barring him from doing anything heroic. That was probably frowned upon here.

Min was shorter in stature, with raven hair cropped close to her head that emphasized the soft points of her face. It was obvious she was lethal, but she was also kind, which Gideon appreciated, since it seemed Keely was liable to run him through with a knife at any moment.

Unless Evie did it first.

His sister flew away from her white wooden desk when she spotted him, eyes wide, her curls pinned away from her face, her anger perfectly visible. "Gideon! What in the deadlands are you doing out of your room again? Lyssa is up here!"

Gideon gave her a questioning look. "Should she be?"

"Fool," Keely hissed behind him.

"Are you questioning how I care for our sister?" Evie narrowed her gaze, and he suddenly felt like a trapped rodent surrounded by hungry felines.

"No, of course not!" Gideon reassured, looking for a shovel to dig himself out of the hole he'd made.

A little girl came around the corner then, and the sight of her knocked the breath from his lungs. It was like looking directly at their mother. "You— I— Hello."

"You're Gideon," Lyssa stated, her small voice high and melodic as she stuck out a hand toward him. "I am Lyssa."

Evie looked pointedly at Lyssa's outstretched hand. *Shake*, she mouthed to him. So he did. "Yes, I know. We've met before." His lips tugged upward as he clasped her small hand in his.

Lyssa tapped her chin. "True, but I was just a baby then, so it doesn't really count."

Gideon crouched down until he was eye level with his youngest sister. "Good point. I suppose this is our first real introduction."

Lyssa regarded him carefully. "Evie said you lost your memory and that's why you didn't come home."

Gideon nodded, noticing the dragon trainer hovering behind them, along with the healer, Tatianna, and another woman he didn't recognize in very large glasses. All that was missing was— Never mind. The Villain wandered out of his office and leaned against the doorway, folding his arms and gazing at her in intense scrutiny. His sisters had a horde of protectors, and they all godsdamn terrified him.

Lyssa spoke again. "When did you get your memory back?"

Gideon was struck silent. He hadn't expected such a direct question. Once he'd overcome his initial shock, he replied, "I suppose it was around…five years ago now?"

The little girl scrunched her nose and tugged at the end of her braid. "Then why didn't you come back?"

Now he understood why he had finally been permitted out of his rooms. This was beginning to feel like an ambush, and not at all an undeserved one. "I think about that a lot, and I don't really believe there is a very good reason. At the time, I felt like I couldn't leave, and then I suppose I was too afraid to face all that I'd left behind."

Lyssa's curiosity turned to a glare. "Evie was afraid, too. She had to do everything by herself." It felt worse than a knife to the gut.

"Lyssa," Evie crooned, brushing back her braid. "It's okay."

Lyssa shook her head, and Gideon knew: his father's betrayal, Evie's struggle to care for them—it *was* all his fault. Gods, when he'd found Evie in the woods, surrounded by knights, he'd thought it was his chance to redeem himself, to finally reunite with his family. How selfish he'd been to think that all those years could be forgotten merely because he wanted them to be. He despised Benedict, but not half as much as he despised himself just then.

"Sage, we need to depart," The Villain said coolly. "Tatianna and Clare are coming along to investigate a lead on an enchantress to fix the manor's defenses. In addition to the visible door, there's now a second-floor window that can be clearly seen from the forest." The man walked forward, past where Gideon knelt before Lyssa. "The horses have been saddled, and I want to get on the trail before the clock strikes ten."

Evie nodded, looking like she pitied Gideon just a little before leaning down to Lyssa. "Go easy on him, Lyss. You are a fearsome adversary."

"Wait," Gideon called, feeling his heart race with desperation. "Where are you two going? Might I join?"

"No," The Villain boomed at the same time as Evie. They glanced at each other and then promptly looked away. "You will remain here," The Villain said.

Lyssa tugged at his pants, and Gideon gave her his undivided attention. "You may play with me while they're gone."

Gideon swallowed through a well of emotion. "That's very generous of you, Lyssa. What shall we play?"

"Flying Guard," Lyssa said succinctly.

Gideon furrowed a brow, as did Evie, and The Villain stiffened. "How do you play that?" Gideon asked.

"You fly off the roof! I saw one of the guards do it just this morning!" Lyssa said excitedly. Gideon didn't know whether to laugh or run at the realization that said guard must have been falling to his death.

But Evie had no such confusion as she turned and smacked The Villain on the shoulder. "What did you do?" she whispered furiously.

The Villain actually looked…sheepish? What had his sister done to the poor sod?

"He was making the other guards discomfited. I don't begrudge cruelty, except when it is careless."

"Who was it?" Evie hissed.

"Damien," Keely cut in from behind them. "I promise you, Ms. Sage, it is no great loss. It's rather a fortunate one."

Evie sighed and shut her eyes tight. "Luna!" she called, and a pixie with purple wings halted. "Can you put the incident board at zero?"

They had an incident board for the boss's kills? *Of his own staff members?*

The Villain grumbled, "That hardly seems fair. Damien wasn't an intern."

"Hush!" Evie scolded. "Tati, Clare? Are you ready?"

Tatianna winked at Gideon, patting him on the shoulder as she passed, which chilled him to the bone. "I deal in secrets, sir knight, and I sense you are holding a great many. I would suggest not waiting so very long to reveal them."

He tried to swallow the lump in his throat that arose at the truth of her words. He could've told Lyssa and Evie of their father's manipulation of him. How Griffin and the king had abused Gideon's own magic to hurt their mother.

It was that ignorance, that naive trust of the adults in his life that had destroyed his family. He turned to look at Lyssa. Tatianna was right; there were so many secrets living in his mind, like traps waiting to be sprung.

Secrets that could topple an empire, if he chose to wield them that way. And perhaps he would.

But not yet.

The Villain called back then, pulling Gideon out of his musings. "Gushiken and Ms. Erring are in charge. We'll be back by the day's end!"

Ms. Erring was the one in the round glasses, judging by how Blade bumped her with his shoulder and grinned.

"You're not qualified to oversee anything, you buffoon. *I'm* in charge." The woman sniffed.

Blade chuckled, but Gideon was then distracted by a large, green frog hopping after the departing group...with a crown affixed to its head.

"This is a very strange place," Gideon said in astonishment.

Ms. Erring folded her arms and grumbled, "You don't know the half of it."

CHAPTER 29

EVIE

It wasn't hard to ascertain that Evie had far overestimated her riding abilities. The first clue being she had the stamina of a goldfish.

"Can. We. Take. A. Break." She huffed out each word between trots. She'd thought riding a horse would be a leisurely experience, but her entire body ached from trying to keep her balance in the seat *and* hold herself up.

"Use your core strength," Clare called from beside her. They'd been on the winding path through Hickory Forest for more than an hour, and by Evie's measure they weren't even halfway to their destination.

She threw an exasperated hand in the air. "What core strength?"

The Villain immediately slowed at her response, waiting for her mount to catch up. The animal had been incredibly patient for the duration of the ride.

He looked at her strangely; it made her feel warm. He opened his mouth, and she held her breath.

"You look ill."

Tatianna, who was riding with pristine posture, not breaking a sweat next to The Villain, gave him an exasperated look. "Who taught you etiquette? A pack of wolves?"

Kingsley was atop Tati's steed, shaking his small head along with Clare.

They all fell into a slow canter, The Villain nudging in beside Evie. "I merely meant that you look as if you didn't sleep last night."

"I didn't."

He spun his head toward her in a flash, gripped the reins of her mare, and halted them both. Clare and Tati glanced at each other, slowly trotting ahead while angling their necks back to hear.

The boss asked, "Why?"

A red bird soared over their heads, and Evie followed it with her eyes as it flew through the trees, sailing for the sun before diving back toward the earth. The forest grew denser this close to the eastern border, with the sun dancing through the leaves in wild patterns around them. It looked like every good dream she'd ever had.

Her eyes didn't leave his as she deadpanned, "I was unsettled by the number of pillows on your bed. It kept me awake for hours."

The Villain glared, releasing the horses' reins. "I do not have that many pillows."

Clare's shoulders shook as she laughed from up ahead. "Still, Tryst? I'd have thought that when you became a dark, murderous figure you'd have rid yourself of the collection."

Evie felt like tiny, joyous butterflies were fluttering in her chest. The sun beating against her back was making her feel warm. "He did this when you were children?"

"Clare. Don't," The Villain grunted.

She didn't need to—Tatianna was already speaking, her fuchsia-painted lips moving a mile a minute. "Remember when we hid them, Clare? He went ballistic."

"Because you were thieves! I bought them with my own money," the boss grumbled, his black stallion chuffing like it agreed with him.

Clare gave him an evil grin. "I thought you were a fan of theft."

He huffed. "Not when it's something that's mine."

Kingsley held up a sign that read, LONELY.

Evie pouted and looked at the boss, her heart swelling at the possibility. "Is that why you have so many? You're lonely in your bed?"

The Villain ripped the sign away from Kingsley before plopping it in Tatianna's pink-gloved hand. "Don't be ridiculous."

"My gods, it was such an odd habit that we couldn't make sense of it. He'd have five to six pillows in there with him at all times. Malcolm thought he was having overnight guests. The four of us even spent the night spying once, but nope, all for him."

Clare brushed her hand over Tatianna's, likely to get her attention, but it lingered. Evie eyed that touch with a small, triumphant smile before realizing the implications of Clare's words. "Four of you spying on him? Clare, Tati, and Malcolm—that's three. Who's the fourth person?"

The Villain's head snapped toward Clare, who stared at her reins, her knuckles turning white. "I—I meant three! Only three of us." But Evie didn't miss her eyes flashing to Kingsley.

Rolling her neck, she was merciful and changed the subject. "My cousin Helena has been to the Heart Village quite a few times. When she wrote to me about it, she said it was a place of innovation and progress. Is that true, sir? I've never been."

Granted, there were many areas of Hickory Forest she hadn't explored, because that would mean leaving the comfort of home, and Evie had never been very good at venturing away from where she felt safest. She loved destinations; it was the journey that always seemed to stifle her. And it did help to have a comfortable place to return to as well—though the small cottage she'd shared with her parents was not her home any longer. The thought sent sorrow piercing through her chest.

You can't be sad when you're trying to be professional, Evie!

But being professional is so sad, her mind argued.

The scar on her shoulder tingled for a moment, and the dagger sheathed beneath her skirt answered it, like the two were having a conversation she wasn't privy to. "Rude," she mumbled.

"Sage, are you listening?" her boss asked.

She frowned—oh dear, had he been speaking? She hated when her mind would follow a thread inside her head, tugging so strongly that she completely missed what was happening outside of it. It made her feel flustered and silly.

Which was why she lied, "I was," all wide-eyed innocence.

"You're all right being bait, then?"

Hold on! "Bait?"

Magical plants and flowers glowed against the mid-morning sun. To distract from how little she'd been listening, Evie reached out to the nearest branch and plucked one. Rolling the stem between her fingers, she lifted it to her nose and took a large whiff.

"What am I to be bait for, exactly?"

A large stone bridge appeared ahead—the entrance into the Heart Village. Evie had heard of this place, and not just from Helena; it sat on the border of Rennedawn and the eastern Kingdom of Kaliora. Because of this, it was often considered to be the heart of Myrtalia, a village with no kingdom—perfectly neutral, and a bustling enterprise of different humans and magical creatures alike. But to enter, you had to pass the bridge entrance.

Suddenly, it became clear what she'd been volunteered for, and her heart started beating erratically. And was the ground getting a little fuzzy on the horizon?

"You want me to be bait for the bridge creatures?"

The Villain rode up beside her. "You're clever enough to solve the entry riddle they'll give us to cross, and you're charming enough to convince them to ignore our differences in favor of finding your mother." He turned, grinning, dimple on full display, then dismounted and helped her do the same.

Magical flower still gripped in one hand, she used the other to balance against his shoulder, which of course was hard enough to rival a boulder.

"That's an apt comparison, I suppose," The Villain said, amused, almost unknowingly puffing his chest. Had she spoken that aloud? Her senses felt dulled, her heart rate abnormally slow all of a sudden.

Tati and Clare dismounted easily, gracefully, and then conferred about something. *Wait…are there four of them?*

The Villain turned, not noticing how she swayed when he released her. He sauntered toward the gold bell hanging from a flowered archway over the bridge entrance. "The bridge creatures hate me. We had a mild misunderstanding a while back, and they have long memories."

Her vision was going spotty, but she felt warm, almost a little giddy. The flower in her hand shined brighter, but the scar on her back was tingling again.

She gave a little giggle, then, oddly, hiccupped. "Always making enemies wherever you go, aren't you, Trystan?"

He immediately stopped in his tracks and spun around with a wild look of alarm. And when he spied the flower in her hand and the unfocused look in her eyes, his face jumped among three different expressions she'd come to know meant the following:

Alarm, concern, and finally, rage.

"Sage! What have you done!" He was in front of her in seconds, ripping the flower from her hand.

"Oh my goodness, I do not know." She gave a wobbly shrug, giggling again, her words slurred, and she snorted at the way they sounded.

Clare strutted over, Kingsley perched on her shoulder, before ripping the flower from her brother's fingertips. "This is a Piony flower. The scent is supposed to make you intoxicated." His sister looked at him with a frown. "She's drunk, Tryst."

"Oh, that's bad, right?" Evie said, scrunching her nose, attempting a step forward but swaying into Trystan's shoulder instead; he caught her immediately. She reached up and touched the stubble at his chin. "This is prickly. I like it."

He looked like a scared owl, and she giggled again.

"We need to get out of here before they see us," her boss said. He turned her around and led her back toward the horses. "You won't be any help in this state."

They were a foot away from the bridge when a gritty voice called from behind them, "Leaving so soon, Villain?"

It was too late.

CHAPTER 30

THE VILLAIN

"Act natural," Trystan hissed.

Sage hiccupped, then promptly giggled at said hiccup.

"She's as natural as a mooing chicken." Tatianna grimaced, holding a glowing hand up to Sage's eyes. Sage scrunched her nose and leaned away, blinking a mile a minute.

"Can't you undo it?" he asked Clare frantically as the bridge creatures climbed up from the deep water that ran through the entire Heart Village. "Is there a plant for this?"

Clare tossed the red flower Sage had been holding in the direction of the woods. "Not for magical intoxication, Tryst. The only way out is to wait, and it can last hours."

"Hours!" He stared at Sage, who was now humming a merry tune and skipping around in a circle. *I won't survive hours of this.* It was suddenly quiet, and he found Sage's gaze intent on his face. "What are you staring at?"

"Your mouth."

Correction: I won't survive minutes.

"Villain. Why did you return? Another bridge you want to destroy?" a creature asked, and Trystan turned to see none other than Reming. He was taller than Trystan recalled from their last fateful meeting, with sand-like skin mostly hidden behind a long tunic and tight trousers. Sea glass shined where human hair would be, a vibrant burst of colors.

"He destroyed a bridge?" Sage almost yelled, and he clapped a hand over her mouth, pulling her against his chest.

"Ignore her—she's not feeling well. Reming, I hope we can put that little misunderstanding behind us. We have important business in the Heart Village, so please serve us with a riddle and we will earn safe passage over the bridge."

In theory, one could make it across the bridge without Reming and his family's permission, but their magic was linked to the architectural structure. So in practice, if they didn't want you to make it across in one piece, you wouldn't.

Reming eyed Clare and Tatianna as his mother and father joined him. "What do you think, Mother?"

Ellia was considered a great beauty among the bridge creatures—a great beauty among all, actually. She was tall, her figure ample and wide, and her long, colorful eyelashes glittered in the sun's rays. "I think that—"

The matriarch was cut off by Trystan's yell. Sage had bitten him to free herself. *Bitten* him. "Did you just *bite* me?" he roared. She stumbled out of his grip, looking so joyous, he forgot how furious he was for a second.

"*Yessssss.*" She drew out the S far longer than necessary, then tilted her head and asked with unfocused sincerity, "Why? *Do you want me to do it again?*" The last question, said on a mock whisper, was heard by every human, frog, and bridge creature within five hundred yards.

The second was over.

Markeith, the patriarch of the family, folded his arms. The sea-glass crown atop his head pointed into an angle that reminded Trystan of a steel blade's tip—a blade he'd likely be stabbed with if he didn't get Sage to cease speaking. "Did she smell a Piony flower?" Markeith asked.

"Oh, you bet," Tatianna said, gripping Sage's skirt before she fell over, like a cat holding a kitten by the scruff.

Markeith pushed past his son and mate. "Very well. You may all cross the bridge to the village"—he pointed a sandy finger at Sage, who was plucking at the flowers on her skirt like they were real—"but she must be the one to solve the riddle. *Without* any help."

"Oh, c'mon!" Clare griped, waving a hand toward Sage, who looked dangerously close to removing her skirt to get a better grip on the embroidered petals. "She barely knows her own name!"

Reming smirked. "It is she or no one."

"Evangelina."

Ellia tilted her head, sun striking against the sea glass to create a kaleidoscopic array of colors. "What, child?"

"Clare said I didn't know my name. It's Evangelina."

Ellia smiled lightly, holding out a hand. Sage didn't hesitate, just wrapped hers in Ellia's and, with the purest look in her eyes, said, "Your hands are so lovely."

They were done for.

Though, to Trystan's surprise, Ellia looked flattered by the compliment.

"We hold much of our life's experiences within our hands. What a keen observation." Ellia's eyes began to glow lilac as a different voice spilled out of her mouth—an ancient one.

"I am a terror many try to hide.
I am a secret that no one will find.
I am only used by the brave.
When issued properly, I will save.
I am the source of everyone's strife.
If you wield me wrong, I will cut like a knife.
What am I?"

"You couldn't have given her something easier?" Trystan asked, though he was interrupted by Sage stumbling back, out of Ellia's grip. He almost pulled a shoulder muscle trying to catch her before she hit the ground. As always, his act of valor backfired. In catching her, she ended up in his arms, bridal-style, and before he could get his bearings, she was nuzzling her nose against his neck, shredding his bearings like the magical goats in the office they used to shred unwanted papers. Her rose-scented hair filled his entire being, and he shut his eyes tight against the onslaught of sensation.

"The riddle chooses its solver. We cannot simply make it easier because your lover doesn't know to not touch plants she doesn't recognize." Reming sneered.

Lover. Trystan choked on the word, but Sage was already correcting them, so quickly he almost felt insulted.

She jumped down out of his hold, waving her arms like a fan propeller. "No, no, no, no. We are *not* lovers!" She whispered behind her hand, like she was telling the bridge creatures a secret: "I'm just his assistant."

She wasn't *just* anything, but he kept that confession behind his lips.

Markeith boomed, "Well, assistant to The Villain. Do you have the answer?"

"Give her a moment to think about it. You're setting her up to fail," Trystan said.

"I thought you told me"—her words were still slurred, her gaze drifting away toward a blue butterfly soaring beyond the bridge—"that you would never make the mistake of underestimating me."

"Sage, you're drunk as a pirate; I'm certain there are many things you feel you could do right now. Flying, perhaps."

She brightened.

"No."

Her bow-shaped red lips pulled down in a frown. "You're no fun."

Markeith cleared his throat. "The answer. Now."

Trystan gripped Sage's arm as she straightened her spine, but she speared him with a look so sharp and keen, it felt like a blade was running lightly over his sternum. She placed a hand right in the middle of his chest, feeling his heartbeat. "I know what the answer is."

Trystan swallowed.

Reming scoffed. "Do you?"

She stumbled but righted herself, saying with a firmness that her body language didn't reflect, "The answer is the truth."

Trystan moved in front of Sage, gripping her shoulders to get a look at her face, because that was—

"Correct. Well done, Evangelina." Ellia smiled warmly.

Tatianna shook her head in disbelief. "How did you know?"

Sage shrugged carelessly. "When you've been lied to so often, the truth becomes easier to discern."

Markeith gestured to the bridge behind him. "You are welcome in the Heart Village, along with your friends." A light shimmered above the archway. Tatianna gasped quietly, then followed Clare onto the curved stone surface toward the other side.

Sage pulled her hair out of its plait, fluffing it as she did so and tossing the ribbon into the air. "Thank you." She stopped right next to Markeith, a magical being, looking bold and fearless. And piss drunk.

"You have a lovely family." It wasn't a haphazard comment; it was a genuine compliment. This was one of the most marvelous mysteries about Sage—that she so readily handed out praise but it was always so *specific*. Like she found her favorite part of every person she came across and then presented it to them. It made him want to ask what she liked about him.

Markeith blinked at her, his green eyes going soft like he was questioning the random admiration. Sage squeezed his shoulder. "The truth," she murmured, walking past him and the other creatures.

She kept going, and Trystan made to follow quickly—gods knew the kind of danger she'd find on her own. Tatianna and Clare were ahead of her already, but the duty of protecting her felt charged to him. A godsdamn problem, that.

But Ellia halted him. "You may enter the Heart Village, Villain. But you must leave your magic behind."

His outrage was swift. "Absolutely not."

Ellia calmly shook her head. "It will return as soon as you leave the village soil, but not before. I will not allow such destruction anywhere near our citizens."

It could well be a trap. He wanted to scoff in her face and turn right around. Let them find another way in, past the magic wards that surrounded it. But then Sage stumbled. He watched closely as she giggled and stumbled again, this time looking to the sky and shaking her head with a light smile, glowing. Unafraid to laugh at herself, unafraid to look upon her missteps with anything but a brave sort of joy. She took each moment of her life with a natural good humor, no matter how painful, no matter how tragic. She trekked on with nothing but her will. No magic to protect her. Just faith and optimism and belief in her survival.

Being a cynic doesn't make you wise. It makes you a coward.

His heart pinched at Sage's accusation.

"Fine," he chewed out. His magic had been finicky lately anyway; one less thing to be concerned about.

Ellia stepped aside, gesturing her sandy arm onward, but not before pointing a finger at him and threatening, "Do not cause any harm."

He climbed onto the bridge, joining Sage in the middle. His assistant was jumping like a rabbit who'd just learned to hop.

Do not cause any harm?

Impossible.

And he proved it as soon as he stepped foot into the Heart Village.

CHAPTER 31

EVIE

Evie wanted to smell flowers every day.

She felt elated, like nothing could touch her, like all was right with the world. Stepping off the bridge, she couldn't stop smiling, awestruck by the splendor of the Heart Village. The stories she'd heard were nothing compared to seeing it with her own eyes.

Little shops lined the cobblestone streets, bustling with children and content-looking adults. An upbeat song played by a group of performers gave her a merry tune to step to as she entered the fray. The entire village was surrounded by channels of glistening blue water, some taking the place of streets with small boats to travel between points. It was like nothing she'd ever seen.

She'd worn flat shoes, the arches of her feet needing the rest from the lift of her heels. It made her quicker, which was excellent news for her and exhausting news for the boss. He appeared at her side in a flash, gently gripping her arm. "Sage, do not wander off in the state you're in."

"We're standing right here with her," Clare argued. Kingsley hopped from her shoulder onto a floating lily pad in the canal, stretching out his small limbs. "Alexander, do not wander," Clare scolded.

Alexander? Did she mishear? "Who is Alexander?"

Clare and Tatianna looked at each other, both biting their lips. Surely she was missing something... But the boss was whistling and turning in the other direction.

"We'll split up. You two see what you can find out about the barrier and an enchantress consult. Sage and I will inquire as to Nura Sage's whereabouts."

Tatianna grinned. "Or Clare could go with you and I can stay with Evie?"

Evie was making herself dizzy, her eyes darting between the two. The boss's face twisted in anger, and she tried to mimic it.

"You think I can leave her alone when she's like this? I destroyed a bridge last time I was here. She'd likely topple the whole *village*."

"Hey!" Evie stomped her foot. But she quickly forgot the insult when the smell of warm butter and fresh pastry danced across her nose—right before she spied a vendor selling large, flaky rolls in various shapes. "Oh, bread! I love bread." She ran for it.

But not before Clare muttered, "Oh yes, a danger to us all."

"Sage! Evie! Hold on!" the boss yelled after her to no avail. She could just barely hear his next words to the others: "We'll meet here in an hour. You two learn what you can in that time, and for the love of the gods, please keep an eye on Kingsley."

Evie had already gotten to the cart when Kingsley held up a sign that said: RELAX.

She giggled when the boss arrived next to her. The vendor was an elderly gentleman with wrinkled skin and graying hair that tipped silver in the sunlight. He grinned when she asked her boss sweetly, "Sir, will you buy me bread?"

His gaze had weight to it—different, somehow, than before he'd been captured. It was intense, breathtaking; it sent chills up her spine and goose bumps along her arms.

And her whole body felt like it was on fire when he said in a soft, low voice, "If you wish."

Before Evie could blink again, a warm roll of sweet bread was placed in her hands, this one in the shape of a cloud.

There was mirth in The Villain's gaze now. "I thought it fitting, in honor of our cave friend."

She laughed loudly, uninhibited. This in and of itself was not uncommon for her. She was often amused, trying to find delight in life where she could. It was her drive, what kept her up when she felt the urge to remain low. But that delight was frequently found while wearing her mask of humor and lightness. In this moment, it was lovely to be happy without effort. She kept laughing until a snort came out of her nose—a loud one. She hiccuped. "I'm a mess."

But the gentle humor had slipped from The Villain's expression now. "You're going to have to sleep this off at some point," he said, guiding her onward after paying the vendor for the sweet bread. A legal purchase by The

Villain, just for her. She almost swooned. "We'll get you a tonic for the splitting headache you'll undoubtedly wake up with."

"I...I've been having trouble sleeping." She sighed, holding out her arms and spinning, letting her skirt float in a circle. She enjoyed the freedom of wearing trousers, but she didn't think she would ever shake the giddy feeling of twirling in a pretty dress. She could have both now, the freedom of choice.

"We'll get you a tonic for that, too," her boss assured her in a hard voice.

"Tatianna said the antidote for the sleeping-death fruit doesn't have any long-lasting side effects, but I'm beginning to question it." She stopped to remove her shoe and shake out a pebble.

The Villain's voice was dark, forbidding from beside her. "I beg your pardon?" Before she could protest, she was being dragged bodily into a small alleyway between shops and gripped by the shoulders, pressed against the wall.

Oh, that wasn't— Uh-oh, that had been a secret.

This was hardly the way to prove to him that she herself could be more villainous, that she was an asset, needed. But her rescue plan had worked out anyway, and she knew he believed in her abilities. His anger was likely due to the reminder of being trapped with Benedict in the first place...or possibly the reminder of having seen her "dead."

"Are you saying that you faked your death by eating a sleeping-death fruit?" The Villain was so furious, the vein in his forehead was throbbing. She wanted to poke it.

"Can we talk about this later, when there aren't three of you ganging up on me?" His figure was spinning in several different directions, and they all looked pissed.

He barreled on. "Do you know how dangerous that is? How perfectly timed the antidote needs to be? There's only one cure! Of all the foolish—"

"Two," Evie interrupted before taking a large bite of bread. The flaky crust melted under her tongue.

"What?"

She chewed for a moment before speaking, which seemed to incense him, so she began to chew slower just for the fun of it. "There are *two* cures to the sleeping-death fruit; everyone knows that."

He shook his head. "The other is a myth, a lie we push for children's stories. It's positively evil, even for me."

She blew air out of her lips, feeling strangely let down all of a sudden. "By the gods, alert the town crier! I've found a man who doesn't believe in love."

He lifted a brow, angling his head down when he responded, devoid of emotion: "I do believe in love."

She stood on her tiptoes to get closer to his face, her heart pounding. "You do? Then why—"

"I just do not believe in it for myself. I am The Villain. Any woman willing to love me would be out of her gourd." He flinched at the words, like the thought of someone that unhinged was terrible to even imagine.

She had to stop herself from raising her hand and saying, *GUILTY!*

Lowering back down, she grumbled, "Yes, an absolute nincompoop of a person." She broke off a piece of bread and chewed it slowly, wanting to change the subject. "Becky had a connection to obtain the fruit, and I waited to eat it until after Gideon had smuggled me into the castle. He slipped me the antidote before I was brought into the ballroom. I wasn't in any danger."

"But now your sleep is disrupted."

She shrugged. "I haven't slept well since they took you. This isn't new."

That seemed to knock him silent. He opened his mouth to speak again, but Evie took the opportunity to rip off another piece of bread and shove it in his mouth. "I ate the fruit, and I survived. The plan worked, and now we are on the road to your ultimate revenge—stopping the king's prophecy and stealing Rennedawn right out from under him. All is right with the world, Your Evilness."

He chewed, even he unable to resist the deliciousness of the flaky creation, eyes shutting as he savored it. As she looked upon his face, memorizing every angle, every dip, curve, and hollow, a thought plagued her. "Gideon... He was supposed to signal to you that I wasn't dead, that help was on the way. He—he *was* able to do that, wasn't he?"

Her boss's eyes flew open, and he swallowed hard. Then waited a moment. "Yes, he did. Fear not. I knew it wasn't real."

Evie exhaled. She hadn't known how The Villain would react to her possible demise, but she wasn't so obtuse as to assume he wouldn't care. He would—probably in a quiet, closed-off way.

She blinked. Her head felt lighter, the effects of the flower beginning to wane a bit. "So where do we begin? Was there a specific spot in the village the map had marked?"

The Villain held out a hand for more bread. She smirked in satisfaction, ripping him off another piece. He spoke after he finished chewing. "No, that would be far too easy. I'm thinking we start in one of the shops, ask a few questions. Mention your mother's name offhandedly so we don't appear suspicious."

She began to argue as she turned to exit the alleyway. "You always look susp—"

An *"oof"* sounded behind her. She turned to investigate. "Sir?"

But he couldn't answer, as several men in an array of costumes—ranging from a jester's garb to a large hat with a feather sticking out the side to a fur cape with pink polka dots—had pinned The Villain to the ground.

The one with a tin crown pointed a sword right at the boss's back, a WANTED flyer in his meaty hand. Only this flyer didn't have the usual cartoonish depictions of her boss. In fact—

That was The Villain's true face, almost exactly, and worse…his true *name*.

WANTED VILLAIN REVEALED:

TRYSTAN MAVERINE

REWARD: A THOUSAND GOLD PIECES.

"We caught The Villain!"

CHAPTER 32

EVIE

"I've never been tied up before," Evie said, "but I am almost certain you could be doing that more gently. I'm going to get rope burn."

"Theodore, gag her like we did The Villain! I can't listen to her squawking any longer."

Anger pulsed as Evie was jostled against her boss, who for some godsforsaken reason had done absolutely nothing to get free of his own bindings. Why wasn't he using his magic?

To his credit, he was not shy about using brute force.

As soon as the largest of the men — Theodore, she believed — yanked her back and shoved a rolled-up cloth in her mouth, The Villain went berserk. His feet, which were not bound, came up and kicked the goon hard in the nose with a loud *crack*. Three other men were on him in seconds, pinning him as he yelled against his gag, a furious, muffled sound.

Evie choked on the cloth as Theodore shoved it even farther in and then covered it with another cloth tied around the bottom of her face. She couldn't talk her way out of this, just listen to the rattling quiet as the boat carried them down an unknown canal to an unknown destination. She felt sick.

Creak, creak, creak.

Her breathing became labored as she felt the bile rising in her throat. The leader of the group, who was being called Fritz by his companions, had silver hair, but he otherwise appeared young, perhaps only a decade older than Evie. He grinned at her, but it wasn't friendly.

"You look awfully familiar," Fritz said as he inched even closer. The Villain began thrashing again, but Evie didn't move. She was through with letting herself be intimidated by men. "Did I take you to bed last month?"

She frowned and shrugged, looking down at the gag still in her mouth. The intrigue in Fritz's eyes only grew as he untied the cloth, and Evie spit the filthy-tasting handkerchief from her mouth. She smirked. "No, I don't think I've ever been *that* disappointed."

Fritz paused, raising his hand like he would strike her, but the blow never came. Instead, he brought his hand down against his thigh hard, then hollered, "That was very good, little lady! Disappointing in bed!" He motioned to a quiet blond man with glasses in the corner. "Write that one down, Douglas. I wanna use it in the next performance."

Performance?

Douglas gave Evie a considerably distasteful look before turning to write in his tiny black notebook.

The boat jostled again, and The Villain finally settled back against the seat. *Use your magic!* she urged him with her eyes. But he didn't. He merely sat there in silent fury.

She didn't have magic. She didn't have physical fighting skills. But she did have her mind and her optimism. They would have to be enough.

Evie pushed her shoulders back. "If it's gold you want, The Villain can double whatever the king's ransom is."

Fritz laughed again and pointed at her like they were buddies sharing an ale over a rowdy game of cards. "Ah, but can he pay his ransom *and* yours, Evie Sage?"

Her mouth parted and her pulse climbed as the man pulled another WANTED flyer from his pocket. This one was a perfect rendering of...her.

THE WICKED WOMAN
EVIE SAGE
WANTED FOR TREASON
COLLUDING WITH THE VILLAIN
ARMED
DANGEROUS
REWARD: 300 GOLD PIECES

The sketch was a semi-faithful rendering of her face, but the eyes were angled in a dangerous tilt, her curls flying wildly about her head like a large gust of wind was drawing them back.

"Sir!" she said, feeling sobered but still lightheaded from the flower. "I have a wanted flyer!"

The Villain looked concerned, glaring at the slip of paper and then back to her face as if he was worried she was about to cry.

"Isn't this...*exciting!*" She grinned, more flattered by the word "dangerous" than she ought to be. "We can certainly pay you both reward amounts, gentlemen. The Villain has been stealing from the nobles for more than a decade and has amassed a fortune from doing...odd jobs, we'll call them." They were hired-out mercenary missions, but these goons didn't need to know that.

Fritz leaned forward, resting his elbows on his knees. "I'm not taking you to the king. I'm taking you to our boss. You see..." He paused. Evie and The Villain exchanged a look before waiting with bated breath to hear what the head goon had to say. "I'm training for my lead role in our autumn theatrical production at the local playhouse. My character is a kidnapper, and I like to be method."

Evie's eyebrows shot up to her forehead before she looked at her boss and uttered, "My guess wasn't even kind of close."

If the boss could've pinched the bridge of his nose in that moment, she had the incredibly strong belief that he would've. Which was nice, actually — there was a comfort in knowing someone well enough to be able to anticipate what they'd say and do next. She had that familiarity with so few people.

The boat rattled to a jolting stop. Fritz leaped up, nearly banging his head on the ceiling.

"Bring them in, and be sure you're not seen. The boss will be right angry if any of the guests catch wind of this."

Firm arms hoisted her up and dragged her out of the rocking boat, back into the burning sunlight. The air was wet with moisture that dampened her skin, making her dress cling uncomfortably to her body. She heard raucous yelling and the bustling of human activity behind the door long before they were pushed through it, and once inside, she was accosted by the smells of sweat and old shoes. A wall separated them from what she guessed was the playhouse on the other side.

The Villain struggled against his bindings and against the three men hoisting him in. It was like the beginning of a bad joke. *How many theater performers does it take to bring down The Villain?*

She chuckled to herself and mumbled, "Douglas, write that down."

The Villain rolled his eyes at her, but before she could blink again, they were down some small side stairs, through a wood panel, and in a small but surprisingly clean cell.

"Used to keep the rowdy patrons down here in the water cellar to dry them out after too much drink," Fritz explained. The water cellar lived up to the name. Long, rectangular windows were spaced evenly along the upper walls, with nothing beyond but the sloshing water of the river canals. They were belowground, below the river line. "Should be nice and cozy for the two of you until morning."

They both stiffened. The Villain made a low noise behind his gag, and Evie's mouth opened. "Did you say *morning*?"

The rest of the men filtered out, but Fritz stayed behind just long enough to give them a little salute. That vicious smile from earlier, the one he'd made when she looked uncomfortable, had returned.

"Sit tight, lovebirds."

CHAPTER 33

BECKY

Meanwhile, back at the manor…

Gideon Sage was staring at her.

Becky narrowed her eyes before squinting back down at the payroll sheets she was signing. It was meticulous work, mindless—her preferred kind.

At least when she wasn't being scrutinized so closely by the knight off in the corner.

Keely and Min had led a contingent of the guard into the woods as extra security against anyone who might stumble upon the manor by accident—in addition to the front door, two errant windows were now visible high up in the trees. This was growing more concerning by the day. As was the fact that Becky was now this knight's babysitter.

"Can I help you with something, Mr. Sage?" She folded her arms, looking directly at him. It would only make the man more suspicious if she hid herself away, and she couldn't have suspicion aimed in her direction. It was far too dangerous.

"No, I apologize. You just resemble someone I saw once in my time with the Valiant." Gideon shook his head, brown hair falling forward toward his dimpled chin. His eyes were boyish—exactly as she remembered them. "When the king traveled south for a diplomacy meeting with a powerful family."

She buried her anxiety under a veneer of indifference. "I don't associate with the Valiant Guard, and I've no experience with powerful families."

Lyssa interrupted, charging in with a tray of cookies in hand, powdered sugar dusting her cheeks. "I helped Edwin make another batch of sweets! But we used caramel pieces and pixie sparkle! He says I'm a natural baker." Her chocolate-covered lips pulled into a wide grin. "Would you like one,

Ms. Erring?"

Becky shrugged at the little girl, though her mouth watered at the smell of baked sugar and butter. "Would you like a cavity? Stop eating desserts at all hours of the day."

Lyssa Sage did not take her prickly attitude to heart. In fact, the girl seemed fueled by the censure as she took another big bite.

"I'll have one, Lyssa, if there's extra," Gideon said. Lyssa tentatively picked one up from her small tray and handed it to her older brother.

Gideon took a bite and made a show of almost falling over, holding tight to Becky's desk for balance. "Holy gods! This is the best cookie I've ever had."

Lyssa looked shy, but her smile was enormous. *Well played, sir knight.* "Really?"

Gideon nodded and winked at Becky just as Blade rounded the corner of the courtyard entrance, shirtless, covered in sweat and dirt, his tanned, muscled stomach glistening—and her mouth watered again for different, much more embarrassing reasons. He should've disgusted her, but he didn't. He never really had, if she was honest.

But of course, she could never admit this. She didn't believe in office fraternization, office friendships, or anything outside of professional distance. "You look vile, Mr. Gushiken—go bathe immediately."

Another voice screeched through the office. "Ms. Erring, the interns are going to kill each other!"

She groaned. *And this is why.* "What is it this time, Marvin?" she asked as the front-gate guard rushed in, pointing toward the ascending staircase.

"They're fighting in the mess hall! One of them found a way to repair the barrier, and they're fighting over who gets to present it to you and the boss!"

She gritted her teeth. "And no one is trying to break it up?" Becky stood, rounding her desk and listening at the base of the stairs. She heard nothing but raucous screams. "Are they...cheering?"

Marvin winced. "There have been bets placed on who will win."

The intern pool was made up almost entirely of disgraced noblemen's children. All spoiled, all insufferable. In a different time, she'd let them tear one another apart. But if there was one thing she took incredibly seriously, it was her role as the head of Human Resources. She was here to be a resource to all humans and magical creatures alike, no matter how irritating.

She pulled out her desk drawer, grabbed her gold letter opener, then headed for the stairs.

"Ms. Erring? Shall I send for the Malevolent Guard?"

"No need, Marvin," she said, walking past a skeptical Blade. "I'll handle it myself."

A warm hand closed over her arm; she turned and saw Blade's whiskey eyes, his brown hair pulled back in a half bun. "Stop, lovely Rebecka. I'll go. What are you going to do? Alphabetize them?"

She smirked, pulling her arm from his grip and starting up the stairs.

"Something like that."

CHAPTER 34

THE VILLAIN

"**D**o you think you could get one of your hands up my skirt?"
The noise Trystan made behind the gag was meant to be *huh?* but instead, his all-too-befuddled reply was much closer to *"herg?"*

"To get the dagger strapped to my thigh," she clarified, licking her lips and rolling back her shoulders, bringing her chest up at an enticing angle.

He decided it would be easier to blame the sound on his dry throat than the memory of Sage's breasts that was seared into his brain for all eternity. His heart rate increased, and he shut his eyes to clear the black spots forming at the edges of his vision. When he opened them, Sage was staring at him with a concerned furrow to her dark brows. With a flick of his neck, he motioned for her to slide closer, maneuvering awkwardly to lift the hem of her skirt. She sucked in a gasp, and he pretended not to hear it or the harsh breathing coming out of his flared nostrils.

The sound of the fabric sliding up her leg was far more sensual than it should've been, the rustle of cotton against bare skin something he knew would be a source of torment for him later. His calloused fingers slid up the subtle softness of her thigh until they hit the leather strap, and all the while he kept his eyes tightly shut.

It was less likely she'd see the yearning that way.

A muffled cry of victory left his lips when he slid the dagger free, but he nearly dropped it when it burned the daylights out of his hand. Grimacing in pain, he made quick work of cutting his binds and spitting out the gag, then tossed the demon dagger to the ground. "What the blazes!" He held tight to his palm—there was a searing burn there, like he'd put his hand to a hot stove.

"Does it burn you every time you touch it?"

She looked at him quizzically, eyeing the burn with a frown. "No, it feels good when I hold it. Like it's warming me."

Bracing himself, he gripped the handle and sliced through her binds, dropping the dagger as soon as she was free. "Whatever magic it was imbued with must repel mine." That, or even weaponry was beginning to turn on him.

Sage rubbed at the rope burn on her wrists, then held her palms out flat. The dagger took the invitation, jumping into her hand like a hound greeting its master. *Absurd.*

She turned the blade every which way, pouting. "Well, that's not nice."

"It's a tool for harm, Sage; it's not meant to be *nice.*"

"Shh, it'll hear you." She grinned. He sighed.

He went to the bars of the cell, which were rusted and old. They could be easily broken if they were lucky. He looked around the cell for a tool, but the only furniture was a spindly wooden chair and table on the other side of the bars, so brute force would have to do. While he worked on shaking them, a thought struck, and he couldn't let it go. "When did the scar stop hurting?" he asked casually.

"When I slit Otto Warsen's throat." Her voice was detached, and he immediately felt a pit in his stomach—he hadn't even asked her if she was all right yet. "The scar stopped hurting after that, but now it tingles and hums, like the piece of me the dagger absorbed answers the mark it left on my body."

"Hmm," he said, sounding noncommittal—one of his many talents. The metal bars were cold beneath his hands as he angled his neck back. "You shouldn't have had to kill him."

Her answer was immediate and succinct. "Oh, believe me, it was my pleasure."

Chills skittered across his spine like an icy rain, the sensation so jarring that he couldn't be certain if it was refreshing or unpleasant.

The smell of vanilla and roses drowned out the thoughts in his mind as she came to stand next to him, her hair tickling his arm. "Don't worry," she said quietly, a smile on her face he'd begun to recognize as false, as much a mask as the hard lines of his mouth. "I survived. Now, move. Let me try." She angled her arm up and brought the dagger down. The two metals reverberated off each other, but no breaks occurred, just an unpleasant clanging—and the bars heating the way the dagger had.

Trystan released them with a yelp, shaking out his hands. Sage winced, dropping the dagger to grab his hand, but when she stepped forward, her heel caught on the discarded rope that had once bound his wrists. Her foot slipped, hitting the weakest part of his ankle and bending it as they both grappled for balance and failed.

Sage fell first, and he fell after her. On *top* of her.

Her body was warm and curved beneath his, his hard muscle flush with her softness. He pushed himself up onto his elbows, gasping. "Did I crush you?"

Her lids were drooped, her eyes on his mouth. He should move—she was likely still under the effects of the flower, and Trystan's brand of villainy in no way extended to women who were too inebriated to know what they were doing. He'd sooner sever his hands from his wrists.

But he was too late.

The door to the basement cellar flew open and slammed against the wall, causing his body to curl protectively over her.

"I heard we caught The Villain! And— Oh, am I interrupting?"

This wasn't one of the deep voices from before but a light, slightly raspy voice, whose next words made Sage go rigid beneath him. "Evie, is that you?"

A young woman stood in the doorway. Her dark-brown brows arched against golden-brown skin, radiant as she stepped out of the shaded doorway and into the dimly lit space. Her eyes were the color of burnished gold and lined with kohl, giving them a catlike appearance, and her long brown hair— even longer than Evie's—was pin-straight and shiny as she pushed it behind one ear.

Sage shoved him, and he moved immediately, helping her to her feet.

His assistant stared at the woman, mouth open. "Helena?"

Helena, the woman in question, stretched her lips into a full, menacing grin.

"It's been a long time…little cousin."

CHAPTER 35

EVIE

"What are you doing here?" Evie asked incredulously.

She hadn't seen or heard from her cousin in years. She remembered so well how she used to wait by the mailbox for Helena's letters every day, just in case a new reply to her missives arrived, but after two years, she'd had to give up hoping.

Helena glided toward the bars, dressed in a lovely sapphire gown that floated behind her as she took a seat in the room's only rickety old chair. She tapped her finger against her chin thoughtfully. "I work here." Her cousin's eyes flitted to her and then her boss, keen interest playing in them. "And what are *you* doing here?" The finger stopped tapping her chin and now pointed around the cell.

Suddenly, Evie felt angry—*so* angry. She'd had no idea Helena ended up in the Heart Village, had no idea she worked in a playhouse, had no idea of *anything* her cousin was doing. Because she'd simply disappeared, like everyone else in her life.

"You didn't hear?" she asked with an eye roll. "I had too much to drink and tried to strip naked on your stage."

Her boss choked behind her, slamming a fist against his chest. He'd been doing that a lot—perhaps she should have Tatianna make him something for heartburn.

Helena laughed—a lovely, lilting sound that matched her countenance. Evie wondered if her boss noticed that loveliness. The thought sent a pounding ache through her skull. "You are still most amusing, cousin."

"Incarceration really tickles my funny bone," Evie said pointedly, looking at the bars and then the keys hanging on a hook by the door.

Helena followed her gaze, nodding, unhooking them from the wall. Both Evie and The Villain stood on edge in preparation for the cell door opening. "Before I do you any favors, though, perhaps you can tell me what you're doing in the Heart Village"—she smirked—"*wicked woman*?"

The Villain grimaced, but Evie jumped and gave a little clap. "Oh, the wanted flyers of me are spreading, sir! How exciting."

"We have different definitions of that word," he grumbled, rubbing at his temples.

Evie shrugged, deciding directness was the best way to address the situation at hand. "We're looking for my mother, Helena, and I'm guessing you've seen her recently, judging by the ghastly look on your face."

Helena flinched. *Got her.* "Yes," she said, not trying to hide it. "Aunt Nura was here for a time."

But not anymore, were the words Helena wouldn't say. The silence wore through the last of Evie's patient kindness. "Helena, as much as I have missed our correspondence, I am through with niceties. Tell me."

"She spent a few months here. Maybe two or three years ago." Helena looked haunted. "I had just moved to the village when she arrived, after my father remarried."

Evie hadn't even known that Uncle Vale had remarried. "And his new spouse?"

"Oh, my stepmother is lovely, if not a little boring. I think that's what my father needed. I just didn't want to be in the way while they started their new life, and I was told the Heart Village was a bustling hub of enterprise and opportunity." Helena scoffed at the words like they were a joke.

The Villain, who had until now allowed Evie to take charge of the conversation, chimed in, quiet but steady. "I take it you do not feel that way any longer."

Helena's eyes flashed. "I work with method kidnappers. What do you think?"

He clicked his tongue as if to say *point taken* and moved back, allowing Evie to continue.

"Did my mother say where she was going? Or why she came to you in the first place?" Evie asked, growing desperate.

Helena shook her head, almost looking sympathetic beneath the guise of her apathy. "I think she thought it safer to come to me than my father. He loves his sister, but you know as well as I he would've sent her right back to Uncle Griffin." Her warm gaze went far away, and her brows knitted together, as if she was trying to remember. "She wanted to know more about the stars, I think? Of what my father taught me. It was the only time she'd speak. Mostly she was truly a ghost, Evie. It wasn't pleasant. And when she did talk, it was nonsensical muttering about wanting to be gone. To be no one. She wanted to be swallowed by midnight. I thought she'd gone mad."

There had been a certain level of detachment that Evie had held on to during this endeavor to find her mother. But she could see it, remember it—the lost look in Nura's eyes. It had been ingrained into Evie since she was too little to understand what it meant. She had watched her mother fade from the vibrant, beautiful woman who ruled her childhood to a husk of a person, and then to nothing.

Evie had been given many things by her mother—the length of her fingers, the curl in her hair, the bow of her lips—but she could never have anticipated being handed down her mother's ability to bury anguish beneath the surface. And like her mother, Evie feared one day…she, too, would break. A tragic inheritance, seeing your mother's flaws crop up within yourself and having the awareness to know it but no idea how to stop it.

"I imagine the guilt drove her to it, about killing Gideon," Helena said, snapping Evie from her spiral.

Her eyes burned. "He isn't dead."

This surprised her cousin but didn't seem to shock her. "Oh, how wonderful! He owes me money."

"Take heart," The Villain said to Helena, but his eyes were on Evie; she could feel them.

Helena laughed and swung the keychain about her finger. "I wonder whether the rumors of The Villain's brutal, destructive magic were exaggerated, if simple rusty metal bars can keep you contained."

The Villain didn't reply, just glared, stepping subtly closer to Evie. "Let us out and I'll be happy to demonstrate for you."

Helena quirked a grin before tossing the keys to the other side of the room, where they landed soundly on the small table near the door. "Unfortunately, I cannot do that."

Evie gripped the bars, furious. "Helena, we're family. You're not actually going to allow your boss to sell us out to the king, are you?"

Helena tsked, the train of her dress floating behind her as she glided to the door. "Oh, goose. You think any of those buffoons upstairs could run anything? Other than their hopeless careers into the ground." Helena finished with a flourish and put a nail in Evie's and The Villain's proverbial coffins.

"The Deadlands Theater is my playhouse, and I *am* the boss."

CHAPTER 36

EVIE

"**Y**our family members make mine look like a picnic," The Villain gritted out after Helena had slammed the door behind her.

Evie stared at him with a blank expression and then asked curiously, "How is Malcolm? We haven't heard from him in a while."

"He sent a letter to the manor while I was captured that said he hoped I didn't get executed."

Both of her brows shot upward. "Oh, well, that's promising." She gentled her voice. "And Arthur? Have you heard from him since he returned home?"

"He sent me a letter as well. It appears both our families have made a habit of poorly timed correspondence."

Evie usually tried her best not to pry, but he looked a little like he wanted her to. *Wishful thinking.* "What did it say, Trystan?" She lightly touched his arm.

The Villain actually appeared to soften a bit at the sound of his name. "I don't know. I crumpled it up and threw it in a drawer. I likely will never open it."

It would be easy to chide him for it. But he didn't need her to tell him how to manage complex feelings. She barely knew how to manage her own. "If you ever want to open it, I will sit with you. You don't have to read it out loud or anything like that. But if you wanted someone there…I'd be there for you."

He moved away, rotating his arm like her light touch had strained a muscle. "I will, um, keep that in mind."

She looked at the keys, out of reach on the small table, and then back to The Villain. "All right." She nodded, swiftly changing the subject, and flicked a hand toward him. "Remove your shirt."

"I beg your p-pardon?" he sputtered. "For what purpose?"

She rolled her eyes. "Relax, Evil Overlord. I'm not trying to offend your delicate sensibilities. I'm going to make a rope to bring the keys over to us." Even as the words came out with ease, though, her face felt aflame.

He untucked his white shirt and pulled it over his head.

Terrible plan. Terrible, horrible, AWFUL plan.

If it wasn't already clear that the effects of the flower had worn off by the beginnings of a headache, this would've sobered her completely. She'd seen him shirtless before, in passing when he was training with the Malevolent Guard, or if he occasionally became overheated during a Scatter Day run. But she'd always avoided staring, at least for a long time and certainly not this close.

Shut your mouth! She clamped it so tight her lips were bloodless beneath the rouge. He looked more menacing without his shirt on, like he'd grown seven feet in the last few seconds. His chest was widened with muscle, his shoulders hard, and... Was he flexing?

"There you go, little tornado," he said quietly, dropping the warm garment into her hands.

Her eyes went to the gold-flecked ink that circled his upper arm, like vines and leaves that had been gilded into his skin. It was nearly identical to the employment ring on her pinkie finger—the one he'd claimed to have given her for trust purposes, so that she'd never betray him.

"It looks like mine," she declared, reaching out, running her finger over his mark to compare. He sucked in a breath, and she looked to his face. It had gone blank, but not the normal disinterest he showed everyone in the office—no, this was forced. He was *trying* to be emotionless.

Interesting.

"A...coincidence." He sounded confident to the untrained ear, but Evie had spent an inordinate amount of time observing his minute tells. He was *nervous*.

She squinted and crossed her arms. "Are you sure it's not because you used the gold ink bargain to magically link us so you'd always know when I was in danger?"

His eyes popped so wide, he resembled a caricature drawing. Exactly as she'd hoped. Better, even. "You know?"

She snorted, bumping her knuckles under his chin playfully. "I'm afraid I've known for a while, Your Evilness."

One hand fell to his hip, the other dragging through his hair till it almost stood up on its own. "You—you— How?"

She shrugged. "I guessed. Clare confirmed."

Words were normally a struggle for him, but now they seemed completely out of reach. She put him out of his misery. "I thought you'd tell me eventually, so I didn't say anything, but I got impatient. Sorry."

The apology, ironically enough, was the thing that sent him over the edge. In a flash, she was in his grip. "You're sorry, not angry? You don't hate me for keeping it from you?"

Carefully, she removed each of his hands, giving him a dubious grin. "Do I hate you for protecting me instead of putting ink on my body that will kill me? Oh, yes. To the gallows with you, you deviant monster." Her sarcasm didn't seem like it was well taken—her boss was still too flabbergasted, too confused, so she added with a touch more humility, "Sir, I'd hardly begrudge you secrets. I have my own, too."

His head angled toward her, his astonishment turning into something sharper. "Like what?"

Ignoring him, she frowned at the shirt in her hands. "This isn't long enough." She dropped it and, without warning, lifted her dress over her head.

"Sage!" the boss roared, his hands waving like he was trying to put out an unruly fire.

"Oh, relax, Evil Overlord. I wear less than this to swim in the pond in my village, and the men there don't startle," she said, rolling her eyes and noting the wildness in his own as she tied the two garments together and promptly removed one of her shoes to give it weight.

"What are their names?" His voice was distant as she focused on her task of wrapping the tail end of the cloth around the shoe.

"Who?" she huffed, finally finishing.

"The men in your village who saw you in your undergarments."

"I don't remember. Why?"

"Just curious." His voice was low.

"Got it!" She grinned at him and then promptly frowned when she saw his face. "You look like you swallowed something bitter."

"I did," he said through gritted teeth.

She hardly noted his response, merely gripped the shoe, holding tight to the end of their knotted clothing, and aimed it in the direction of the keys— but instead knocked over a chipped vase about four feet in the other direction.

Biting her lip, Evie looked at her boss sheepishly. "I was so excited to get the shoe knotted that I forgot I have terrible aim."

He held out his hand for it. "If you were aiming for the vase, you are an excellent shot." His dimple appeared. Every barricade she'd begun to build around her heart to keep him out, to protect herself, collapsed. She could deal with the grumpy villain, the murderous villain, the torturous villain, but the charming villain? That was simply unreasonable.

He began his own attempt at aiming, standing with the same posture he had on Scatter Day with the interns. Focused attention, like he was blocking out everything but himself and the keys. He tossed the shoe, and Evie sucked in a breath, watching as it sailed through the air and…overshot the keys by a yard, knocking hard into one of the windows. It cracked, and water slowly began leaking in.

Evie tilted her head and said nothing, just let her smug expression speak for her. The Villain dragged the shoe back, glaring like it had personally offended him. "It's lighter than I thought."

"So you took that out on the window?" she replied.

He set up to aim the shoe at the keys once more, where water was now troublingly puddling around the table. "I'll get it this time, now that I have the mechanics squared away."

"Sir…the water," she said nervously.

"It's a little leak, Sage. Leave the theatrics to Fritz and his troupe." He tossed the shoe again, once more slamming into the window, and the crack got bigger. "Damn it."

She glared at him. "You hit it on purpose that time!"

"I have too much force in my throw," he muttered grimly.

"Yes, your strength is such an encumbrance—however do you bear it?" she replied sardonically, but the effect of her words was lessened by her heart rate rising at the water now pooling at her feet, soaking up to her ankles and chilling her toes.

She took a deep inhale, trying to assure herself that someone would hear all the noise, that the water was leaking in slowly enough that there would be plenty of time.

Until a terrible, sharp sound filled the room. The glass of the window was fracturing as cracks covered the entire clear surface, and then it burst. Water rushed in without reservation, streaming in waves, and they were trapped.

With no way out.

CHAPTER 37

BECKY

Meanwhile, back at the manor…

It was two men fighting. Of course.

Banging into each other and knocking tables and chairs over as they went. The damage reports for the broken furniture would fall to Becky, and they would take *forever*. Before, she was annoyed, but now, she was *furious*.

She strutted into the room, footsteps pounding behind her.

"Rebecka, you could get hurt!" Blade's voice echoed up the staircase, but she was too angry to care. *Little rats.*

"Cease at once!" She didn't scream it; she simply commanded it in a louder tone than her normal volume. *Proper and proud*, her grandmother had always called her.

The two interns were slamming fists into each other's guts, blood dripping down their faces, while other interns lined the walls, throwing food along with obscenities. Some noticed her command and stopped, while others were too lost in their mutiny to give a damn. The two fighters looked like if someone didn't stop them soon, they'd kill each other.

Fine. She'd tried it the proper way.

Now it was time for proud.

She reached down, tore her skirt up the middle to allow for more movement, and dove into the fray against Blade's and now Gideon's yells. She gripped the first intern by the hair and used his surprise to her advantage as she slammed her elbow into his face before sweeping her foot out to knock him to the floor, where he fell with a *thud*. The second, shorter intern, still high on adrenaline, charged her, but he was using brute force and she agile intellect. She dodged away from his grab easily before knocking him in the back and pressing against a nerve that made him howl in pain before collapsing alongside the other one.

She took a step back and straightened her glasses. "If this hall isn't spotless before the end of the workday, I will be certain to tell the boss in great detail who was responsible and what sort of punishments I would deem appropriate—starting with switching to the non-energizing cauldron brew." There were panicked murmurs, but nobody moved. "Now!"

A flurry of bodies ran frantically to the exit. Nodding, satisfied, Becky spun on her heel, her thigh partially exposed to the cool air in one of the highest points of the manor. She moved what was left of her skirts to cover it before glancing up and finding Blade standing before her.

He was gaping at her, his perfect white teeth visible as his mouth hung wide open. "What in the deadlands was *that*?"

She'd be lying if she said she didn't enjoy the astonishment on his normally confident face. "That was me doing my job."

"No, no, no. Hold on, soldier. Where did you learn to fight like that?"

She grinned to herself, finding a nearby mirror to fix her hair. She slid the falling pins out, and thick, silky brown waves fell down her back. Pulling her fingers through the strands, she began pinning it back up. "You'd be surprised how paperwork strengthens the muscles." She dropped a pin, and it was fished up quickly by one of her favorite pixies. "Thank you, Nalia." She gave the pixie a small smile and began pushing the pins back in, the skin on her face yanked tight.

Blade laughed, wagging his finger behind her. "Oh, no. You're not getting out of this that easily, lovely Rebecka. I'm not giving up until you—"

But he was cut off when one of the interns who had been fighting, Caden, stood up and gripped her by the shoulder hard enough that she yelped in pain. "I was going to win! This was my chance for a promotion, you frigid witch!" he screamed in her face.

In seconds, Blade was pulling the man away from her and restraining him against the brick wall with seemingly no effort. When the intern tried to break free and reach for her again, Blade shoved an arm into the man's chest, pinning Caden in place. "Apologize," Blade thundered. "Now!"

The intern sneered, blood still dripping from his nose. Becky watched, motionless, her hairpins forgotten.

"I'm sorry," the intern mumbled, still squirming, though he stopped when Blade pressed his arm tighter across the intern's chest.

"Louder." The dragon trainer smiled, but it was a far cry from the jovial man who charmed everyone and flirted in the office day after day. This was what lay beneath the surface. This was just for her. "So she can hear you."

"I'm sorry, Ms. Erring," Caden said loudly, humbly. Blade released him, keeping his body between Caden and her, then pounded the man on the back.

"There. Now, that's better, isn't it? Do we see why manners are important?" Blade then gripped the intern by the collar and tugged him close. "Speak to her like that again and I'll throw you to my dragon and let him pick his teeth with your bones."

The intern cried, sprinting away as soon as he was released.

Becky could only stare, slack-jawed.

But Blade had already moved on, like the encounter had never happened, straightening his sky-blue vest. "So? Where did you learn to fight like that?"

"I, uh…need to get back to work," she said hesitantly, backing away.

Blade frowned, scratching his head. "Of course. Maybe later?"

She swallowed. "Maybe!" But she was already sprinting toward the stairs, where Gideon Sage leaned against the wall, a knowing look in his eyes.

"So I was right," Gideon said, shaking his head. "It is you."

"If you say a word, I will deny it," she hissed, angry at herself for being so careless. Of course he'd recognized her; she'd just given him blatant evidence with her showmanship.

Gideon flattened his mouth into a grim line. "I understand secrets, Ms. *Erring*." He emphasized her name, knowing now that it was false. "I won't say a word. Don't worry."

She turned back and noted Blade's frown, the way he eyed the small space between her and Gideon. He was misunderstanding, and she had to let him. Her secret must remain just that—a secret.

Or her whole world would topple.

And the life she'd built for herself with it.

CHAPTER 38

THE VILLAIN

"I heard drowning is the most painful way to die," Sage said unhelpfully as the water in the room pooled around their calves.

He was still attempting to get the keys but had only managed to knock them closer to the edge of the table. "Speaking from experience, are you?"

Sage kicked up water; the downpour from the ceiling had soaked her, soaked them both. Her undergarments clung to her like a second skin, and Trystan thought quietly that there were many far more painful things than drowning. Like dying without his hands molding to her two perfect—

"Are you having performance anxiety?"

The shoe slipped from his hands and made a *plop* sound as it hit the water.

"I'm sorry?" There was no way he'd heard what he'd just heard. But when he turned to stare, she was smiling sympathetically.

"It's all right, sir." There was no mirth in her tone to indicate that she was joking, but Trystan often misread others' humor. "Tatianna told me it happens to everyone." Was she serious? *Godsdamn deadlands.*

Irritation caused his jaw to twitch, water splashing against his legs as he stormed over to her. The intimidation factor was perhaps dampened by the squishing sound of his boots. But he was satisfied when he caught her cheeks reddening as she admired his chest. There was a clear, sobered focus to her eyes that hadn't been there when they'd entered the village.

"I can say with the utmost assurance"—his eyes raked over her, and she stopped breathing—"when given the privilege, I have no issue *performing.*" Water dripped down from her hair onto her lips, the red smeared a bit against her cheek.

Her breaths were coming in short gasps, her chest moving quickly as she reached up a hand and placed it against his bare chest, right over his heart. A twinkle—he was begrudged to call it so, but that's what it was—a twinkle appeared in her eyes and a small, amused tilt at her mouth. "I was speaking of your magic, sir."

Good for you. I'm not.

Clearing his throat, noting the water had made its way past his knees now, he said with a large amount of exasperation, "I surrendered my power so that I could enter the village."

She pushed him with no force—just censure. "That was incredibly foolish!"

He didn't look at her, picking the shoe back up and aiming once more for the keys. "It was their only condition upon my entry, and I didn't want you to be alone."

He aimed again, missed. Again, missed. Aimed again—and this time hit the keys dead-on…right into the water, where they sank like a stone. Along with his heart.

Someone from the playhouse above would come. He had to believe that. They would not die here, right? Sage would not die here. But the panic raking nails down his spine was spinning a different tale.

"I wish you'd stop doing that," she said quietly.

The water was to his waist now, nearly swallowing Sage up to her chest. He rushed for her and gripped her hips, hoisting her above the water to give her more space to breathe. But it brought their faces inches apart as her hands fell limply to his shoulders. "Stop doing what?" he asked, embarrassingly out of breath, but he hoped she would assume it was from the exertion.

"Being so nice," she said calmly, casually, like they were having a normal conversation in his office and not trapped in a cellar beneath the water that was imminently going to lead to their demise.

His face twisted with disgust. *Nice?* "Well, now you're trying to offend me on purpose."

It was the twitch of her red lips that started the prickling sensation in his face and neck. Then the squeeze of her fingers against his shoulders, freezing him in place as he stared at the smattering of freckles faintly dusted across her elegant nose. Her eyes were fixed on his mouth, something desperate in them when she looked up at him.

"We're going to drown," she whispered.

He squeezed his eyes shut and saw her laying in her coffin, then saw her standing atop the stairs of the king's palace with the color back in her cheeks. He felt a tingle in his lips, and Sage removed a hand to shake out her knuckles, as if reliving an unwanted sensation there.

He forced emotion below the surface, tried to kill every feeling within him so he didn't need to cope with defeat. He was numb. Until Sage—until *Evie*—placed the hand she'd been shaking out against his cheek and said with a crack in her voice that fissured his soul, "Please kiss me."

There was nothing for the agony as she leaned her head closer to his, as all his muscles froze out of necessity, for if they thawed there would be no more holding back. And why should he? If she wanted reprieve in these final moments, why should he not give it? She couldn't know what that small request was doing to him, how desperately he wanted to.

How he'd always wanted to.

Her sweet breath brushed against his mouth, and it made him feel drunk— And that word shattered everything. *Drunk.* The flower effects. That could be the only reason she would ask him for such a thing. His desperation could not extend past the final measly scrap of honor he had left—honor that seemed to only extend to the one person he wanted above all else.

He wondered if she could see the sorrow in his eyes as he said, "I—I can't do that."

The wounded look in her own eyes nearly changed his mind, but then, without warning, another window high above them in the corner shattered. Sage screamed, and Trystan pulled her head into his chest, using his body to shield her from the falling glass—as something small and slimy landed on his head.

"By the gods—"

"Kingsley!"

CHAPTER 39

EVIE

"**M**y hero!" Evie called happily, picking up the amphibian.

She was inches away from pressing her lips to the frog's cheek when he was yanked from her hands. The boss gave her a dark look. "We should not reward defiance, Sage." Though his words came out choppy, he still managed to glare at the frog. "You weren't even meant to come, you little nuisance."

Tatianna appeared through the shattered window, her lovely face a welcome sight after their moment of hopelessness. And the mortification Evie would be buried with for the foreseeable future. And the words she'd hear every time she had even an inkling of self-doubt.

I—I can't do that.

It had been her one surge of confidence, and it had been buried beneath painful rejection.

"Oh, thank goodness you two aren't dead," Tatianna said, soothing her rampant thoughts.

The Villain frowned. "Was that up for debate?"

Kingsley leaped into the water and swam toward the corner, where the keys had sunk. "Smart boy!" Evie cooed, treading water, her toes unable to meet the ground without her head being swallowed. The boss grunted, curling his lip in distaste, then wrapped a hand around her hip and hoisted her up.

Tatianna disappeared and was replaced by Clare, who had an awed look as she took in the room. "Goodness, you two are incredibly destructive."

Evie grinned. "It's routine at this point."

Clare rolled her eyes. "And that doesn't explain why you're both basically naked."

Before Evie could come up with a plausible explanation, Kingsley returned with the keys in his little froggy mouth. The boss unlocked the cage door, pushing with all his might against the pressure from the water. The muscles on his back rippled with the force, moving in a way that made her want to douse her head below the cool surface. She couldn't believe that mere seconds before, she'd had her hands all over his skin...

When she finally found it in herself to look away, Tatianna and Clare were staring at her...and chuckling. She flipped a finger at them—the not-nice one.

When he'd successfully opened the cage door, The Villain turned to where she was treading water behind him, seemingly not noticing her exchange with his sister and the healer. "You first, Sage." The boss helped her through the bars and lifted her toward the broken corner window. She felt two hands reach in to tug her out and up onto the wooden sidewalk above the water. Gasping, she flopped onto her back, spitting and coughing. The hot sun overhead warmed her skin as she caught her breath.

Her hands were still clasped in Tati's and Clare's. They all breathed heavily before Clare said into the quiet, "I really don't know how we got here. We had such a normal childhood."

A fit of giggles took over, and Evie squeezed her fingers around each of their hands. Feeling warmth and affection for her rescuers, she released them quickly to reach for Trystan.

But he wasn't there.

And of course, as the gods commanded, she knew that when things were too good, that was the moment they were about to get very bad.

"Trystan?" Clare leaned over with her, reaching into the overflowing water. "Where is he?"

"Did he manage to get the door open from the other side? Perhaps he came up the stairs of the cellar and took the normal exit?" Evie asked, panicking, angling her head in to look and promptly banging it against the upper edge of the window.

It was then that a voice called from behind them. "He did."

It was Helena and her actors holding The Villain, who was shirtless and wet, his face seething with anger.

And Evie's dagger at his throat.

CHAPTER 40

EVIE

"That's mine, Helena," Evie said softly.

She was sure Clare and Tati would assume she was talking about the dagger, but the dagger was not what she was looking at—or rather *who* she was looking at. Trystan was held between two of the larger goons, struggling in their grip.

Please kiss me.

Not now, she begged herself. Her lingering mortification would have to wait until she was alone and could properly scream into a pillow.

Clare stepped forward. "Release my brother this instant, ruffians."

"Actors," Fritz corrected, the rest of his companions nodding.

This knocked everyone silent. Helena groaned into her hands. "Fritz, not now!"

The man looked hurt and loosened his grip, and that opening seemed to ignite something inside her. Her scar tingled, but instead of just the sensation, her whole shoulder glowed, as it had before she'd dispatched Otto Warsen—but this time, the glow was an array of rainbow hues. Her shoulders were bare, with only the corset holding up her chemise, so not only was it visible, it was seriously *bright*.

"Gods, Evie!" Tati said, covering her eyes.

"Mine," she said again, eyes still not on the dagger, but it answered her call anyway, glowing the same rainbow hue—and then soaring out of Fritz's hand and back into her own. The Villain didn't waste the opening created by the men's surprise; he shouldered away, bolting to her side. Evie angled her body in front of his, gripping the dagger tightly in her hand.

"It's over, Helena. We're leaving." Evie waved her dagger in the direction of the goons, who covered their heads and ducked away from the glowing magic blade that had answered her call. She was prepared for a fight, if that was what it took. Nobody would harm her *or* Trystan again. She knew how to use her dagger and would readily discard her heavy morality to—

Helena's full lips went into a pout before she looked down and picked at her nails. "All right."

Evie's racing mind ground to a halt. "Wait, that's it? 'All right'?"

Helena shrugged and combed a hand through her hair, looking like she was over the whole thing. "I was going to let you go anyway. I just wanted to see how you'd fare locked up together for a little while." Her cousin leveled a smirk at their soaked undergarments. "I had ten coins on clothing being discarded."

She held out her hand to Douglas, who stood to the side, book still in hand. He glared at Evie as he emptied his pockets and handed a pile of coins to Helena.

The Villain's anger radiated off him. "You planned to sell your cousin and me out to the king—and you gambled on us as well?"

Helena snorted. "It was a sure bet. And I was never going to sell you out. The king's the reason our theater is nearly bankrupt."

Evie frowned. "How do you mean?"

Helena maintained her haughty stance, but Evie could tell her eyes were haunted. "This theater used to be blessed by the gods' magic. Objects coming alive, animals joining the crew, the sets practically building themselves. But lately it's like the magic is…"

"Fading," Evie finished.

Helena didn't hide the pain in her eyes this time. "Exactly." She ran a hand down the side of the building. "The Deadlands Theater is dying."

"And you blame the king?" Clare asked, picking up Kingsley before he chased after a fly.

Playing with the ends of her hair, Helena said, "It's his fault. He's been rumored to be pushing the bounds of magic for years—clearly the rumors are true. And now we all must pay the price."

Evie walked over to her cousin and gripped one of her hands. She'd admonish herself later for forgiving too quickly, but she had so little family left to spare, and as careless as Helena was, she was still a part of it. "What do you mean? The king claims to be trying to enact the prophecy to *save* Rennedawn."

Helena sighed, her shoulders drooping, but she didn't release Evie's hand. "There are whispers in the Heart Village about Benedict. Not everyone is as loyal as you think they are. Benedict has destroyed families by tampering with magic, and if you want my opinion, I think he plans to steal it all."

Evie's heart raced, thoughts coming all at once instead of one at a time. Benedict's desperation to fulfill *Rennedawn's Story*...could it be a ruse to mask his true intention? Was The Villain merely a scapegoat to hide his own evils? But her thoughts paused when Helena dug a pouch from her skirt pocket and dropped it in Evie's shaking hands. "Aunt Nura left this behind. I should've sent it, but she asked me to wait for the right time. I suppose that's now."

The velvet pouch felt like it weighed at least ten pounds.

"I think she knew you'd come looking for her, goose. The day before she disappeared again, she handed it to me with this note." A small, rolled-up scroll, no bigger than Evie's index finger, was attached to the pouch, wrapped in a red ribbon. "I didn't read it," Helena added.

"She didn't say where she was going?" Evie asked, far gentler than she'd been a moment ago. It felt like there were two versions of herself at war. One who was screaming at the top of her lungs with rage and anger and the other sitting quietly, hurting deeply, waiting for someone to notice. To care.

Helena shook her head, finally showing a small amount of sympathy. "No. She just said to be sure you had it."

Evie frowned but decided to take the high road. "Thank you, Helena." And she meant it.

Helena nodded and dipped into a dramatic curtsy. "You should go. I may not be willing to turn you in, but there are plenty here who would."

She was right; they needed to leave, but she couldn't resist saying goodbye. "Helena?" Her cousin stopped, shiny hair glossy in the sunlight. Evie continued. "I'm sorry the magic fading...has hurt you."

Helena's voice was hollow. "It's hurting everyone, Evie."

She gripped the pouch in her hand, along with the scroll, as Helena and her actors started for the back doors to reenter the theater.

Helena halted, turning back to her cousin. "You should check the house. I always had a feeling she'd try to go back there."

Evie shut her eyes tight, holding the dagger close to her chest. "She never came back, Helena."

Her cousin shrugged. "Just because you didn't see her doesn't mean she wasn't there."

The dagger vibrated in her hand, her scar answering it, like they were both warning her not to creep too close to the darkness warring in her heart. Like they were urging her to hold on to herself, on to hope.

But as they all walked silently back to the bridge, with no Nura and even more of the world unveiling its ugliness to her, Evie couldn't help but wonder if she should be warring with it at all.

CHAPTER 41

EVIE

Once again, they were without any leads.

The ride home was solemn, quiet. Evie ignored the burning pain in her stomach from holding herself upright on the horse and the itching chafe of her thighs. It was odd how discomfort could be ignored when a greater problem presented itself. Her mind was wandering too far away, and Tatianna and Clare's bad news wasn't helping.

"The innkeeper said the enchantress who resided in the village hasn't been seen in eleven years," Tatianna said, flicking a braid over her shoulder, barely breaking a sweat.

The boss was gripping the reins of his black stallion tightly, all cool composure, almost like he was making an effort not to look at Evie. That was fine—she'd likely never make eye contact with him again anyway.

"Well, that's wildly unhelpful," The Villain grumbled. "Is that all the information you obtained?"

Clare looked freakishly like her brother, avoiding eye contact with Tatianna as she spoke, spine rigid. "The enchantress resides in the southern kingdom now, Trystan. Imprisoned by the king and queen for killing the crown prince."

There was a fierce, unsettling look that passed among all three of them. Even Kingsley, whose expression was normally sweet and innocent, seemed... sharper. She was missing something, and watching them quietly communicate with their eyes made Evie feel even more like an outsider.

Tatianna seemed to notice the frown pulling at Evie's lips, because she continued speaking where Clare had left off, looking at Evie to include her in the conversation. A kindness. "In any case, the innkeeper mentioned the enchantress's daughter as another viable option. She was just a girl when she and her mother were in the Heart Village, but she'd be an adult now—twenty or so. Children of such powers usually inherit."

Kingsley perked up, and he stared at Tatianna.

Trystan shook his head. "We do not have the time to traipse through the southern kingdom on a whim. There must be a better solution."

Tatianna gave a shallow nod. "Yes, sir. We'll keep looking."

They rode on in silence, but Evie couldn't seem to pull her eyes from Kingsley, who she'd think, if she didn't know any better, looked quite sad.

. . .

T he night grew dark as they neared the manor. Tatianna and Clare, upon their return, opted to investigate the growing manor concealment issue tomorrow, and the rest of them convened in the kitchens to plan out the next steps in finding Nura. The boss had donned a shirt, tragically, and Evie herself had changed into a comfortable pair of heels to help her stand taller and a warm red wool gown, still feeling chilled from the water and from the revelations of the day.

The smell of fresh pie crust lightened her mood as she wandered into the cozy kitchen space, smiling at her favorite window. Blade lifted a mug of cauldron brew in greeting from where he stood stiffly next to Gideon, who was sipping the brew and wincing at the taste.

"You get used to it," Becky reassured him, downing her cup in heaving gulps. Gideon looked at her like she had several heads. And Blade glared at Gideon like he wanted to remove his. That was…new.

"You've returned! Wonderful! Just in time for pie," Edwin called, turning toward them. A white chef's hat sat precariously upon his blue head, and his small glasses had a slight fog on the lenses from the oven's heat. His cheeks were flushed to a deep purple as he put plate after plate on the wood table, each with a piece of gooey apple pie.

"Welcome back, conquering heroes!" Gideon grinned, looking far too at home in an office he'd not been at yet a week, but he shrank when he saw the boss's glare. "Or conquering…villains? I'll stop talking."

"Thank the gods," The Villain muttered, yanking out a chair and gesturing to Evie. "Sage? A seat?"

Her cheeks matched her dress as she sat down, aware that every eye in the room was on the gesture. They couldn't read what had happened between Evie and her boss as the waters rose around them...could they?

Please kiss me.

She almost put her hands over her ears and screamed.

Lyssa turned away from the stove, fawning in dreamy delight. "He's such a gentleman!"

Blade chuckled in the corner, taking a sip of cauldron brew, then mumbling under his breath, "Oh, sure, when he's not severing heads and plucking eyeballs."

But of course, Lyssa heard, because ten-year-olds seemed to hear none of the things they were supposed to and all the things they shouldn't.

"I saw an eyeball in the hallway! It was huge!" Lyssa screeched with a little hop, just as Edwin plopped a tiny chef's hat on her head.

Blade winced. "Oh no."

"Lyssa! We have cinnamon rolls to prep," Edwin said cheerily, giving Evie a wink, and she mouthed a quiet *thank you* for the distraction.

"Has there been any change to the map, sir?" Evie asked, gently pulling the velvet pouch from her pocket and reaching two fingers inside.

The Villain grimaced before striding to the hall and dragging the large map-that-was-once-his-desk to the table. No longer glowing, no longer marked in any way. "I'm afraid the stardust wore off."

Her fingers halted on something cold and hard inside the pouch. She frowned and looked up. "It can wear off?"

The Villain set the large, useless slab off to the corner. "Apparently so. We do have a small thimbleful left. We could take a chance and pour it on to see if it lights up with another lead."

The object inside the pouch was pointed on one end, with a textured surface, and Evie felt her heart stutter as she dumped the contents into her palm.

Becky wandered over, looking at the object with confusion. "What is that?"

"It's from my mother."

In Evie's palm laid a large corner piece of a gold frame that had been broken away. It was lavish, with swirled inlays she remembered tracing as a little girl... Evie quickly turned it over and stiffened when she read what was etched on the back.

Property of the Sage Family

Gideon almost dropped his cup as he moved closer. "I recognize this."

The Villain's ears perked up. "You do?"

Gideon held out a hand to Evie. "May I hold it, Eve?"

She licked her lips and dropped the gold chunk into his waiting palm. While Gideon inspected it, Evie untied the scroll affixed to the ribbon. Her fingers went to her lips when she read the words etched there. *Find me here, hasibsi. I'll be safe. I'll be with my friend.*

She frowned, her brow furrowing as she rubbed a hand down her cheek. "Her friend?" She looked up to her brother. "Gideon?"

"This is from a painting in our house, Eve. Father had a ton of these frames, remember? Got them all specially made from a vendor in the village for Mama's birthday, for her art collection."

The words pulled a memory from the depths of her brain, like it had been archived until this moment. Her mother had loved art, had loved portraits and landscapes of people and places that held meaning to her, but her father had put nearly all of them into storage when her mother disappeared. He said he couldn't bear to look at them, but now she wondered if his motives were less romantic and more nefarious. It was always that way, she pondered. When someone revealed themselves to be something worse than what you thought, you were then tasked with sorting through what good parts within them were real, if any.

"Are you implying she could've been in our village the whole time? With the vendor? Were they friends?"

Gideon shrugged, handing the frame piece back to her. "If that's what the note says, it's possible."

"Then we must find the vendor at once! We'll go to the village, and we can ask—" She leaped up but was interrupted by the boss's heavy hand on her shoulder, pushing her back down in her seat.

"Sage, you aren't going anywhere. You're a wanted woman, as you so joyously celebrated. If you go to your village asking questions, you'll be arrested and taken into custody."

There was a stab of defiance in her gut at being told what she could or couldn't do. Even if it was reasonable, even if he was right. "I can be subtle," she argued, setting her chin in a stubborn line, climbing to her feet, and removing his hand from her shoulder.

"You are as subtle as a battering ram," The Villain responded dryly, his jaw tightening.

Gideon winced, and Blade took a hearty step back. Lyssa and Edwin seemed to be purposely ignoring them, hands pushing dough to and fro.

Evie wouldn't let him do this—bar her from continuing this investigation, cutting her out now when they were getting so close. He may have soundly rejected her in the cell, but she would not allow him to reject her here, professionally. "Sir, I plead with you to see reason. Don't leave me out of this." There was warning in her words, in the lift of her brow, in the upper tilt of her red lips. All these signs were a reflection of the anger pooling in her stomach like poison.

A lighthearted smirk curved his mouth, and it made her want to knock a fist into his smug face. "Come now, Sage. Pleading is beneath you."

She reeled back with a gasp.

Gideon slapped a hand to his head, and Blade pulled his body away like he had wandered too close to a fire.

Kingsley hopped up on the table, holding a sign. Danger.

Evie was too shocked by the offense to say anything at first, just parted her lips, her words stifled by hurt that he'd so readily harp on her vulnerable request that she'd made when they were near death. He even had the nerve to furrow his brow in confusion when he read the pain on her face—and beyond that, to act *surprised*, eyes wide as he sliced a hand through the air.

"Sage, no, that isn't at all what I—"

"I don't care what you say. Your judgment nearly got us killed in that cellar; I'm hardly going to adhere to it now. I'm coming." A vein throbbed in her head, along with a pounding in her temples. Her cheeks flushed, and her eyes narrowed into slits.

The Villain recovered quickly, huffing an incredulous laugh. "No, you are not. I will go *alone* and bring back whatever information I find."

She let out a growl of frustration. "You're wanted, too! *You'll* be arrested on the spot!"

"No I won't, Sage." He crossed his arms. "I have death magic. Anyone who recognizes me beneath my hood will find themselves face-first in the dirt."

"I'm going!" she screamed, not trying to temper herself any longer.

He glared at her, starting to shake, too. "No, you are not! It's too dangerous!"

"You can't tell me what to do!" she cried.

His hands flew in the air in a frustrated gesture. "I am your employer! I absolutely can!" He turned to Becky. "Right, Ms. Erring?"

Becky was already out the door, waving behind her as she yelled, "Nope, not getting involved in this. Goodbye!"

The boss frowned, losing some steam as he turned back toward Evie. "You'll remain here. You...you aren't needed for this. My decision is final."

He couldn't have hurt her more if he'd literally reached over and slapped her across the face. Her entire life was being needed—it was her value; it was her feeble placeholder in this world. She was his assistant. Not being needed by him was robbing her of her purpose. It was cruel, and he knew it.

He's The Villain, Evie.

The reminder didn't calm her anger at all. She merely managed to stop her body's shaking as she smiled dangerously. The boss gulped, and Kingsley held up a sign that read: RUN.

"Well then. As you wish, Mr. Maverine." She curtsied dramatically. "If there's any other way I can better assist you, please let me know."

The boss looked wary at her formal use of his last name. "Evie...please understand..."

She looked up at him with a dangerous glint in her eyes. "Oh, as your *assistant*, I understand perfectly, sir. Don't give it another thought."

As she turned and glided from the room, she heard Blade's voice call to her. "Evie, hold on!"

She turned around and snapped, "What do you want?" and then immediately regretted it. Her anger wasn't with him. She sighed heavily. "I'm sorry, Blade. I'm not good company when I'm upset. It's just that I feel so— And he just—"

Blade grinned, taking her gently by the arm. "There are two animals downstairs with a similar affliction. Why don't we go say hello? It'll make you feel better."

Unlikely, but she allowed him to guide her all the way down to the cellars anyway.

Both guvres seemed content. Blade had just fed them, and the male curled his beautiful, colorful body over the female protectively as Evie inched closer to the bars, smiling at them. Wondering quietly to herself why looking at such deep devotion made her chest ache painfully.

"I wonder what it's like to be happy like that. So content, together with the one you love," Evie whispered, but the cellar was quiet enough that she might as well have yelled it. She glanced at Blade, but he stared ahead with a half smile that didn't reach his eyes.

"Yeah. I wonder that, too. I wonder all the time."

Evie leaned her head against Blade's arm, and he glanced down at her. "The boss was unwise for not letting you go, Evie. I'm sorry."

She didn't answer, just shrugged before patting his arm in farewell and making her way back up the stairs.

The ache in her chest didn't waver, but she'd keep it—it was fuel. Her heels clicked off the stone hallway as she strutted forward, comforted by the knowledge that Trystan Maverine was about to find out just how unwise it was.

CHAPTER 42

THE VILLAIN

The pixies were glaring at him.

Every ten minutes on the dot for the last three hours, he'd heard the twinkle of their wings floating past the crack in his door, which he'd left slightly ajar only so he could hear the goings-on in the office. Certainly not because Sage hadn't spoken to him in three days and he was desperate to hear her voice. Every morning in the days past, she'd enter with a blank expression, placing his cauldron brew as he liked it on his desk, her old, weathered notebook in her hands. The one with sketches of kisses inside. Sketches that made him burn with curiosity, but he couldn't ask her about them. She was painfully—and unnaturally—silent.

It was a welcome change. Delightful, even. He was rather enjoying it, clenched teeth notwithstanding.

She hadn't hummed, hadn't laughed. He hadn't even seen her pop a vanilla candy in her mouth, and he'd been watching her to the point of absolute embarrassment. He noticed everything. When she got up, when her desk shifted, when she played with a lock of hair, when she fucking *breathed*.

And all he could do was replay her plea all over again.

Please kiss me.

Chivalry wasn't dead, but it ought to be, with the abysmal situations it put him in.

The memory of Sage's quiet request was driving him mad. Had she meant it? Was it the stress of the moment and nothing more…? Did she truly want him? Was that why she was so angry now?

Or maybe the anger was solely due to him steamrolling her into remaining at the manor.

"It doesn't matter," he grumbled, trying to get a hold of himself.

This was why a romantic entanglement was a mistake, always. It led to all this messiness, or worse yet...*feelings*. Him hurting her when all he'd desired was her safety.

As his assistant. Nothing more.

Trystan had received a raven that morning—a tip that Sage's village was having a festival. It was the perfect time to slip in unnoticed, but he couldn't even rejoice in the victory. He had no one to enjoy it with. Everyone was angry with him. *Everyone*. His own workers, his own family. Even Rebecka Erring gave him disdainful glances every time she passed him on the floor.

Kingsley, his only remaining ally, sat on his desk, ever the reflection of everything Trystan wasn't. Kind, good, gallant.

The frog held up a sign, this one reading: BEWARE.

"I don't have time to decipher your codes, Kingsley. Beware of what?" Trystan pulled a hand through his disheveled hair. He'd barely slept the last three nights, and it showed. There were shadows under his eyes and an overgrowth on his chin. He rubbed his tired eyes with his hands, leaving them there to block out the light.

"Sir?" Sage's lilting voice floated in through his cracked door. His hands left his face, and he stood so fast he knocked his chair over. Clumsiness was a trait he'd thought to be completely commandeered by his assistant, but it appeared to be catching.

He picked up his black chair and glared at it. Clearing his throat, he stood up straight, trying to appear unruffled. And failing.

"I was wondering if there was anything you needed me to do to help prepare you for your trip into *my* village."

She sounded cheerful, which for some reason gave him a horrid feeling. He moved around his desk and fixed his eyes on her face. Her warm black curls were pinned back by two golden butterfly combs, and her white tunic hung over a loose pair of trousers. The combs matched a butterfly pattern painted onto the design of her corset. She looked put together and well rested.

He had a sudden urge to pull the combs out and muss her hair, just to undo her as she did him.

"No, Sage. I believe I have things well in hand."

Kingsley held up two signs behind her back.

A and MESS.

Little traitor.

Sage lifted a brow and folded her arms across her chest, drawing his attention there for a second before he forced his gaze back up to her face. "Well, then," she said curtly, "I suppose you don't need me at all."

His body screamed the contrary.

But it was good. They needed this careful distance between them if they were to have any sort of professional future. If he was going to have any hope of forgetting he'd nearly kissed her in the water cellar—not to mention accomplishing his takeover of Rennedawn without interference—this was for the best.

The pain in his chest would go away.

"I'm taking my carriage; Keely and Nesma will ride behind me just as a precaution. I'll continue the rest of the way on my own," he finished, though he felt very much like he was being quizzed on an exam he was entirely unprepared for. And by the look in his assistant's eyes…

He'd gotten every answer wrong.

But her eyes were the only place to reflect this. The rest of her face stayed in that nearly perfectly pleasant mien, like she'd stuck a hanger behind her teeth. "Excellent. Well, I hope you have a pleasant trip, and I wish you every success." She moved in a flurry to leave, and all things considered, he was in the clear.

There was no explaining why he lurched forward, though, almost instinctually, to clasp her hand in his. The touch sent a shock through his hand and up his arm, angling right for his heart…and other, less polite places.

She swallowed. "Was there— Is there something else you needed, sir?"

You.

His thoughts were committing treason now, railing against him and everything he was endeavoring to conquer. His feelings, his body, his heart, his *memories*—they were all warring, and the object of their ire and desire was so close he could count the gray flecks in her irises, buried beneath the blue.

She is your employee, he thought desperately.

But his heart shortened it.

She is yours.

"No!" he yelled aloud. *Damn it.*

Sage ripped her hand from his, probably because he was acting like he'd just been struck by lightning. She took his outburst as a response to her question, thankfully. Or perhaps not thankfully, by the silent fury in her now-pained expression. "Very well. Have a pleasant evening."

He would have a more pleasant evening ripping off each of his fingernails. But he responded, "I will return successful."

Her eyes softened before she shook her head. "I'm sure you will."

"And how will you spend your evening?" he couldn't help asking.

She clasped her hands behind her back and tilted her head. "Some of the guards invited me to join them for drinks."

He didn't like the airiness in her voice. "Guards? Which ones?"

"Dante, Amar, Daniel…"

"Daniel is a philanderer," he warned.

Sage winked playfully. "Let's hope so."

She shut the door behind her, and he fell back into his chair, squeezing the armrest so hard, a piece of wood cracked off.

Kingsley held up two more signs: Regret This.

"I already do, old friend. I already do."

CHAPTER 43

THE VILLAIN

Trystan couldn't stand the sound of laughter.

Laughter reflected joy, and unfortunately for any person who came into his path this evening, he was determined to squash joy under his foot like a bug. With his hood pulled high over his face, he entered the village fray. Lanterns were strewn about every street corner; music was playing, couples dancing. Children were watching puppet shows, and there was even a stage off to the side with some sort of playact performance of love lost and tragedy.

How maudlin. How truly ridiculous.

Vendors lined the street. There must have been more than two dozen, and as he walked the line, he listened, feeling struck when he heard a name that ripped the air from his lungs.

"Poor Otto Warsen. I heard The Villain fed him to his wolves!"

"The Villain has wolves?" the other voice said.

"Rest in peace, Otto! It just goes to show that no good deed goes unpunished. I told Otto not to hire that strange Sage girl, but he said he took pity on the creature, and this is how she repays him! The treacherous wench. I always knew something was off about her. Working for The Villain! And all the while, her sick father is missing!"

Keep walking, he ordered himself. *Do not draw attention to yourself.*

He took a hard step forward, pulling his dark hood farther over his eyes. His magic was seeping out already, gray mist surrounding him, waiting to strike. *No*, he commanded. *Not yet.*

"She was always a pretty little piece. But the mouth on her! If I could've wired it shut, I would've enjoyed her for far longer."

Wait. He knew that voice.

Okay, he told his magic. *Go ahead.*

It seeped out toward the men near him who were drinking against one of the shop windows. The man speaking had his knee light up in vibrant red—it was Rick, Sage's unfortunate ex-paramour. Trystan's magic struck the point on his knee hard, and the man cried out, falling to the ground with a satisfying *thud*.

"My leg!" he screamed. "Something's wrong with my leg!" The group of men surrounded him, murmuring concern. Trystan smirked and walked on until an elderly woman tugged on his sleeve.

"'Scuse me, sir? Might you want a face paint?" The old woman had a weathered smile and long gray hair. Her station was a sad sight compared to the other vendors with large carts and opulent signs—all she had was a tiny table with paints and old-looking brushes, and not a patron in sight.

It would be decidedly unwise for him to expose his face to this woman. The chances were high that she would scream or cry out for the guards, effectively ruining any chance he had at finding Nura Sage. But she looked so hopeful, and her hands shook as she waited for his reply. "Please, sir? I promise I'm good! And I'll only charge you one copper piece."

A copper piece was hardly enough for a small slab of bread. *Dammit.* He'd become a weak sap with no sense of judgment. But he sat down on her stool anyway. "Can you make me into a wolf?" he asked, voice low and strained.

The woman looked so happy, he almost smiled with her—almost. He still had some self-control. "Certainly, sir!" She began dipping her brushes into paints, her hands shaking as she went, squinting so hard, it relaxed him. There was no chance she would recognize him; she could barely even see. "A right handsome wolf you'll be!"

As she painted, he looked along the streets, trying to find a stand that sold portrait frames of any kind. He didn't see a single one, but this was only one side of the street. The woman made quick work for someone with such an unsteady hand, and when she held up the mirror, his mouth opened in awe. She wasn't a face painter; she was an artist. His entire face was etched in dark swaths of gray, black, and white. He looked transformed. He looked nothing like himself.

Perfect.

"What do you think, sir?" the woman asked nervously, smiling slightly. "I can redo it if you like."

"What is your name?" he inquired, attempting to gentle his voice.

"Edna, sir," she said, plopping her brushes back into their cups.

He pulled a pouch from his waist—one filled with thirty gold pieces—and dropped the entirety of it in her hands. "You made a masterpiece of my face."

"But, sir!" Edna said, opening the pouch with a fervent expression. "This is far too much."

His lip twitched. "I am of the belief that art is the world's most valuable commodity. Please take it. I can't think of a single thing that would be worth more."

Edna's eyes watered, which made him so uncomfortable he looked away, but it was too late. Her hand was grasping his. "Thank you, sir! I wish you every blessing! Every happiness!"

He gently pried his hand from hers, finally finding it in himself to look into the woman's lovely eyes. She was beautiful. And he knew he'd done a good thing for once. "Thank you, Edna. I wish the same for you."

She went back to her table, rounding her seat and ripping a sign down from the wall behind her. It hit the lantern lights, and he saw his WANTED flyer. She winked at him before tearing it up and throwing it to the wind.

I'll be damned.

With a gallant bow and a crooked grin, he bade the woman farewell and continued his search, not quite as wary of being discovered with the face paint. "Excuse me," he said to a gangly young man walking by with a large cone of fairy floss. "Do you happen to know of a vendor here who sells portrait frames?"

"You're thinking of Mr. Gully. He's right up that walkway! Likes most of the street to himself," the boy said through a sugar-coated mouth.

Mr. Gully. "Thank you." Trystan wandered in the direction the boy had pointed, trying to prepare himself to ask questions as inconspicuously as possible.

But when he arrived at the cart, someone was already there.

A young woman with her back turned to him stood at the cart, asking Mr. Gully questions. Her long silver hair cascaded down in flowing waves. Her dress was tight enough that he had a perfect view of the lines of her back. A cut-out dip in her waist revealed a soft patch of skin that made him swallow, and when she turned, he saw them.

Two golden butterfly combs pulling back her hair and a face painted like a rabbit.

He cleared his throat in surprise. The sound caused the woman to turn.

"Oh, I'm sorry, mister. Would you like to cut into the conversation?"

Her red lips were cocky as she propped a hand on her exposed hip.

A man passed, whispering to him in jovial camaraderie. "Aye, she's a looker, ain't she? Get in there, son."

Of course she was a looker.

She was Evie Sage.

CHAPTER 44

EVIE

E vie Sage had been told many times in her life that she was stubborn. And while she was aware of this flaw, she knew it wasn't her biggest—not by a long shot. No, Evie Sage's greatest affliction in life was *spite*.

She'd spitefully learned to sew perfectly when her brother had called her patchwork *hopeless*, she'd jumped headfirst into the deep end of the pond when the boys in her class called her a chicken, and she'd found a job working for a villain when the employment market told her it would be impossible. It had occurred to her many times over that "impossible" was merely a word people used to describe limitations they wished for you to adhere to, so you wouldn't upset the balance.

It was why, in a carefully played coup, she had enlisted Tatianna's help in procuring a dress and wig—ones that would essentially hide any traces of the woman she'd been when she lived in this village. Strangely, she felt very much that she didn't need the disguise, as she *wasn't* the same woman.

She was worse—and all the better for it.

"I've just learned of the most interesting pieces from Mr. Gully, mister. Would you like to hear about them, too?"

The Villain stood there, hidden from the town's view in face paint of his own, likely from Edna. Their elderly neighbor had always been so kind about watching Lyssa when Evie was away at work. Edna liked the company, and Evie liked Edna a great deal. Especially when Evie had arrived that evening and asked for her to disguise her face. Edna had known her immediately and assured her that she was amply protected.

"I would," the boss answered her inquiry, his voice so low and gritty, her instincts were giving warning flares. "If you please."

Mr. Gully, seeming to sense the tension, pulled at his collar before stepping away from the cart. "I need to use the facilities, but please browse what you like. I'll be back promptly for any payments."

As soon as Mr. Gully was out of view, she was airborne. She yelped and squirmed in the boss's grip, stopping for the tiniest of seconds to enjoy the view of his annoyingly perfect hindquarters as she was slung over his shoulder like a sack of potatoes. "Have you lost your mind? Put me down!" she screamed, banging on his back as he lumbered with her down a small stone side path that led between two buildings.

"Quiet!" he ordered, his grip tight on her hips. When they were alone and away from view, he dropped her uncourteously to her feet. She stumbled, righting herself and straightening her wig, chagrined. "What in the deadlands is this?" He gestured to her disguise, to the paint on her face, to her in general.

"A wig," she grumbled.

"A wig!" he repeated, raking a hand down his face before tugging on the ends of his hair. "Why would you do this? Why would you risk yourself in such a reckless, obtuse manner? Please explain exactly *what* you were thinking!"

She folded her arms and said the most dangerous thing she could think of. "Come now, sir. Pleading is beneath you."

In Evie's experience, there were different levels of anger. Annoyance, irritation, and then came the real stuff. She'd finally hit the highest point on the boss's anger threshold: the quiet kind.

There was such a harsh coldness to him that Evie almost grabbed hold of her arms to push her goose bumps back in.

"Are you implying that I am a hypocrite?" he demanded in a whisper.

She wasn't sure where her boldness had come from. Yes, she'd always been one to say exactly what was on her mind, but usually she tempered it, withheld it, or analyzed it ad nauseam. Always so desperate not to offend, so worried she'd say the wrong thing. But she never worried about how her words would be taken with Trystan; he somehow always knew exactly what she meant.

But his coldness after she'd nearly kissed him changed everything. It made it easier for her to say, "'Implying' would mean I am merely alluding to your hypocrisy. No, sir. I'm telling you that you *are* one."

"I could fire you for insubordination."

The words should've scared her, but it was so obviously an empty threat that she looked to either side of her in a show of confusion before shrugging and replying, "Do it."

He sputtered. "I-I'm not actually…going to fire you! I just cannot believe you'd ever be so defiant."

She gave him a dubious look. "Really?"

He groaned and pressed his head against the brick wall above her, bringing his body much closer than it ought to be. "No, I believe it. I suppose I even expected it."

She bounced on her gem-studded heels, which were pinching her toes so uncomfortably she'd have blisters the size of crystals come morning. "Well, now that we've gotten our niceties out of the way, follow me." Despite the pain, the heels made a satisfying clicking sound on the cobblestones as she walked, making her stand straighter.

"The whole purpose of this little excursion was to question Mr. Gully about your mother's whereabouts. Where could you possibly be going?" he asked but followed immediately behind her.

"My home—or the place I grew up, anyway," she said with a steadiness she was proud of. Her relationship to their family cottage had been altered so drastically, she wasn't certain how to feel about it at all. It was difficult to hate a place where the etchings of how tall she'd grown year over year still stood in the doorway. "And I already questioned Mr. Gully."

They moved through the main village square, his hand on the small of her back as they bustled through a thicker portion of the crowd.

He spoke sarcastically into her ear, sending a shiver through her. "Well, don't leave me in suspense, Sage. What did you find out?"

"Mr. Gully never even met my mother."

"I hope you didn't just flat-out ask him and draw every ounce of suspicion to yourself." Well, now he was just being insulting.

She rolled her eyes, brows coming up to salute her hairline when they passed a crowd hovering over Rick, who was gripping his knee and crying. "My goodness! What happened to him?"

"How should I know?" He responded far too quickly for comfort, but she let it go, because it was actually fairly pleasant to see that little weasel in pain. She wanted him to hurt more. As if it knew, her boss's gray mist that only she could see hovered above Rick, pressing harder on his knee. Rick cried out harder as well, and she turned on her heel to face her boss, who'd halted, looking confused as his mist returned to him.

"Sir, why did you do that?" she asked, feeling a strange hum in her dagger and then her scar.

He cleared his throat, putting a hand to the small of her back, urging her to continue. "I didn't… Never mind it, Sage. Come on."

They moved off the main path, their footsteps now softened by grass. She slipped her heels off, lest she sink into the dirt—that, and her toes could only take so much abuse.

"I merely said I had always admired Nura Sage's collection," she informed him, "and what a travesty it was about that poor woman. I couldn't get him to shut up after that. It's easy to encourage people to gossip about my family in this village. We were the object of censure for years."

The Villain did not seem to appreciate this. "That is what happens when people are bored of mundane existences. They have to pick at extraordinary ones."

She stopped, running a hand down her dress. "I'd hardly call my family's history extraordinary."

"I was referring to you."

How she was expected to not attempt to jump him—again—right there was beyond her. It was like dangling chocolate in front of her face and telling her to just look at it. But she knew she had to respect whatever professional boundaries he was choosing to put up. "That's kind of you."

"It's not kind," he pressed, blessedly distracting her from the cottage cropping up in the distance. "It's simply true. Though I don't know how you could reveal your mother's name to that man and not worry he'd recognize you on the spot. It's a small village."

She shook her head, skipping up the pebbled path she used to walk every day. "The disguise was merely precautionary. The truth is, I could probably saunter through the village just as I usually am without much notice at all."

"I can't imagine that."

"What?" she said as they arrived in front of the door.

"Not noticing you."

What a delightfully awful thing to say. Was this man trying to kill her?

She yanked open the door and moved inside without looking at him. The door was unlocked, but the cottage seemed for the most part intact. Edna had kept an eye on things. "In any case, I remembered that my mother had a painting of two little girls playing together. I suspect this corner of the frame is from that portrait, and I'm hoping that if we find it, it'll give us a clue as to where this friend resides."

He grunted, and when she angled her neck back to look at him, he had a strange glint in his eyes. "Very well. We'll have to search the house."

She gave him a wary look, dropping her heels by the door and pulling the scratchy wig from her head. "Yes, I suppose we will…"

Her eyes widened, for suddenly The Villain looked well and truly evil as he said, "Shall we check your childhood bedroom first?" Oh, he was attempting revenge for all the fun they'd made of his pillows.

"No! I can look there; there's no need for you to— Sir! Trystan!" she screamed as he barreled past her up the stairs.

"It's only fair, Sage," he called as he ran. "No need to be embarrassed."

"I only have one pillow! Why would I be embarrassed?" she screeched, scrambling after him.

He rounded the corner and somehow guessed the first door correctly— because of course he did.

She huffed, out of breath behind him, pulling the tight pins to unravel her hair. The locks glided down her back, cluster by cluster, and when she glanced up, her boss didn't look amused at all anymore. He looked dangerous.

And they were in her bedroom.

CHAPTER 45

THE VILLAIN

*F*uck. *Fuck. Fuck.*

It was like a repeating jingle in his mind. This was his punishment for trying to be playful—it somehow caused a heavy tension in the room. After everything that had happened, he should have known better than to allow himself and Sage to be alone together in a room with a bed. He had to leave. But when he turned, he saw a sketch sitting on the desk: it was of a man with a high collar and large, dark eyes. It was poorly done, but even Trystan could tell who it was.

"You drew me?" He lifted a brow, a satisfied half smile curling his lips.

She sneered at him, and her face flushed his favorite color as she ripped it from his hands. "Yes, but I forgot to add the horns."

He grimaced. "Well played." Then he did a full sweep of the small...not-very-tidy space. Though it was incredibly difficult to see in just the moonlight. "It's a bit dark—is there a candle?"

She jumped, rushing for the drawer as she pulled the final pin out of her hair. "Yes, of course! I'm so sorry; that was so inconsiderate of me. Are you well?" She fumbled with a match and quickly lit several candles sitting on her windowsill and small side table.

He opened his mouth to ask her why she was apologizing, but then he realized. It had been dark, nearly pitch-black, and he hadn't even thought about it. Not once. When was the last time that happened? *Ten years ago.* What was different about him now?

"I'm fine," he said, even though he really wasn't. He pulled a gold handkerchief from his pocket and rubbed it down his face before tucking it back into place. "Where shall we look first?" He pulled open a drawer of the cabinet off in the corner.

"Don't!" she screeched.

But it was too late. He'd opened it and reached in, finding…something silky, with ivory lace. He panicked and chucked it out the open window.

She slammed the drawer shut with her hip, glaring at him. "My undergarments are not going to detonate."

"One can never be too careful." He ducked, chuckling, when she lobbed a pillow at him.

Fun—he was having fun with her. That's what this giddy, elated feeling within his chest was. He kind of hated it almost as much as he was enjoying it, because he knew it had to end eventually.

"Why didn't you want me to come here, really?" she asked. And it seemed the end had already arrived.

An honest answer was ill-advised. A curated, villainous one would keep her away and set them on the right course forward. "It was too risky." He opted for safety.

"What was?" Sage asked. "Me coming? Or simply admitting that you think me an encumbrance?"

Hold on a minute. "I don't know what scenarios you're playing out, Sage, but I can assure you I do not think you an encumbrance. I merely felt… cautious regarding your safety."

But she crossed her arms, looking like that wasn't even close to enough of an answer for her. Her dress was making it damn near impossible to focus; there was so much of her glowing skin exposed, and the black shimmer in the gown made her look like midnight. "You were never shy about me going on field missions before."

"You weren't a wanted woman before," he replied.

She scoffed, gesturing to the white lines of her face paint. "Clearly, that problem was easily remedied."

He didn't respond, running out of excuses that would divert her. What could he say? That he couldn't bear the thought of putting her in danger? That she was murder for his focus and his self-control? No, those were all thoughts that needed to remain tightly contained, but they were bubbling to the surface with every step she took toward him.

"I don't understand why you suddenly have so much concern for my well-being when nothing bad will happen."

But something bad *had* happened.

"Sage, drop it," he warned, feeling the last thread of his control pull taut.

"No, I won't drop it. My safety wasn't in question at all. There was no reason you should've pushed so hard for me to remain behind."

"I couldn't take the chance," he argued, pleading with whatever gods watching that she'd stop before it was too late.

"There was no chance. There was no danger! I was fine!"

And though he shut his eyes tightly to stave off the memory, as he'd been desperately trying to do since it happened, in this moment, he couldn't take it any longer. The confession spilled out before he could stop it.

"YOU WERE DEAD!" he roared, his chest moving up and down like he'd just done battle—and he had. With his mind and his foolish, foolish mouth. And he'd lost.

He opened his eyes to see Sage's face drop, astonishment pulling back her shoulders. "What? What are you talking about?"

"You were dead." He curled his lip. "I thought you were dead. I ran into a room at the Gleaming Palace, and I saw your corpse."

"But Gideon was supposed to— You said that he told you I wasn't. Why would you lie?"

He took a large step closer. This entire room smelled like her—it was attacking every one of his senses. "I did not wish to speak of it. It doesn't matter." He couldn't relive it.

She let out a sigh of frustration as she pulled a hand through her curls and shoved her desk chair out of her path to move in front of him. "This is the problem! In one breath, you imply I'd be a hindrance. In the next, you tell me I'm extraordinary! Hoisting me over your shoulder, acting like I matter to you, when you rejected me outright and then taunted me with it!"

"Rejected you?" He was going to blow a gasket. "I wasn't going to kiss you when the request was made under duress!"

She huffed cynically. "Duress? Please! Admit it—right when we get close to the crux of it, you always pull back! Are you trying to confuse me? Is this part of villainy, playing games? Pretending to care about me and then ripping out the rug with something cold?"

He went as still as a statue. "You think I *pretend* to care about you?"

Sage realized her error far too late. Her eyes widened as if she sensed the danger, and she took a step back.

He charged after her. "You think I do not care? As if thoughts of you and your well-being don't plague me daily. Nightly. Every second we are apart! I watched you *die*! I thought I'd never see you again! I have never known such darkness, and I never wish to again. If you think that makes me overbearing, so be it. But do not ever claim I do not care about you. You are wiser than that, Evie. Do not be a fucking fool."

His harshness was meant to cow her, but it didn't work. She just stared, quiet and confused, like she was looking at a painting that remained out of focus.

Placing a hand to her chest, she blinked at him and said, "Plague? Are you comparing me to an illness?"

That final thread of control snapped.

"Damn it!" he growled.

He moved, and before Sage knew what was happening—

He kissed her.

CHAPTER 46

THE VILLAIN

Trystan supposed there was only so far you could bend something before it broke, and he was broken, shattered, when his lips settled on Evie's mouth. Both of his hands landed on the sides of her face, cradling her head gently in a stark contrast to the fervent kiss.

He would regret this—losing control, giving in to it, in to *her*. He'd resisted. He'd hoped and willed away the desire to be near her, willed away wanting her. But she was inevitable, from the moment he first saw her and every moment since.

He loved her. It was a never-ending echo that he'd vowed to never say aloud. And surely later, when the kiss ended, when he pulled away and made his awkward excuses, stumbling over his words to avoid the truth, he would loathe himself for taking this taste of her.

But not now.

Now, he would simply enjoy it, pouring every ounce of love he couldn't say into this moment, this woman, this kiss. She hadn't moved, hadn't pulled away—hadn't kissed him back, either, come to think of it, and this gave him such pause he ripped his lips from hers.

How could he do this? He'd probably frightened the wits out of her. She was rigid beneath his hands. He took a large step back, leaning away from her. "Sage," he breathed. "I'm sorry—"

"It came true," she said, looking at him in a daze. "I didn't think it ever would."

He was struck by the words, but he couldn't figure out why. "What do you mean?" Her eyes flicked to the window, to the stars, and then he remembered.

That first week. The late night in his office. Her wish.

I'll let you know when it comes true.

He couldn't fathom what she was saying, what her words meant. His usually organized, efficient brain was jumbled. "You wished for— Your wish was—"

She dove toward him, pressing her lips back against his. His eyes widened for a moment, watching as she clutched for his shoulders like she needed something to hold on to. Like *she* needed *him*.

And this time, he froze.

This is, quite honestly, the worst game of tag ever played.

But when she hummed against his lips, any remaining frigidness thawed. Only heat remained.

I'll let you know when it comes true.

A low sound built in the back of his throat as he wrapped his arms around her, pulling her close. What had started as gentle passion turned wild with wanting. He'd been built to covet his control, and this woman seemed to be built to unravel it.

And he let her.

She clutched at the back of his head, playing with the hairs at the nape of his neck, and it felt so. Fucking. Good.

In answer to her, he gripped her hair, tugging quickly but gently until her neck was exposed. When he opened his eyes, he found that her light eyes were darkened, her lids only half open.

His lips found purchase against her pulse, peppering small kisses there, and all the while, he listened for her cues. Making sure this was all right—that she was all right.

He bit lightly into her skin, and she gasped, sighing once more when he soothed the spot with his tongue.

Too far, his mind warned. *You're going too far.*

He didn't care. He was drowning in her, drunk on her. He wanted to live here, kissing her for the rest of his days, the rest of his life—and suddenly, it wasn't enough. He needed more. His mouth returned to hers, and he almost growled in relief when their lips met. Bending low, he gripped the backs of her knees and hoisted her up, placing her gently on her desk and moving between her thighs.

The black gown was pushed up just over her knees. He gripped each of her thighs, feeling them through the soft fabric of the dress, committing their shape to memory. For when he was buried beneath the dirt, when he no longer reigned as the villain of this land, he would have this one memory to carry him.

Without breaking their kiss, he began to trace her body, starting at her neck, where he swirled a finger until he was torturing himself. He dipped lower, running a careful hand over one of her breasts. She gasped, and he kissed her harder.

But the urgency within him slowed, and he reached up to cradle her face again. He kissed her tenderly, like he dreamed of nightly, like he'd always wanted to, like he'd imagined doing ever since the first time he saw her in Hickory Forest. With her soft hands and her amused smile. Her gentle defiance.

It was at this moment, of course, when he was savoring her—when he wasn't ready to stop and reflect on what he'd just done, the line he'd just crossed—that a voice called defensively from beyond her partially closed bedroom door: "Who's in there? I have a weapon!"

They were caught.

CHAPTER 47

EVIE

Evie was not one for melodramatics (yes she was), but she did startle rather easily. So, when a voice shattered the most erotic and passionate moment of her young life, she screamed. Very loudly.

The door was yanked open, and a man stood in the entry. It was impossible to make out his features in the dark hall, but it didn't matter. Trystan had already begun to charge at him, though the man was gone before Trystan reached the doorframe. "Stay here, Sage!" he yelled.

She snorted. "Yeah, right."

She hopped off the desk, landing on shaky legs. Weak in the knees—he'd made her weak in the knees with one measly kiss.

The real issue being, there was nothing measly about it.

Still trying to catch her breath, she grabbed one of the candles from the side table and rushed down the hall after them. The intruder had sought cover in her father's study, but the boss did not relent, following in after him and tackling the man to the ground, hands tight around his throat.

There was a fire lit in the hearth, which was odd, considering she'd assumed her old home abandoned. The room was warm, though, despite the terrible events that had occurred in it. She fought the chill in her heart even as she felt her cheeks heat. "Sir, are you— Hey!" She knew the man below him—knew him immediately.

"You blithering nincompoop!" Trystan screamed in the man's face, releasing his neck with a ragged sigh. "I could've killed you."

The man went to his knees, coughing and rubbing at his throat. "Well, that's not so out of the ordinary for us, is it, brother?"

Malcolm Maverine hadn't changed much, save for the once long and lustrous brown locks now shorn close to his head. He was still broad shouldered, still carried an easily amused expression, and still seemed to annoy the ever-loving shit out of his older brother.

"Malcolm, I don't mean to be rude or a poor host," Evie started, extending her palm toward him, "but what are you doing in my house?"

Malcolm rubbed his head, taking her hand and standing. "May I pour us all a drink before I tell you? I fear it's far too painful to reveal without liquid courage." He went to a sideboard that she didn't recall being there before and poured three glasses full.

A drink was just the ticket. It would allow her body to catch up with her mind, though both parts of her seemed to agree that she was still upstairs, still kissing Trystan, The Villain, her *boss*. The kiss had been entirely mutual, though he'd been the first to pull away, and then she'd promptly…mauled him. But he'd seemed to enjoy the mauling. He'd seemed to enjoy *her*—but there was so much distance in his expression, she'd begun second-guessing it all.

Yes, a drink. She took the glass of amber-colored liquid from Malcolm and downed it in one gulp, then could not keep herself from coughing. "Oh, that's disgusting!"

Malcolm frowned. "I'm afraid it's all I have left of the Redbloom Tavern."

She cringed, feeling mildly guilty at the thought that if this was the last of that horrendous liquor, it was rather a good thing. Trystan remained off to the corner, arms crossed over his chest, his face stony. He was silent and barely looking at her.

It was terrible.

But Malcolm's words caught up with her. "Wait, what do you mean? What happened to the Redbloom Tavern?"

Trystan carefully took his drink from Malcolm's hand and downed it in three long sips. He didn't flinch. Unbelievable. "Lose it in a game of cards, Malcolm?"

Malcolm glared at the accusation, finishing his own glass and refilling hers, which she hadn't asked for, and under any other circumstance, she would have refused—the stuff tasted like copper-tinged medicine—but it was warming her gut and washing away her frenzied overthinking of that kiss. She took another large swig.

"I lost it because of you, Tryst," Malcolm said quietly.

The boss went rigid. "What do you mean?"

"When they found out The Villain was my brother, people stopped coming. Never mind that I have no association with you or your business. The Maverine name was enough for them to *hate* me. A few nights ago, I was away, and a group of retired Valiant Guards banded together and burned it to the ground. It's…gone."

Her heart twisted at the pain in Malcolm's voice. "Oh, I'm so sorry, Malcolm. That's evil."

The boss's face flinched like he'd been struck, and she regretted her words almost instantly, knowing how he'd take them. She took another sip of the horrid drink; her head felt lighter, floaty. It would be wise to put it down.

She didn't.

"I will pay for you to rebuild. Wherever you wish," Trystan said quietly. He offered it readily, humbly, with a downturn of his head, like he was submitting to his transgressions with utter defeat. "I'll help you stock the finest liquors, the best mead, the richest wines. Whatever you want, it's yours."

Malcolm laughed without humor and without patience. "As much as the offer tempts me, I have no interest in rebuilding an establishment the public is only going to scorn or use as kindling. It's okay, Tryst, really. I knew it wouldn't last. There's no need to atone for it."

Trystan didn't take this well. She could tell by the way his shoulders fell, like he'd defeated one demon just to be battered by another. "Allow me to apologize, then, for your having to suffer me as a brother."

Malcolm stepped forward, reaching up and placing a hand on Trystan's shoulder, cockiness slipping away to reveal familial sincerity. "I assure you, there's no need to apologize for that, either."

She almost died for the sweetness of the sentiment, watching in the corner like a creepy spectator. Until she heard, "Sage, for the love of the gods! Are you crying?"

Her drink sloshed in her glass as she waved her arms around. "What do you want from me? This is cute!"

Malcolm laughed, and then the boss did, too—smaller than Malcolm's, but she saw the dimple, so there was no need for complaints.

"Oh," Malcolm said with a snap of his fingers. "As for my rather unorthodox entrance, Evie, I was looking for a place to hunker down for a little while. I'd heard from local gossip that your house was vacated, so I thought it would be safe to lay low here until I figure out my next move. I'd hoped you wouldn't mind. I'd actually sort of hoped you wouldn't find out at all."

She smiled and patted Malcolm's cheek. "I don't mind. Please stay here as long as you like, but you're of course welcome to come join us at the manor. Clare is residing there, too; I'm sure she'd like your company."

Malcolm's light-brown eyes widened. "Clare is staying with you? Our *sister* Clare? Next thing you know, unicorns are going to be giving birth to rabbits."

Trystan gave Malcolm a pointed look before uttering one word: "Tatianna."

Malcolm digested the information immediately with a decisive snort. "I should've guessed."

Licking her still-swollen lips, Evie pulled the piece of frame from her pocket. "We came here looking for a painting of my mother's. Have you happened to see it around in your time here? It's an outdoor landscape with two little girls playing."

Malcolm gasped. "Oh, yes! There's a few in the small cupboard off your kitchen. I'll fetch it for you." He flew out the door, and for a moment it was just her and Trystan again.

The air grew thick, his eyes roving every inch of her face until he landed on her lips. He lurched forward and halted like he had to physically hold himself back from her, like he wanted her too badly to move. Evie had never felt so overcome in her life.

But then Trystan slammed himself back against the wall when Malcolm stormed in, portrait in hand. It was in a gilded frame with one corner missing.

"This is it!" she exclaimed, her focus now completely on the painting. She brushed a finger down the rough canvas and stepped back to better view the picture. Two young girls, perhaps no older than Lyssa, frolicked in a field surrounded by strange and large-looking plants. Vines twirled around every inch of open space, and the colors were so liberal and vibrant they almost distracted from the people in it. It was obvious her mother was one of the little girls—she looked exactly like Lyssa. Like her sister had been placed right into the art.

Pinned-back braids; round, dark eyes; golden-brown skin; hand clasped with that of the little girl next to her. The other had braids, too, but they were dark red, like fire. Her eyes were a light brown that reminded Evie of toffee, her pale skin was dotted with freckles just across her nose, and she held a gilded gold key in her hand. Evie searched for an artist's mark, an inscription, any clues as to who the redheaded girl was or where this was painted. But there were only two faded *F*s at the bottom.

She assumed they didn't stand for *freaking fucked*, but it felt rather appropriate anyway. "Do you know where this is, sir?" She took the portrait from Malcolm and angled it toward the boss.

He squinted hard and rubbed his chin. "I'm afraid not, Sage. I don't recognize it at all. But perhaps someone in town will. We'll ask around."

She shut her eyes tight. She knew exactly what needed to be done, but her bravery wasn't up to the task, her heart not yet healed from the battering it had taken the last time she'd challenged it this way. But emotional scars sometimes demanded to be reopened—to let out the remainder of the pain, to free you from it.

"No, we can't waste any more time," Evie said, a pit of dread pooling in her stomach. "We're working against the clock with the guvres and the manor's wards failing, and there's only one person I am certain will know exactly where this portrait was painted and who this little girl is."

Trystan tilted his head at the artwork, then sent a questioning look to her. "Who?"

"My father."

CHAPTER 48

EVIE

"I can't do it," Evie whispered, staring at the cellar door.

The boss stood on one side of her, Tatianna on the other, smiling, hand clasping hers. Warmth seeped through the touch, like the healer was sending her magic to every broken piece of Evie's heart. "Come now, little friend. You've done far harder things than this."

Evie wanted to argue, but Tatianna always tended to speak in hard resolutions, like her beliefs were facts and not subject to argument, and, annoyingly enough, the healer was usually right.

Evie and the boss had ridden back to the manor in discomfiting quiet, both avoiding the giant in the room like their lives depended on it. They'd left Malcolm to continue his residence in her home after he'd declined the offer to join them at the manor.

"Probably for the best that I stay here. Tryst and I tend to brawl when we're in too close quarters."

"The manor is huge," she'd argued.

"Not huge enough," the boss had grumbled.

So, they returned alone, and all the heated wanting that had made the room thick with tension had dissipated into something frigid and confusing. They'd both agreed to retire to bed and begin questioning her father in the morning, and Evie had been certain that come sunup the subject of their kiss would reemerge with a vengeance. But he hadn't sought her out, hadn't brought it up again, just avoided eye contact and oddly pressed the back of his hand to his lips every so often. Like they stung.

Now that the workday was well underway, things had seemed to just revert to normal, and she decided it was likely best for the both of them if she just stopped thinking about him at all.

The only problem being that she *was* still thinking of him—and in a way that would likely send him and his proper manners into heart failure.

She returned her gaze to the door before her, the marks in the wood taunting her as she tried to focus on the task at hand. It was foolish of her to think she could've avoided this forever, avoided speaking to her father again. It had been foolish to think she might instead just move on with her life with the dignity he'd attempted to steal from her. But there were some things that couldn't be buried, and the search could not continue without him. It had to happen today, and it had to be her.

The boss whispered in her ear, "At what risk would my vulnerable areas be if I offered to do this in your stead?"

"That depends." She did not turn to look at him, but she felt the heat radiating off his body, smelled the clean scent of his shirt, freshly laundered. She wanted to bury her nose in it. "Which vulnerable areas are we speaking of?"

He bent low, cupping a hand over his mouth like he was going to say something scandalous, but the delivery was flat and dry. "My ear."

Oh no. A laugh burst out of her, fast and *loud*. The sound echoed down the empty corridor. The only ones to hear were Tatianna, The Villain, and now Blade, who was rounding the corner with a jovial expression.

"The female guvre's gestation is moving along nicely, everyone, and by the looks of her abdomen, I'd say there's at least a month before we have a baby. The male also seems to be nesting"—Blade's expression turned indulgent as he smiled—"if the amount of scales and leaves piled up around the cage is anything to go by." Blade's lemon-yellow vest shimmered with red embroidered roses, his color scheme matching the daylight. He halted and frowned. "Did I miss a joke?"

Tati leaned against the wall, one of her gauzy pink sleeves rising as she lifted her forearm. "The boss made one."

Blade pretended to faint.

"Can you leave?" The Villain bit out before looking back to Evie, checking for cracks in her joy, waiting for her sadness to return.

But she felt lighter with her friends here. "I will be going. Alone." She said it pointedly to the room as a whole, reaching to lift the latch of the door, but her fingers stopped over the handle.

Do it, she urged herself.

But she stayed in place, arms locked, fear coursing through her at the possibility of losing any of the softness she had left. She didn't want to be hardened by her experiences—she wanted to defy them by remaining just as she was. Kind, gentle, forgiving. How could there be a way forward? How could she do this without losing those parts?

Two interns passed by the dungeon door, snickering at her.

A bold move in front of the boss—however, it was not Trystan who called out to them but Rebecka Erring, who had appeared around the other corner, running directly into them.

Her tight bun pulled her features back into a severe expression, as usual, but it was strange how comforted Evie felt to see it.

Becky turned to the interns and said, "I was hoping to run into you two; you're on muck-out duty for the dragon today. Mr. Gushiken's got his hands full with the guvres, and Fluffy's cleanliness is of the utmost importance."

Both interns began sputtering. "Ms. Erring, we cannot possibly take on a task that large," one of them complained. "That animal is a mess."

Becky rolled her eyes as she leaned toward them and mock whispered, "Then I suggest you get started."

"But—"

"She gave you a command," Blade said, an uncharacteristic hardness in his tone and expression. "I suggest you follow it."

They scattered. Becky's lips pulled slightly up in Blade's direction, and an answering smile was aimed back at her.

Evie had to force her mouth closed, but Tatianna had the same giddy expression beside her. There was nothing quite so hope-inducing as a budding romance.

Becky's heels clicked against the stone floor as she walked toward Evie, resolve in her expression. "Do you remember what I said to you on your first day?"

Evie searched her mind, trying to remember, but she was flummoxed, not used to this direct address with no sarcastic insult included. The only thing she came up with was, "I think you said, 'You're going to fail'?"

Becky's eyes shined. "But you didn't."

And Evie was certain in that moment that Becky saw right through her pasted-on smiles, right through to the core of her, and Becky didn't turn away. Right now, for Evie, it was safe to just be.

Becky nodded toward the door and smiled at her—a real one, for maybe the first time. "You won't fail at this, either. I promise you can do this."

Evie gripped the handle and turned, opening the door.

You can.

So she did.

CHAPTER 49

EVIE

It was dark.

A fitting scene for confronting what was arguably the ugliest part of humanity: betrayal.

The first night after her father had been imprisoned in the dungeons below the manor, she had been too grief-stricken by the boss being taken, had been aching with despair and a worry so pervasive that she hadn't slept well since. She'd imagined what they were doing to him, how they were hurting him, and it had nearly killed her. She'd thrown herself headfirst into planning his rescue just to survive it, hadn't wasted time on anything else. She had made sure everything was executed down to the last detail.

But Trystan was back, she'd succeeded, and now it was time to face the music.

Hurt tugged her heart into two mangled pieces as she walked down the dimly lit corridor beyond the cellar door. It was dirty, dark, and cold—an apt place for her father—but she railed against the twinge of pity she felt nevertheless. Love shriveled and disappeared differently, sometimes slowly, sometimes quickly, but she realized now that it was the most brutal, the most *painful*, when it was abandoned.

Her love was too big, and it had been given too freely to people who didn't deserve it.

She swallowed as she approached his cell, where he was kept isolated from the other Valiant Guards in their custody. The Malevolent Guards had left for their rotation, and the boss was keeping the next group from coming down until she was through.

As she passed the single torch hung on the wall, she saw a silhouette of a man sitting on the floor of his cell, knees pulled inward. She was cloaked in shadow, so he didn't see Evie when she first approached—not until she tripped over an uneven slab of cement, knocking into a table with a metal tray atop it. The leftovers from his latest meal.

Griffin's head snapped up, but his body remained still, until he saw that it wasn't another Malevolent Guard. She dug her nails into her hands, placing them quickly behind her back so he wouldn't see her discomfort and use it against her.

"Hello, Papa." She sounded stronger than she felt, and she kept the point of her chin angled upward so that he might see that she was looking above him, beyond.

His face was the first thing to hit the light when he walked closer to the torch. The sight of it, which had once been a comfort, now only brought stinging pain. His laugh lines were so deep, one might look upon him and think he'd spent his life in constant humor. No one could have guessed that that humor was merely a distraction from his cruelty.

He looked surprised but oddly healthy. His complexion had more color than it had in the last few years, when he had been doing everything possible to convince Evie that he had caught the Mystic Illness to hide his involvement with the king.

He looked like a deception, a lie. It made her wonder what he saw when he looked at her—if she seemed changed, too, with her unbound hair tucked behind her ears, her loose trousers tapering down into her boots, her mother's rouge on her cheeks and lips.

If he saw the changes, he didn't acknowledge them. "Ah. So my daughter finally deigns to grace me with her presence."

Sharp. There was a sharp feeling in her gut—not at the fact that she was finally facing him or that he had caused so much hurt, but because he didn't seem at all remorseful. Worse still, he looked smug.

She was unable to pretend. Her face reflected her anger. Ice was flowing through her bloodstream, chipping away at the torn pieces of her heart until nothing remained. With her chin high, her heartbeat steady in her chest, she took one step toward him and responded, "And how little you deserve it."

Scoffing, her father shook his head. "And yet here you are. I thought you were resolved to leave me below to rot."

Evie's mouth stayed in a flat line. "I think we both know you were rotted well before you got here."

He rolled his green eyes, infuriating her, thawing the ice into a boiling rage. "Now, Evangelina, really. The dramatics. I truly thought having you find employment for the family would lead you well into adulthood, but even now, you act with such immaturity."

Don't, she warned herself. *It's what he wants.* Someone in his position didn't want to hear reason, just emotion. He wanted to know he had affected her. But he did not control her. He couldn't. Not anymore.

"I have questions for you, and I will have answers," she said. "But I will be gracious and give you options." Stepping closer to the cell, she let one hand fall to her side, the other remaining behind her back. "You can either tell me here and now—"

Her hidden hand whipped around while the other grabbed for his dirtied shirt, and she yanked him forward hard enough that the sharp edge of the dagger dug against his throat. The skin there bobbed against the hard metal.

It was a point of satisfaction that made her drunk with power. "Or you can take a visit to our lovely torture chambers. It is, of course, included in your stay with us. We're known for our...*amenities.*"

Griffin's mouth pulled into a sneer, but there was a smidge of fear in his eyes. She was getting to him. A point for her.

"What do you want to know?" he asked.

She pressed the dagger closer, trying not to feel satisfaction when a drop of blood slid down the side of his neck. She was a little alarmed by the feeling—and by how difficult it was to ignore. "The painting of the two little girls that Mama had before she disappeared. One of them was clearly her. Who was the other girl? Where was it painted?"

Astonishment shot through him, and he jolted against her blade. "How did you—"

"Tell me," she commanded, her dagger humming in her hand, the scar on her shoulder answering with a tingling sensation.

He narrowed his eyes. "Your mother didn't have many friends. I don't recall any painting."

She pressed once more with the dagger. "I'm sure it was hard to keep good company with a belittling ass for a husband."

"The apple didn't fall far, did it?" Griffin Sage smirked, eyes on the knife at his neck. "Despite my best efforts, you turned out much the same as her."

The accusation was too close to her deepest fears—that she, too, would break, that she, too, would destroy the lives of the people she loved. And to have the accusation made by the person who'd hurt her the most, who'd left scars on her soul that would never heal... She did exactly what her father had just accused her of.

She snapped.

The dagger thrummed in her hand, and then she buried it in his thigh.

"Son of a bitch!" he screamed, clutching the bleeding wound as she removed the weapon swiftly. She was torn between her empathy and her satisfaction that the man who'd caused her so much pain was hurting, too, as he fell to the ground, holding both hands to his leg to try to stop the blood.

She pulled the cell door keys from her pocket, then pulled open the door and slipped inside. Her father began to crawl away from her. She'd spent years of her life minding his health, caring for him in the way only a child could; that feeling didn't leave so easily, but neither did her spiraling anger or yawning hurt.

"Oh, don't leave so soon. Please stay awhile." She laid her heel against his hand and listened with quiet gratification to the scream that tore through him. It reminded her of the sound of one of the animals he'd slaughtered for the butchery when she was a child. A memory flashed of her father then. How he'd held her while she cried for the animals, how he'd carried her on his shoulders the whole way home.

She removed her heel so fast she almost fell over, gripping her chest, breathing heavily in alarm at her sudden cruelty. He deserved it, but...he didn't deserve the power to change her this way.

He sat up, and she helped him, lifting his shoulders until he was sitting against the wall, his blood smearing across her clothes. "What do you want?" he asked warily.

Evie hardened her voice. "I want you to tell me what you were doing with my mother. I want you to tell me what you and the king did to her magic, and more than anything, I'd like to know why the gods cursed me with someone like *you* for a father." She removed her hand from his shoulder, watching warily as Griffin backed himself to the wall on the other side, far away from her, hands returning to the wound.

He closed his eyes tightly before opening them once more, a tired resolve in their depths. "The little girl in the portrait was your mother's childhood best friend, Renna Fortis."

This surprised her. "Renna Fortis? As in the Fortis family?" The Fortis family was well known throughout the kingdom as warriors of valor, and a line that dated back to the very beginnings of Rennedawn. It was said that the land their fortress resided on was so magically touched that even the plants came alive. Evie had had a meager education, but even she knew them well; they were the stuff of legend.

Griffin looked pale, as if his false sickness had become real—probably from the blood loss. She'd ask Tatianna to do her best to repair the damage she'd done, but Evie would take her time. She had the information she wanted, a steady lead, and a damn good chance of finding her mother with the most noble family in Rennedawn—not by blood, but by honor.

But she wasn't done. There was more to what happened to her mother all those years ago, more to the power that had nearly overtaken her, and one of the only people with the answers she needed was bleeding out in front of her.

He looked so weak. "Have mercy upon me, Evie. I am your father. That should still mean something to you." He was apparently under the impression that he could have Evie play into his hands, but she would not be manipulated any longer.

"What did you and the king do to my mother?" She stepped closer, standing over him, the bloodstained dagger dripping at her side.

Griffin's eyes were on his hands, and they stayed there as he replied, "I did what I thought was right." It was the truth. She wasn't certain how she knew, but she could feel it in the shame now creeping into his expression.

"You destroyed her," she replied, feeling hollow.

He looked up at her. She didn't think it was possible for him to sink lower in her esteem, but then he whispered, "I didn't mean to."

The words made her heart drop to her stomach, because this wasn't a lie either; she knew he meant it, as useless as it was now.

Suddenly, she was through with the conversation, through with him, and uncomfortable with how strongly she wanted to hurt him the way he'd hurt her. But it would get her nowhere. There was nothing he could give her now but sorrow.

"You won't see me ever again," she said coldly. "I will forget about you. I will move on and be happy, and you will be here. Rotting, weak, and alone, with only your valiant honor to keep you warm." She shook her head. He looked so small, this man who had once been a mountain in her eyes. "I hope it was worth it."

Blood from the tip of her dagger dripped onto her boot. The cell gate creaked as she pulled it back open, almost gone, almost away from him, almost escaping the torment. But his next words halted her, cooled her ire into something new — an almost unrecognizable feeling, like she was watching an atrocity be committed upon her open heart with no means to stop it.

She'd only dropped her guard for a moment, but it was too late.

"If you'd like answers to what the king and I did to your mother's magic…" Her father paused, like a fist slowly pulling back for a great blow.

Her eyes were wide, unguarded, and Griffin Sage looked as though he couldn't wait to say, with a sickening grin: "Perhaps you should ask your brother."

CHAPTER 50

THE VILLAIN

Trystan stood waiting outside the cellar door for twenty minutes.

Gods knew why. There were plenty of other things he could be doing: managing mercenary requests, torturing the new workers with something truly cruel—like an icebreaker activity. But instead, he paced nervously, waiting for the cellar door to reopen.

That kiss had rattled his brain loose.

He'd tried to forget it—the way one tried to dodge a brick flying at one's face. Inevitable, painful, and impossible to truly escape.

He needed a distraction. A disruption. He needed…

Kingsley! The frog entered his line of vision, shortly followed by Gideon Sage, who looked mussed and sweaty as he dove after the frog, only to fall hard on his stomach. The amphibian landed at Trystan's feet, looking up at him with satisfied golden eyes.

"What are you playing at, Kingsley?" Trystan untucked his arms and crouched, waiting patiently as the frog jotted down a word with his free foot, then held up the sign the animal had been keeping who knew where.

Fetch.

Trystan snorted, and Gideon glared as he stood, pointing an accusatory finger at Kingsley. "Real nice, you deranged turtle."

Trystan looked at Sage's brother blankly before lifting an eyebrow. "He's a frog."

A patch of sunshine dipped in through the stained-glass window, shining right over Kingsley and his tiny crown. Gideon clicked his tongue. "Are you always this literal, Maverine?"

Trystan frowned and looked at Gideon as he said, "Yes."

Gideon chuckled. "I see why she likes you."

Trystan sniffed and began inspecting one of the water-hose installations that Sage had put in months prior for safety. To ensure that it was in working order, certainly *not* to hide the red tinging the tops of his cheeks.

He didn't need anyone—particularly not Sage's brother, a man who'd worked for his enemy—to become aware of the...attachment Trystan had formed to his assistant. Once someone else was made aware of a feeling, it became real, inescapable. Chasing you down like a monster on the hunt.

Like Scatter Day but far less entertaining.

"Sage likes everyone," Trystan muttered.

Gideon rubbed the back of his neck, still grinning. "Evie doesn't like *everyone.*"

He opened his mouth to argue, but Gideon barreled on. "When we were children, she was always agreeing, always doing what she was told. Going above and beyond to ensure both of our parents were always pleased. It never seemed right to me, but they were more critical of her, I think. Expected more."

After shaking his head and coughing lightly into his hand, Gideon continued, a glassy sheen in his green eyes. "She always hated making a fuss, to the point of her own discomfort. One of the neighbors made her a shawl once that was so itchy she developed a rash, but she refused to take it off because 'it was a gift.'" Sage's brother rolled his eyes like this story was endearing and not pinching the daylights out of Trystan's tiny, unused heart.

"But don't misunderstand," Gideon said. "Agreeableness doesn't always mean true affection, especially for Evie. She's kept her heart guarded all these years."

Trystan looked at his feet. "I don't believe you know her well enough anymore to make such an assessment."

"Maybe not," Gideon said, "but I can see she's not afraid to disagree with you, to argue with you, to say how she really feels. She trusts you not to turn on her."

She trusts you.

Well, why in the deadlands would he tell me that?

Trystan swallowed and began to pace in front of the door again, Kingsley clinging to his boot now as he walked. "Well, that's just prudent. I'm her employer, and there needs to be a certain level of trust and honesty for us to have any measure of success."

Gideon looked at him almost piteously. "You are so far gone, aren't you?"

Rebecka rounded the corner then, trying to look casual as she eyed the still-closed cellar door. "Has she come out yet?"

A knowing smile curved Trystan's mouth, and it made Rebecka scoff.

"I am *not* asking for myself! Nobody is getting any work done! Word of her confronting her father has swept through the office, and it's causing an uproar. She needs to hurry it up down there." Rebecka parked her hands on her hips. "If one more guard asks me where the provolone cheese is, I'm going to break my glasses against the cement just so I do not have to look upon them any longer!"

Another head bobbed around the corner, interrupting Rebecka's rant. "She's still in there, then?" Gushiken shifted nervously.

Trystan pinched the bridge of his nose. "I gave an order for everyone to return to work."

Tatianna didn't sneak around the corner as Blade and Rebecka did but floated around with an authority that Trystan seemed to no longer have. "I thought that was just a suggestion."

Trystan growled. "Apparently!"

Tatianna smirked and nodded toward the door. "How is she?" But the healer's immovable composure crumbled for a moment when Clare brushed past her.

It would've been more nauseating if even the whisper of a touch from Sage didn't also make him weak in a way that disgusted him.

And intrigued him…but mostly disgusted him.

"No word yet," Rebecka said. "But if she's not out of there in the next sixty seconds, I'm sending all of you back to your desks."

The door burst open then. Almost as if Rebecka's ire was so powerful it had conjured her, Evie barreled out into the hallway, blood running down her cheek and neck.

"Sage, my gods!" Trystan yelled, immediately searching her for injury.

"Oh, thank goodness," Rebecka said. "Can you please tell everyone you're fine so that they may return to their— Evangelina!" Rebecka yelled, clearly having just noticed the gore smeared across Sage's body and face. But Sage seemed to only have eyes for Gideon, who was waiting against the wall.

Sage raised her dagger, a wild look in her eyes, and stalked toward her brother, shoving him hard until his back hit the surface. "Eve! What are you doing?" Gideon yelled.

"I've just been to see our father."

Gideon's eyes darted around before he moved to leave, shouldering past Sage so hard that she stumbled backward, tripping on the uneven ground and slamming to the floor with a pained yelp.

In every life before he'd met her, Trystan would have gone after the knight now darting down the hallway, escaping for reasons that couldn't have been favorable. But the only thing his body recognized was her hitting the ground—and immediately after that, the uncomfortable sensation playing within his chest at seeing her in even an ounce of pain. He dropped to his knees beside her on the floor in a panic.

But by the time Trystan had shoved enough wisps of curly black hair out of Sage's eyes to see the violence there, she was already darting to her feet, dagger still in hand.

"Sage, the blood..." he started, trying to sound emotionless.

But it didn't matter—she was clearly not interested in his concern, just the path she was now tearing down the corridor after her brother, calling back behind her before she distressingly disappeared: "It's not mine."

It was like a lightning strike to his skin, sudden and hot. He stared after her with too many tangled bits of feeling that couldn't sort themselves. Wonder, pride, concern. But it was the concern that stood out in the harshest clarity.

Ellia's words before he'd crossed into the Heart Village washed over him like frigid water. *Do not cause any harm.*

Sage was trending closer to darkness, and as much as he enjoyed her deserved ruthlessness, as much as he admired her perseverance and strength, that voice in his mind—the one that reminded him every day that he was only good for one purpose...

That voice wondered if the worst harm he'd ever commit would be to the one person he wanted to save.

CHAPTER 51

EVIE

Evie chased her brother into the open office space, interns and pixies darting out of their path. She knocked into a desk, and papers flew, one of them sticking stubbornly to her face. "Gideon, stop!" she yelled.

Thank the gods he was halted by Marv, who just so happened to be entering right as Gideon was about to escape. They danced around each other for a second. "'Scuse me, sir," Marv said politely.

"Marv, don't let him leave!" Evie screamed, rushing forward. The workers around her eyed the blood caked to her skin and watched the scene with open-mouthed shock. Even though blood wasn't an abnormal sight here at Massacre Manor (especially during intern orientation), she couldn't fully blame them. She probably looked like a nightmare.

Marv, bless him, didn't need to be told twice. He threw his short, stocky form right into Gideon, tackling her brother to the ground. "Got 'im, Ms. Sage!"

She softened for the man as she walked forward, appreciating that he hadn't batted an eye at the blood or her dishevelment. "Thank you, Marv."

"And who do we have here?" Marv asked.

"Gideon Sage. A pleasure," her brother choked out—Marv still lay flat on top of him.

Marvin smiled like they were shaking hands and not getting intimately acquainted on the office floor. "Lovely to officially meet you, Mr. Sage. We're all very fond of your sister around the office."

Gideon smiled. "Our mother will be thrilled. Employee of the month, is she?" Though she knew it was a jest, it was in poor taste, all things considered.

She huffed as she sat on the floor beside them. "If he lets you up, will you tell me the truth?"

Gideon nodded, looking at Marv and smiling. "Well, kind sir, I think that's your cue."

Marv's cheeks pinked, but he quickly jumped off her brother. "I was coming in to tell you and the boss, Ms. Sage: Keely and the others said there were Valiant Guards getting closer to the manor borders. The Malevolent managed to distract them and lead them in a different direction for now, but parts of the manor keep becoming visible again."

Evie's heart pounded double time. Clare and Tatianna had still had no luck finding an enchantress to reset the barrier, and though non–magic users could still set invisibility spells, they didn't seem to be sticking for very long. It was obvious they were only buying themselves a little bit of time.

"Thank you, Marv." Evie smiled gently, not wanting to alarm the guard any more than he already was.

Marv's cheeks pinked again as he scurried out of the room and back to his post.

Evie remained on the floor, watching Gideon as he watched her. "Well, we could continue to stare awkwardly at each other, or you could tell me everything you've been keeping from me," she said.

Gideon folded his lips inward. "Staring awkwardly sounds delightful."

She rolled the dagger handle in her palm and scrunched her nose. "Even if I carve out one of your eyes?"

Her brother frowned. "I don't recall you being this bloodthirsty."

"Hazard of the occupation."

He adjusted his shoulders, setting them back. "I always wanted to be a knight, Eve. Surely you remember that."

She did, vaguely, along with her own aspirations to be a queen or a sheep herder. Or the summer before her tenth birthday, when she'd tried her hand as a fire-wielding trapeze artist and had promptly fallen off the roof.

And burned a hole in the grass that never grew back.

But those were childhood notions. Evie had always thought that Gideon would settle within their village, perhaps take on the butchery for their father when he grew older. She hadn't thought their youthful ramblings could make any sort of way for actual employment.

If that were the case, she should have a herd of sheep following her and a crown on her head, which, admittedly, wouldn't be the strangest sight this office had been witness to, but it was far too close to the week's end to give her boss a burst blood vessel. Though she likely already had, darting out of the cellar and chasing her brother down the hallway like she did, coated in blood that did not belong to her—because she was tracking it on the floor, not because of the blood itself. Her boss hated mess.

"Before I continue…" Gideon frowned. "May I ask: Did you murder our father?"

"Gideon, that's a horribly rude question."

"My apologies. Shall we first sit and ring for tea?"

She slapped him on the shoulder and wiped some of the blood from her chin. "I didn't murder him. I merely stabbed him in the thigh."

Gideon blinked. "And then decided to use his blood for face paint?"

She rolled her eyes in exasperation. "I slipped on my way out of the cell, and this was the result. Are you happy?"

Her brother's hand flew over his mouth. "You slipped?" Though he was attempting to hide it well, she knew he was laughing beneath the shaking appendage. "In the blood of your victim?"

She rolled her eyes and crossed her arms. "I don't see why that's so amusing. Blood is slippery. Isn't it, sir?" she inquired, having felt his presence coming up behind them.

The Villain cleared his throat, probably finding the whole spectacle unsavory. "I suppose it could be described as such."

Gideon lifted a brow and leaned an arm against his propped knee. "But have you ever fallen in it?"

The Villain scoffed in indignation. "No, that would be ridiculous." But when his eyes fell upon her pinched features, his face took on an uncharacteristic panic. "Not that you are— I did not mean—" Her boss sighed and rubbed a hand down his face. "Would you like me to kill your brother for you?"

"No." She smiled sweetly, and The Villain took a step backward. "That would be *ridiculous*."

But Gideon interrupted their back-and-forth by pushing himself to his feet and reaching a hand down for her. She took it hesitantly, trying not to stumble over the heel of her boot. "After I recover from the carriage wheels I've been thrown under, shall I continue?" he asked.

The rest of the workers returned to business as usual, or at least pretended to. Evie caught more than one of them pretending to write, their quills hovering about an inch from the actual paper. This interlude would no doubt be a source of gossip for employees to speculate on beside the fountain that magically spewed water tucked into the back corner of the office. All the best rumors started there.

"I was doing schoolwork in my room when Father first came to me about the king. I was perhaps twelve or thirteen." Gideon shifted nervously. "I had dreamed of being one of the Valiant: noble, brave, beloved by all. I remembered seeing them ride through our village, and I couldn't believe such men existed outside of the stories we were read at bedtime. I wanted it so badly, Eve."

Her brother turned away and sauntered toward the nearest window, clearly not wanting to face her during whatever he said next. "All magic awakens from a trauma, and mine was awoken after I'd caught that fever from one of my teachers." Evie knew this of magic, as well as the myth that magic could also be awoken from the purest joy. But that wasn't real, just a fable. The real magic in this world was always brought about by pain.

It hadn't been the Mystic Illness, according to the healer who had come to evaluate him. But Evie remembered how worried she'd been for her brother—and her mother, who was well into her pregnancy with Lyssa. Gideon had survived the fever, but he grew distant from her after that; she'd thought it was her fault. She'd been in the habit then of thinking everything was her fault.

"After that, Father had me begin training with a magical specialist in secret. He said it was too small a village to let anyone know about how powerful my magic was. It was a blocking magic of sorts—I was able to suppress other people's magic, no matter how powerful, no matter how strong, and it made Father wary. He wouldn't even let me tell Mother, said it would cause stress to her and harm the baby." Gideon was facing the other direction, but she could see his body shudder, like regret was a physical torment.

"And then I met the king," Gideon said. Her boss stiffened beside her, clenching his fists tightly. "He was thrilled by my magic and even more so by the development of Mother's. She'd just had Lyssa, and her starlight magic was flourishing. He said it was the magic of a savior…and that it would be too powerful for her to wield all on her own."

Warning bells rang in Evie's head. She knew where the story was going, knew it had a tragic end. Because unlike the beauty of fairy tales, real life didn't end in a neat and tidy bow.

"They asked me to use my magic to suppress the fullness of Mother's power so it wouldn't overwhelm her. They told me it was safe and I was doing my duty to the kingdom. So, every night after she'd fall asleep, I'd use my magic on her. She'd been withdrawn because of Lyssa, and once her magic evened out, after I'd helped her, I thought all would be well again. But I fell asleep early one night, and when she woke, her power came out full force."

That early morning, dawn, when everything changed—the dandelion fields, the day her childhood had ended.

Gideon turned around and ignored everyone else, looking only at her with genuine tears in his eyes, and it broke something inside her. She saw him at fifteen, then at twelve, then at seven, until the earliest memory of her brother slammed into her.

"It's my fault. What happened to Mother," he said. "Her losing control of her power. I tampered with her magic for the sake of the kingdom, for the sake of the knighthood... And then I destroyed her."

CHAPTER 52

EVIE

E vie didn't knock when she entered The Villain's bedchamber, unless her shoulder slapping against the wood as she shoved it open counted. "Sir, you left before I could tell you about my lead! And now, to boot, I can't find Lyssa."

She *definitely* should've knocked, or whistled, or sent out a raven call at the very least, because what she was witnessing was…truly something. The Villain was holding himself like a plank over the ground, shirtless, his back muscles rippling all the way down to the top of his rear end as he lowered to the ground and pushed himself back up. He froze when he heard her voice, the motion causing the muscles in his arms to shake as he held his stance.

"Sage, I hope I didn't give you the mistaken impression that I enjoy company in my chambers."

She replied with teasing amusement, "Sir, you're doing push-ups alone at four o'clock in the afternoon. Nobody would get that impression."

He glared as he stood, unwinding the white canvas wrappings around his palms and dabbing sweat off his neck. He eyed her now-clean attire, the blood washed from her skin. "What of your father? What did he say? I fear your brother diverted my plans with his little confession."

My. Not *our.* It was a purposeful distinction. She could tell by the subtle shift in his face.

She wanted to blame her brother for her mother's disappearance and all the events that followed, for the revelation that seemed to drive a larger wedge between her boss and her, but it wasn't fair. Gideon had been a mere fifteen years old, just as much a victim of their father's and the king's machinations as she. And anyway, her brother was not the sibling she was most concerned about at the moment.

"Later. I can't do anything until I know where Lyssa is. I asked Edwin, Becky, Blade, and the guards. Edwin said she usually disappears around noon to write her stories in our bedchamber—she takes writing time quite seriously—but she's not there."

He frowned, crossing the room to open the armoire and retrieve a shirt, then shutting it quickly like he didn't want her to see inside. He slid the dark fabric over his head before speaking. "With Tatianna, maybe?"

"I can't find her, either." She gave him a suggestive look. "Or Clare."

"You're kidding," he said with a small grin. Suddenly, they were two old friends gossiping over tea.

She clasped her hands together, grinning. "Nope!" Her smile fell. "Wait. Focus. Lyssa. Lyssa is missing."

Trystan nodded, solemn, before pulling an amethyst from his pocket and ordering into it, "I need everyone searching for Lyssa Sage and reporting to me with any sightings of her." He put a reassuring hand on Evie's shoulder. "She's around here somewhere. You needn't worry."

"I'm not worried; I'm murderous."

"Don't be that, either," he advised, contemplating her. "Tati said that you stabbed your father in the leg."

She didn't deny it, merely shrugged.

"Are you okay?"

"Nope!" she said cheerily, then looked around desperately for something to change the subject while they waited for any reports.

His room looked different during the day. She could see more lines of detail along his quilted comforter, the million pillows on his bed. She turned around and flopped back onto it—it was brutally uncomfortable. Her boss was a sociopath.

"This is outlandish," she grumbled.

"I was going to say that about you lying on *my* bed," he said in a strangled voice, one hand on his hip, the other pressed over his eyes like he couldn't bear to see it.

Her sister was missing, likely up to gods knew what mischief—probably toppling an army or creating a potion that would turn her into a worm—but that didn't stop Evie from acknowledging the dragon in the room. "Okay, so are we going to talk about our kiss? Or is this a sweep-it-under-the-rug sort of situation?"

"Sage," he gritted out, looking up like he was hoping for the sky to tumble down.

"I don't see why you're so outraged. You kissed me first!"

"It was an accident!" he objected and then winced, probably realizing how silly that sounded.

An accident? She deserved a better excuse. With a raised brow, she looked him up and down. "A fairly long accident, if I recall."

His gaze narrowed on hers. "*If* you recall? It happened yesterday. Do you forget so easily?"

She looked at him boldly. "Do you?"

He went rigid, his muscles so tense he seemed like he was turning to stone. There was an intensity in his expression that she'd spurred, but now she glanced down at her hands instead, unable to hold his gaze with hers.

"A momentary lapse, perhaps. Like eating something spicy because it looks good and then it makes your stomach sick," she said, nodding succinctly.

When she looked up, he was staring at her hands, sounding acutely uncomfortable when he replied, "Spicy food would never make my stomach sick."

They weren't speaking of spicy food, but that hardly mattered. He looked haunted.

So she decided she'd give him the smallest bit of mercy. "I'll let it go if that's what you want. But I demand we revisit it after my mother's found. No matter the outcome."

He hesitated. *Coward.* "Fine," he finally agreed. "What did your father say? Who was in the painting?"

"Renna Fortis," she said, walking over to his drawers and starting to riffle through them. She pulled out an oddly colorful pair of socks. She held them up, biting her lip. "Polka dots?"

"Give me those! You're worse than a racoon," he griped, ripping the socks from her hands. "Renna Fortis is the matriarch of the Fortis family. If your mother is at the Fortis Family Fortress, that…could be a serious problem."

She frowned, wandering to the armoire. "Why?"

Next thing she knew, she was over his shoulder again, being gently flopped onto the bed like a rag doll. Though she had the sudden, foolish hope his body would land on top of hers, it didn't. Instead, he was already across the room, leaning against the armoire doors. There was something in there he didn't want her to find.

Which meant she wouldn't rest until she knew what it was.

"For one thing, the fortress is completely inaccessible to the public. And…"

She sat up on her elbows. "And what?" she prompted.

He looked uncomfortable, but it was a toss-up as to whether it was due to her presence in his bed or whatever it was he was hiding in that damn armoire. "It's not my place to say. Let me make some inquiries, and we'll go from there."

Suddenly, Marv stormed in the room, causing Evie to startle so badly, she fell off the bed. "Problem—big problem—huge problem!"

It was too much to hope that Marv hadn't seen her. And he couldn't keep a secret to save his life. Fantastic.

"A fire has been deliberately started in the courtyard!" Marv yelled.

The Villain furrowed his brow but otherwise kept his composure. "It isn't the first time, Marv. Use one of Sage's prized hoses and put it out."

"They're not prized," she said, affronted. "They're safety precautions!"

Marv shifted nervously. "Sir…I fear the Valiant Guards are behind this."

The blank expression on The Villain's face morphed into a determined set of his jaw as he sailed from the room, Evie following hot on his heels.

Marv could be right; there had been knights sniffing around the barriers of the manor. But Evie had her suspicions as well, and none of them were aimed at the Valiant Guards.

No, she had a terrible feeling the person responsible was someone else entirely.

CHAPTER 53

THE VILLAIN

Trystan used to like being in charge.

Ordering people about and having them bend to his control was his duty, his destiny; the one thing he could strive to be good at was evil-doing, committing crimes against the kingdom. But if he were being truthful, he thought as he and Sage raced through the manor, if he allowed himself to acknowledge that long-held hope he'd pushed off to the corner of his mind so long ago, he could acknowledge that fulfilling the prophecy, that saving Rennedawn…doing something to save instead of destroy…might make him deserving.

Of peace, of friendship, of family, and maybe even of—

"Fire!" The word left his mouth rather without warning as he and Sage ran into the back courtyard to find the trees ablaze.

Sage startled, clutching her side, out of breath, panting, skin dampened from the exertion— His mind went to a horrid place, and it involved his bed… and a few of his pillows. "I think it knows, sir," she gasped out. "You don't have to scream at it."

Trystan gripped the sides of his head. "Just get out the hose. So I can find—and *severely* punish—whoever is responsible for this."

She tried to lift a cement slab in the floor of the courtyard. It didn't budge, and so she frowned at it. "Huh. I was sure that was the one I put it under."

He gaped at her. "You don't know where it is? You, the rubber hose enthusiast?"

She pointed a finger in his face. "Planning for safety in case of an emergency does not make me an enthusiast, Evil Overlord."

Trystan lifted a brow and crossed his arms, contemplating her. "Did you buy a book about it?"

She looked away guiltily. "…Yes."

"Ha!"

She threw her hands in the air. "I did a little reading on safety! It's a palate cleanser after my last bodice-ripper book."

He didn't need to be a genius to surmise what those books entailed.

"Wh-What was the title?" he asked.

She looked up, her nonsense wheels clearly moving. "I think *Fire Hoses for the Workplace* or something to that effect."

Yes, he had most *definitely* been referring to the hose book. Trystan pinched the bridge of his nose, turning away from her in an effort to regain his footing.

The movement caused a slab to loosen under his boot, catching him by such surprise that he lost his footing completely. Which was unfathomable enough, but then…he *flailed.* He didn't think he'd ever flailed once in the span of his entire life. His ass hit the ground hard enough to rattle his skull in his head. But the slab had lifted, revealing the end of a long rubber tube.

Sage squealed, "You found it!" and clapped her hands. Then she pulled it out, holding it expertly, and her efficiency at her task, the focus on her face was…oddly arousing.

The woman could sharpen a pencil and he'd go into an apoplectic fit.

He frowned down at his position on the ground. "Sage, I fear your lack of equilibrium is catching."

She ignored him, pulling a nozzle at the top of the hose, and water came out in a rush. As he jumped up, the force of it knocked her backward and right into his chest. His hands went up instinctively to grip her elbows, and though he couldn't see her face, he felt her stiffen, planting her feet firmly to keep from moving. "I do not lack equilibrium," she argued. "The ground merely lacks the courtesy of letting me know when it is coming closer."

It was with patent disbelief that he said, "Do you think you could argue your way through anything?"

The flames were dissipating under the onslaught of water, though a few flickered still. But it wasn't the fire that was causing all the warmth in the air. It wasn't the sun beating down on them or the flowers coming up through the cracks in the stones that were layered throughout the back courtyard. It was Sage, looking at him with her mischievous smile and her kind eyes.

"I argued my way into this job, didn't I?"

She said this, of course, not knowing that the job was hers the moment she'd said she needed one.

That he would've found a way, any way, to ease the burdens she clearly carried in her slender shoulders, in the gaunt hunch of her frame, like she had been undereating when they first met. How he'd stayed up late that first night wondering why.

There was a standing order for vanilla candies at the manor, the start date of which had been—coincidentally—the day after her first shift, after he'd seen how much she enjoyed the ones hidden in a tin atop his desk. He could use one right about now, in fact, to calm the fury that rose within him when he saw the charred wood of the back gate.

"Finish putting out the fire, Sage. I need to find who is responsible for this."

Sage put the hose down. "No need."

A wash of confusion swept over him, dampening his ardor for revenge—nearly ruining it, in fact. "You may do as you please, but I haven't killed anyone in nearly a week, and I believe I am due. The incident board misses me dearly."

She squeezed her eyes shut tight. "You cannot injure the person responsible."

He leaned forward menacingly, trying to take on his air of forbidding evilness. "Sage, I will do whatever I please."

The look she gave him could only be described as a challenge, a dare. "Lyssa!" she called. "Get out here *now*!"

The authority Sage commanded in that one parental order made his back straighten. Like he, too, would come running should she tell him to do so.

"It wasn't a Valiant Guard," Sage said with silent disappointment in her face and posture. "It was my sister."

CHAPTER 54

EVIE

E vie Sage had always known her parenting skills left much to be desired. It was an eternal weakness that she could never overcome. She'd taken on the caregiver role too young, at an age when her biggest problem should've been a difficult topic in school or worrying which of her friends was whispering about her behind her back. An age when she should have been climbing trees and making wishes, pretending the world was bright and open and fun.

She grew nostalgic at times for the childhood she'd lost too soon.

But regardless, she'd done her best to keep believing that the world held goodness, and hope, and joy, so that Lyssa might believe it, too. She perhaps leaned a bit *too* far into her optimism—as a means of survival. Perhaps this wasn't the parental presence her sister needed? Considering she was now committing arson?

Lyssa's small, dark-haired head appeared from behind a gap in one of the back walls. "How did you know I was out here?" she asked as she rounded the wall and approached them cautiously. Her brown eyes were wide, her button nose and round cheeks covered in black soot that coated not just her face but her hands as well as the hem of her knee-length dress.

Evie lifted a finger, displaying a purple ribbon that she'd found on the ground. "Lose something?"

Lyssa's hand shot for the end of her braid as she realized the strip of silk was missing. "Rats! The first rule of villainy: never leave evidence behind."

Evie's boss smothered a laugh beside her. She gave him an incredulous look, and the laughter died. He was serious when he said, "She's correct. Though it is on occasion permitted to leave a calling card."

Lyssa looked at Trystan with stars in her eyes, nodding like she was cataloging everything he said for later. *Good grief.*

She pushed at her boss's shoulder. "Stop giving her tips!"

A bone-aching exhaustion wrapped around her limbs, the expectations and responsibilities draining life from her body. She pleaded with Lyssa. "What the deadlands were you thinking? How did you even do this?" Evie tried to keep her relationship with Lyssa light; she lived in a balance of being her big sister, her friend, and her parent only when needed.

This was a parenting moment.

Lyssa rubbed at the soot on her face, softening Evie's heart, but before she could move, her boss edged forward, handing Lyssa a black handkerchief from his pocket. Her sister rubbed the sides of her face but missed the soot completely. "Did I get it?"

Evie watched him visibly fight his lips pulling up in a grin, keeping his expression serious, his tone professional.

"You look like a chimney sweep, little villain." He took the handkerchief from Lyssa's small hands and lifted it in front of her. "May I?"

Lyssa looked at him shyly, but she warmly nodded. It was a startling thing, watching her boss, whom she'd seen in different states of violence—from torture to arson himself, to breaking bones, breaking hands, hanging heads... She could go on.

But this man was different—or perhaps he was the same, just softer, safer. He rubbed lightly at the soot spots on Lyssa's cheeks until the black had transferred to the handkerchief and he was standing, tucking it back into his pocket. "There you are," he said with a heartbreaking grin.

Or rather, heart-mending. Like with that one small act, he'd taken a needle and thread to the two broken pieces of Evie, slowly pulling her back together, slowly making her whole.

She considered the absolute atrocity of kindness he'd just committed in front of her. How was she supposed to stay detached when he did things like that? She wanted him to reassert himself as the big bad in her life, but it was too late. He had already become too dear in her heart—so dear that losing him would eviscerate her. She'd never recover. Her feelings were threatening to swallow her.

Shove them down. That *feels healthy.*

She shouldered her way past him to stand in front of her sister. "All right, I'll be the bad guy, then, while you play him like a fiddle."

Lyssa chuckled into her hand.

The Villain blinked. "What do you mean?"

Evie nodded sympathetically. "You were conned by a ten-year-old."

He blinked in disbelief before saying in a low, graveled timbre, "No one can know of this."

Leaving him to his existential crisis, Evie turned her attention back to her sister, crossing her arms. "Lyssa. The fire. How?"

Lyssa looked down, wiggling her toes in her shoes. "I was helping the dragon."

The Villain cocked his head. "Fluffy?"

Lyssa nodded. "It's so funny that we call him Fluffy. We had a dog with the same name!"

"I know," The Villain said darkly.

Evie frowned. "Continue— Ah!" she shouted, gripping her chest when Fluffy himself appeared over Lyssa's shoulder, his green and purple scales bright. "For such a large animal, he has abnormally quiet footsteps."

Fluffy's head angled down and nudged Lyssa's shoulder. She patted his nose, and he hummed into her hand like a cat.

"Lyssa…" Evie started. "Did you get the dragon to breathe fire?"

Her sister stopped petting Fluffy, who gave a little growl in protest. "Yes, I did! I'm sorry that he burned down the back wall, but since I've been here, it's become very clear to me that everyone in the office needs my help. So I'm afraid it was just collateral."

Evie stared at her with skepticism. "Do you even know what collateral means?"

"Something you sacrifice so you can do something even greater." Lyssa, as she always did, put seemingly complicated things in the most simple terms.

The Villain nudged her arm with his own. "That was fairly well put, actually."

Evie hissed at him. "Whose side are you on!"

Just then, Tatianna and Clare burst into the courtyard, looking bedraggled and furious. "Lyssa Sage! You are in big trouble!" *Ah, at last—allies.*

Lyssa dove toward Fluffy, who hovered his head over her, prepared to safeguard her from all harm. Evie got a peek at Kingsley atop the dragon's head—he was holding up a sign that read, INNOCENT.

Not likely. "What did you do to *them*?" Evie asked her sister.

Tatianna seethed, her normal composure frayed, clothes wrinkled, hair tousled. "She locked us in a cupboard!"

"Lyssa!" Evie turned to her.

"I was trying to help them fall back in love! I'm sorry!" Lyssa winced. "I wanted to do it with Ms. Erring and Blade, too, but sometimes it's hard to tell if she actually likes him, so I wasn't sure if I should."

Clare glared. "Oh, and with us it's so obvious?"

The Villain arched a brow. "Clare, do you have pink lipstick on?"

Clare coughed, rubbing the fuchsia color from her mouth—the same one Tatianna was wearing. "No."

Oh, when this was over, Evie was *definitely* looking into that further.

Lyssa had taken the distraction as an opportunity to slowly creep away, but Evie tugged her back by the collar of her dress. "Oh, no you don't. Who else did you 'help'?"

Her sister's face got red; she looked like she'd swallowed something that burned her throat. "I may have...helped you a bit, too."

Then it clicked. Her missing journal appearing on her boss's desk. She'd thought it a prank by one of the interns, but no, it was her little sister on a matchmaking spree. "Of all the ridiculous things! Lyssa, I understand that your intentions were good, but it is not nice to meddle in other people's lives."

Lyssa's mouth turned down. "But this group does it all the time."

This struck everyone silent. Until Rebecka Erring stumbled into the courtyard next. "There was a fire? Did they find Lyssa? I can't—" The HR manager stopped in her tracks when she saw them huddled, shoulders dropping when she found Lyssa in the middle, safe and sound. Instead of appearing relieved, Becky somehow knew to look suspicious instead. "You started the fire, didn't you, Lyssa?"

Lyssa approached Becky with a sheepish grin. "Technically speaking, it was Fluffy."

Blade bolted out next; this was beginning to feel like a poorly done skit. "Yes it was!" Blade picked up Lyssa and spun her around. She giggled, small hands around Blade's neck in a sweet hug. "Lyssa Sage, you little genius. How did you do it?"

Lyssa shrugged, replying gleefully, "We just worked on his confidence. Kingsley helped, too!"

Kingsley hopped toward Lyssa, hiding behind her when the boss began to glare.

Becky seemed put off by the whole thing. "Wonderful. And where were you two"—her accusatory gaze landed on Evie and The Villain—"when she was helping 'build the dragon's confidence' and setting fire to the architecture?"

Evie answered first, knowing they had to keep their friends and coworkers in the know. "We were discussing Renna Fortis."

Becky stiffened, color draining from her face. "What? Why?"

This was an odd reaction from her. Evie stepped closer, feeling concerned, as she said carefully, "Renna Fortis was the woman in the painting with my mother. They were best friends. We believe she's with her now at the Fortis Family Fortress, but we have no means of finding it."

Becky swallowed, but the boss cut in to say quietly, "You do not have to if you do not wish, Ms. Erring."

Oh, what am I missing now?

Blade's eyes sharpened on Becky. "What's going on?"

Becky smoothed back her bun and pushed her glasses up her nose before addressing them all. "I can get us to the fortress."

Tatianna didn't look surprised, but Clare's jaw slackened. "How? It's inaccessible to the public."

Becky's eyes found Evie's, and what she observed there was so reminiscent of what Evie saw in the mirror every day that she almost took Becky's hand: Fear. Reluctance. Worry. But also…strength. Conviction.

All warred in Becky's expression as she said, "It's not inaccessible to me… because Renna Fortis is my mother."

CHAPTER 55

EVIE

It was a bad time for her brother to be bothering her. The group was waiting for her in the courtyard, and she was already late. As usual, she'd overpacked.

"Keep an eye on him while we're gone, Keely—a close one," she said as she lugged her stuffed suitcase through the corridor. The head of the Malevolent Guard, who was back on Gideon guard duty after his secrets had been revealed, gave her a quick nod.

Gideon's cheeks reddened. His head was downcast. "I deserve that."

She didn't want him to be self-pitying; it made it that much more difficult for her to hold on to her hurt. It was a terrible feeling to be angry with someone and want to comfort them at the same time, and she wished that her brother would be just a bit more awful so she wouldn't feel the need.

They reached the stairs, and Gideon took the suitcase from her hands, gesturing for her to precede him down. Damn chivalry. "You do not deserve my ire for being manipulated," she allowed. Evie knew what it was like to be played by their own father. It wasn't right for her to be angry, but she was human. Emotions didn't always know right or nuance; they just knew to be hurt when someone caused pain.

They reached the bottom of the stairs, and Gideon carefully handed over her bag. "Here you are. I know better than to ask to join, but if you might tell me where Lyssa is, I'd like to spend some time with her while you're gone."

Evie nodded, feeling a sting behind her eyes. "She's baking with Edwin. You should go help—I'm sure she'd love it."

Gideon brightened. "Excellent! I'll head there now. Keely, will you join me?"

Keely remained on guard behind him as she rolled her eyes. "Unfortunately."

They were interrupted when Tatianna stormed down the stairs, thick brows pushed together, mouth turned down in anger.

It was very different from Tatianna's normal unruffled confidence. "Everything okay, Tati?"

Tatianna flung a braid out of her eyes. Her face looked perplexed, and her brown skin glistened with a sheen of sweat. "Your menace of a sister stole my diary."

Evie set her suitcase down and clamped a hand over her mouth. "Oh no!"

Tatianna's dark lashes fanned out as her lids went half closed. "Are you smiling under there?"

She shook her head, not wanting to speak, because she was, in fact, *laughing*. As was Gideon, who barked out a "ha!" before masking it by rubbing a hand over his mouth and down his chin.

Tatianna adjusted her pink sleeves. She had changed into long, silky pink trousers to better accommodate traveling. She narrowed her eyes, which were dusted with vibrant pink shadow. "I think it's a family trait."

Evie looked at her friend closely and pursed her lips. "Tati, did something happen in the cupboard?"

The healer froze, growing more rigid as Clare made her way down the stairs behind her. "I'm coming along, too," the youngest Maverine announced.

Every strand of hair on Clare's head was out of place. Every. Single. One.

"Unnecessary," Tatianna grumbled as she made her way for the door, Clare following behind her. They were near each other but apart, like opposing forces that didn't want to touch but couldn't help but remain close.

Once they were gone, Gideon broke the silence first. "Our sister is… something." His laughter barked out before he could stop it.

Evie moved her hand from her mouth, putting both over her eyes. Her echoing giggle was light; it calmed her immensely against everything that was currently trying to weigh her down.

His low laughter harmonized with hers, and when she removed her hands and looked at her brother, his smile faded. She watched as his eyes went red and glassy. "I'm really sorry, Eve. For everything. I can't tell you how much I wish I could do it over. You might not believe me, but I promise I will make it up to you."

It was enough.

She threw her arms around her brother, burying her face in his neck. "It's okay. I love you. It's okay."

Gideon sniffed quietly into her shoulder, gripping Evie the way a child would a mother's skirts, like he was the little boy once more, with so many fears and no way to manage them. "I'm sorry."

She shushed him, rubbing circles on his back. "No one will ever hurt us again. I vow it."

They pulled apart slowly, watery smiles and drying tears making both their faces sticky and red. Keely had moved off to the corner, clearly uncomfortable with the display.

Evie picked up her bag. "Make me something tasty with Lyssa and Edwin for when we return? And look after things while we're gone."

"Count on it." With a trembling chin, Gideon gestured a hand toward the back door. "Now get out there and find our mother."

She was nearly to the door when she halted and spun around. "Gideon."

He looked at her, ever the gilded hero. He was good—a different sort than her.

This was why she said carefully, "I want to hurt the king. Not because he's done bad things. Not because he's bad for Rennedawn. I want him to hurt because I hurt, because he hurt all of us. Do you think that makes me a villain?"

He smiled hesitantly; even Keely appeared surprised by the question. "No, Eve. It's okay that you feel that way."

But as she walked out to the now-saddled dragon for their long trip to Becky's family home, she noted something she'd seen behind her brother's eyes, behind his words.

Fear.

CHAPTER 56

THE VILLAIN

Trystan wasn't nervous.

So perhaps the nausea and stomach twists were merely a result of the dragon dipping and diving through the sky, occasionally opening his mouth to light a tree aflame—something Sage took very strong objection to, as evidenced by her nails digging into her palms every time a sprig of green went up in an orange blaze.

"Gushiken, kindly tell Fluffy to cease making ash of Hickory Forest," he said. "I enjoy destruction, but I bear the trees no ill will." He did not move his gaze from Sage's hands, willing them to loosen so that he didn't reach over and do it for her. That would violate the spirit of the agreement between them.

I demand we revisit it after my mother's found.

He shouldn't have agreed to it, because now, on top of the guvres and the failing wards, he, too, was on a ticking clock, with an unknown outcome looming when the time ran out. Nothing could happen between them— nothing good, anyhow. Sage's life was already in shambles just *working* for him; he couldn't imagine how he'd destroy her if she became anything else, anything *more*.

It made him envy Blade, that the dragon trainer had the freedom to pursue whomever he chose without fear of destroying them by accident.

Gushiken gripped the reins tighter, his eyes on Ms. Erring, who was leaning with her chin in her hand and looking as far away as a person could be. No doubt she was dreading their destination. Though Trystan couldn't understand the weight on the woman's shoulders, he could imagine the nerve-igniting dread of returning to a place fraught with terrible memories. He'd feel the same returning to his own village, to his mother's house, to the woman who, instead of accepting his power, had sought to destroy it.

Had sought to kill him.

Rebecka Erring was someone Trystan understood. It was why he'd so readily offered her employment three short years prior, when she'd been a desperate, far less composed version of the woman she was now. The woman he'd first met stumbling away from home, seeking— He wouldn't say "rescue," as that wasn't in his repertoire, but his hiring of her came at a time when she'd sought escape. He'd known she'd be a fearsome ally, and she'd more than proven herself since.

Blade frowned at Rebecka's forlorn expression and used what seemed to be the dragon trainer's favorite tactic: diversion. "Lovely Rebecka, would you like to steer?"

Ms. Erring glanced at him, emptily shaking her head, before going back to staring off into the distance. Sage's hands loosened, and Trystan internally exhaled, deeply affected by the small actions of her fingers. *I demand we revisit it after my mother's found.*

At this rate, she'd be revisiting it at his grave.

Sage scooched closer to Ms. Erring, sliding a hand toward her but not touching her. "It's not too late for us to turn back. If you don't want to face them, you do not have to. We can find another way."

Ms. Erring frowned. "You want to find your mother, don't you?"

Sage pushed a wind-whipped lock of hair behind her ear. "Not at your expense. You're not collateral, Becky. I don't want you to be hurt simply because of who your family is."

Tatianna chimed in, too. "This isn't a requirement, Rebecka, it's a choice. Whatever you want to do, we will support you in it."

Becky looked between both women, mouth pinching, suppressing emotion. He knew because he often made the same face when he was holding back. "I…appreciate the sentiments, but I cannot run from my family forever. If your mother is there… If finding her will help us defeat Benedict, then we are doing it." Chin bobbing, she lifted her hand to lightly hold her throat. "But I warn you to not be dazzled by the grandeur of the fortress. It is not all that it seems, and neither is my family."

Clare, on the opposite side of him—notably as far away from Tatianna as humanly possible—said, "We know of family complications, Rebecka. Don't worry; we'll be on guard. I know I always am any time I'm with any of mine."

Trystan's power snaked out, knocking into the side of his sister's leg. When she turned accusatory eyes on him, he looked away, whistling.

"I know that was you, Tryst. Must you always be so hostile?"

He answered flatly, without hesitating. "Yes."

Sage quietly placed something warm, wrapped in parchment paper, in his lap. He did a double take before unwrapping it and inhaling a large whiff. It was bread, much like the kind they'd shared in the Heart Village. "He's always crabby when he's hungry," Sage clarified. "I once stopped him from razing a village to the ground by offering him a cupcake."

He glared. "That is not true."

Sage looked guilty. "You're right." She grinned at Clare. "It was a cookie."

It was acutely unflattering to be spoken about like a recalcitrant child, but he was more taken aback by how well and easily Sage knew exactly what he needed, exactly what he would want.

That's her job, you dolt.

It was nonsense that thinking of her carefully packing a loaf of bread caused disgusting sentiment to pull at the strings in his chest.

He cleared his throat, willing the sentiment to disappear. "Thank you, Sage. It will fuel my evildoing for the afternoon." She huffed a laugh.

But her laughter faded when Rebecka adjusted her glasses with sobering grimness. "There will be no doing of evil once we arrive at the fortress. It'll be a wonder if they even allow you two entry, with your faces so revealed to the world."

She slid two scraps of parchment across the saddle into his and Sage's waiting hands. Their WANTED flyers—the very same that had been held by Helena's henchmen in the Heart Village. One had a recounting of his crimes and his real name, a now-tripled amount of gold pieces, and a sketch of—

"Well, this is absurd—my head is not this big," he grumbled.

Sage peeked over his shoulder, her breath tickling his ear and making him see stars. The ugly kind that were bright and irritating behind your eyelids after being struck hard in the face. "Really?" Her blue gaze took measure of the head in question. "I think they made it smaller."

The sun beat down harder upon them, reddening Sage's cheeks and bringing a smattering of freckles out on the tip of her nose. He wanted to tap it. More so when the color on her cheeks deepened.

Biting her lip, she continued for reasons he could not fathom. "Not that your actual head is large. It's more proportionate to the rest of your body, which is also fairly…large." She choked, and so did he—nearly. "Not all your body, of course! How would I know if other things are also…large? Although I would assume, based off the rest of you, that everything else is also proportionate in size…"

Tatianna smiled into the tiny mirror she was holding up to do her lipstick. "Evie, dear, quit while you're three feet belowground."

Sage saluted and scooted away from him—exactly what he needed. Irritating that his hands itched to drag her closer.

A large gust of wind whipped back his hair, and he held up a hand to shield his face as he shuffled to the second WANTED flyer: Sage's.

THE WICKED WOMAN flyer was a near-perfect and lovely depiction of Sage. Her dark curls were blowing away from her face, flying in every direction, like the artist had caught her in a stiff breeze. Her lips were quirked, and her eyes seemed to shine with a sinister glimmer.

She looked like the most beautiful nightmare he'd ever seen.

But her list of charges had grown longer since the last flyer.

TREASON

KIDNAPPING

THREATS TO THE CROWN

CONSPIRING WITH THE ENEMY

APPRENTICE TO THE VILLAIN

Suddenly, she ripped the paper out of his hand. When she looked at it, her eyes widened and a small yelp left her mouth, her fingers coming up to brush against her lips.

"Sage…" he said, placating. Perhaps someone in the Massacre Manor Relations Department could find a way to spin Sage as a prisoner, so that she may still lead a normal life in Rennedawn when this was all over, when the chips finally fell into place and she was ready to leave him and his business behind forever. He ignored that his heart suddenly doubled in weight and dropped toward his feet; it was merely because the bread was dry. Never mind that he hadn't taken a bite yet.

Fluffy sailed upward, as if sensing they needed to be lost among the skies, but the abrupt rush of air couldn't drown out Sage's scream.

Trystan was not a reader of emotions. He could barely interpret his own, with how little he endeavored to use them. But was the woman who drew nearly every ounce of his attention…bouncing?

"They…they *promoted* me!" Her smile was so wide that she beamed. It was like rays of color spilling out of her: red on her lips and her cheeks, blue in her eyes, a white sheen bouncing off her plaited hair and finally settling against the glow of her skin.

Did she want more flyers printed? He could arrange it.

Blade loosened his grip on the reins, leaning over to look at the paper she extended to him. "Apprentice, huh? Very official. Honestly, it's about time. You've done far more than just assistant tasks in the office as of late."

"You're right," she said smugly, snatching it back when Clare reached for it. "Don't rip it," Sage warned before handing it to Clare.

His sister lifted a dark and sardonic brow. "Oh, I wouldn't dream of it." She *hmph*ed before looking back to Evie. "Whoever the sketch artist is, they're halfway in love with you."

"Is there a credit to the artist at the bottom?" he inquired without thinking.

"Yes, at the bottom corner," Clare answered.

He snatched it away from her, and the parchment tore a bit, earning an outraged cry from Sage as he said, dry and emotionless, "I will see him about my head measurements."

Sage glared at him with murder in her eye before grabbing the WANTED flyer back and clutching it to her chest. "This is so exciting. I'm practically on your level now!"

He smirked, feeling an amusement that he knew would fade into dread minutes later, once the enormity of this had settled in. But he allowed it for the moment. "Not quite, Sage."

Though he knew she'd earned the title and then some.

"You're merely an apprentice," he went on. "You have a ways to go before you're a villain."

CHAPTER 57

EVIE

"We're here," Becky said. "This is my family's fortress."

Except they weren't near an estate of any kind, just an empty clearing surrounded by fog right outside Hickory Forest. Silence befell the group as they all looked around. The boss's normally blank expression was changing to reveal frank skepticism. Evie merely blinked, waiting to see something appear from the fog, but nothing did. Was Becky playing a trick on them?

Blade broke the silence first. "It's really nice, what they've done with the place."

They all groaned.

Becky ignored them, walking forward, fishing out a golden key from her pocket, twisting it in the open air, and then standing stock still, waiting for… something.

"Do Rebecka's glasses give her heightened vision? There's nothing there." Tatianna scanned the air with concern, her long fingers lighting up, ready to use her magic if need be.

Blade crossed his arms and hissed back at them, "Could we all just give her a chance to get herself sorted? She doesn't need our censure. Can't you see she's terrified?"

Evie could see it in the slight, almost undetectable shaking that ran from Becky's shoulders all the way down to her outstretched hand. A pang of tenderness gripped Evie's heart as she surged forward and placed a gentle palm on Becky's shoulder. "Remember what *I* said to you on my first day?"

Becky's eyes rounded as she contemplated the question. "You said that it was nice to meet me and that you hoped we'd be friends."

Evie grinned. "What else?"

"I don't remember anything else. I stopped listening after you said *friend*."

Evie sighed. "I said that you seemed fearsome and in control of yourself. Your family, no matter what, cannot rob you of that. You are in control. And more importantly, you are *not* alone."

Evie still saw fear as Becky squared her shoulders, angling the key up. She admired the woman for it, because it wasn't thoughtless bravery that won the fiercest battles—it was welcoming the fear that lived inside your heart, in your mind, and harnessing it to carry your feet forward, knowing it couldn't control you.

Rebecka Erring—or rather, Rebecka Fortis?—moved forward, not turning the key now but thrusting it up into the empty air.

And then the world around them cracked open.

CHAPTER 58

BECKY

Rebecka Eriania Fortis had never thought much of the deadlands.

But she decided it would be a preferable location to where she was now, at her family's fortress—a place to which she thought she'd never return. The group behind her *ooh*ed and *ahh*ed, wowed by the splendor unfolding before them. Already forgetting her warnings, already hypnotized by the beauty.

She wished she could be surprised by that.

Large magenta gates swung open, and beyond was the colorful glamor of her former life. The fortress was huge—not as big as the manor, but the grounds were wider, open, and far more colorful. Plants and trees were everywhere, so tall and full of splendor that even she marveled as a tree branch reached down and brushed her cheek in greeting.

She hated to cry, certainly didn't make a habit of it, but she felt the stinging burn of tears now. Her family wasn't innocent, but their land was: the trees, the grass, the dancing mushrooms lining the front walk, making little murmured sounds when they saw her walking up the flower-lined path to the fortress entrance. The sound was equal parts comforting and foreign after so many years. The front doors to the house were the same, with gold vines wrapped over every inch, and her family's crest was etched into the front of each door—a large magenta flower with green leaves falling from it.

Archibald, the Fortis family's tried-and-true butler, appeared as the doors swung open, greeting her with unbridled warmth. Undeserved, in her opinion, considering the last time she saw him, she'd slammed that very same door in his face.

"Lady Rebecka. You've come home to us," he said, his voice cracking. The butler was older than both of her parents; he began his service to her family when her grandmother was just a little girl.

"Come in, come in! All of you, please," Archibald urged. She'd always envied his manners and decorum, and she'd attempted to mimic them even after she left.

He ushered them into the foyer, his uniform matching the bright colors surrounding them. The vibrant pinks, greens, and yellows were meant to be an ode to Myrtalia, the continent on which they lived. It was the Fortis family's subtle way of declaring their loyalty to the land and not to any ruler. They were not believers in *Rennedawn's Story* or its prophecy. Or at least...they weren't meant to be.

Her mother had never mentioned Nura Sage or starlight power, but it was not so out of the ordinary for the family to harbor wayward souls. There were many people who had come and gone through the fortress, looking for protection, looking for safety.

"I've sent for your parents. Your father is out minding his spice garden, and your brothers are training in the Trench." Archibald looked at the people filtering in behind her—*my people*, she thought with some pride—and with a pinch of dismay. "You and your *guests* may wait in the green room for them. I'll bring refreshments."

Blade whispered in her ear, "Isn't the whole house a green room?" She elbowed him but stifled a laugh as they all shuffled down the hall after Archibald.

Wild plants straightened as she passed them. A rose in a hanging vase reached up and nudged her hand to welcome her.

She tried to ignore it, and the stem of the flower wrapped around Becky's wrist, playfully tugging her closer in retaliation. "Stop that!" The group of roses flinched and wilted for a moment, and Becky scoffed. "I know the lot of you better than your very poor playacting." The stems perked up immediately, and the roses bounced.

She smiled despite herself, heart softening inside its hard shell. She may have missed them, a very little bit. "I'll say goodbye before I leave again," she whispered.

Clare reached out to touch them, and they leaned gently into her fingers. "I've never seen anything like this! And I deal in magical plants."

"The magical plants in the fortress are blessed by the land. We sit atop the most powerful point in Rennedawn." The words rolled off her tongue easily after years of rote memorization.

When they entered the green room, the first thing they heard was a crash—and then a deep-sounding croak.

"Kingsley!" The boss reached out, gripped the frog by his middle, and hauled the amphibian away from spearing a fly with his tongue. "Who brought him?"

Becky waved a hand. "Oh, never mind him—my family will hardly notice. This house is filled with animals. Listen." Chirping sounds danced through the space, along with squeaks, chatters, and even a bark in there somewhere.

No. The bark had come from the hall, along with a hum of voices that made goose bumps rise along Becky's skin. Her throat grew so tight she forgot to swallow. She looked to one of the potted ferns, which waved at her, then shook when a loud crash sounded outside. The voices came closer and closer to them, growing louder and more boisterous with each passing second.

Evie's lips pulled down, and her eyes widened. "What…or I suppose, rather, *who* is that?"

Becky sighed, rubbing at her temples as the door crashed open.

"My brothers."

CHAPTER 59

EVIE

A man and a small child spilled into the room.

A room that Evie could not seem to stop marveling at, despite Becky's earlier warning. The walls were *alive*. It wasn't like the magic within the manor but something else, something that ebbed and flowed. Every flower, every leaf greeted them—when she entered, a small vine from the largest plant off in the corner had curled out and around Evie's ankle, as if it were saying hello.

What an enchanted place.

And what seemingly enchanting people lived here.

The older male was handsome. He looked like Becky—light-brown skin, wide cheeks, his hair shaved down, and his most notable feature: the set of round glasses sitting atop his regal nose, almost hiding the short scar that ran across it.

"Bex!" The younger of the two—perhaps a year or two older than Lyssa, with longer dark, curly hair—barreled into Becky, throwing both of his arms around her. "You came home! I missed you."

Becky wrapped tentative arms around the little boy, her mouth pulling up into a small smile. "Rudy, I saw you two months ago, and I send you letters every week."

"But we never get to see you *here*!" Rudy unfurled his arms, and the plants in the room moved and sniffed at his feet like loyal hounds and laid against his shoes in an affectionate manner. "You always make us come to you!"

Becky's smile faded when she looked toward the older man, who had a soft look in his friendly expression. The lithe line of his shoulders told Evie he was a warrior, someone who would fight with honor, but his eyes and the curve of his lips told her he was kind.

One of the vines snapped against her foot—probably because she was staring. "Ow!" Evie hissed at it. She swore it shook as if it was laughing at her.

"Sage." A hard voice behind her made her freeze. "What are you doing?"

She blinked at her boss with an innocent expression. "I'm being made fun of by the houseplants."

"That means they like you," a gentle voice cut in from the very man she'd been admiring, and the plant slapped her foot again.

Becky winced only slightly when the man moved forward and wrapped his arms around his sister. "We missed you, Bex."

Blade's throat bobbed as he adjusted his vest, trying to keep a steady expression when he questioned, "Bex, eh?"

Becky rolled her eyes as she and her brother parted. "An old nickname. How are you, Roland?"

Roland—Becky's brother, older if Evie had to guess—stepped back and assessed the rest of them. His eyes arrowed in on Blade with suspicion, protectiveness in his gaze.

Good. She liked that there was someone to look out for Becky the way she seemed to always be doing for other people.

"I'm well," Roland said. "But I suspect you didn't come all the way here just to ask after my health." Roland lifted a brow and folded his arms, stretching the gold-lined white fabric of his tunic. "How did you get in? I thought Mother confiscated your key."

Becky looked different for a second—more alive, more determined. "I stole it back when I left. If she takes issue with that, she can pry it from my fingers herself."

Roland adjusted his glasses, looking to the side. "You never shy away from saying something unpleasant, do you, little sister? Mother misses you dearly; she'll be thrilled that you're here. She doesn't care about the key."

Becky lifted a brow. "I'm sure."

It surprised Evie to hear that a family who thrived on goodness and honor would try to cut out one of their own, but then she remembered Rebecka's warning and the danger of their coming here. It could very well be that Becky had deserved to be ousted from her family for actions Evie wasn't aware of, but it didn't matter. She was firmly planted on the side of the HR manager, no matter what.

"There's already a dinner being planned with all of your favorites. Father is arranging it for our guest of honor, or I suppose…" Roland smiled toward the rest of them. "*Guests* of honor. And Grandmother will be so happy to see you. She's missed you most of all, I think."

"How is she?" Becky asked quietly.

"The Mystic Illness wears on her, but she perseveres. You know she has a good attitude about these things."

Becky absorbed the information with a neutral expression. "And where are Reid and Raphael?"

"Where our brothers usually are." Roland grinned playfully. "I couldn't pry them from the Trench. But they're eager to see you, too."

Evie rounded on Becky. "You have *more* brothers? Are they all this handsome?" She gestured to Roland, and he looked upon her with interest.

So many things should stay in her head. Most things, in fact.

She blushed, and the boss glared as Roland took her hand and planted a kiss on the back of it. "Evie Sage, I take it? Rebecka writes of you often. It's a pleasure to meet you."

Evie folded her hands in front of her, grinning at Becky, who was staring at her brother with treacherous fury. "Becky, you write about me?"

"He didn't say it was nice," she grumbled.

Roland laughed, a hearty guffaw. "As for our older brothers, Ms. Sage, I assure you they are far more handsome than I."

Scrunching her nose, Evie said coyly, "I think I will be the judge of that."

Roland's eyes sparkled behind his glasses, and Becky glared in tandem with The Villain. "Stop flirting with my brother."

"Yes," The Villain said through clenched teeth. "You're making Rebecka uncomfortable."

Tatianna's eyes dipped down to where their boss gripped the back of a wooden chair. "You're bending the wood, Trystan."

Roland's face signaled alarm as he turned in Trystan's direction. "Wait, you're The Villain? We have to get you away from—" But it was too late.

Plants from every corner of the room shot out at once, wrapping tightly around the boss like a serpent wrapping around its prey. And then they squeezed.

Clare yelled, Tatianna's hands began to glow, and Blade pulled a switchblade from his boot, ready to cut at the vines, but Evie was quicker.

"No!" she screamed, her dagger already drawn as she ran to cut at them. Kingsley ran alongside her, leaping on the first vine and biting just the way she'd taught him. The vines didn't take well to being attacked; they slithered around, trapping the frog along with her boss.

But Roland grabbed Evie's hand and twisted until she dropped her blade. "You can't hurt them!" Roland pleaded, apology in his tone.

An anguished shout came from Trystan, his eyes never leaving hers as one of the vines wrapped around his mouth, and before another word was said, the plants enveloped him completely, dragging him across the room and through a hidden passageway behind the bookcase that shut tightly as soon as he was through.

He was gone.

"Let me go!" Evie cried.

Roland didn't release Evie's wrist until Becky landed a hard punch to her brother's face. He dropped her, and Becky tugged Evie close. "What the fuck is wrong with you, Roland?" Becky screamed. "That was my *boss*!"

Clare sprinted to the bookcase, trying to get it to budge, but to no avail. "Where are they taking him?"

Roland held his now-bleeding nose, glasses dislodged. "Where all villainous intruders with dark magic are taken if they enter Fortis land."

The entire room stood still.

Becky finished his sentence, whispering in horror: "The Trench."

CHAPTER 60

THE VILLAIN

Trystan was going to die.

Vines and leaves closed over his nose and mouth, cutting off his air, wrapping around his middle and squeezing at his lungs. Black spots clouded his vision, and a chant began in his mind.

Don't pass out. Don't pass out. Don't pass out.

But his body was failing him. If he didn't get a breath of oxygen in the next few moments, his eyes would close, and there was no telling if they would open again. His mind reached for something to hold on to, something to sustain him against the creeping darkness.

Revenge. If he didn't stay alive, Benedict would continue playing the gallant leader adored by all. Doing whatever was necessary to stay on the throne, even if it meant infecting his people with an incurable disease. The prophecy was Trystan's to fulfill—he had to live so he could continue to seek revenge.

But he was letting go…

Evie.

Her lovely face appeared before him: her lips, her eyes, her smile. The snorts that came out of her and the shock on her face that always followed, like she didn't realize herself capable of such untethered amusement. He saw her face pale, lifeless on a marble table, her hands clasped over flowers, her eyes closed.

Black spots. No air.

She was alive. She was alive, and the makers of this world were in for a true surprise if they believed he would ever be separated from her again.

Heavy lids weighed down over his eyes, but his power didn't sleep.

It woke up.

Black mist angled itself like a blade, cutting at the vines and releasing the ones around his middle and his mouth, allowing him to choke down sweet air. He'd never take simple breaths for granted again. He drew another and another, regaining his control, regaining himself as he coughed.

Sage had tried to save him, but she'd been forcibly stopped.

A cry of fury left him.

The surge of anger was enough for his magic to finish slicing away at the vines until they freed him completely, dropping him to the hard dirt ground. Stumbling to his feet, he blinked in the dim light of—

Where in the deadlands had the blasted weeds taken him?

He was in the middle of what looked to be some sort of arena, raised walls all around him. There was no clear means of escape. A skylight above let the sun beat down on his face. His shirt was torn in the middle, like he'd just done battle with a behemoth and not an overgrown houseplant.

On the far wall, there was a lowered gate. He walked toward it. Black mist searched around him, his power feeling ahead for anything living among the darkness. He'd never been as grateful for his magic as he was just then.

"I wouldn't go any closer to that gate if I were you," a low voice called from beyond the raised wall.

Trystan was searching for whoever the voice belonged to when an animalistic growl echoed out from the blackness beyond the gate, causing him to fly backward. *What in the deadlands was that?*

"State your name!" the same voice commanded, and Trystan looked up to find two men standing outside the arena, perched on a viewing stage, staring down at him with crossed arms. Trystan would hazard a guess that they were Rebecka's other two brothers.

"I'm The Villain," he said without feeling. "Cower in fear, and when you're done doing that, kindly lower a ladder." Something plopped onto his foot, and when he looked down, he nearly wept for the frustration of it all. "Kingsley, you are killing me."

The frog stared up at him, and he sighed and pulled him up.

"Is that a frog?"

He tossed Kingsley, his friend, upward as gently as possible. The amphibian's foot gripped the side wall. Success. "Sort of," he replied. "Let me leave and you can have him."

A chuckle sounded from the curly-haired man. "I'm afraid it's unlikely you'll leave here at all, good sir. Or—rather, evil sir, I suppose." The man stroked his chin and ignored the glare from the other Fortis sibling, who looked upon Trystan with the most disdainful expression imaginable. His HR manager would likely frown upon him maiming these two dolts with his magic. That was a shame.

"I am merely here on business, not to harm you...Raphael?" The quiet man nodded curtly. He'd guessed Rebecka's oldest brother's name from the meager information she'd shared of her life when he'd hired her. Trystan always remembered names, even when he wanted to forget them.

"And I'm Reid." The curly-haired brother bowed. "Since we're exchanging pleasantries."

Trystan crossed his arms over his ripped shirt. "You find this pleasant?"

Reid shrugged, nearing the wall's edge. "I do. It's been rather boring around here, and I'm not the one in the Trench of Anguish."

"Reid. Shut up," Raphael snapped, moving toward a lever that looked too menacing to initiate anything good.

Trystan cleared his throat, looking at the two men and back to the gate with the unfriendly growling beyond. "I assume the anguish comes from whatever is in *there*?" He pointed toward it.

Raphael let the question fall unanswered. "You shouldn't have come here, Villain. Nor should you have brought my sister."

Reid shifted, uneasy. Trystan filed that unease away; it looked deeper than familial obligation.

"Your sister's affairs are her own to express to you," he called back to Raphael. "I am here because our merry chase through the kingdom looking for answers has brought us to your doorstep."

"You're looking for a star," Reid guessed. *Was that the blasted rumor spreading?* They may as well have said he was looking for a birthday candle— it would be better for his reputation.

He had to correct them. "I'm looking for a woman."

Reid's mouth flattened. "Aren't we all?"

"Reid! No more talking." Raphael's commanding voice boomed through the room, as did the creak of the lever he angled backward. "Villain, your magic is a scourge to the people of Rennedawn." The gate raised, and a low rumbling prickled the hairs on the back of Trystan's neck. "I do not wish to hurt you. But you brought yourself here and left us no choice. Now you will be tested by the hands of destiny, the world's oldest magic."

Trystan felt a wash of fear as booming steps echoed in the dark. "And if I don't pass…?"

Something appeared—worse than Fate's creatures, worse than death itself.

He barely heard Raphael finish his sentence.

"You die."

CHAPTER 61

BECKY

This was all her fault.

She should never have allowed their boss to walk across the entry. She'd foolishly thought her family's belief in unconditional acceptance would extend even to The Villain. This place was meant to be a refuge, but it was to be his prison.

Though he could survive the test, could be deemed worthy. There was a chance.

"Rebecka, my goodness! You've only been home twenty minutes and the house is in an uproar. Whatever is the matter?" Renna, her mother, glided into the room, her long red hair cascading down her back in auburn waves. "My sweet girl, you've come home." Renna took a step toward her, and Becky took four large steps back.

Renna flinched.

Blade moved next to Becky, angling his body slightly in front of her, shielding her from her mother's hurt. His purple vest oddly fit the scene, like he was the one who belonged here, not her. Tatianna and Clare drifted slowly toward the bookshelf in the back corner of the room, like they wanted to escape from the familial conflict. Becky wished she could escape it, too.

"Mother." Becky folded her lips and nodded, feeling far too much like a girl of twelve, not a woman of twenty-five. "The fortress has taken my boss as its next victim. If you've any ideas on how to reverse it, now would be the time." She kept her composure in the question, as she always did. But there was a jittery panic at the thought of her boss being hurt and the trickle effect it would have on the others. There were few people who mattered to her, well and truly. Inconveniently, nearly every single one of them was under this roof.

Renna's eyes widened as Becky's father tumbled in after her. Julius Fortis had married into their family when he'd met her mother at a local fair. He'd been selling flowers, her mother had made them dance, and the rest was a fairy tale. Her father's love was instant and intense, as he loved everyone — as he loved Becky. It was a discomfiting thought to Becky rather than a comfort, to be so consumed by affection for another that it compromised all your sense and restraint. Becky far preferred to remain in control of her life, of herself. Never mind that her eyes kept searching for Blade. That feeling would pass, and any hints of affection would ease. Her father did not hold such principles.

Julius didn't give her the chance to back away, just moved his tall frame over to her before lifting her from the floor and spinning her around. "My little Becky! How I've missed you!" He dropped her and frowned. "You're too thin. Is The Villain starving you? Is that one of his methods?"

"Julius!" Renna scolded. "Show some sensitivity. Your daughter is quite worried for the man. He's been taken to the Trench for judgment."

Julius frowned, removing his gardening hat to reveal a thick head of shiny black hair. His brown skin was covered in sweat from the blaring sun's heat. "Oh dear." He whispered to her, "Could you get another job?"

Becky slapped her forehead, and she heard Roland groan into his hands. "No, Dad," Becky said, looking to Evie, who was watching the scene, bewildered. "We're going to err on the side of optimism and assume he will survive till supper." She assured her coworker, "He *will* survive, Evie. I'm certain of it."

She wasn't, but if there was one thing she couldn't tolerate, it was Evie's sadness. It was the equivalent of watching a baby deer be pushed down by a stiff wind: sad, helpless, and a little pathetic.

Renna's head turned slowly toward Evie, and a small gasp escaped her lips. "Oh. It's you. Oh, my dear." Her mother was in front of Evie in seconds with her hands clasped around her cheeks. Evie looked too stunned to move, eyes darting to Becky's. They seemed to say, *What do I do?*

Becky threw her hands up as if to reply, *I don't know!*

"Um, hello, Lady Fortis," Evie said with a shaky smile — one that didn't reach her eyes. They were too spun with worry. "Do you, um… That is to say… You know who I am?"

Renna beamed, pushing one of Evie's loose hairs back. "You have your mother's curls. She told me you did, but it's another thing entirely to see them upon your head."

Evie softened, Becky's mother melting her like butter left too close to the fire. Her mother often had that effect on people. Becky rolled her eyes.

"My mother?" Evie asked. "So, we were right. She's here?"

Renna released Evie and took her hand, pulling her over to sit. "Archibald, would you go fetch Reid to update us on The Villain's welfare for the daughter of my dearest friend?" Archibald followed the command posthaste, and her mother turned back to Evie with a sympathetic expression. "I wish I had better means to assist in the matter. The Fortis magic can be unruly and unpredictable at times. As much as we can manage it, it simply cannot be controlled completely. The Villain, I'm afraid, will be no exception to ancient destiny's tests if he possesses the power he's rumored to. But hope is not lost."

She eyed Evie with calm curiosity. Becky's mother had always been able to see through people, right to the core of their feelings; Becky had hated it as a child. She hated it even more now, watching it be used on someone so vulnerable. "I can see you care for him a great deal."

Evie's eyes watered. "I…I do."

The door to the green room opened farther, and her grandmother, Ramona, was wheeled in by a footman, who bowed and promptly left the room. Her grandmother smiled wide, the high planes of her face lined and spotty. But she looked more lively than she had the last time Becky saw her.

Becky reached her in two strides, leaning down to plant a gentle kiss on Ramona's wrinkled cheek. "I'm glad to see you up and about, Grandmother."

Ramona Fortis was a spitfire with very little tolerance for nonsense. When she'd fallen ill, it had devastated the family so tremendously, it created tensions that never dissipated, opened wounds that never healed.

"You think a little magical illness can keep an old girl down?" Grandmother laughed, then coughed harshly into her arm. But her grandmother lightened the weight of the worried glances from everyone in the room by observing, "This illness is a bitch."

Becky barked a laugh and clapped a hand over her mouth. "Grandmother!"

Her grandmother's brown eyes twinkled as she pulled a strand of hair from her pulled-back bun. The gesture made Becky feel like she'd swallowed something thick as she twined her fingers together.

Renna leaned down and kissed her mother on the cheek, too, then smiled up at Evie. "Mother, this is Nura Sage's daughter, Evie."

Ramona's eyes widened, a gasp sounding on her lips. "Oh my. There is a likeness between them, isn't there?"

The pleasant smile on Evie's face was forced, and her fingers were squeezing into her palms in a way that looked painful.

Becky couldn't take any more. "Enough, Mother. You're torturing her. Where is her mother? Where is Nura Sage?"

Renna frowned. "Rebecka, do not be rude. I still expect you to use your manners when under our roof."

Becky's face heated, the sensation climbing up her neck; she felt like she was a mere child once again, scolded for stealing a cookie. But the next thing she knew, Blade was objecting. "Excuse me, Lady Fortis, but you will not meet another person on this continent with better manners than your daughter."

Oh, she wished he hadn't done that. Because now her mother's and her grandmother's hawk eyes were on him. Sharp and shrewd, they assessed him as Renna asked, "And who might you be?"

Blade didn't cower, merely stepped forward with a gentle bow. "Bladen Gushiken, Lady Fortis. Of the Gleaming City Gushikens."

Bladen? Becky snorted into her hand, and she watched Blade's eyes dart to her at the sound. There was a look of astonishment on his face, like he couldn't believe it had come out of her.

Renna looked impressed. "A politician's son for a partner, Rebecka? And here I thought you had no interest in such pursuits." Her mother made a point to be aware of all the noble families in Rennedawn. Of course she'd know Blade's family name immediately, his father being one of the king's valued advisors. Even more reason why Blade should've kept his mouth shut.

Becky waved a hand through the air. "Mother, he is not my partner. He's merely a colleague: a beast trainer at the office." He wasn't *merely* anything, but Becky couldn't say that—not when it could so easily be used against her.

Blade seemed to take it in stride, though. "It's true, my lady. I have no association with my father any longer. I am disowned with no footing in society. No title. I am a beast trainer, nothing more, and certainly *not* your daughter's partner."

Renna absorbed the information with a nod. Becky frowned, and Blade grinned as he tacked a word on the end: "Yet."

Her mother laughed, and her grandmother whistled, eyeing Blade like a prized piece of meat. "I'll tell you, if I was sixty years younger..."

Becky's eyes flared, and Renna chuckled behind her hand. "Rebecka, please reconsider. Good with animals *and* charming are the most admirable traits."

"The arms." Her grandmother whistled again, and Becky buried her face in her hands.

"Deadlands bury me," Becky grumbled.

When she finally peeked up, Blade was grinning so wide she thought he'd split a lip, and her mother and grandmother were smiling right back. "So, Mr. Gushiken, I take it the dragon currently destroying our lawn is yours?"

From two decades with her mother, Becky knew when she was trying to change topics. "Nura Sage, Mother? Your dearest friend? Where is she?"

Renna brightened. "Of course. Forgive me—too much excitement. It riles the blood." Evie was wringing her hands so hard, Becky half expected water to escape them. "Your mother was with us for some time, Evie. It's been such a blessing to have my dear friend so near again. But I'm afraid she is away with one of our healers at our second home by the Lilac Sea."

Becky was incredulous. "Why would you send her away? Don't you know the king is looking for her? The danger she's in?"

Renna's eyes flared, too, as she stood to match Becky's height. "I have known Nura longer than you've been alive. I have seen her at every stage of life, and you do not know the ghost she was when she fell at our doorstep. Even the boys were appalled. Right, Roland?"

Roland fidgeted with his glasses, wincing. "She was rather worse for wear, but the poor woman has been through a lot," he said gently.

"She was vacant behind the eyes. A husk. The woman I knew was full of laughter and light, but it was as if all those things had been sucked right out of her. The specialist said he'd never seen a person so badly mutilated by magic. We tried everything we could to help her but eventually decided to send her to the very best place with the very best care, and by all accounts, she is improving." Renna exhaled, tension leaving her shoulders. "Now that her daughter is here, I will have word sent for her to return at once. She should be here in two days' time at most."

Renna looked at Becky then, motioning toward the corner to speak privately. She followed her reluctantly, rubbing at her arms as her mother spoke in hushed tones. "When Nura returns and the rest of your coworkers leave, might you consider staying, even just a few extra days?" Her mother was so hopeful, it hurt.

Becky sighed, running a finger over her loose strand of hair. "I can't just forget what you did, Mother, no matter how much you want me to."

In her mother's desperation for a cure to the Mystic Illness, she'd taken it upon herself to extend an invitation to King Benedict, to see if their combined resources might lead to a solution. Becky had been a different person then, with her colorful clothes and her unbound hair—even her glasses had been brighter, a magenta pink to match the flower on the front door. Her greatest crime was being eager to please.

The heir to the Fortis family's magic had to be perfect. She'd been chosen by the land to inherit. Her oldest brother, Raphael, had been angry at the revelation, and by all accounts it should've been him. But Becky had been born with exceptional gifts. This land called to her, and she called to it.

Benedict had seen that gift—and an opportunity. He'd made large claims of a cure to the Mystic Illness, promising that all Becky had to do was offer the use of her magic. Her mother had agreed for her; it hadn't occurred to her to ask what Becky wanted.

"I followed all the rules you ever gave me," Becky told her mother now in a low tone. "I walked a narrow line my entire life, and the only thing I got in return was censure for not wanting to give away what belonged to me."

Renna flinched. "That was a terrible day. I let Benedict manipulate me into believing that your magic was the only way to cure your grandmother, and I was so desperate then. You know how we repel the crown; it was misguided. But things are different now. I've learned from my mistakes."

Becky steeled herself, putting iron bars around her resolve. "Which ones? Letting Benedict leave after I refused you? Or when you tried to steal my magic anyway?"

A tear slipped down Renna's cheek, but she quickly swiped it away, eyes darting to the far corner of the room. "Oh, please don't touch that, dear," Renna called to Clare, who'd wandered away from the bookshelf and was reaching out toward a large, stemmed flower by the window with pearl-like petals.

Clare tilted her head and moved her hand away. "This is a memory plant, yes?"

Tatianna frowned, still staring at the bookshelf. "What's a memory plant?"

Becky remembered the rare flower from her childhood, tarnished as it was now in her eyes—there were only three left in the world, and two of them resided in the fortress. "It holds memories the way people do; it can even mimic them on occasion." She pointedly looked at her mother. "And some people have attempted to use it in the past to siphon magic."

Her mother flinched.

Clare leaned an ear down to listen to the flower, not reading the distress coming from Becky or her mother, but they all startled when Reid stormed into the room, boyish and rugged as always. "Hey, sis!" Reid waved at her, never overly affectionate. He'd always been her favorite. "We, um. The Villain is…"

Evie perked up, panic written all over her face. "He's what?"

Reid's eyes widened when he saw her, and he swallowed. "I think he's dying."

CHAPTER 62

THE VILLAIN

Trystan woke up with a start.

A wooden table sat in front of him, where his head had rested before he jolted awake. A dream. Had he dreamed the whole thing? Even the monster about to attack him from the dark?

The clanging of pots and pans rang in his ears until he was out of his seat and taking in the room.

This wasn't the manor kitchen—this was...

"Make anything good today, brother?"

Malcolm?

His younger brother wandered into the room—and he was indeed younger. A teenager of no more than seventeen. Malcolm's hair had been longer then, tied back from his head with a red bandana.

This was a hallucination. Something had put him here, but he couldn't remember what or how, could barely remember details about himself. Anytime something solid formed, it fell through his fingers—like dust or happiness or dark, curly hair— Wait, whose hair?

Speaking of which, now that he noticed, his fingers were closed around something warm. It was a pie tray filled with sugared crust, and the intense smell of blueberry bloomed into a delicious aroma that warmed the small space of his childhood home's kitchen. Someone was showing him a memory, though he couldn't pinpoint this specific one.

"He is not going to work for the king, Arthur! I refuse to allow it!"

Deadlands save him, that was his mother.

"You're going to wreck the boy's future over a petty feud. This will be good for him, Amara. He'll socialize at court. All he does now is keep to his room and make up recipes all hours of the night. His only friend is Edwin! Don't you hear the whispers about him from the rest of the village? Doesn't it bother you?"

Oh. He did remember this now. The way one remembered being hit over the head with a large rock. "Tryst?" his little brother asked, concerned, already helping himself to a piece of pie.

"It's nothing," he whispered against the echo of his younger voice, his younger self.

It went dark again.

A familiar smell and the sound of agonized cries surrounded him—his cell; the darkness. His breath came in heavy rasps, and the memory of his cries came out of his mouth with no warning. "Benedict! Please! I'm sorry! I'll be better—I swear it! I'll give up my magic! Please come back! I don't want to be evil!" He yelled and slammed his fists against the bars, sliding his hands down them until he fell to his knees. "Please come back for me."

His eyes fell shut again.

When he opened them once more, he emptied his stomach on a large patch of grass, wiped his mouth on his black sleeve, and then blinked. Sunlight burned against his pupils. There was green shrubbery all around and...a running stream. Hickory Forest.

"Argh." He clutched his pained middle and came away with sticky redness—blood. A jostling at his waist made him grab for his satchel, and he opened the flap to see Kingsley sitting inside. This was—he was seeing—

Her.

Against the lining of the trees, light shone off someone walking along the edge, a shock of color coming in through the cracks. So bright, he nearly walked toward it, until he heard the call of male voices. The men who were after him, after Kingsley. He dropped to the ground to hide among the plants, ducking his hands over his head... He'd hide there, and he knew he'd be fine.

A moment passed, and he could feel the person from before moving closer. The sounds of a blade being unsheathed made him tense, but when he glanced up from the cover of his black cloak, he saw gently curved hips and sensible boots. Nothing else... He couldn't risk moving his head up. It was a foolish village girl. What a nuisance.

His arm darted out, grabbing her wrist, and yanked hard. She fell, and his hand closed over the softness of her lips. Sage—it was Sage. The lucid part of his mind was peeking through, but then it was swallowed again, replaced with his current reality.

This was their first meeting.

He pulled her down and against him, struggling to remember that this wasn't real. This was a vision of things past, a test. *A test.* But the memory played through anyway. "Be quiet, you little urchin, or you'll get us both killed."

She was struggling against him, wafting the smell of roses about them like a heady mist.

Everything went dark again.

His eyes closed and opened.

This time, he was in his office, at his desk, but this didn't feel like a memory; the room grew hazy under the smoke from the candles lit all about the room. The night sky was dark as the moon shone through the windows, alongside one shining star.

Why was he here? He paused, trying to remember. This wasn't real. Was it? What was he doing in his office?

Disoriented and confused, he heard a pained whimper on the other side of his office doors. Something about it caused the blood to freeze in his veins. He yanked the doors open.

Standing at the end of the hall, half hidden in darkness, half illuminated by candlelight—the sight so foreign in his safe place, his empire—stood King Benedict with a crown perched atop his regal head.

And a knife against Evie's throat.

CHAPTER 63

EVIE

Trystan's screams shoved her heart up into her throat as she rushed down the arena stairs toward what seemed to be an elevated viewing platform, followed by his other employees and friends.

"It's killing him!" Evie cried. "Trystan! Snap out of it!"

Whatever the creature in the arena was, it wasn't human. Gleaming white shimmered off it, making it almost impossible to look at. The form it took was hardly a form at all, just an array of shine that reminded her of the sun's rays descending to the earth, unnatural and a signal that the world had been turned upside down. Just looking at it made her feel sick to her stomach.

Becky grabbed Raphael by the collar. He'd been standing sentry over the scene when Reid led them to the Trench. "Stop this. Stop this now!"

"Or what?" Raphael's eyes narrowed coldly. "You'll kill me? Ruin the family? You've already made fair attempts at both, Rebecka."

Becky reeled back, and Evie turned to him, directing all her anger at the man. "You're an asshole!" She went to charge at him, dagger raised, but Becky tugged her back by the wrist.

"He's a Fortis warrior, you ninny. He'll eviscerate you."

Trystan's cries rattled the entire space from the arena floor below, turning her ire into debilitating pain.

"I have to help him," she whispered, a tear falling freely down her cheek. She'd become no better than a watering pot. But tears were a quiet problem... if the sniffling didn't start.

She sniffled and glared inwardly at the betrayal.

Stepping up, she gripped the side wall of the viewing platform, just as

Raphael gave her a genuine warning. "No person has ever tried to stop the creature of destiny and lived. Its magic is older than time itself—it *is* time itself. Right now, it's wrapping The Villain in every moment of his life touched by such magic. By destiny. If you interfere, you'll get yourself killed!" Raphael was shouting at her now—annoying, since she'd only met him five seconds ago. A new record.

She sighed a shaky breath—but he was right, of course. Raphael knew the magical creature far better than she. But she had one powerful and far more ridiculous tool in her arsenal.

Spite.

She flung herself over the edge of the platform, falling ungracefully to the dirt. She looked up and smirked at the outraged oldest Fortis brother, who was leaning over the edge. She approached the light and the ancient magic froze, turning its sickly shimmer on her. It didn't have eyes or a face...or a head. But she could feel it watching her, could feel it sense her awareness around the shocked ray of light gleaming off it. If she didn't know any better, she'd think it a silvered sun—impossibly large and impossibly dangerous. This had been a miscalculation.

"The destiny creature is searching for any ounce of goodness worth saving," Raphael called down to her. "It will test his resolve, his soul—and judging by his screams, he will not be saved. The creature will consume him *and* his soul. What can you possibly do?"

She shrugged against the panic trying to consume her and reached Trystan in three long strides, hovering her hand over his. She closed her fingers around destiny and its overwhelming light as she said with a sureness that was absolutely faked:

"I'll give him mine."

CHAPTER 64

THE VILLAIN

If this was a dream, he'd like a refund. Or a drill to his skull to pry the thought from his head.

The man who'd stolen his future stood before him. The one who had set him on a course he had never planned to pursue. *You were crafted to be evil*, Benedict had told him, his magic made for pain, for hurt. There would be no other path for Trystan.

Except there had been. One that led him to the stream at the edge of Hickory Forest, where tall trees hid the greatest of misdeeds. There had been no path other than the one that led him to Evie.

"Release her," he said with enough anger that it felt as though it shook the walls.

Benedict grinned as he tightened the knife against Sage's throat. "I *could*. Or I could save you the inevitable and end her life right here, right now."

Sage whimpered, which was a bit odd, but all his mind could focus on was her pain—especially when she whispered, "Trystan, help me."

He could feel his gaze soften. He wanted to reach for her, to comfort her despite knowing he was terrible at it. She had him so torn apart that he wouldn't mind the fumbling awkwardness of it, of trying to warm someone despite his coldness. She made it impossible not to try at things, even when he knew he would fail. He liked to try, liked trying with *her* even more.

Loved.

Not that word again, he thought, mentally swatting at himself.

"I'll do anything you want," he said solemnly, resigned.

Benedict's eyebrows shot up, his interest piqued. "I think I want to hurt her. She can see your magic, Trystan—she's making you weak. I'd be doing you a favor."

The knife was drawn tighter against her skin, and a single drop of blood eased down her throat.

"Stop!" It was agony. "Whatever your price, I will pay it. I do not care who I need to kill, what I need to destroy; if you release her unharmed, I am at your disposal."

The king smiled, and Sage did, too, as Benedict released her. She flew across the empty office and into his arms. But it felt…wrong. Something in him flinched at her touch, but she trembled, and he couldn't resist holding her tightly against him, breathing in the smell of her hair.

Wrong! his body screamed.

But Sage angled herself up, pressing every inch of herself into him. He may be The Villain, but in this moment, he was only a man—one with plenty of weaknesses. One of which being that he'd need to be six feet belowground to not respond to the heat of her body, to the feeling of her hips, her breasts, the beating of her heart. He counted the beats: *one, two, three, four.*

Bumps rose along his skin as she pressed up farther against him and whispered in his ear, "Destroy the Fortis family, free the hands of destiny from its cage, and you can have me."

Wrong, his brain argued as Sage arched up on her toes, her sweet breath brushing against his lips.

Shut it, he argued back as her lips dusted over his, and he bit back a groan until her mouth was fully upon his and he was lost. There had been a threat in the room before—a part of him knew this—but whoever that was, they were gone now. His only thoughts were of her, her voice, her lips, her body beneath his hands, which slid tentatively over her waist.

Wrong.

Wrong.

Wrong.

"Do you think"—he spoke quietly against the warmth of her lips—"that I would fall for such an obvious, *vile* trick? That this *farce* could ever compare to the real thing?" He pushed her away, wiping his mouth with the back of his hand.

The fake Sage reeled back with wide, innocent eyes. They weren't hers. He could clearly see that now. When he looked into them, he felt nothing.

"Even so," the fake Sage said, the voice sounding different, too—wrong.

"This is your chance to be with her fully. You won't ever have that in the real world. She won't ever have *you*. I am crafted from destiny, and I can see resistance from her *and* from you. She will turn away from you eventually. Or you can have all of her, in a way, now."

He nudged the fake back farther, gently, having difficulty causing any actual harm to a figure who resembled her so. It was another display of feebleness.

At this point, he was collecting weaknesses like deranged little knickknacks.

"I would sooner take the scraps she lay at my feet," he stated, "than commit myself to a cheap imitation."

The fake Sage's lip curled into a snarl, but not before an object soared through the air, knocking her in the back of the head.

They both turned in the direction it had come from, and there, covered in grime, her hair unbound and her face furious, was Evie—the real one. He knew, down to the marrow of his bones—deep within everything that made him human, made him whole—that she was real. And she was here, in his dream. How?

She smirked. "I do take the 'don't beat yourself up' sentiment quite seriously, but you are making it awfully tempting."

He smiled despite himself, and the word he'd been keeping at bay echoed again, but this time he didn't shove it away.

Love.

He'd fight for it—for her—no matter the price.

CHAPTER 65

EVIE

It was a new low, in every sense, having to stare at one's own backside.

When she first saw the impostor, she'd panicked. Then, when she saw how close the fake was to her boss, she got…very angry. Enough to pick up the first object she could find and chuck it—hard.

Had that been a paperweight? She *knew* they'd make a good weapon. She giggled.

"I'm sorry, did that really hurt?" She winced at the hand that covered her impostor's head.

"Sage?"

She stood at attention. "Yes, sir?"

"Don't apologize to the ancient monster, if you please." He didn't sound exasperated, as he usually did at her antics, but rather…relieved.

She scrunched her nose. "But I hit her with a paperweight."

Fake Her hissed and ducked backward, snarling in the corner.

"Take note," her boss said, moving swiftly in front of her. "That's what you look like before you have your cauldron brew in the morning."

She gripped the back of his arm as the creature hissed and snarled again. With a sour expression, she said, "I should've thrown the paperweight at *you*."

A voice came out of the body that was now changing back into what had appeared in the Fortis arena: the unnatural white light that had no face. As reassuring as having Trystan's arm in her grip was, she still felt her heart pounding erratically in her chest.

"You're too late—he's already failed," the light taunted. "His dark soul is mine. Hand it over or you'll remain trapped here forever, tormented by great evil."

Evie curled her lip and nodded earnestly. "That's a pretty average work week in the office, honestly."

The boss's gaze flicked down to her. "Why, thank you," he deadpanned.

"You're welcome!" she said with a playful grin.

"Cease!" the voice hissed again. Even without a face, she could feel its impatience.

The boss sighed, holding his hands up in surrender. "Hands of destiny, I surrender. Take my evil essence and allow her to leave."

Right, like she'd thrown herself into this just so he could play the self-sacrificing hero. "Don't be ridiculous. Here." She removed the dagger from her waist and held it out toward the light. "How about a trade? This dagger is magically imbued and weirdly linked to the scar on my shoulder. You could probably make me dance like a puppet."

The hands of destiny—which, sure, why *wouldn't* Becky's unfairly attractive family have a room for something called "the hands of destiny"?— flinched away from the dagger, hissing again. *Noteworthy.*

But the boss's voice drowned out her musings. "You are not bartering your dagger for our freedom, Sage. It's hardly an even trade."

Destiny spoke again, interrupting them. "You would offer your most precious possession to save such twisted evil?"

She rolled her eyes. "I've suffered more at the hands of those who claim to be good than those who are deemed to be evil." She held the dagger up high. "Take it."

"No." The Villain's face was seething with anger. "No, Sage. You cannot argue your way out of ancient magic. As convincing as you think yourself, you cannot defy natural law. Take the deal and get out of here."

He turned to the light now.

"I'm evil," he told destiny. "I've killed countless people, tortured a dozen more for information, and tormented and struck fear into the hearts of nearly every person in Rennedawn—and likely the whole of the continent, too. I shouldn't pass any test of goodness."

Evie interrupted him by clapping a hand over his mouth. "He's like a teddy bear that got hold of a kitchen knife."

The Villain pinched the bridge of his nose, shaking away her hand, but destiny's creature cut in, a hint of amusement in its ancient voice. "No need to continue arguing. I forgot how tiring humans can be. You already passed."

Her boss looked like he wanted to argue again, and she pressed her shoe over his boot and furiously shook her head.

He, of course, ignored her. "How is that possible? What was the test—who can bicker the longest?"

The hands of destiny shook its illuminated head. "No, Trystan Maverine." He stopped short, and so did she as the light hovered over them, leaning down and whispering something in the boss's ear that made him stand so rigid, it looked as if his bones were about to crack.

The next thing she knew, she was being flung against the dirt of the arena ground. Evie turned over and coughed and coughed until she blinked the world back into focus. She felt like some haphazard artist had taken her body apart and put it back together in all the wrong places.

She felt around for Trystan, but instead of catching the softness of his shirt or the warmth of his skin, the back of her hand landed somewhere near his forehead, which felt like it was on *fire*.

In the background, she could hear the gate of the cage closing, but all she could focus on were his closed eyes, his chest rising and falling too slowly.

"Sir?" She shook his shoulder. "Trystan?" His eyes fluttered open, and he looked at her so curiously, Evie wanted to shake his head to see what words would fall out.

Trystan's eyes remained unfocused as he stared at her. "It can't be."

"What? It can't be what?" she asked quietly, pushing damp strands of hair off his forehead and moving to cradle his head in her lap. "What did it whisper to you? Are you sick? What's wrong?"

"I wish it was different. I wish… I wish…" he murmured, eyes fluttering shut.

I wish…what?

Evie swallowed and stared at their onlookers. Renna and Julius were ushering down servants with a medical gurney. While Tatianna kneeled beside her, hovering glowing hands over Trystan's still form, Kingsley appeared, tapping a webbed foot against the boss's forehead.

She addressed no one in particular. "I think…we will be late for dinner."

The boss's fingers twirled around hers, grabbing tight to her hand, eyes shooting open on a gasp as he was loaded onto the stretcher. "Don't leave me."

She gripped his hand as hard as she could. "I won't. I promise."

But just as she said the words, there was a prickling feeling on the back of her neck, like she was being watched by someone. And in that moment, she feared very much that she'd just made a promise she wouldn't be able to keep.

CHAPTER 66

EVIE

The sunset was spilling an array of pinks, oranges, and golds into an otherwise dreary room.

"Evie, dear? Are you in here?" Renna Fortis's gentle voice filtered into the airy space of the infirmary, where only two sick beds were occupied: the first by Trystan and the second by Becky's grandmother, Ramona. Both had been asleep the entire time she'd been up there.

Evie turned toward Renna, damp rag in hand. "I'm here, Lady Fortis."

"Oh, I wish you'd call me Renna or even Ren. That's what your mother calls me."

It was strange to have a connection to her mother so close; so many questions floated up, threatening to boil over.

Renna grinned. "I know that face. Ask whatever you'd like."

But her question was somber. "Do you think she'll be okay?"

Renna's grin slowly dropped, her eyes darting to Ramona's sleeping face. "I think —" She sucked in a breath. "I think your mother is one of the strongest people I know. You'll be the best sort of reminder and motivator for her to get better. The best parts of her live in you." She squeezed Evie's hand.

And the worst parts, too.

"I wish I saw more of myself in Rebecka," Renna admitted, walking over to her mother and re-tucking in her blankets, then laying the back of her hand to her mother's head. "She's such a mystery to me. Always so quiet and reserved. I worry she'll shut herself off from happiness because she's so difficult."

"Becky isn't difficult," Evie said, her cheeks heating at the unfairness of the statement, at how little Becky's mother truly knew her daughter. "She's stern, of course, but her job sort of demands that."

Renna smiled placatingly. "Please do not think that I am trying to say anything negative. Rebecka is my daughter, and I love her more than life, more than breath. I am merely used to her ways of being, and not all of them are good for her."

It didn't matter then that Renna was her mother's friend or that she was kind to her. Evie plopped the rag in the bowl and stood. "Forgive me, but you know an entirely different version of your daughter than I. Becky is fair-minded and shows kindness in ways so subtle you almost don't even know it's happening. She doesn't need the credit for it. She's not showy or boastful even when she should be. She makes the office safe. Do you know how rare that is? I've *never* had that. You think I'm the best of my mother? Well, Becky is the best of The Villain's office. Without her rules, that place would be in shambles, and while I appreciate your kindness and hospitality, I wish you would extend all of it to your daughter instead."

Evie exhaled and sat back down. The boss's hand moved slightly toward her own. Even unconscious, he could read her distress.

Renna looked mortified. "I, um—" Evie felt a small twinge of guilt. "Would you excuse me? There's a plate of food for you just there, and one for The Villain when he awakens." Renna was gone before she could blink a second time.

"As far as speeches go, I can't bring myself to regret that one," Evie said, dabbing more cold water against Trystan's burning forehead. She hoped her mother's friend would listen.

"Why did you lie?"

"Argh!" Evie dropped the cloth right onto the boss's face with a hard *plop*. "Oh, sorry, sir." She giggled nervously before swiping it off. He hadn't awoken. "Deadlands, Becky, the bats in the office don't lurk the way you do."

"Stop changing the subject, you ninny. I was in the hallway and overheard what you said."

Evie waved an accusatory finger. "You were eavesdropping."

Becky folded her arms with a dubious lift to her lips. "Your voice carries. I would've heard you if I was standing clear across the estate."

Fair point. She shrugged. "Regardless, I didn't lie. I meant every word."

Becky looked vulnerable behind her lenses, her hair looser than usual, like being around her family unraveled her normal staid composure. "Y-You think my rules are important?"

Evie smiled softly, folding her hands in her lap. "Becky, without you, I likely would have died twelve times over by now." She chewed on her lip. "I think I've gone most of my life without any sort of structure, and when you presented it so steadfastly, my first instinct was to hate it. But that isn't fair, especially when it's come to make me feel so secure and safe. Most of my life, I've been attempting in haphazard ways to fashion myself into a safe person for others, but I hardly realized when someone else was trying to be that for me."

Becky looked deeply uncomfortable. "Well…I love structure." She winced. "But I understand why it would be a difficult adjustment for someone who is not used to it. I'm…also…*sorry*."

Evie laughed so hard she felt like she might cry.

When Becky saw the tears, she held up a frantic hand. "I beg you not to weep!" She pulled up another stool and sat beside Evie, rolling her eyes. "Even when I try to pay you a compliment, you are difficult." Evie mimed zipping her lips shut. Becky rolled her eyes again, but Evie could tell it was in good humor. "I mean to say that when you first began working in the office, you were unprofessional, disorganized, and chaotic—"

Evie interrupted. "I'm still those things."

"Can I finish?" she said pointedly, and Evie shut her mouth. "But I realize now how much those things are needed, how balance is needed. There was truly no one better for your job."

Evie winced, feeling past regrets boil to the surface. "Becky, it should've been you. We both know you're far more qualified than I am."

This time, Becky did laugh—very loudly. Just as Blade walked in with a leftover dinner plate, fork poised halfway to his mouth as the sound halted him in place.

"Evie!" Becky said. "Don't tell me you believed that stupid rumor!" She clutched her stomach, tears coming from her eyes. "I never wanted your job! Could you imagine?"

Blade wiped his mouth, putting the plate down, still looking a little dazed. "Then why did you move into her desk after she quit?"

Becky smacked her forehead. "Because, you fool, it's the only desk that's isolated from the others. I merely wanted to be alone. Not to make cauldron-brew runs for the boss."

Evie's head spun. "I'm so confused."

Becky gripped her hands, commanding all of Evie's attention. "Let me be clear, then. My entire existence is getting to organize and order people about. It is my dream come true, and I would *never* want to do anything else. I have the highest salary and command a level of fear and respect I only ever dreamed of accruing. I am content where I am—and just to clear any remaining doubt…"

Evie leaned closer as Becky said in a hushed tone, "There was no villain's assistant position…until he met you."

Her breath stalled along with every thought she'd ever had. The world around her moved at a sluggish pace, save for the branch tapping against the window and the draft that seemed to follow, spreading goose bumps up her arms. "What? That can't be true. He'd been searching for an assistant long before me."

Becky looked at her with pity. "Evie, before you, the only thing that man had been searching for was solitude and quiet. The other workers weren't allowed within five feet of his private office, and frankly, they were all too scared to get within ten feet of it regardless."

Evie squeezed Becky's hands, still clasped in hers, feeling a tinge of desperation. This was not at all how she remembered her start. Or how she'd been hired. Or…anything. It made her feel like there was a large bubble expanding in her head, inches from popping.

And it did when Becky saw the look on her face and whispered, "The day he hired you, he ordered custom chairs for his office. Very discreetly, but I saw the report, and he made a note that they needed to be comfortable for a woman of short stature."

Evie wasn't sure what to say, so that left the only thing she knew to do when she was uncomfortable. She laughed. It was an ugly, strangled sound.

The boss groaned beside them, still too weak to open his eyes. "Stop." He groaned again. "Telling her things."

Becky looked at him and then at Evie with a thoughtful expression. "I'm gonna ignore that order."

Evie clapped her hands together and nodded earnestly. "Good for you."

Becky rolled her lips inward. "Would this be a good or bad time to tell you that I shortened the leg of your desk chair in the hopes that you'd fall?"

Evie jumped up. "I knew it!"

They both broke into a grin at the same time—so big it felt like safety, like coming home. It felt in part like she'd just gotten a piece of her lost childhood back.

The simple joy of making a friend.

A voice rasped across the room. "All this chatter, and my Becky still hasn't brought me the cookies I asked her to sneak." Ramona had awoken.

Becky gave Evie one last smile before going to her grandmother and handing her a wrapped-up bundle from her skirt pocket. She murmured low words in soothing comfort, a soft grin playing on her lips, a few pieces of her hair tumbling out from her pins.

When Evie turned back to Blade, the dragon trainer was focused on Becky in wonder and then possessiveness, like he'd fashion himself a thief just for the excuse to have that smile for himself.

It was sweet, and if she remained in that room in that moment with all her confusion and hurt mingling together, she'd ruin it. She needed air and space and something she couldn't quite name.

She charged for the door abruptly, knowing if she glanced back at her boss it would only complicate her feelings further. She just needed a moment, *one moment* to herself. She called back to them when she was nearly out into the hallway. "Might you two look after him while I step outside for some air?"

Blade plopped himself down on the stool she'd been sitting on. "Not to worry, Evie. I'll keep sentry at his sick bed. I'm sure Tatianna will be by soon to look in on him as well."

This comforted her enough to enter the quiet hallway and take a deep, shuddering breath. She kept walking until she hit a flight of stairs, then wandered down in a daze, and before she knew it, she was outside, the dusk air so sweet, she took heaping gulps of it as she gripped her hips.

The peace didn't last—because she had terrible, terrible luck. The clanging of metal in the distance was not so discernible from the ringing in her skull; she almost didn't notice it.

She looked hard through the trees and overgrowth and spotted a group of men. She squinted harder—Becky's brothers. They'd taken their training outdoors. The exercise was a good aid to digest their dinner, likely. Her stomach groaned angrily.

Eat before you storm out in a huff, Evie!

She should return inside, for many reasons. For one, she was incredibly hungry; for another, she worried for Trystan and didn't want him to be alone for too long after she'd made him a promise to stay. And if that wasn't enough, she knew as well as anything that she couldn't be around this many handsome men at once without saying something that would haunt her at three a.m. in a cold sweat.

Moving to leave, she then heard Reid call after her. "Little assistant!"

She turned slowly, wincing when she saw all three of Becky's older brothers staring at her, weapons in hand.

Reid stepped forward with a wide, welcoming grin. "Care to try your hand at combat?"

Her mouth dried out and her heart did an odd stutter at the prospect, but the dagger at her thigh hummed, the scar on her shoulder with it. "Oh, no thank you. I'm not much of a fighter."

Raphael stepped forward then—the one who seemed to like her the least, perhaps because she'd called him an asshole... But his hazel eyes weren't angry, merely stern as he assessed her with a speculative glance. "Perhaps you should change that, Ms. Sage."

She took a step toward them, a sharp clarity cutting through the fog that had fallen over her senses, along with a pounding resolve.

Perhaps she should.

CHAPTER 67

EVIE

"Remember, you want to get the dagger from me."

"I *want* you to get off me. So I can stab you with it." Evie glared at Reid hovering above her, his boyish face grinning as he pinned her to the ground for the fourth time in the last half hour. Her training thus far had the success rate of a wet blanket.

The night had grown dark beyond the torches circling the sparring gardens. Stars twinkled above in greeting, as if waving down to the lush gardens below; the brightest star seemed to glint harder when she looked at it. The back garden was clearly designed for training and combat. Even the plants that sprouted up from the ground were as deadly as a Fortis warrior—and as pretty. Reid had explained that the pink flowers twisting up in the air caused instant death the moment they hit a person's tongue…or instant healing. It depended on which one you picked.

Becky had wandered out shortly after Evie to watch her flounder. She'd nearly had a heart attack when Becky plopped one of the pink flowers right in her mouth. *I've yet to choose wrong*, she'd said.

The HR manager stood off to the side, rolling one of the weapons from the small armory cart in her hands. "Reid, your knee is about to go into her kidney."

"Reid, your knee is already in my kidney," Evie gritted out as she shoved at him. The scene was almost uncomfortably reminiscent of when Otto Warsen had her pinned to the ground, hands wrapped around her throat. The memory brought back the panic, the fear…the rage.

She brought her knee up to his groin—hard. Every man within a twenty-foot radius winced as Reid toppled over and Evie climbed to her feet. Reid wheezed, "That was a cheap shot."

Evie pouted. "I'm afraid there are no cheap shots when one is defending themselves." She leaned down, and Reid gulped. "The last man who pinned me down like that has his head adorning our rafters. I think I was gentle just then...all things considered."

Reid crawled away, nodding gratefully.

One of the torches encircling the sparring grounds flickered, drawing her attention to a tree that was dotted with glowing fruit. One she recognized.

"The sleeping-death fruit you got me came from here?" Evie asked Becky, wandering over and plucking the peach-like fruit from the lowest branch. The soft fuzz tickled her palm. She smiled wistfully, shaking her head. *A poisoned peach.*

Raphael ripped the fruit from her hand and squashed it under his boot, waving a finger at Becky. "I told Reid not to honor that request, Rebecka. What in the deadlands would ever goad you into eating one of the world's most deadly magical fruits?"

Evie stared at him, deadpanning: "I thought it would taste better than regular poison."

Raphael clutched his head with both hands. "You keep odd company, Rebecka. What manner of beast is she?" The man was incredulous, clearly not used to being challenged—on anything.

Becky picked at her nails. "I don't know. I've been trying to figure it out for months."

A cry sounded from behind her as Reid slammed into her back, and Evie panicked. She hadn't realized they were still sparring! Her arms flew everywhere until her elbow connected hard against— Oh gods. Reid's nose. He released her instantly, blood dribbling down his face.

"You're bleeding!" Evie sounded a little too delighted. She hoped no one noticed.

"Amazing," Reid said, bringing a handkerchief up to dab at his nose. "What would you call that move?"

"Flail until you hit something."

Reid playfully slung an arm about her shoulders. "If it works, it works! Right, Raphael?"

Raphael grunted, moving to pick one of the pink flowers. The color made her realize something odd.

"I haven't seen Tatianna—or Clare, for that matter—since the Trench. Were they at dinner?"

Reid and Roland shook their heads.

Evie found she was enjoying all the members of the Fortis family. She'd watched their affection, their candor, even their humility, and wanted to cram herself right in the middle. Still, there was something in Raphael...something secret...something rather *formidable* in how he carried himself. "I believe I saw both of them retire to their rooms for the evening."

When he would have seen that, Evie had no clue, since the others had just admitted neither woman had gone down to dinner.

"I think I'll go check on Tati, and I'm sure Clare wants an update on Trystan. If you would return my dagger, please?"

Her path was blocked by Raphael, who glowered at her before saying, "We are not done. You've yet to spar with me."

Because I don't want to die.

But it felt like a challenge, and she wasn't one for backing down. "Fine, but I'd like to use the thinner swords over there," she said, knowing she had zero chance of winning any sort of sparring match with the oldest of the Fortis siblings, but holding something sharp would certainly help her chances. The tips were capped, of course, for safety purposes, but she was sure they wouldn't be difficult to remove...

Raphael's jaw tightened, but he nodded to an incredibly large footman with hair so yellow it rivaled the sun. She moved to grab one of the swords, but she didn't account for the constant movement of the vines that curled across the sparring grounds. Her foot caught on one, and it took the opportunity to tug her down the rest of the way.

Her back slapped into the dirt, her arms thrown wide in a disturbed *T*. The stoic footman above her was holding the sword almost over his shoulder, the hilt resting there.

The footman blinked at her. "Miss?"

"Would you believe me if I told you this happens a lot?"

The footman replied too quickly: "Yes."

Reid went to stand next to the footman, bumping the large man with his hip as he asked Evie, "Shall I join you down there? Or will you come back up here for a little *sword play*?"

Evie narrowed her eyes. "Is that a euphemism?"

Reid waggled his brows. "Do you want it to be?" He kneeled and gripped her hips, preparing to haul her up, but he froze, peering at something past her.

Her breath caught when she tilted her head back against the ground and saw heaving shoulders and black diamond-chipped eyes.

Trystan.

He was watching the scene unfold, sweaty, raw, and perfect. His molten gaze locked on to where Reid's hands were still molded against her hips, then to the large footman standing over her with a sword raised above his head. It didn't look...*good*, per se.

But she was far too relieved to care that the men standing over her were likely in imminent danger. Trystan was alive—the man she'd sacrifice anything for was okay.

The same man with the vein throbbing in the side of his sweaty hair–slicked forehead. "What the fuck are you doing?" He was glaring at the footman and Reid.

The footman—the quiet, unassuming one—chose that moment to say, "We were discussing euphemisms. For swords."

Evie's lips pulled back in a wince.

But she should give Trystan more credit. The boss was a master in subtle displeasure. His largest bouts of anger were quiet and subdued, allowing the fear to build and flow in startling, frightening waves.

His brow twitched, his jaw flexed; his eyes flared, and the fists at his sides tightened. As he took a slow step toward them, she was sure he'd take the time to think and not do anything rash.

"I'm going to kill all of you."

Never mind.

CHAPTER 68

THE VILLAIN

Trystan's skin was aflame.

In part due to his fever just now breaking, but it could mostly be attributed to the scene playing out before him—a scene that included two large men standing over his apprentice like she was quarry.

Sage leaped to her feet, standing in front of both men. "Sir, don't be rash. It isn't as it appears."

Trystan was on her in seconds. The delirium of sickness still fogging his thoughts, he tugged her arm toward him when he spied blood from a scrape on her elbow. His face darkened, and so did his thoughts.

"What. Is. That?" He pointed to it calmly, disguising the rage behind his words. His mist called to her, coiling around her, climbing up and circling the wound. It lit red. It was fresh.

Sage furrowed her brow. "Would you believe me if I said a plant did it?"

His head felt like it had a twenty-pound weight on it and his eyelids were heavy, but he fought against the sleepiness to answer, "Unfortunately."

Sage reached down and picked up the thin sword that the footman had dropped. She sighed. "The Fortis brothers were teaching me how to fight 'properly.'" She put air quotes around the word.

Becky snorted.

Raphael cut in, commanding attention the way a leader would. "Your assistant lacks coordination and any sense of finesse—"

"Apprentice," Trystan corrected coldly. "If you're going to address her like she isn't here, I caution you to at least do it with her proper title."

Even though he was lashing out, Trystan knew he wasn't truly angry with

Raphael. In fact, he appreciated them giving Sage some self-defense training; gods knew she could use it. But her mother was set to arrive in the very near future, which meant that she would want to revisit their kiss, revisit the possibility of…what, he still didn't quite know. But what the destiny monster had whispered to him… He shuddered.

There was no way forward with Sage. No hope. And worst of all, he wasn't even surprised. This was his life—had always been his life, in all honesty.

This was being The Villain.

Raphael huffed, tossing a sword back into the cart.

Roland sighed, removing his glasses and buffing them against his shirt. "Forgive Raphael. He has not a romantic bone in his body. I think it's very gallant you want to ensure she is properly recognized for her advancements. There's clearly a great respect and love between you."

It was as if a hand had reached out to slap him before diving into his chest to rip out his heart. "I am The Villain," he said with a calmness he did not feel. "I do not have the time or the patience for love, and I certainly would not pursue such a useless emotion with someone who works for me."

He looked directly at Roland. Anywhere but at Sage.

Trystan had witnessed a carriage accident as a boy. Watched the wheels twist and bend against a stone wall, the doors and roofing bowed and gnarled. Watched it and wondered quietly to himself why nobody could've stopped it. But now, he understood it with stark clarity.

Because he was no longer watching a carriage accident.

He *was* the carriage accident.

A cloud broke, and a light drizzle began to sprinkle down upon them; it felt as if the rain were trying to extinguish the flames he'd just made of his life, of his relationship with Sage.

It had to be done.

Because he was a glutton for punishment, his eyes landed on her. She didn't flinch at the raindrop running down the slope of her nose, just stared at him with no expression on her face.

"Come now, Roland. It *would* be nonsensical for The Villain to find love," Raphael said, a scoff in his voice. "With his bevy of enemies? Always living life on guard? It would be a disaster. A nightmare. I'm certain one couldn't find someone more difficult to love."

"I didn't find it difficult at all," Sage whispered.

Everything froze.

Trystan's head slowly turned toward her in the painful quiet, his mouth falling open. The bees stopped buzzing; the plants didn't sway. Nothing else existed. Just her. Just Sage. In all her splendid color.

He said his words with such carefulness, like he was treading on glass. "What did you just say?"

She took a step away from him and pulled in an anxious breath. She made a fist, then released it. A sharp sound of swinging metal cut the air as Sage's discarded dagger flew into her waiting hand.

Raphael frowned, likely shocked at her ability to call the powerful weapon. "I don't have time for this," he grumbled as he stalked back toward the house.

Sage's knuckles went white around the dagger, and the torchlight illuminated pure anger etched in the lines of her mouth. "Perhaps you all should join him."

Nobody moved.

"Now. Please."

Trystan had never heard a plea sound so threatening. He'd be impressed if he wasn't so shaken.

I didn't find it difficult at all.

How did one move on from such a statement? How could he ever move forward when those words replayed on an endless, agonizing loop in his mind?

All the others moved immediately at her words, however, scattering back to the fortress. Becky leaned in toward Sage as she passed. "There is a very brave person standing here, and it's not The Villain."

"Ms. Erring!" This was mutiny.

Instead of looking remorseful, the woman just spared him a quick glance before scurrying after her brothers, a lightness to her steps that was different from the usual weight in her gait.

When his attention turned back to Sage, he was met with the tip of a dagger. The drizzle and the torchlight created an ethereal glow over her dampening curls. He arched a brow, his eyes going to the steel and then to hers.

I didn't find it difficult at all.

"Sage...are you...all right?" *Did I destroy you, just as destiny said I would? Have I already fulfilled destiny's prophecy?*

She picked up one of the stray thin swords and tossed it to him; he caught it easily. "Do you mean am I embarrassed of unrequited feelings? No, I am not. And since all I am to be is your apprentice, then I demand that my learning begins now."

Unrequited? What a fucking cosmic joke.

His lips parted. The rain mixed with the sweat from his broken fever on his skin. "Learning what, precisely?"

She stepped toward him, stretching her arms high above her head, loosening her shoulders, and bringing her chest up. The top curves of her breasts were peeking out from her corset. He looked down at the grass and the tops of his shoes.

And that was when Sage demanded: "Teach me to fight like The Villain."

CHAPTER 69

EVIE

"You want to learn to fight like me?" her boss asked with a healthy dose of skepticism.

"I don't expect to ever be an expert, but yes, I'd like to learn to fight like you, or at least like the Malevolent Guards." Evie was still reeling from her indirect confession of love and how foolish it had been to show her hand at the exact moment he'd toppled the whole deck.

"Then have the Malevolent Guards teach you!" he argued, the rain soaking his white shirt and pressing it to his chest. Internally, she sighed. There was nothing like a man in a puffy white shirt, and wet to boot. *And* in a picturesque setting underneath the night sky. This was very not fair.

The stars were still visible through the rain clouds, and the torches surrounding them hadn't gone out. They had an evening to kill, and if she wasn't going to spend it in his arms, then she would take some delight in throwing sharp things at his head.

She made a show of looking at her nails. "Very well, then. I'll ask Daniel the Philanderer." She twirled away from him, only to be snatched back against hard muscle and locked into place. One large arm fell across her middle and the other over her upper chest, just below her throat.

"Firstly." His voice was low in her ear, making her toes curl in her boots. "Don't turn your back on me. I am your adversary. If I'd been a real opponent, I could've killed you a hundred different ways already."

She went to jam her heel into his foot, but he caught her thigh in his hand, making them both breathe heavier—from exertion, surely; nothing else. Yet there was a pooling warmth in her stomach when his breath brushed against her neck. It made her blush everywhere. "Your leg is not a wind-up toy. You're giving the person the chance to stop you."

"But I need the force—" she started breathlessly.

"Screw force. One quick jam of your heel into their toes is all you need. Now show me."

"I can't!" she squeaked.

He *tsk*ed, slightly mocking. "Now, Sage, I've seen your heel do a fair amount of damage. Surely—"

"I meant because you're still holding my thigh, sir."

He dropped it like it burned, and she stumbled and turned, her foot slipping and tangling with his. His entire body bowed, hands catching her waist just as she fell into him, gripping his shoulders for balance. He went stiff and uncomfortable where they touched.

She started to back away but gasped when he jerked her toward him, fingers tightening against her, his warmth pressing through the thin cloth of her corset. When she looked up, dark pain shadowed his face, stronger than she'd ever seen before. "What have you done?" His eyes were searching hers for something he couldn't understand. "What enchantment is this?"

The desperation in the whispered plea hypnotized her. The dagger slipped from her fingers...and landed on his foot.

The hilt end hit first (thankfully), and then she was free of his fierce grip (miserably).

The crackle of the flames was easier to hear as the rain dissipated. The fruits on the trees surrounding them seemed to emit a soft orange glow, like little lanterns. An owl perched on a branch above watched them, making small noises as unicorns trotted by, free of saddles and free of stables. This land was beautiful freedom. A place to untether yourself and exist as completely free.

So few people did—herself included.

Trystan dropped a sword into her hands. "Simple blocking." With deliberate slowness, he brought the blade down, giving her ample time to come up with her own and stop it.

She managed to block him again, and again, and again. "Trystan." His name fell out of her mouth like she used it all the time, but she didn't, obviously, or her boss wouldn't look like he was on the brink of losing his marbles. "Did you hire me because you felt sorry for me?"

The sword came down harder this time, but she blocked once more, both hands on her hilt. He drew away and said coolly, "Do you not recall me telling you I am not in the habit of charity? What makes you think I'd make an exception for *you*?"

She scrunched her nose and tapped her lips with her finger, thinking he'd earned this.

"You kept my scarf."

Slam.

He did not hit her blade head-on as he had been—this blow caught closer to the tip, nearly knocking it from her hands. She could see the realization dawn on him with startling swiftness. It hit Evie at the same time what that knowledge revealed about *her*.

"You little snoop! Did you go back into my chambers to riffle through my things? What next? Do you intend to peruse my undergarment drawer?"

She furrowed her brow. "That would be silly." She paused, then added, "Any sensible person knows to always look in someone's sock drawer first."

He seemed alarmed. "Did you look in my sock drawer?"

Her mouth twisted. "No—wait, why? What do you have in there?" she asked, a little intrigued.

"Nothing."

"Yeah, that vein in your forehead definitely concurs with that statement."

Slam.

She blocked him, and he continued: "I did not keep your scarf, Sage. I stole it. I do it with lots of things. Artifacts, money, jewels, food."

She snickered.

Trystan slammed his sword down, his loose shirt sticking to the muscles in his arms and chest as he moved, dampened by a combination of sweat and leftover rain. He twisted his blade against hers, and she stumbled closer to him, his sword locking hers into place, their faces inches apart.

"Okay. Focus," he said, a quiet command, all business. It made her sick with giddiness, with unequivocable glee. This closeness was dangerous; she was forgetting what he said, how he'd dismissed her barely an hour ago. "Break free of me, Sage."

Oh, that I could.

The doubt must have been drawn in the twisted curve of her face, because he pinched his mouth in defiance. "No. Stop. I can see you overthinking. Your mind is a terrifying wonder, but it is not always needed in situations like these. Sometimes, you can rely on instinct. You can trust yourself. How would you get free?"

Her face went blank, and then she kissed him.

CHAPTER 70

THE VILLAIN

Trystan had asked her how to get free, not how to ruin his fucking life.

Was he still in destiny's test? Could this be a dream?

No. He knew the feel of her mouth, the taste, the way his whole body lit like a match at even a whisper of her touch. This wasn't a whisper, though; this was burning, flaying him open.

It was torment. It was the deadlands' punishment sent to damn him for all the evil he'd wrought. She hummed, as he'd heard her do so many times outside his office, except now it was against his lips. How many times had he imagined tasting the gentle sound? How many times had he imagined quieting her ramblings with a hard kiss?

He'd imagined silencing her for hours.

But after the smallest response of his lips, he opened his eyes and shoved away hard, grappling for his sword…which was now in Sage's hands. Satisfaction danced in her eyes as she angled it in his direction.

He was dumbstruck in love with her.

Shit, shit, shit.

"What was that?" he inquired with an impressively detached steadiness.

"An accident?" she said sardonically—a clear dig at the pitiful excuse he'd given her back at the manor. She smiled—the scary one; her rouge was slightly smeared. Because of him.

Well, that was it. He'd held out long enough. Damn the consequences.

But before he could dive back onto her, she lightly poked the capped tip of the sword into his chest. "It was a distraction. You told me not to think."

"And *that* was your first instinct?" He turned his head away so she wouldn't see how he touched his lips to quell the sensations.

"It was," she said casually.

He thought of a million things he could say to scold her.

Sage, that was irresponsible.

Sage, that was unprofessional.

Sage, if you kiss me again, you'll kill me.

Maybe not the last one.

"That wasn't what I had in mind," he settled on, shifting his weight. Which was true—what he had in mind was flipping her on her back and stripping her naked.

"But it worked," she said with a wild gleam in her eye that he refused to extinguish.

He gently tilted his head, acknowledging her victory, and then said carefully, "You are correct, but why don't I show you a few maneuvers to get out of that position that don't include kissing?"

"I suppose I could—"

"Save one for us, sweetheart." The new voice jarred them both, and Trystan swung himself around, maneuvering Sage behind him.

They were met with shiny silver armor, the king's crest, and raised weapons poised to kill. Four Valiant Guards had entered through the hidden veil of the Fortis Fortress.

Trystan's power climbed from the depths of his body, already dark, already searching. He couldn't help but smile at the men who had made him suffer. "It's about time you boys caught up."

His power flared out.

And then everything went horribly wrong.

CHAPTER 71

GIDEON

Meanwhile, back at the manor…

Gideon wasn't certain what he'd expected when he abandoned his post with the heroes to join up with The Villain's team, but it certainly wasn't eating pastry with an ogre and discussing severed heads.

"How long do you keep them up there? Is no one concerned for the smell?" he asked with a mixture of disgust and curiosity.

Keely threw something at him, and he dodged it, then picked up the foreign object—and dropped it with a cry of revulsion. "You threw a finger at me?"

"A middle one." She turned up her long, elegant nose, revealing the loveliness of her profile. For the leader of brutal killers, she really was adorable. He supposed that's what made her so dangerous.

"Can I see?" Lyssa charged for where he'd dropped it, and Gideon scooped her up.

"Nope. Sorry, baby sister." He plopped her down next to Edwin, who reached over to ruffle her hair. Pixies floated in and out, enjoying the small cookies Lyssa had just made, which were no bigger than a fingernail—the perfect size for the twinkling beings who played with Lyssa's hair in thanks.

"I'm not a baby," she objected, handing one to a pixie with ice wings. The being kissed her cheek. She smiled wide, then looked at the window in the corner and frowned. "When will Evie return with Mama? I hate waiting."

Gideon sauntered over to the window. There was a strange familiarity to the artful stained-glass piece. "I've seen this before," he observed to himself. The window was a depiction of a book with the sun shining down on it, and when he looked closely, he saw it bore a startling similarity to…*Rennedawn's*

Story. "Huh. What are you doing here?" he asked it.

Edwin laughed, stirring the dark liquid in the cauldron. "Your sister has the habit of talking to it, too, like it's sentient."

Lyssa skipped across the room and plopped a tiny cookie in Keely's waiting palm. "Evie does that with everything. She used to scold the front door when it wouldn't latch! She called it a lot of different words."

"I think you should not repeat them," Gideon said, turning just as Lyssa knocked into him with the full plate. The cookies tumbled to the ground. "Shoot. I'm so sorry, Lyssa. Let me—" A silver key lay on the ground, apparently having fallen from Lyssa's apron pocket. "What's that to?" he asked curiously.

Lyssa's brown eyes widened as her face went white. "It's for our bedchamber," she said, rushed and jumbled, shoving the key in her pocket before Gideon could investigate further.

He was amused, folding his arms across his wrinkled cotton tunic. "If it's more of your schemes and you're planning on locking someone in…just be sure that you let them out eventually?"

There was no accounting for the strange glint in his sister's dark eyes. "Don't worry. I will." The words were light, but they made his muscles jump uncomfortably, like his body was warning him.

"Lyssa…is everything all right?"

She didn't look at him, just at the window with the mysterious depiction of the book of prophecy. "It will be."

He wanted to ask more questions, but right as he opened his mouth, Marv came charging into the kitchens.

Keely was already handing the panting man a glass of water. "Marv, I beg you to start taking the lift."

There's a lift? Like the ones that move on belts? Why does everyone take the bloody stairs, then?

Marv huffed, holding his stomach with one hand as he chugged the water, then straightened with alarm. "The barrier…"

"Isn't in top condition, we know," Keely said. "None of the cloaking spells we've found have been sticking, but it's still just a window here, a doorway there—"

Suddenly, loud bells rang through the air, clanging so hard they shook the entire room. Lyssa gripped her ears, and Edwin, too. "What is that?" Gideon yelled over the noise, wincing with every toll.

"The manor is completely exposed!" Marv shouted. He pulled his hand away from his middle, revealing a gaping, bloody wound as he dropped to his knees. "The Valiant Guards have found us."

By the looks of Marv's wound, they certainly weren't here for peace negotiations.

But without The Villain and his power, Gideon had a bad feeling this wouldn't be a fight at all.

It would be a massacre.

CHAPTER 72

EVIE

Someone had betrayed them.

The realization was like a thick poison curling over Evie's heart. She held out her hand, and her scar stung as her dagger jumped from the weapons rack into her waiting palm. Holding it high, she stepped out from behind the boss, widening her stance, ready to do battle with anyone who dared cross them. She'd fell these troublesome enemies, and then she'd find the traitor among them.

Two more knights had appeared from the darkness—that made six total. She and Trystan were outnumbered, but they had death magic on their side.

The curling mist spilled out of Trystan's hands and wrapped around the guards—but not completely. It split in two, one half aiming for the knights, the other swirling in her direction. Circling her ankles.

"Oh dear," she said. "Shoo!" But no amount of waving her hands into the mist would make it obey as it twisted around her feet like a lap cat. Her boss hadn't even noticed the power splitting off; he was too busy dispatching the first knight with startling swiftness. "You're very cute," she told the mist, "and we can play later—after you kill those men."

The power splitting was weakening Trystan; she could tell by the way he hunched and the sweat lining his temples as he moved to dispatch another knight. One snuck up from the side and landed a fist to his face, causing him to fall.

"Trystan!" she yelled, glaring at the mist. "Go help him!" But it wouldn't budge, and when another guard rushed toward her, the mist took on a mind of its own, slicing forward and enveloping the knight completely. The knight didn't even see the magic coming.

But Trystan did.

His brow furrowed in confusion as he grabbed the first felled knight's sword and drove it through the man who had sucker punched him, gaping when he saw the mist still swirling around her even while it swarmed the knight near her. "Sage, don't panic," he called carefully.

"Why would I panic? Just because of your weird foggy magic adhering itself to my ankles?" she called back, a note of hysteria in her tone.

The knight beside her screamed, until the mist slipped down his throat and cut off his air. Trystan stalked over to her, taking hold of both her arms, and her dagger slipped from her fingers as he said urgently, perplexed, "I didn't do that…did you?"

She furiously shook her head. "I didn't do anything!"

The mist finished choking the life out of the guard. The remaining three gaped in horror at the invisible killer, but her and Trystan's attention was on the receding gray now playing in the curls of her hair.

"Stop it this instant," he boomed.

The mist shook like it was chuckling, and Evie put her hand over her mouth to keep her own giggle in.

Trystan glared at her. "Are you laughing?"

She bit her lip. "*No.* That would be inappropriate."

But the humor died when a remaining knight aimed an arrow right for Trystan's heart.

He couldn't turn fast enough; his magic wouldn't protect him before the arrow struck true, she realized. Her frantic words died on her lips. Time seemed to slow and then nearly stop as a hundred memories flashed before her eyes.

Trystan offering her a vanilla candy on her first day.

Trystan and his grim, sheepish expression when he apologized for something.

Trystan with his bed full of pillows and his little tornado nightlight.

Trystan keeping her scarf, clean and neatly folded away…like it was precious to him.

Trystan humbling himself, begging Benedict—the man he hated—on his knees to save her life.

There was no time to think, no time to second-guess. She merely *did.* With a piercing cry, she dove in front of him. As the arrow flew, she held up her hands instinctively, and Trystan let out a low shout of outrage behind her.

The next thing she knew, the dagger was in her hand. It began to glow, as did her scar—an iridescent shimmer that seemed, in the dark of night, to blaze with a thousand different colors. She felt warmth so strong and powerful it brought tears to her eyes as she fell to her knees, gripping her chest. The arrow had broken in two when it struck her—but it hadn't even touched her skin.

Well, that was a nice little trick, she thought, suddenly wickedly tired.

Her lids drooped, and she fell forward.

CHAPTER 73

THE VILLAIN

Evie had been fatally wounded. There was no doubt in his mind as he watched her body fall forward, lifeless. An anguished yell reeled out from the very depths of his soul.

Trystan's mist swirled, his anger and panic making it stronger, seeking a weak point on his enemies—anyone who harmed her. It struck the knight with the crossbow in the leg, and his armor clinked as he dropped like a stone. The remaining two fell back, though not before one of them called out, "More of us are coming, Villain. You cannot win against the entire Valiant Guard!"

Then they retreated into the darkness.

Trystan continued forward, considering for one heartbeat chasing after them, but only for one heartbeat. In the next, he was on the ground in front of Sage.

Her eyes were open. She still breathed. Thank the gods.

His voice was frantic, his hands panicky as they searched her chest, her shoulders; his breath was ragged when he came up empty. "The blood—where's the blood?"

"Sir," she said gently.

"We must stop the bleeding. You'll be all right, Sage. Tatianna will heal you, and all will be well. Where is the blood? I can't find the blood! I can't see the wound!" He needed to stay calm—he didn't want to panic her until the healer could arrive. Her muscles were already shaking. No, wait—she was perfectly still. *His* muscles were shaking.

Bloody brilliant.

"Trystan," she said again, firmer, gasping when his hands traveled up to her cheeks, holding her head in place. She whispered, "It didn't touch me." And she held up the arrow, which had broken clean in two but with no traces of having harmed her.

Wonder, relief, and befuddlement ran through him in equal measure as he crinkled his brow and angled his head. "How?" he breathed out.

She shrugged, wide eyes blinking at him. Alive. Unharmed. "I don't know." And she told him about how the dagger had emitted a light, her scar had burned, and then nothing. There was no explaining it, but the dagger—and whatever magic lay within it—must have protected her.

And she'd nearly traded the blasted thing away to save his life, just as she'd done now.

That had to stop. It all had to stop. "No more attempts at saving my life, Sage. As it stands, those acts of misguided bravery seem to be ticking years off my life rather than tacking them on."

Her brow furrowed in the way that he adored, though the feeling was followed quickly by nausea. He wasn't meant to adore things. He was meant to sneer in disgust. Speaking of which… His eyes followed the knights retreating in the distance.

"I let the last of them get away," Trystan lamented. "They'll tell the rest where we are."

Evie's upper lip curled as she looked directly into Trystan's eyes, chilling him as she said, "Then why don't you stop them?"

His eyes bored into hers, and a heated sensation climbed the back of his neck as he smiled, feeling truly villainous. "As the lady wishes."

The gray mist sprinted across the land, over plants that shied away, until it reached the first guard, who was just visible at the edge of the fortress gates, illuminated by the torchlights. The man fell, and after a short pursuit, so did the next, both dropping from an angled death blow to the neck.

Good riddance.

But his relief was short-lived as his easy stance waned. He fell to his knees.

"Trystan! Are you all right?" Evie was suddenly next to him, rubbing a hand down his back. He could feel the color draining from his face as he sighed out of dry, cracked lips.

"I'm never this weak after using my magic," he croaked out. "Never. Something is wrong with it. Somehow, it's making me sick. I feel it…changing." He couldn't help it; his eyes darted over to hers. A look of realization passed between them, and the truth of it was unpleasant.

She stumbled back, away from him, and his body immediately missed her warmth, her proximity. "You think it's me? You think it's *my* fault?"

He shut his eyes tight, fighting two different kinds of pain. "You're the only one who can see it. And ever since it revealed itself to you, it hasn't been the same. I can't risk it failing me like that again. Without my death magic, I cannot fight Benedict or my enemies. Without it…am I even The Villain?"

He'd never felt more tired in his life. His body hurt; his *heart* hurt. But he had to protect Sage and he had to protect himself, and this was the only way he knew how.

"We should— We should keep our distance for the foreseeable future. Just in case. Just to be sure."

The look on her face was one he never thought he'd see there—let alone be the cause of. It was betrayal and shock and pure, true hurt.

He called the mist back, and it left Sage slowly, almost begrudgingly. He knew how it felt. "We have to go to the house to warn Lady Fortis and the rest of them."

Sage nodded, tucking her dagger back into its holster tied with leather about her ankle. As they made their way toward the fortress, she committed the most heinous act a person could in his presence.

She started to cry.

He'd never felt smaller than he did in that moment.

"Sage." He tried to gentle his voice, stepping a little closer as they walked. "Please don't cry over me."

"I'm not crying over you!" she insisted with a sniffle. "You're so self-centered."

He cleared his throat. He didn't know why Benedict was working so hard to destroy him; all it took to fell The Villain was the sound of his apprentice crying. "Would it make you feel better if I let you try your hand at torture?"

She side-eyed him. "You're trying to make me laugh, and it's not going to work."

"Well, that's fortunate. I'm not very funny." He got closer still, then bumped her shoulder. "C'mon, Sage. Ripping off some fingernails? Listening to the knights' screams? I'll even let you use the torture rack."

She kicked a rock, sullen, but he thought he could see the tiniest beginning of a smile. "What's a torture rack?"

"It's a device that stretches your limbs apart until they snap off."

She gagged. "What? That is so gross!" She slapped his arm. "You always assume that the only way to get information out of someone is pain. But I'd be far more willing to spill all my secrets if I felt pleasure."

He coughed, hard, banging on his chest. It was a wonder he still had any oxygen left around this woman.

She frowned at him. "Are you well?"

"No."

The smile grew on her lips, and now it stayed there. Though he turned away, he could feel her eyes on him still as they moved.

They were nearly to the doors of the fortress when a scream wrenched the air—high, piercing, and bloodcurdling—and Sage startled, a look of pure horror on her face.

"Sage? What is it? Are you all right?" he asked. The scream sounded again, louder this time. "For the love of the gods! Who in the deadlands is screaming?"

She shoved the fortress's door open and said without feeling: "My mother."

CHAPTER 74

EVIE

Evie raced down the halls of the fortress in an unseeing haze, focused only on finding her mother and fixing whatever had broken her. She barely heard the boss's voice in her ear trying to reassure her, barely saw as a door creaked open in front of her. Her eyes were fuzzy. Everything was.

Panic. She was in a fog of panic. Her mother screamed again, causing Evie to collapse to the ground. "Make it stop! Make it stop, please!" She curled up, trying to get so small she hoped she could disappear. "Help her. Someone help her!"

Then suddenly, she felt something warm and slimy plop into her hands.

She blinked as if waking. "Kingsley?" The frog prince peered up at her, stark concern in his golden eyes.

At that moment, Clare and Tatianna flew into the room, the screaming growing louder with them. Evie flinched and closed her eyes, but she felt someone lifting her up in his warm arms. "I got you, sweet Evie. I got you," Blade said as he placed her upright in a chair, where she sat with Kingsley in a death grip.

Tatianna nudged Blade aside, then began pushing Evie's hair back and off her neck, tying it with the pink ribbon Tati always wore around her wrist—her first one, her favorite one. "No, Tati," Evie protested weakly.

"Hush, little friend. You're only borrowing it. Take deep breaths. There is no danger. It's only the memory plant. Hold Kingsley close—animals can help calm the mind."

It took a second for her to process what her eyes were seeing. The screaming wasn't coming from her mother; it was coming from the long, delicate-petaled flower Clare had dropped in the corner of the room. It was a memory flower.

A memory flower that echoed her mother's screams.

"What is that? What's wrong?" Becky slammed the green room doors wide, then closed a hand over her mouth when she saw the memory flower. Renna came in after her, looking panicked and frazzled.

"Poor Evie! Please, we must silence it somehow!" Renna cried. "Evie, please don't listen. Don't look at it."

Tatianna glared. "We got it from a secret room hidden in the hall. There are hundreds of these things. We were conveniently locked in until Blade heard us banging on the walls."

Evie felt her heart rate calming, her fingers loosening around Kingsley, who remained in her hands as if sensing she still needed his support.

"We were about to leave when one of the plants started shrieking the most terrible sound I'd ever heard," Tatianna finished.

It was the most terrible sound Evie had ever heard, too.

Becky shook her head, moving a vine out of her way. "No, that can't be. Memory flowers are extremely rare—there are only three documented living specimens! And it's dangerous to produce them. Nobody in my family would ever be so reckless."

Raphael came in as if on cue, followed by the rest of the boys and Julius. The screaming halted for a moment, giving Evie a much-needed reprieve.

Raphael spoke first, shaking his head in disgust. "Tell them. Tell them what you've done."

Evie followed his eyes.

Right to Renna.

Becky stumbled away from her, aghast, as a vine wrapped carefully around her wrist. "Mom? What does he mean? What did you do?"

Renna stayed silent, but tears were pooling in her eyes now. The sight of them sent Evie's heart plummeting toward her feet.

"What did you do!" Becky screamed.

Evie stood up and looked at Blade. "Go," she offered. Blade was up and over to Becky in seconds, a gentle hand at her elbow to hold her up.

Renna broke down in heaping sobs then. "I didn't mean to. I didn't mean any harm! Rebecka, please." She reached for Becky's hand, but her daughter slapped it away.

"Renna." Julius put a reassuring hand on her back. "It's enough now."

Renna looked at her husband, seeming to absorb strength from him.

She stood taller, her loose auburn hair moving with her as she pushed her chin up. "We have been aiding King Benedict in fulfilling the prophecy for some time."

Raphael bit out, "You, Mother. *You.*"

Renna licked her lips, folding her hands primly together. "I've been trying to find a cure for my mother. That is not a crime! That is not wrong! And everything I've done has been in service to Rennedawn and the Fortis line."

She addressed the group as she continued. "We've been working to develop a plant—a hybrid between the memory plant and another rare flower we grow on the estate to siphon magic. To relieve the burdens of overbearing power." Renna looked to Evie. "Like your mother's."

The boss, who'd been quiet, leaning against the wall in the corner, stood up and moved next to Evie, spearing Renna with his coldest, most threatening look. "Nura Sage isn't coming tomorrow morning, is she?"

Renna looked to Evie and only to Evie. She cried out, "Your mother was my very best friend! Please know that I loved her as if she were my own sister. My own blood. I have never in my life sought to hurt another human being." She inhaled hard. "Nura arrived at our gates, asking for aid. I knew of the accident; I knew of her power. I knew the king was looking for her, too, so instead of turning her over, I tried to siphon her magic away. I wanted to help her *and* the kingdom."

Evie stood, lip wobbling as hot, angry tears slid down her cheeks. "Then why...was she screaming?"

Renna got up, strode to the other side of the room, and pulled out a small vial of dark-silver dust. "I used the flower on her." She handed Evie the vial, which felt weightless in her hands. "But her magic had already been so abused, it was like trying to repair an already-stopped heart."

Evie looked up from the midnight vial. "Was. You said she *was* your very best friend?"

Renna's neck strained—Evie could tell by the veins protruding out. "Your mother's starlight enveloped her, Evie... She screamed for mercy one moment, and in the next, this stardust was all that was left of her. I'm so sorry, dear one. She died."

CHAPTER 75

GIDEON

"**F**ortify the borders!" Keely commanded. "Move, sir knight!"

Gideon jumped out of the way, searching for any means to assist, but this was a siege unlike anything he'd ever seen. The front of the manor was lined with Valiant Guards striking the gates with a battering ram as others shot arrows over the walls. But the Malevolent Guards showed no fear. With raging battle cries, red dove against silver. The Malevolent were less in numbers but not in ruthlessness.

On the high rampart at the front of the manor, Keely held a match to a glittering pumpkin projectile. The king didn't have them in his arsenal, but Gideon had seen them in action. One light of the magical vegetable, and it would flame as many as fifty knights in one drop. Gideon gripped Keely's wrist out of instinct, for he knew the men below. "Don't—they'll burn."

Keely sneered at him, shaking her wrist from his grip and shoving him till he fell. "Until you know what side you're on, go mind your sister. It's the only task you can be trusted with." She looked right at him as she ignited the charge and hurled it over the edge, her face glowing orange in the flames.

It would be inappropriate to find her lovely just now, during a brutal battle, but she was rather splendid in the light of the…flare…that had likely just injured or killed his former colleagues… Oh gods.

Edwin appeared at the flank, holding a tray of bread, interrupting Gideon's spiral. One of the Malevolent Guards jumped down from the rampart's raised edge, sweaty and covered in blood. "Edwin, I don't think we're in need of bread just now, but perhaps cake for when we're all done."

Edwin shook the tray. "This bread isn't for eating—it's stale. Harder than a rock." His eyes twinkled. "Perfect for throwing."

Gideon grinned. "Attaboy, Edwin." He gripped one of the loafs and chucked it down, knocking a knight clean off the ladder he'd been attempting to climb. He turned to Edwin with wide eyes. "What did you make them with? Cement?"

Edwin smiled and chucked one of his own over the side.

An office pixie fluttered out, plugging her tiny green ears to block the sounds of battle. "Keely!" the pixie screeched, voice high-pitched like a bell. "The back gates—they're getting through! They're lifting the grate to the guvres' enclosure!"

Keely paled. "I'm coming." She screamed to the crowd: "I need any available Malevolent with me!"

Gideon gripped her arm before she could run. "I'm available."

An arrow whizzed by, and Gideon didn't think, just pulled her into him and covered her head protectively, feeling the thickness of her braid doubled up underneath her helmet. To hide the length? That was strange. But she smelled of lemons and sweat, and that wasn't strange at all. It was glorious.

Her hawk eyes were on the arrow on the wall, then on him. "Okay, sir knight. Let's see what you can do."

He saluted, then jumped down from the rise first. And when he looked up at her, he couldn't help it—the moment demanded it... "Keely, oh Keely, let down your—" A hard piece of bread hit his gut. *"Oof."*

Keely grinned as they ran back down into the office corridors, taking the stairs two at a time. She called into a ruby, which Gideon had slowly gathered wasn't a ruby at all but a device for communication—or lack thereof, judging by Keely's growl of frustration.

"Wherever the boss is, he's out of reach," she muttered.

Gideon pulled a sword from a mount on the wall before they dove into the courtyard swinging. Knights charged him, and he dodged until he could no longer, felling men he once guarded and protected one by one. He panted at the small reprieve when they were no longer flanked, his back bumping into Keely's. When he peeked over, he saw that she had blood caked to her cheek and stray wisps of hair free. His hand itched to push them away.

"I'm sure he'll return to the manor soon enough," he told her instead.

But as he scanned the courtyard, with countless knights far outnumbering the Malevolent Guards desperately trying to fight, to push them back, Gideon feared there may not be a manor for The Villain to return to.

CHAPTER 76

BECKY

"How could you?" Becky whispered, hissing to the rest of the family. "How could *all* of you?"

Her father looked more solemn than she'd ever seen him. "The boys only just found out, Rebecka. If you are to blame anyone, blame your mother and me."

Becky almost spit at his feet. "Believe me, that's not difficult." Her mother was crying, holding her chest, and Becky knew why—she felt like doing it, too, to keep the sorrow from spilling out. Blade's hand was on her back, grounding her. "Get Fluffy, Blade. We're leaving." Blade gave a stiff nod, avoiding looking at Renna as he passed her.

"Why would you lie and say her mother was on her way?" Becky demanded. "Why give Evie false hope?"

Renna smoothed out the front of her gown, clearly trying to compose herself. "I only wanted to keep my family together. I wanted you to stay, and I thought it might be better for Evie to think there was still a chance her mother was out there. Tomorrow morning, I was going to gently tell her that her mother needs more time and allow her to go on believing that she still *exists*."

"Oh, Mother, what a horrible thing to do."

Becky saw Evie flinch out of the corner of her eye. There was a blank, lost look on her face as she stared at the vial of dust in her palm. Blankness in her expression was something Becky could hardly bear from the larger-than-life Evie.

Renna straightened, eyes roving to a dark crystal slab in a strange, jagged shape propped up on one of the shelves. She walked over, grabbed it, and beelined for Evie. "She wanted me to give this to you. I think she always knew you'd end up here. Please take it."

Evie reached out shakily, taking the smooth slab from Renna's hands. "What is it?"

There was a suspicious tone to Renna's voice. "It was someone else's for a time, then it was mine, and then I gave it to your mother."

Evie didn't look up at Renna, didn't have it in her to ask any more questions, just stared down at the dust and now the slab and whispered words that were shaded in heartbreak. "You were her friend."

Renna reached a hand for her, but The Villain moved in front of Evie, walling her away.

"Go now, Rebecka, and hurry," Raphael cut in, his voice hard and unfeeling. "Mother is neglecting to mention that she sent for the Valiant Guard. A battalion is on its way here now to arrest The Villain."

Her father's eyes widened. "Renna, you didn't."

Another vine twined around Becky, like they had when she was a little girl. When she would fall or get hurt, when life would knock her down, they were there.

She'd miss them. But they had to go—*now*.

Renna whispered brokenly to no one in particular. "I thought she might stay. I thought if they took him, she would have to stay."

The Villain swept his hands up under Evie's legs, hoisting her against his chest and holding her there as they walked toward the door, Kingsley still burrowed into her. "Come, Ms. Erring. Let's go," he said with a tinge of distaste. Clare and Tatianna filed out after them.

Becky took one last look about the room; she likely wouldn't see it again for a very, very long time. Her brothers stood in the corner, grim expressions on their faces. With a pained cry, she folded her arms around them, and they held one another tightly. "Come visit me, okay? Tell Rudy and Grandmother I said goodbye," she told them, tears running down her face.

Roland was red-faced, as was Reid, and Raphael had a somber glint in his eyes as he said, "I'm so sorry, Rebecka."

Becky smiled at them as widely as she could manage through her tears. "Don't be." Brothers were a curious thing, somehow able to lighten even the heaviest of hearts.

She was halfway out the door when Renna grabbed her hand. "Rebecka, please understand. I didn't want to hurt anyone. I wanted to protect the fortress. I wanted to protect Nura. That doesn't make me evil."

Becky stared at her mother with pity. A flash of black hair through the open door caught her eye. Evie stood waiting for her in the hall. "No, Mother, it doesn't."

Her mother whispered, "We are your family, Rebecka."

Evie held out a hand for her. Becky kept her eyes on it. "You are." She kissed her mother's cheek. "But so are they."

And then she brushed past Renna, clasped her hand in Evie's, and together, they ran for the front doors.

Her mother cried behind them, but Becky ignored it. She ached for Evie at this terrible news, and she knew their mission to her family's home had ended in failure, but still: she finally felt free of her burdens. Of perfection, of expectation, of being anything other than herself. Her family loved her, and one day she would return to claim her place as heir to the Fortis Family Fortress. But for now, she would remain Becky in HR. And she would be happy.

Fluffy waited outside, and Blade grinned at her softly from his back. "I warn you—he reeks of basil. He ate an entire bush."

Becky shrugged, pausing before a genuinely wide smile tugged at her lips. "I love basil." He smiled back.

The clanging of armor sounded in the distance.

Blade started waving his arms. "Let's go, let's go, let's go! Show a little urgency, people!"

They climbed atop the dragon and then soared through the skies, solemn and quiet the entire way.

No Nura, no starlight. No prophecy. Which meant no magic. Which would eventually lead to no Rennedawn.

Life as they knew it would end.

They returned to the manor.

And what they found there changed everything.

CHAPTER 77

THE VILLAIN

He'd never seen the manor in such an uproar. At least, not when he wasn't the one causing it.

As soon as the dragon was near enough to the ground, Trystan had jumped and rolled, immediately throwing himself into the fight beside his Malevolent Guards. Blade had been tasked with landing Fluffy somewhere safe, where Evie and the others could remain hidden. He would have liked to have had his trusted colleagues beside him—Tatianna's magic, Clare's inks, even Fluffy's newfound fire—but the Valiant Guards had nearly conquered the manor already, and his employees' safety was far more important than extending a losing battle.

Her safety. She was far away, and still his magic wouldn't yield to him as it once did.

In all his years as The Villain, he'd never fought so tirelessly, with as much fury as his body allowed. "Argh!" he cried, slamming into another knight. And another. His power aided him, but it wasn't enough, and there weren't enough Malevolent Guards to match the king's numbers.

He spied Keely beyond one of the pillars, slicing and maneuvering away.

They kept falling back and back, until they were nearly under the awning over the rear doors of the manor.

The grate to the guvres' enclosure below had been opened. His heart stopped. "No!"

Trystan ran for them and swept out his power, but his mist was dwindling as his exhaustion grew. It only made it a few feet before he was swarmed by more knights. He fought, one eye on his opponent and the other on the knights dropping a noxious smoke past the open grate.

He and the other Malevolent Guards struggled helplessly as the knights hauled an enormous net into the enclosure and lifted the female out. Her large eyes were shut as she was dragged without care onto the sturdy wooden cart.

Trystan sliced through several more Valiant Guards, pushing his power until he felt like his veins would burst through his skin…but it was too late.

The female was strapped down, too far away, with too many obstacles between them. But just before they wheeled her into Hickory Forest, into the night, one yellow eye opened for a moment, and a light whine came from her chest as she stared at Trystan.

Help me, she was saying.

I can't, he thought in anguish. Villains didn't help. They only destroyed.

He watched in the most wretched pain as they took her away…and then she was gone.

The sky opened up and rain poured down, along with one hot tear running down Trystan's face.

The male flew out, screeching after his mate, the sedation from the guards' gas making him stagger. Trystan's heart caught in his throat as he realized the knights had propped up what looked like a catapult, and attached to that…a very large spear.

"NO!" Trystan was too far away.

But Gideon Sage wasn't.

Across the back courtyard, Evie's brother saw the catapult at the same time Trystan did.

Gideon cried, "Don't!" He ran through the line, tackling the knight about to fire and knocking into the catapult just as it launched. The spear was diverted but still clipped the male guvre's wing; he fell, slamming hard into the ground.

Gideon locked eyes with the creature. The guvre cried out as the carriage containing his mate and his unborn let disappeared into the forest. The desperation of the cry was so strong, the despair rippled through the entire courtyard. Everyone seemed to jolt at once, Trystan included, as he staggered toward Gideon before falling to his knees and clutching his chest.

He got to his feet, but it was too late.

Gideon had been knocked to the ground by several knights. He tried to escape, but one of the knights pressed his boot into Gideon's chest to stay him. Trystan squinted. He knew those boots. But he didn't have time to linger on that, because another knight was already holding a sword high, ready to plunge it into Gideon's heart. "You'll regret betraying your king, deserter! There are no villains to save you now."

The knight thrust his sword up just as Trystan swept out his magic, but it was moving too slow; it wouldn't make it to Gideon in time. He cried out but was cut short when the knight jerked to a halt, eyes rolling to the back of his head. He fell beside Gideon, a silver dagger in his back.

Gideon smiled, and Trystan nearly did, too.

"Gentlemen," Gideon said to the Valiant Guards surrounding him. "Have you met my sister?"

CHAPTER 78

EVIE

The dagger flew out of the knight's back and into Evie's waiting hand. She smiled, wiggling her fingers. "Hello, boys! Did I miss all the fun?"

They charged toward her, but she was ready for them. She felt no fear, just ice in her veins as she threw the dagger with a flick of her wrist. It spun and guided itself right into another knight's shoulder. Down he went. The rest closed in on her, and Gideon leaped to his feet…but there was no need to protect her. Someone else was already there.

The Villain clutched a knight by the head as his mist took care of the others. "Were you going to hurt her?" he asked casually, calmly. Which Evie knew for The Villain was the equivalent of alarm bells calling, *DANGER! DANGER!*

The knight stuttered beneath his hand. "No, no, I—I—"

The Villain squeezed his head hard. "Answer honestly. I detest liars."

"Yes, I was, sir," the knight finally admitted, shaking.

"I'm afraid I will have to hurt you, then." It was a resolute statement.

"Please, sir! Have mercy!"

The Villain's eyes flickered down to the man's boots before calmly climbing back up. "The boots you're wearing were stolen from me during my stay at the palace." Evie blinked in surprise at the statement and even more when the knight yelped, tugging the boots off and muttering apologies and something about winning them. It was, all in all, a confusing exchange.

Or it was until The Villain swung an arm and knocked the shaking knight clean out. That was normal. Evie took the opening and rushed for him. "Are you okay?" she asked, but then stopped cold. The male guvre was still lying there, all alone; he looked at Evie with a whine. The sight, his pain, what it meant for their mission… In that moment, she was re-shattered all over again. She could practically feel the pieces of her falling away. "No." She gripped the sides of her head. "No, I can't take any more."

Gideon was there, putting a reassuring hand on her shoulder. "We'll get them back, Eve."

More fighting roared around them, but Evie no longer had any motivation to join the fray. Her dagger felt as useful as a pencil. Gideon looked like he was ready to fight, but Evie put a hand over his, stopping him. "Just watch," she said.

The Villain was walking to the center of the fighting with the same dark, calm, and cold expression. He was ready.

And so was she.

One by one, every knight began choking and then fell, attacked by a mysterious force they couldn't see. "His magic really is invisible," Gideon whispered, sounding awed and a little bit terrified.

"To everyone but me," Evie admitted.

And as the remaining knights caught on to the danger, they scattered, clearing the courtyard as fast as they could. They nearly made it to the entrance of Hickory Forest.

But it was too late.

A rumbling rattled overhead as a wave of fire spread from the courtyard to the tree line, turning the escaping knights to ash. "Oh, that's right," Gideon said. "We have a dragon."

Evie grinned, nudging his shoulder. "Fluffy."

Fire shot across the courtyard in celebratory bursts, and the Malevolent Guards cheered as they claimed their victory. Fluffy swooped down with Blade and Becky atop him, Ms. Erring gripping Blade tightly as he pumped his fist.

The Villain stood alone, with bodies littered around him, staring at the destruction, expressionless. Hunched over, weaker—because of her.

Gideon nudged her with his shoulder. "I'm okay. Why don't you go see if he is, too?"

Evie licked her lips, shutting her eyes briefly. "He prefers it that way, I think—being alone."

Gideon nodded once, and then a contemplative expression took over his face. "Eve, could we talk? I have something important to tell you."

Her heart felt like it was weighted with lead, bottoming out to her stomach at what she had to say, the failure she had to admit. "Me too."

But their discussion was paused by Edwin barreling in, arm sliced open and bloody, but he barely seemed to notice. "Miss Evie!" he yelled.

Tatianna was working her way through as many Malevolent Guards as she could to triage any wounds; she and Clare shot haphazard glances at each other as they healed and patched them up, already looking tired, but Tatianna jolted when she saw Edwin, reaching him in seconds. "Edwin, what happened? Give me your arm."

"Don't fuss, Miss Tatianna. I'm all right."

Her glowing hands hovered above the wound, gently molding the slabs of skin back together. Tatianna smiled softly. "I'll always fuss over you, dear Edwin."

He turned to Evie, and they locked eyes. "Miss, it's your sister."

Everything around her seemed to come to a grinding halt at the realization that Lyssa could have been anywhere near the battlegrounds. Was she okay? Evie would never forgive herself if something happened to her—

"She's okay!" Edwin assured, and everyone visibly exhaled. "But we found her below in the dungeons… It seems she's been sneaking there to visit with your father."

Evie groaned in anguish, her heart breaking anew for what this must mean. "Oh, Lyssa."

Edwin winced. "There's more, Miss Evie. She wasn't just down by the dungeons—she was locked in your father's cell."

Gideon took her hand as she braced herself for Edwin's next words.

"Your…your father escaped."

CHAPTER 79

EVIE

"Lyssa?" Evie called from the doorway to their room with no small amount of fear.

Gideon was behind her, fidgeting. "Should I stay out here?"

Evie softened. "No. No, she'll want to see you." She hadn't yet told Gideon about their mother, hadn't fully processed it herself. Becky's hand had remained in hers for the entirety of the flight back to the manor; it had kept her grounded. The boss had stayed farther away, though she caught him sneaking peeks at her when he thought she wasn't looking.

Move on, her mind begged her.

Nope, her heart said with a wild laugh.

She'd deal with it all later, when her sister didn't need her so much.

Lyssa sat on their bed, feet swinging off it, dress dirtied and hair unkempt. It reminded Evie of all the days she'd come home from work to find Lyssa filthy from playing outside with her friends. Now the only beings she interacted with were pixies, trained killers, ogres, and villains. *Oh my.*

But her sister hadn't complained, not once—not about missing her friends, not about Evie spending so much time on work, not about never seeing their father. And that was Evie's fault.

Lyssa's eyes welled with tears when she saw them come in. "Do you hate me?" she asked in a tiny voice.

Evie was beside her in seconds, her arms wrapped around her sister's head, cradling her against her chest, the way she had when Lyssa was a baby.

"There is nothing you could do, *ever*, that would make me hate you, my love." Evie kissed her sister's head twice. Then Gideon sat on the other side of her, and Lyssa didn't hesitate—she immediately buried her head in Gideon's neck and wrapped her small arms around him. Gideon sniffed, using his free hand to tug Evie closer.

It was the one beautiful thing Evie could find in this mess: being held by siblings who had been hurt by the same set of hands that had hurt her. She would never be known like that by anyone else.

They separated, and Evie swallowed hard, feeling trepidation at the thought of pushing matters forward, but there were questions that begged for answers. "Lyssa, how did you get down to the dungeons in the first place?"

"Someone slid a note under my door. It was from Papa, saying he wanted to see me." Her sister looked away, guilty. "So...I stole the dungeon key from Ms. Erring's desk and would pretend to come down to our room and write my stories at noon in between guard rotations, but really..."

"You were down conversing with Papa," Gideon finished with a disbelieving laugh. "Our sister is an evil genius."

Evie nodded gravely. "It would appear that way."

Lyssa beamed, taking it as praise. "Do you really think so?"

Gideon rubbed his chin like he was stroking a long, scholarly beard. "Oh, yes. Very impressive." Gideon was serious then, sterner than she'd ever seen her good-humored older brother. "Lyssa, did he hurt you? How did you end up in his cell?"

"No, I'm okay." Lyssa frowned at her hands. "The first time I went down, I yelled at him, Evie, I swear." Lyssa hopped off the bed and wandered over to the window. "But then he apologized and said it was all his fault, and I thought that if he was really sorry, maybe everything would be all right and we could let him out."

It wasn't her sister's fault; she couldn't blame Lyssa for falling for the machinations of a manipulative monster. But she *could* blame her father—and she would make sure he paid for every moment of pain he'd caused Lyssa, caused all of them.

Lyssa tugged on the curtain. The early-morning light was just peeking over the horizon. They all needed to sleep. But Evie couldn't rest until she shared with her siblings the last bit of grief-inducing news.

"Lyssa, can you come over here and sit with us? I must tell you both something." Lyssa wandered back, and Gideon hoisted her onto his lap.

Her brother knew—she could see it on his face. "She's gone, isn't she, Eve?"

She gripped Gideon's hand. "Don't blame yourself. I beg you."

Lyssa frowned. "Mama? She…died?"

Evie's breath hitched. She was unable to fight the burning in her eyes any longer. She pulled the vial of dark-silver stardust that was all they had left of her and handed it gently to her little sister. "Yes, Lyssa. I'm afraid her powers overcame her. I'm so sorry. You deserve so much better."

Lyssa put both of her small hands up to Evie's cheeks. "But, Evie, I still have you."

Her heart twisted, and Gideon moved Lyssa from his lap gently and got up from the bed, trying for a small smile. "How's anyone supposed to keep it together with all this sweetness?" he joked. But she could see he rubbed at his eyes.

"Lyssa, you're not sad?" Evie asked, wanting to borrow some of that strength for herself.

Her sister smoothed out her skirt, feet kicking again. "I think I am very sad. But I won't be forever."

Words to live by.

And so they all retired to sleep.

Evie finally settled into the pillows, so weary, so unsure of what the future held beyond her hurt and grief.

Until she shot up, clutching her chest. The small nagging reminder she'd forgotten had become a sharp stab of realization. Lyssa continued to sleep soundly beside her as Evie's quiet thoughts turned to a roar.

Who in the deadlands slipped Lyssa that note?

CHAPTER 80

THE VILLAIN

"If you're wondering if this is a healthy way of dealing with your emotions, boss, let me clear it up for you. It's not."

It was too early for Sage to be awake and pestering him—for *any* of them to be, after the harrowing night. But here she was, with her quick words and her knowing eyes.

He hadn't slept, so he'd decided to relieve some stress, and Sage was effectively ruining it.

A sharp knife hovered inches away from the Valiant Guard's eye. "I wasn't wondering," Trystan said dryly, keeping his focus.

The manor protections were being refortified as best they could by the staff. Their magic was not nearly as strong as that of an enchantress, but beggars couldn't be choosers, and this was now a matter of life and death. The patch job wouldn't keep the manor truly safe—not effectively, anyway. Even if they could have it recloaked, the once-secret location was compromised, likely being whispered into Benedict's ear as Trystan stood here hovering a knife over his knight's eye.

No matter. He'd refortify the barrier and then marvel at the small fortune he'd just sent off to his black-market gardener, who had offered the rather gracious solution of large, thorny hedgerows to be planted all around the manor.

If he couldn't hide the manor, he'd make it the most dangerous place in all of Rennedawn. To the Valiant Guards and anyone else who dared to cross him. But right now, he'd focus on the knights. Particularly the one on his table saying the same boring drivel over and over again.

"Do whatever you like to me, Villain. It is an honor to die for my king!"

the knight cried furiously, but Trystan could see he was shaking on the table.

Sage stepped forward and addressed the knight directly, with a friendliness that both impressed Trystan and enflamed him beyond measure. "Would you mind waiting here for five minutes while I speak with this one?" She angled her thumb at Trystan, who threw his hands in the air at the ludicrous request.

The knight sputtered, "O-Of course, miss. Take as long as you like."

She patted the knight's hand, enraging Trystan further as she said with sickly sweetness, "Thank you."

There was nothing sweet about her grabbing his ear and pulling him from the room like a dog on a leash. "Sage!" he growled, unable to stop it as she pushed him out into the dimly lit hallway and shut the door. "Are you having a breakdown?"

"Always," she said far too cheerfully, "but that's not why I came down here." *Don't push me*, he begged. *I cannot take it.*

He deadpanned, "I'm on the edge of my seat."

"Someone in the office slipped Lyssa a note to meet my father, which was ultimately what led to his escape. He had an accomplice."

Trystan's headache was making it hard for him to process the information. "Meaning someone in the office…"

"Conspired with my father, yes. They could have even helped him when he was sabotaging your shipments."

Ice. He was ice; everything was ice. It was in his blood, in his heart, cooling all the emotions trying to burn through him. "Is that so?" he said, low, dangerous.

"I know this is hard to swallow right now, with the guvre taken, your magic acting up, my mother…dead, and *Rennedawn's Story* being… Well, I know everything is absolute shit, for lack of a better word, but I had to tell you right away."

His fist clenched, the other gripping the doorway so hard his knuckles went white. "Thank you for your candor, Sage."

"Sir?" she said warily. "There's one other thing I'd like to ask."

He rolled his shoulders as his magic tried to seep out, to greet her; he shoved it down and away.

"What did the hands of destiny say to you? It must have been something bad, right? You looked so startled." There she went again, finding every uncomfortable button on his person and pushing them until he felt like he was going to let go and do something he couldn't take back.

He ran a ragged hand down his face before tucking in a loose flap of his shirt and taking a steady inhale. He kept his reply brief, unfeeling. "A giant white blob was whispering in my ear, Sage. Of course I looked startled."

She pointed a finger up at him. "You're trying to avoid giving an answer."

"Yes," he freely admitted.

Her shoulders dropped as the knight in the room's voice called out: "Um, excuse me? Mr. Villain, sir? I have to go to the restroom…"

"Hold it!" Trystan banged a fist against the door, and Sage covered her mouth, amused. Never afraid, never fazed, taking everything with a smile and a witty rejoinder. He was sure it was the lack of sleep that made him ask, "Sage, do you ever regret walking in the woods that day? Do you ever think that… it set you on a course you were not meant to go down?"

Her nose pulled up in her normal scrunch, her pink tongue darting out to wet her lips. He watched it with an interest that was undignified. "No, of course not. If I never went in the woods that day, I never would've gotten this job. Never would've been able to give Lyssa all the books and toys she wanted. Never would've had my wounds healed by Tati, or my heart lightened by Blade, or my mind challenged by Becky."

She put her hand right over his heart. *Step away, Trystan.* He could've; he simply didn't have the will. "I never would've met *you.*" *I never would've met you.* "If asked to do it over, I wouldn't hesitate."

"Damn it."

She frowned. "What? Not what you wanted to hear?"

He closed his eyes, banging his head against the wall. "I can hardly cut a man's eyeball out after hearing that. You've ruined the mood."

She pushed him without force, laughing. "You asked!"

They both leaned up against the wall, and Kingsley appeared below their feet, holding up a sign that said: DESTINY.

Trystan's eyes widened.

Sage frowned. "What's destiny, my little prince?" Sage bent down to straighten Kingsley's crown.

Now was as good a time as any, he realized. "Sage, while we are sharing things, I suppose it might be pertinent for you to know that Kingsley isn't just a magical frog… He was once human. My friend. He was turned by an enchantress more than a decade ago, and I've been trying to find a way to undo it since with no luck."

Sage brought her hands together, as if in prayer, and held them to her lips. "Kingsley was once a human?"

He nodded stiffly, waiting for her anger that he'd waited so long to tell her.

But she merely frowned and said, "Oh dear. Then perhaps I shouldn't have changed in front of him so many times."

"What!" He turned a scathing glare on the frog.

"I'm kidding, Evil Overlord!" She laughed until tears pricked her eyes. "I already knew."

His breath caught, and his lips parted. He felt stunned. "What? How? Clare is sworn to secrecy. There's no way she would've told you—"

Evie cocked a hip. "Nobody needed to tell me! Clare has called him Alexander in front of me on multiple occasions. And Alexander just so happens to be the name of the southern kingdom's prince who 'died' about ten years ago—coincidentally around the time you became The Villain. And if all of that wasn't slap-you-in-the-face obvious, you call him by the dead prince's last name. Not so dead after all?"

He threw his arms up again. "Why didn't you say anything?"

"I didn't want to be rude." She tilted her head. "You seemed to so enjoy your secret."

He was going to die young, and it would be all her fault.

"I am curious, though," she continued. "Why was this enchantress so deadlands-bent on changing a gallant prince into a creature with webbed toes?"

He hesitated; the memory of the day it happened still haunted him. He spoke almost mechanically. "It wasn't the enchantress's fault. She was merely following orders."

Sage's brow furrowed. "Whose orders?"

"My mother's."

She flinched and gasped, her hand coming up to cover her mouth. "Why would she…?"

He smiled, but there was no joy in it. Just long-buried hurt. "My mother didn't take too well to how I came out after my time with Benedict. I had returned home looking for sanctuary, and instead I found her waiting for me, along with Clare. It was perhaps the first rift between my sister and Tatianna. Alexander Kingsley was in the wrong place at the wrong time. He came in just before I did. It was supposed to be me, and it was supposed to be death."

Sage's eyes flared. The nonsense wheels in her mind were turning and turning, this time in a fury. "What a bitch—"

The knight called again. "Hello? Are you coming back? Bring the pretty maiden with you!"

Trystan turned to the door and kicked it before roaring, "Apprentice!"

She bit her lip and started back for the stairs. "Well, as fun as this has been, I have to return to Lyssa. Last night was rough for her, and I don't want her to be alone this morning."

There was a pang of emotion for the girl, right in the center of his chest. He used to be able to keep track of the few people he cared about with one hand; at this rate, he'd have to expand to...two? Odious.

Still, an idea began to form. A way to help Lyssa heal from her pain.

The pang was replaced by a sting as a question curdled from his lips—one he'd been holding back. "Sage. That day we met, did you first come across an older woman with three children?"

She stilled at the bottom of the stairs and turned to face him. She narrowed her eyes at him, though not in suspicion. More in confusion. "...Yes, at the job fair. I was almost offered a maid position, but she clearly needed it more, so I gave it to her in my stead. How did you know about that?"

Grains of truth could usually carry you through a lie of omission. "The destiny creature told me."

She smiled. "What an odd thing to share." She paused, then asked, "Sir, shall I... Shall I look into finding another starlight user?"

He sighed, his shoulders sinking. "Take time, Sage...to mourn your mother. I'll work on getting the guvre back in the meantime. The male isn't doing well, but I think he's grown to trust us."

She looked grateful, and he hated himself for it. "And then back to it! Stealing the kingdom!" And with that declaration, she turned on her heel and left. Her footsteps echoed off the stairs, and when they fully faded, he slid down the wall, elbows on his knees.

Kingsley sat there, unblinking, ever faithful. "Should I have told her, old friend?" Trystan asked him quietly. "That there was no older woman at the job fair—that it was one of destiny's enchanters in disguise, guiding her right into my path?" Kingsley hopped closer, ribbiting. The rest of destiny's words felt as if they'd been burned onto Trystan's soul.

You were always supposed to meet Evie Sage, Trystan Maverine. Just as Evie Sage is meant to be your downfall, and you her undoing.

The second he'd heard destiny's words, he knew the truth of them. So it was decided, as painful and heart-wrenching as it would be—he had to keep his distance from her. Lest she ruin him and he her.

No more. He was through.

Just as soon as he finished one more very important task...

CHAPTER 81

EVIE

Night had fallen on Massacre Manor once again. The Malevolent Guards were all recovering, as was the office—the damage from the fire and the battle was being repaired to restore the manor's former glory.

"Maybe we should go in there," Tatianna said warily, kicking out a stiletto boot, arms folded across her chest as she cocked an ear toward the door.

"Give him a chance! It sounds like it's going well," Blade said with an optimistic gleam in his eye.

Crash.

Gideon and Evie shared a glance before Gideon nodded toward the room and gave her a look that said, *Get in there.*

Evie grimaced and lightly pushed against the door. "Perhaps I'll just make sure everything—"

The door slammed open, nearly knocking into her head.

And what they saw on the other side— Blade gripped her arm to keep himself from falling over. "How quickly do you think we could get a portrait artist in here?" he asked.

No artist could ever do the scene justice; there was simply too much to capture.

Standing in the doorway of Evie and Lyssa's chambers was The Villain, face reddened with anger. The color was a contrast to the large pink hat that sat atop his head, feathers coming out of it from every direction. He looked like a deranged pink chicken. Kingsley sat upon his shoulder, crown still perched on his small green brow, but it was now paired with a tiny handkerchief fastened into a dress.

Evie bit her lip so hard she tasted blood. "That's, uh…a good look for you, sir," she said, sounding strangled, stepping forward and reaching up to pluck a fallen feather from his shoulder.

He gave her a warning glance as he loomed over her, pointing what was meant to be a threatening finger in her face. "Be careful, Sage." He seemed to remember himself and moved away as quickly as possible. It stung.

"Lord Trystan! The tea is almost ready. Please return to the table at once!" Lyssa ordered from inside the room.

Edwin came around the corner of the corridor. His new glasses were a perfect fit against his nose, and Evie thought he stood a little prouder for it as he handed Trystan a tray of artfully decorated pastries.

"Thank you, Edwin," Trystan said quietly.

Edwin's smile stretched wide as he tipped a blue hand in salute. "Only the best for Lady Lyssa and Lord Trystan's tea party. Is this enough?"

Trystan nodded, inspecting each one with careful attention and focus that made Evie feel like the butterflies in her stomach were trying to make their way up her throat. "These will do nicely."

He took the tray from Edwin's hands and returned to the room. Edwin made to leave, and Evie called after him. "Edwin, I'm sorry, I never thanked you for making up a plate for me when I slept through dinner. It was delicious." She grinned. "Some of your best work. I meant to tell you sooner."

Edwin turned, face softened, glancing at where Trystan had been standing. He spoke slowly, as if he were trying to make her understand something. "*I* didn't make any plates, Miss Evie."

She shut her eyes tight, sucking in a breath as his meaning struck her. Her smile was sad, she knew, because her eyes burned.

Shaking the thoughts away—*all* of them—she entered the room, giving Blade a look of amused censure when he tried to follow before she shut the door. Lyssa sat in the middle of the bedchambers at a small table with even smaller chairs. She had no idea where Trystan would've scrounged up such a thing, or if he'd had someone go out and retrieve it specifically for this purpose, and she wasn't certain which would defeat her heart more.

Everything he did now was dangerous. But he was pulling away from her; she felt it.

Don't give your heart to the boss, Evie!

Too fucking late.

What an ill-fated pair the two of them were. She was so lost in that bittersweet ache, she was jarred when Lyssa screeched at Trystan, who had his teacup halfway to his lips. "No, Lord Trystan! You must pour for Miss Halliway first!"

He furrowed his brow adorably in confusion, his face such a comfort to her. It took all of Evie's will not to lean forward and kiss him. "Who is Miss Halliway?" he asked. It was Kingsley who lifted a foot and pointed to the doll seated in the chair with a rather frightening expression plastered on her porcelain face.

"Oh."

This was it. This was the line he'd draw; Evie was sure of it. He'd humored Lyssa this long—she'd give him the credit. The pain of betrayal and loss might never be gone, but at least her sister had been thoroughly assured that she was safe, treasured, and loved. Evie started to move toward the table to give her own attention to Miss Halliway, both to protect Lyssa's feelings and to spare her boss the painful awkwardness, but she was stopped...

As Trystan Maverine, Evil Overlord, in his large, ridiculously frilly hat, picked up the flowery teapot and poured the tea, saying with a sternness that made her heart twist all over again, "My sincerest apologies, Miss Halliway. I usually have better manners."

By the gods, she loved him.

She loved his smile and his rare laughter. She loved that in one moment he could be fiercely protective and in the next he could be soft and unsure. She loved that he understood her, perhaps better than anyone she'd ever known, that he made her importance known without placation. That he'd given her a reason to wake up in the morning, a reason to rush to get ready—not only to get to work (though she loved her work) but to get to *him*. There could never be another person in the whole of the world she could feel this way about.

And then she remembered *his* words.

We should keep our distance.

And as if he heard her thoughts, he turned to look at her with a grim expression. "Sage, I've been meaning to tell you. Along with your promotion, I took the liberty of having your desk moved to the alcove with all the windows, until we can have a proper office built for you."

She gaped. The alcove was lovely, airy and spacious, and possibly as far away from his office as one could get. It had begun already, the distance. It would've hurt more if she didn't notice that for someone getting their way, her boss looked like he'd just swallowed a thousand tiny shards of glass.

Something had happened. Something with the destiny monster—something he wasn't telling her. She'd find out what it was, though, because if there was one good thing that she could wrench from all the pain, it was this. It was *them*.

And she was through not fighting for what she wanted.

She looked to him with pity. "You will regret that choice, I think."

He speared her with a glare before turning to pour himself more tea from the pot. "I never regret anything."

"Hmm," she said, smiling wickedly. "Then I suppose I'll just have to make you."

He looked so startled, he nearly dropped the teapot as he returned it to the table with a clatter.

Lyssa didn't notice. She was too busy tipping a teacup to Miss Halliway's lips.

His dark eyes found Evie's. He wet his lips before speaking, causing heat to spike in her blood. "You— I must have misheard you. What?"

It wasn't a game; the confusion was genuine. But he'd heard her. Just was discomfited by the words. He wanted to run from her so fast that she'd see smoke coming out of his heels.

She didn't repeat her declaration, just looked at him with disgruntled fondness. This was her first crack in his defenses. The first of many, she knew. "You heard me fine."

His whisper back sounded painful, his eyes struck by surprise, befuddlement, and heart-stopping fear. "Do not start this, Sage."

She laid a gentle hand over his, and a shock blazed up her arm at the contact. He flinched under her fingers but didn't move away as he normally would—just sucked in a breath, his eyes intensely on her face as she said, "Worry not, Your Evilness. It's already begun."

He's petrified.

She recalled a wish she'd made on a star not long ago and how it had come true. How the star had answered her... The words struck something, something nagging in her mind.

"I love this plate! It's such a funny shape," Lyssa said innocently.

Evie had allowed Lyssa to have the odd, dark crystal slab her mother had left behind for her. All signs of magic from it were gone, if there ever were any. Except perhaps the joy it gave to her younger sister. The shape *was* funny, Evie had to admit—and somehow familiar.

Lyssa dropped the plate and frowned down at the sugar bowl. "We are out of sugar!"

The Villain's face was panicked for just a second before he checked himself into a neutral expression. Clearing his throat, he said, "I think we've already added a sufficient amount to our tea in any case."

Lyssa pouted. "But the table doesn't look as cute!" Her brown eyes widened as she snapped her fingers and pulled the vial of her mother's stardust from her pocket. "We'll use this!"

"Lyssa, don't!" Evie called, frantic at the prospect of losing that last bit of her mother. But it was too late—in her haste to stop her sister, Evie had startled her instead; Lyssa dropped the vial, and it smashed right onto the oddly shaped crystal.

And then the room went startlingly bright.

Lyssa screamed, and so did Evie as they were both yanked to the ground and tucked beneath Trystan's arms. "What happened!" he yelled as the light simmered out.

Evie was the first to peek her eyes open, scrambling up to look at the table and the slab of crystal, too. It glowed so brightly—but not brightly enough. "Sir, do we still have that bit of stardust left from the caves?"

He nodded, gently helping Lyssa to her feet before pulling the small vial out of his shirt from a thread around his neck. "There's barely a thimbleful left." He uncapped it and tapped the rest of the dust onto the jagged slab, and it glowed, complete and vibrant, changing from a dark, opaque nothingness to—

Midnight, with one bright glimmering star in the dead center.

Lyssa squinted over it. "It looks like a piece of sky."

A piece of sky. And it struck Evie all at once. Every clue along their journey to find her mother. It had been written plainly in front of her the whole time.

The daughter of wishing stars.

She wanted to be swallowed by midnight.

Your mother's starlight enveloped her.

Oh gods.

I have no name…by natural law, I can take none.

Wanting to be no one.

Harvested from the stars themselves.

The words and pieces filtered in all at once. Goose bumps rose on Evie's bare arms as she knocked a small chair over, pacing the floor as one more defying sentence clattered in her mind.

I hope you will return to see them.

She knew why the shape of the slab was so familiar.

A large hand closed over her shoulder, and she turned to see Trystan's face. "The daughter of wishing stars," she whispered. "We have to go to the caves. I'll explain on the way."

Trystan's eyes widened, shock and questions in his own fathomless gaze. "All right. Let's go," he said urgently, removing his tea party attire and carefully placing it on the table by Lyssa, and Evie's heart warmed at his immediate trust.

Lyssa was incredulous, of course. "Why are you taking my plate? And what about our party?"

Evie knelt to be level with her sister. Kingsley hopped up beside them, holding up a sign that had a question mark on it. She placed a hand on her little sister's cheek. "Lyssa, I promise Lord Trystan will have a tea party with you at least once a week from now until the end of time, but I'm afraid we need to end it early today. And I need to take this."

Lyssa was confused but seemed satisfied with the bargain, since with a bite of a teacake she said, "Okay!"

When Evie finally looked up at her boss, he wasn't moving with urgency any longer, just staring at her with a strange expression she couldn't figure out. He cleared his throat, unreadable emotion on his face. "I'm following you, Sage."

She nodded, and they both bounded into the hallway, where the others still loitered, waiting to get another look at the boss in all his finery. "Blade, how soon can you have Fluffy ready to go?" Evie asked.

Blade looked startled, but only for a second before his face set in a look of resolve. "Ten minutes, maybe fifteen? Why? Where are we going?"

Gideon's eyes were searching her face. "Eve?"

"Ready him now, Gushiken," Trystan boomed, looking ready to do battle on her behalf while lifting Kingsley onto his shoulder.

Blade was gone in a flash.

Gideon gripped her arm as Evie made to follow. "Evie, please. What's happened?"

She held both of her brother's hands before saying with as much gentleness as she could manage, "I know where our mother is."

CHAPTER 82

EVIE

They were in the sky.

The sun set behind them as darkness descended, following them back to the beginning, back to the cave. When they landed, she saw that the landscape was different now: the kissing trees, once whimsical; the land, once vibrant; it was all transformed—and not for the better. Everything was duller, grayer, like someone had come to leach the color away. The kissing trees, once forever touching above the cave, were separated, cracked down the middle.

"What happened here?" Evie whispered.

"The magic is dying, with the guvre's capture, and Fate's consequences can only be worsening it… I fear this is only the beginning," Trystan answered, helping her jump down from the dragon.

"Blade?" Evie called up to him, unsure.

Blade frowned. "You want me to stay here?"

Evie spoke gently. "Our friend in there doesn't know you, and I don't wish to startle it."

Blade nodded, rolling his shoulders and then waving a hand. "Go, go! I'll be right here."

They approached the cave entrance, where torches were still lit on either side. But twisted brown vines had spread across the opening.

The sentry was gone. All that remained of him was his spear, abandoned on the ground. The magical crisis had clearly seeped through the land, consuming this place and all that it had. The area was run-down, ravaged.

Evie sprinted forward, pulling her dagger out, and began to slash away at the overgrown vines covering the entrance. Trystan, beside her, pulled a long sword from his own belt and brought it down hard against the foliage. He chopped away with furious cries until a path was cleared.

"Go!" he ordered. She dove through, and then she was falling, Trystan right after her. Her scream was swallowed in her throat as she went down, down, down, until she once more bounced on a floating, dewy cloud. But this one was tinged by night. She didn't hesitate this time, merely hopped off and rolled as the boss tumbled after her.

Evie jumped up, pulling the slab from her pocket. The stars in the cave mimicked the ones now shining from its crystal surface.

A large voice boomed above them as the crown of clouds was revealed even in the darker lighting. The giant gleamed like a star itself, the midnight clouds clustering to form its crown. "Evie Sage. I hoped you'd return."

She stepped forward. Trystan's hand shot out to stop her on instinct—she could tell by how he coughed when he released her. "Go on," he said, raking a hand through his hair and looking away. She could see what it cost him to trust her with this, to fight his instinct to protect her. Her heart warmed.

She held up the crystal—the one that she now knew was not merely the magicless slab of rock it appeared to be. It belonged to the creature before them; the rough-hewn edges were an exact match to the gaping hole in the sky of its lair. She offered it up to the creature with a humble bow. "Your missing piece of sky."

The creature was surprised, gasping as it reached down a giant hand and pulled the slab from her fingertips. "My sky. My beautiful sky." The creature wept as it held the piece close, like it had been so lost without it. It reached toward the crack in the surface and pushed the slab into place. And the room *boomed*.

The ground shook, the gleaming stars around them dancing and celebrating at being rejoined, at being whole once more.

The creature stared down at her, smiling; its teeth were so large they could've been used as stones to repair the ramparts of the manor. It bowed back to her. "Whatever you want, Evie Sage, it is yours."

She swallowed and breathed out, "You said that you couldn't interfere with human affairs. But my mother..." Evie looked up through the skylight of the cave to that one bright star, her constant companion beaming down at her. "My mother is not human now. Her magic enveloped her, and she left behind stardust because she became..."

The creature finished with a gentle smile. "A wishing star."

It began twirling its hands about, and air followed its motions, whipping and growing until an almost cyclone appeared between its giant palms. "Now," the creature said, "she will be free."

The creature sent the rush of midnight clouds in its hands up and up and up, through the skylight, out of the cave, soaring all the way to that brightest star above—and plucking it from the soft, vast expanse of the night sky.

It swirled down in a whirlwind. The gale was so strong that Evie's hair flew back, tugging against her scalp, and her yellow dress molded to her. Trystan gripped her hand to steady them both, holding his other palm up to shield his eyes.

When the whirlwind touched down on the grass before Evie and Trystan, a light shined so bright it was warm against her skin, her eyes, as that one shimmering, gleaming star transformed. A flash of silver, white, and then golden light swooped up in a rush of shine—an unearthly, unbelievable sight, impossible to look at. Evie turned her face into Trystan's shoulder, gripping his hand with all her might.

That flash of light spread in an explosion of multicolored brilliance, and when Evie looked up, it dimmed, fading until it was nothing more than a woman.

Her mother.

Standing before her in a dress so white, it reminded her of the moon, was a woman she never thought she would see again—but she was there, and she was smiling.

"Mama?" Evie choked out, the word foreign on her lips.

Her mother's golden skin glowed in the starlight, her arms held out as tears glistened in her warm brown eyes. "You found me, hasibsi."

A sob left Evie's lips, and in it, every pain, every heartache; all the overwhelming collapse of grief poured into the sound as she bounded for her mother and fell into her arms. Nura clutched her head, whispering soothing words of comfort in her ear—ones she hadn't heard since she was a child.

That comfort unlocked everything. A key to the closed door of her childhood, which had been locked tight since she'd lost her mother and Gideon, through all those years of torment without them.

But she hadn't lost them. Not truly. Not anymore.

Fingers raked through her hair, and she felt the warmth of her mother's neck, smelled the summer air after a rainstorm on her skin—so comforting she ached. "It's all right, my darling girl." Nura shushed her gently, and Evie was finally able to pull herself away, sensing her mother's attention shifting to the person over her shoulder.

Trystan stood there, hands tucked into his pockets as he frowned down at his wrinkled shirt and then back up to them. Evie smiled. "Mama, this is my, um— That is to say, he's, uh…Trystan Maverine."

Her mother's eyes were kind and delighted, and Evie's heart swelled with gratitude. Trystan deserved someone who was happy to see him; he so rarely was granted that. Nura reached her hand forward to shake, but Trystan was already bowing deeply over her hand. Ever the gentleman.

"I'm so happy to meet you, Trystan." Her mother went right into using his name, like she'd known him far longer than this moment.

Trystan winced, clearing his throat nervously. "I'm afraid you wouldn't say that if you knew who I was…if you knew what your daughter does for me." When Nura lifted a brow, he fumbled, and was he blushing? "Forgive me. That was poorly worded. I meant to say her profession. What she does in my *offices*."

Her mother let out a twinkling laugh as she patted Trystan's cheek with maternal affection. "I'm afraid I already know. I've been watching you all for quite some time."

Trystan swallowed, blinking fast. "You've been watching?"

Nura looked at Evie, then at Trystan, then at the sky, winking. "I had a very good view."

Her mother had seen, had been watching. And so Evie had to ask. "Mama, then you know that Gideon… You know that he's alive?"

Nura's hand came up to clutch her chest, her smile watery as she replied, "Yes. I do."

Evie pressed further, knowing that she probably shouldn't. "And Papa? You know about…him, too?"

There was no force in the world, no wrath greater than the burning rage in Nura Sage's eyes. Her voice was as hard as granite. "I do."

But at that moment, the time for questions had ended, as the cave around them began to rattle and shake like the earth was quaking. "What's going on?" Evie cried, holding tight to her mother's hand.

"I don't know!" Trystan answered. He turned to the creature. "What is happening?"

"The magic is fading." The creature's voice was booming in its sadness, and the room seemed to weep with it. The stars surrounding them dripped with silvered drops, almost like tears. "It's found us. Go—you must go now!"

A dark cloud bumped into Evie's knees from behind, causing her to fall back onto it alongside her mother and Trystan, whose arm wrapped around her, pulling her the rest of the way onto the creature's platform. They soared up as the cave shook again, the stars winking, the clouds misting into the air.

The cave was going to collapse, and the creature with it. She couldn't stand any more destruction, couldn't bear losing another thing that was pure and good. "Stop!" Evie screamed. The cloud halted as she pleaded with the creature, "Come with us. Please."

The creature shook its head. "I will not abandon my piece. I'm sworn to protect this land for the rest of my days—no matter how numbered. But please: save Rennedawn, save the magic." They were lifted higher still, and Evie cried out in despair. As they continued toward the exit, they heard one last refrain from the creature, and Evie knew it would haunt her for the rest of her life. "Think of me...when you're with the trees."

The cloud soared out of the cave, back to Blade, back to the dragon. They all fell to the ground, the very air around them shaking with debris and dust. It was impossible to see; Evie clung to Trystan's arm, to her mother's hand, and when the smoke cleared and they finally opened their eyes...

The cave was gone.

CHAPTER 83

EVIE

Nura Sage was hugging Gideon so tightly and fiercely that Evie was certain her brother would never escape their mother's clutches.

It had been agreed, upon their return, that they would wait until Lyssa woke in the morning before breaking the news. The poor girl needed at least one good night's sleep before her world turned upside down *again*. At least this time, the changes were for the better. Her mother was alive, her power subdued for the foreseeable future. As a star, she'd exerted so much energy that it had put her magic in periods of dormant sleep. Plus they had The Villain and his power, no matter how fraught. As soon as they got the mother guvre back, every tool they needed to fulfill the prophecy of *Rennedawn's Story* would be in their arsenal.

Or so she'd thought.

"What do you mean, there are four parts of the prophecy?" Tatianna asked as she examined Nura for injuries.

Nura took a sip of tea before gently placing the cup back on the table and answering Tatianna with a small smile. "I did not see everything up there. There were periods of unconsciousness, stretches where I wasn't awake, and I could only see so much at a time even when I was. But I do know there are four objects to make the story real. I heard Benedict name four during one of his meetings. The Villain who was once kind; the youth of Fate's creatures, the guvres; the wishing starlight; and there is one more…"

Trystan was trying to temper his patience—Evie could tell by the way he started to say something and immediately stopped himself. "What is it?"

Nura looked forlorn. "I am sorry, but there are still pieces of my memories that I can't quite grasp. I'm certain it will come back to me."

Evie held her mother's hand. "I'm sorry we didn't find you sooner. Your letters were ruined, and we couldn't sort it out."

Her mother smiled shakily, mischief in her eyes. "Hasibsi, my darling love. The letters wouldn't have given you a single clue to find me anyway. I knew they could fall into the wrong hands, so I left clues only my clever girl could solve." She tilted Evie's chin up and planted a kiss on her forehead.

Gideon stood near his mother, keeping determined eyes on her and then on Trystan. "I'll find out what the fourth object is. Evie's done enough. I'll go back to the Gleaming Palace and get the book."

"No!" Evie said defiantly. "That is too dangerous. We'll find another way. We'll steal the book, rescue the female guvre, find the fourth object, and fulfill the prophecy before Benedict."

Gideon raised a brow. "Oh, is that all?" he asked dryly.

Trystan stared at her from where he leaned against the wall, eyes hard, jaw shadowed, and so much passed between them as he nodded. "Get some rest, everyone. We'll begin our work first thing tomorrow."

As he walked by her to leave the room, the back of his hand brushed hers, and he stumbled like the sensation had stung him. He only paused a moment, though, and then was gone.

Evie breathed in slowly. That one touch felt a little too much like a goodbye. A farewell from everything as they knew it.

She walked toward the window and peered out at the night sky. The brightest star was no longer there—the one she'd wished on so many times. She smiled, looking over to see her mother being worked on by Tatianna's healing hands.

As she leaned into the window, Gideon appeared at her elbow. He looked worried, a crinkle in his brow and a frown pulling down his lips.

Her heart started to race. "What is it, Gideon?"

"I've been trying to tell you something," he admitted, "but it never felt like the right time."

Warning heated her cheeks as she motioned for him to speak. He bit his lip, leaning a hand on the sill.

Speaking low, he murmured, "You remember how I was supposed to give you the antidote to the sleeping-death fruit? So you'd awaken."

Her eyes widened. "Yes, Gideon. A most important step." She laughed nervously.

Gideon took her hand and dropped a vial into it. It rolled back and forth on her palm, glowing.

The antidote.

"I couldn't get it to you in time. I kept being blocked by guards."

She ran her other hand through her curls to hide how it had begun to shake. "This makes no sense. If you didn't give me the antidote, how did I awaken? There's only one cure."

Gideon smiled, like this wasn't going to alter the very fabric of her world. "There are two."

"It's a myth. Such magic, such power—it doesn't exist," she said fearfully.

Her brother shook his head, closing her fingers around the bottle with a lift of his brow. "Are you certain?"

The memories during her death sleep: the gentle voice, the one that called her back to living, and…the whisper of a kiss against her knuckles. She pushed any joy from the revelation away, shoving it deep within herself. It wouldn't serve her now.

She slipped the antidote into her skirt pocket and turned to the window, gripping the sill tight with both hands. Looking up to the night sky, she surveyed all the stars and didn't make any wishes, didn't make any more requests of a world that only sought to confuse her. Instead, she made a vow to it. One she hoped would shake the earth all the way to the Gleaming Palace. To King Benedict. To her father. To Trystan Maverine.

She smiled and made the declaration.

Beware the wrath of a kind heart.

EPILOGUE

GIDEON

One week later…

The office had returned to its usual disarray at a rapid rate. Or at least Gideon assumed the disarray was usual. He hadn't borne witness to any other kind of office function. His mother had been glued to his side for the last seven days, taking the most careful, tentative steps with Lyssa.

Who seemed very keen on evading her. Something their mother was putting on a brave face for, but Gideon could see the pain at not having been there to watch her children grow up. At missing the things she should've been a part of. Only time would mend such hurts. Only new memories could soothe away the loss of the old ones.

Evie and The Villain were avoiding each other the way mermaids avoided ships, only sparing each other passing glances anytime they were within ten feet of each other. That bubbling pot would hit a boil fairly quickly, but Gideon didn't dare say that to either of them.

Keely had gone back to her usual glares, which suited Gideon just fine, as the woman was far too prickly for his tastes. Any sense of rightness he'd felt embracing her or fighting alongside her had merely been due to a rush of adrenaline. It had already passed, and he hardly noticed her—even now, when she was walking toward him with a murderous expression on her lovely face. She slapped a scrap of paper down onto Evie's desk, which Evie let her brother use while she was doing inventory—of spiderwebs, most likely.

"Do I look like an errand girl to you?" Keely rolled her eyes and crossed her arms, her ridiculously thick braid swaying behind her. He was surprised she didn't topple over from the weight of it.

Gideon contemplated her, tapping his chin. "I don't know. They wear silly little hats, don't they? Put one on. Let's find out."

"I hope the dragon eats you," she sneered. "Clean up your own scraps of paper, sir knight." Then she turned and walked away with ground-eating strides. He was surprised and annoyed to find himself staring after her retreating curved form.

Then he looked down at the page he'd torn in haste from *Rennedawn's Story* and smuggled to Evie alongside their mother's letters. The glowing seal at the top was a sign of the book's power. He read the words over again, hoping the fourth object might come to him if he thought hard enough.

The person who saves the magical lands will take fate's youngling well in hand; when fate and starlight magic fall together, the land will belong to you forever. But beware the unmasked Villain and their malevolent dark, for nothing is more dangerous than a blackened good heart...

A confused grin pulled on his lips, something persistent tugging at his mind.

He read the line again, this time aloud. "But beware the unmasked Villain and their malevolent dark, for nothing is more dangerous than a blackened good heart."

And then it hit him.

His eyes widened, heart pounding with dread as he peered down at the words in disbelief.

Gideon had been relegated off to the corner of the king's ballroom all those weeks ago, pushed there by the other guards and quietly panicking as he watched King Benedict's taunts and The Villain's desperation. He'd stared at the glass casket that held his sister and feared that Evie wouldn't awaken, that he would be too late with the antidote.

But she *had* awoken.

And she had revealed herself to the entire room. To the kingdom. To the world.

Gideon felt the dread pool like ice in his belly. He could sense it now, how everything was about to change.

Trystan—The Villain—hadn't been the only one revealed to all the world at the king's ill-fated event.

Evie had, too.

Gideon sucked in a breath.

She'd been...unmasked.

The End.

Until we meet again...

ACKNOWLEDGMENTS

I'm almost certain I could write another novel with all the people I have to thank for making this book a reality, but for the printer and the paper's sake, I will do my best to be brief. When I began writing *Apprentice to the Villain*, I was going through many changes in my life. Change is good, wonderful even, but it unmoors you a bit and helps you to lean on what's grounded and familiar.

For me, that's always been my family. My favorite thing about rereading anything I've written is seeing the pieces of them within a story, especially this one. Thank you to my mom, Jolie, who is all that is good and kind; to my dad, Mark, who is the reason I can laugh at things that sometimes make me cry. Thank you to my grandparents Rosalie and Jim for their ever-constant support and for cheering me on. Thank you to my Sitto Georgann, without whom Evie's good heart would not exist, and thank you to Giddo Richard for passing the author hat down to me. I wish you could've been here to read my books, but I have a very good feeling you're looking down on me and smiling. I hope you have the very best view.

Thank you to my aunts and uncles. Aunt Kim and Uncle Glenn — extra special thank-you to my uncle Glenn, who has the very best ideas! Aunt Nicole, Uncle Brian, Aunt Miriam, Uncle Karl, dearly departed Uncle Brian (yes, there are two), Aunt Chrissy. Thank you to my countless cousins, who I will name here because it's my book and I want to! Kristen, Katie, Brian, Sean, Ashley, Marshall, Richard, Gabriel, Samuel, Nicholas, and Anthony. And to my best girl friends who married in and made me feel like I finally had sisters: Ally, Katie, Amanda, Iman, and Mara. Please don't ever leave me alone with the boys again.

exhales I told you I had a big family. I would say an extra thank-you to my brothers, but this book is dedicated to them, can't get greedy. But in all seriousness, any warmth and fun and laughter you felt while reading about Becky's brothers or Gideon is the joy I feel when I'm with mine. Immeasurable and irreplicable.

Thank you to my best friend Lexi, who's been reading my writing and enjoying it for years, and all the friends who supported me through *Assistant to the Villain* and all through writing *Apprentice*. I am so grateful for you. Thank you to my found family, who I text almost a hundred times a day and who soothe my soul like they are medicine. Maggie, Sam, Kaven, Amber, and Stacey. I love you all so, so much.

And of course, last but not least of my clan, my Michael. Who's driven me to nearly every event, every signing, and made sure I felt safe and loved through every change I went through this year. Thank you for your patience, kindness, and love. I love you as much as The Villain loves sweets. And thank you to Michael's family, who are an extension of my own with their constant support this past year.

Then, of course, we have the people who made this book a possibility and who made all my dreams become my reality. Thank you so much to my wonderful agent, Brent Taylor, whose constant enthusiasm, optimism, and unwavering belief in me was the reason *Apprentice* turned out so beautifully. Thank you to Liz Pelletier, who changed my whole life. Your advice and wisdom through any challenges this year made me a better author and a better human. Thank you for everything. Thank you to my entire Entangled and Red Tower family! All the people who worked tirelessly on this book to make it what it is now and for every ounce of kindness! Thank you so much to Stacy Abrams, Rae Swain, Hannah Lindsey, Molly Majumder, Heather Riccio, Meredith Johnson, Ashley Doliber, Curtis Svehlak, Brittany Marczak, and Jessica Meigs. Thank you so much to Elizabeth Turner Stokes for yet another beautiful cover! Your talent makes my world feel real. Thank you to Lizzy Mason, who answers every single one of my panicked text messages, and my entire team at Kaye Publicity. Thank you to the team at Macmillan and all the foreign publishers who have so lovingly brought this series to their readers around the world.

Thank you to the bookstores and booksellers who have put my book in front of so many readers and for their contagious excitement over my work. Thank you so much to my readers. (It's still so wild to have readers! But I digress.) Thank you for making me feel like the things I make matter. Thank you for the privilege of making you all laugh. I hope *Apprentice* did the same (sans any teary moments). Balance is important! Thank you for reading *Apprentice* and continuing Evie's journey.

And finally, once more, thank you to Evie Sage. This past year was full of new experiences and new challenges. But as always, through it all, Evie was my safe place. She's always been there to reach out a hand for me, to pick me up and dust me off. This story and my characters are my light in places where all I see is dark, and I hope some of that lightness made its way to you.

Thank you to anyone who picked up this book. I hope it made you smile, but most importantly, I hope it made you do the most valuable thing a human can.

Feel.

Percy Jackson for adults meets *The Hunger Games*,
with a slow-burn romance between a contestant
and Hades himself.

Don't miss Abigail Owen's breathtaking
New Adult romantasy, in stores and online
September 3, 2024!

1

A REALLY BAD IDEA

A sizzling zap of electricity snaps directly over Zeus's temple, and I flinch while the crowd *ooh*s and *ahh*s. People from all walks of life, cultures, and gods live in San Francisco, but there's no denying this is Zeus's patron city, even if not everyone is thrilled about that.

Me in particular.

And he is very proud of the lightning thing—this being the only god-powered city in the world. Although, bad news for the people who live here: if Zeus is in a pissy mood…well, it tends to affect the lights. I can only imagine how much time those who enjoy uninterrupted power must spend on their knees in that temple.

I'd rather live in the dark.

"We shouldn't be here," I mutter under my breath as I tick a checkbox on my tablet.

My only job tonight is to observe and assess, but that doesn't make me feel any better. Of all the piss-poor schemes my boss, Felix, has come up with over the years, this one ranks right up there with trying to capture a pegasus to sell on the black market. That put our den on Poseidon's shit list for years. Yes, den. The name isn't exactly creative, but we're thieves, not poets.

Actually, they call us pledges.

All of us have been pledged as collateral to work off a debt of some sort. I was so young when my family surrendered me to the Order of Thieves, I don't even remember my own birth name. But I'm twenty-two now, so that was a while ago and not something I like to dwell on.

A strobe of light illuminates the low clouds overhead a heartbeat before a loud crack sets car alarms blaring and babies crying.

This time I really jump but manage to force my gaze to remain straight ahead. I don't need to spare the temple a glance to know what it looks like—a pristine white structure with its classic, fluted columns aglow in purplish-white flashes and sparks cast by the never-ending arc of lightning captured above the roof. Logically, I know it's unlikely Zeus is taunting me for coming here. He's just showing off for everyone.

Do the job and get out, I tell myself.

"Scared of a little lightning, Lyra?" Chance, a master thief to my left, chides. He's acting as the drop point for all the lifts in tonight's exercise but takes his attention off the pledges long enough to toss me a condescending smile. Asshole.

One of the older thieves, Chance should have paid off his debt by now but hasn't—and the fact I'm his architect and know exactly how much he still has to go pisses him off. It also makes me his favorite target.

But the best way to deal with his brand of dickhead is to ignore him.

So instead, I focus on the unsuspecting, sycophantic multitudes as more and more crush together at the base of the temple, filling the winding street that circles up the mountain to it. They're all here to get the best view of the opening ceremonies of the Crucible Mysteries tomorrow. The opportunity was too good for Felix, our boss, to pass up—perfect for a rash of pickpocketing. Stealing so close to a sacred building is a big risk, but he reasoned away hazarding the gods' wrath by saying this exercise is both a test for the newest crop of apprentice pledges and a chance to rake in one last score before tomorrow.

He is going to get someone killed. Or worse…cursed.

Only, Felix isn't here to bear the consequences if we end up offending the gods. The poor pickpocketing apprentices will, and that's just not fair. A situation I'm regrettably and intimately familiar with. And Felix, as my old mentor, knows that. He's the *only* one who knows.

I carry the curse of a god—Zeus's curse, to be precise.

But I'm pretty sure it's why Felix has me, in particular, up here babysitting this pet project. He could have picked any of the other architects. As project managers, we never participate in the scores. Instead, we work behind the scenes researching, planning, and executing the logistics. On rare occasions, we come out to observe, which is what I'm doing tonight. Given the added danger, Felix needed an architect who would, and I quote, *be invisible*, end quote.

My picture might as well be engraved in a stone dictionary next to that word.

With a subtle hand signal pledges know, I gesture for Chance to move forward again, giving me enough distance to be able to accurately judge his work tonight. It's a power move I know I'll pay for later, but when he grits his jaw but heads back down the hillside as he was told, I breathe easier to not have him so close.

"Excuse me." The first young pledge to return tugs on the sleeve of Chance's overcoat, then scoots by him. Even though it's summer, it's chilly enough that no one looks twice at the master thief's clothing choice, which is good. He needs lots of pockets.

I didn't even see the drop, and I was looking closely for it. Without a backward glance, the apprentice melts into the crowd, no one around us the wiser. Chance slips his hand into a pocket, then frowns. It takes fishing in two more pockets before he discovers the loot. Which means even he didn't feel the handover.

The new pledge is good. Then again, her mentor is the best of us.

For a second, I indulge in picturing what it would be like to be out there with him as one of the thieves, rather than back here keeping score. But that's not my lot in life. I've made it this far without starving, ending up in the gutters, getting myself murdered…or worse.

I do all right.

I even have my own stash of coin tucked away in a place where no one will ever find it. Cold cash, not some numbers on a screen. I'm so close to paying off my parents' debt they pledged me to work off, the sweet scent of it is a tease.

Just one or two more big scores. That's all I need. Then I'm out. No more Order.

Not even Felix knows how close I am.

You'll be even more alone, though, a tiny, doubt-laden voice whispers inside me.

I shift on my feet. *Yeah, well…maybe I'll get a cat. Or, no. A dog.*

No one can be lonely with a dog, right? Especially not in this city.

I glance toward the iconic Olympus Bridge, with its brilliant white Corinthian columns, matching the temple and supported by massive suspension lines. At midnight, they'll close the bridge to traffic and allow the people piling in to cover it. The bridge stretches from the Minos Headlands where the temple sits across the mouth of the bay to the dazzling city on the other side. The twinkling lights beckon while the bay itself is black as night, the darkness broken only by the lights of ships floating by.

Out of the corner of my eye, one of the younger apprentices waves her hand eagerly. "Hey, Boone!"

I force myself to not immediately turn and look.

Boone's is the one face I search for every day, but that's *my* business. After making a note on the tablet to talk to the girl about not drawing attention while on a job, I let myself peer around and see him off to the left.

Boone Runar.

Master thief. Every person's fantasy and every parent's nightmare. My longtime, very pathetic crush.

There's nothing I can do to stop my heart from clumsily tripping over itself at the sight of him. Especially when he grins at the apprentice, kneeling down to her level and saying something that makes her laugh before they both turn serious. He's probably reminding her about drawing attention.

I lower my tablet and take the opportunity to enjoy the view.

Well over six feet of muscle, brute strength, and a fuck-with-me-and-find-out air thanks to, again, the muscles and the recent addition of a scruffy brown beard a shade darker than his hair. Then there's the way he dresses like a biker. Lots of jeans and leather. The vibes he gives off aren't a lie, either. He can handle himself.

To look at him, you'd think he'd be a total dick twenty-four seven. Many of the pledges, like Chance, are. It's a defense mechanism. Survival tactic. But not Boone. It's the way he is with the apprentices, a patient guide, that I like the most.

After a second, he sends the apprentice on her way. When he rises to his feet, he searches the area, and my stomach tightens in anticipation. Not that he's looking for me. No doubt he's either trying to find his own apprentice, the first girl who already made her drop, or one of the other master thieves.

Despite the fact that he looks right in my direction, Boone's gaze sweeps over where I am twice before he finally locks eyes with me. Triumph lights up his features and he grins in that way that always reminds me of a cocky pirate. All he needs is the sword and the hat.

My stomach flips again.

It really needs to stop doing that.

Two nearby pledges follow his gaze. Boredom washes over their features when they discover it's me he's looking at, and they turn back to keeping an eye on the job, uninterested.

Boone points at himself, then at me, and winks. Yep. My stomach should join the circus at the rate it's tumbling. The man is a born flirt. I *know* it doesn't mean anything. And I'm probably asking for ridicule from the others later, but I can't help myself, putting on a show of looking around in wide-eyed confusion and then pointing to a random guy nearby.

Him? I mouth, eyebrows raised.

Even this far away, Boone's low chuckle wraps around me like a warm sweater.

The thing is, I probably would have gotten over him a while ago if he wasn't always so darn nice to me. The only one who bothers. Not that it means anything.

He makes his way through the throng of people, many of whom take one look and give him space to pass until he sidles up beside me. Brown eyes twinkle at me over his crooked nose, broken before I met him.

He's so close. Too close. I take a deep breath and hope my voice comes out steady. "You're not supposed to be near me. It could give us away."

He ignores my warning and crosses his arms. "Remind me why the fuck we're here."

2

IT ONLY GETS WORSE

Boone doesn't usually stop to chat with me. No one does. But then again, my curse doesn't make me hated, it just makes me inconsequential. A non-player character.

I tap on my tablet to cover my urge to fidget. "There are several reasons we're here."

He huffs a laugh. "Bad ones."

I shoot him a closer look. I've also never heard Boone question orders before, even subtly. "We'll be quick."

Sobering, he casts a grim look toward the temple. "Yeah. The quicker the better."

Then he tucks a hand in the back pocket of his jeans and leans closer without touching. None of us likes being touched—pickpocket training does that—but Boone even less than the rest.

"Felix told me you denied my request?" he asks, one eyebrow raised.

I startle, then fight to keep my expression neutral as my stomach sinks. So *that's* why he stopped to talk. I lower my voice. "That's right."

He leans back a little, like he wasn't expecting such a bold admission. Probably because I go out of my way to approve his jobs if I can.

"Why?"

I blink. Is he angry? I get that the score was a big one. Too bad, too, because that job would've put me over what I need to buy my way out.

I glance around pointedly at the crowded streets. "You know why," I say.

No criminal activity during the month-long festival of the Crucible Mysteries—an edict from the gods themselves—and it starts at midnight tonight.

Boone rubs his thumb over the thin white scar that runs from the corner of his mouth to his ear. He had that before he came here, too.

"Son of a bitch," he mutters. At the ground, not at me.

I feel his disappointment all the same. Luckily, an apprentice makes a drop, eyeing the way Boone is standing next to me as he walks away from Chance. Checking off another tick allows me to hide my own disappointment. "You should go."

He doesn't move.

"It's a bullshit rule, and you know it," he says after a second.

It is, but that won't make me change my mind. "I'm not risking you."

Wince. That sounded too personal. Hopefully he'll think I mean I'm not gambling with our best thief. And he is. The youngest ever to earn the rank of master thief.

He tries a different tack, offering a cajoling grin. "Come on. I thought you had more vision, Lyra-Loo-Hoo."

Gods, that nickname.

I can't stand the way it makes my cheeks heat and my heart pinch at the same time. He's used it since we were kids, I think because he figured out how much it bothered me that I never earned a nickname like the other pledges. All theirs having to do with luck—Felix, Boone, Chance.

Back then, he was trying to be nice, but to me, his nickname is just one more reminder that I don't *belong* anywhere.

Irritation sneaks in under my soft spot for him. "I could say no in a couple different languages if it helps."

I've been told I have zero charisma and a tendency toward sarcasm. Sunny sarcasm—I did say it *nicely*—but I don't get the impression Boone appreciates the nuance right now. I witness Chance take another drop and make note of the apprentice who needs to work on softer hands, then cringe at another snap of lightning.

"I've checked every angle at least three times," Boone says, forgetting the charm, eyes hard, suddenly the trained thief he truly is. "This is worth breaking a few rules."

My problem is sarcasm and humor are *my* defense mechanisms. It gets worse when I'm nervous, and Boone always makes me nervous. "I don't bother arguing with foolish."

"Damn it, Lyra."

I swear the people around us go quieter. Including the pledges nearby. I can practically see their ears pricking with interest.

Hades take the man. Couldn't he have waited to have this conversation somewhere more private? "Don't swear at me, Boone," I manage to say calmly.

"I didn't schedule the Mysteries. Maybe try after they end."

He makes a sound in the back of his throat, then turns away, running a frustrated hand through his hair. "My window is narrow," he says under his breath. "I can't wait for *this* foolishness to wrap up. The gods choosing a new king or queen to rule Olympus for the next century has nothing to do with me."

He must really need this score.

Just for a second, I allow my gaze to soften as I stare at the side of his face. I wish I could give in, be able to offer him what he wants.

But the gods are one of the few things criminals truly fear. And the upper bosses who run the North American network of dens have been clear that we will honor the edict or pay their penalties. I'm not planning to find out which consequence would be worse—the bosses' or the gods'.

"You know I'd help you if I could." I say this in a low voice.

"Lyra—"

"I'm busy, and you're breaking form." It comes out abrupt, and Boone's eyes widen slightly.

He runs his hand through his hair again, then shoots me a disappointed, lopsided smile. "I get it. It's your call."

Then he leaves.

I blow out a long, slow breath and watch as he makes his way back through the crowds until I can't see him.

"Holy shit…" Chance barks a laugh right in my ear.

I jump because I had no idea he'd moved closer again, let alone right next to me.

"I see it now," he says in a sly aside. "Lyra Keres, are you in love with Boone?"

His words drop between me and the rest of the pledges nearby like little bombs.

Each one exploding in my chest. Direct hits.

I've been cursed since my mother was pregnant with me and her water broke in Zeus's temple, so you'd think I'd be immune by now. But can anyone ever "get over" wanting to be loved—and incapable of being loved in return? If the pain ricocheting in my chest is any indication, the answer to that is a resounding no.

Ripples of smothered gasps and murmurs loud enough to be heard above the constant noise in this sea of people surge through the pledges, and at least two glance in our direction with wide, curious eyes.

Don't give him the satisfaction of a reaction.

Unbearably aware of our audience, I stare at the tablet in my hands, humiliation crawling over me like ants.

Damn him.

All I can think of is escape, but I can't just run. But…oh gods…I'm starting to tremble. This really needs to be over before anyone sees. Weakness will always be exploited.

Pulling my pride around me like a tattered cloak, I cock a hip and offer him my most sugary smile. "You have your entire life to be an asshole, Chance. Why not take a night off?"

A few sniggers sound from the pledges, or maybe it's from the total strangers surrounding us, and a vein pulses in his neck. I'll pay for that one later for sure. I don't care, though, and he knows it.

"Do you think he knows?" he sneers. "No wonder you always give him the best assignments. Would he want them if he knew you had a thing for him?"

"You should be farther into the crowd," I say, my jaw tight. I'm standing off to one side, slightly up the incline of the mountain, and step a foot to the left as though to get a better view.

Of course, he ignores my attempt at putting some distance between us and steps closer again. "Don't worry," he says. "I'll be sure to tell him the next time I see him. Who knows? Maybe he'll throw you a pity fuck."

It takes a lot not to curl over as I absorb that hit.

Screw it. I'm not sticking around for this.

Tucking my tablet against my chest like body armor, I walk away, knowing that, as the drop man, he can't follow.

"Nah, I don't think you could ever be anyone's pity fuck," he calls after me. "Someone would have to actually care about you enough for that to happen."

Every single part of me freezes and then goes blazing hot. Chance might as well have taken out the bow he's so proficient with and sent an arrow straight through my heart. Clean kill in one shot.

And he said that so loud. No one within a wide radius could have missed it.

Feeling the eyes of the surrounding pledges on me is like the training exercise where they lock us in a box and fill it with bugs. The idea is to desensitize the thieves for when they need to crawl through tunnels or into walls for our jobs. And as architects, well, they make us do it just so we know what we're asking our pledges to overcome. Not my favorite exercise.

I breathe through my nose, chin held high with fake confidence. Without glancing back, I throw Chance the middle finger over my shoulder and force my legs to function and carry me away.

He won't be the only one meting out punishment for this exchange later. I just broke one of the cardinal rules. Never abandon the job when pledges are still in play. Felix will be *pissed*.

But I don't care.

Head down, I keep walking, away from them, away from the crowds, and up the mountainside into the woods that surround the temple, where it's blessedly empty and quiet. The second I know I can't be seen anymore, all the starchy pride that got me here disappears and I sag against a tree, ignoring the knot that digs into my back.

No one comes to check on me.

Because Chance was right about one thing. I don't have any friends.

Worse, Boone is going to hear about this. Which means I'll have to face him every single day until my debt is paid, knowing that he *knows*.

Underworld take me now. I'd even prefer a corner of Tartarus.

I swipe away the tears that manage to escape my stranglehold and glare at the moisture on my hand. I promised myself a long time ago, after Felix yelled at me for ruining a street scam because the other apprentices locked me in a closet, that anything that happens to me as a pledge isn't worth my tears. And yet here I am...

"That's it," I mutter.

Something's got to give.

Whipping my head around, I glare at the temple sparking above the branches. Fuck Chance. Fuck this curse. And definitely fuck Zeus.

I push off the tree, the burn of anger heaping coals onto my hurt and humiliation but also filling me with a new sense of driving purpose.

One way or another, I'm putting an end to this damn curse...and I'm already in the perfect place to do it.

Time to have it out with a god.

3

THE LAST MISTAKE I'LL EVER MAKE

Raw emotions bubble inside me like a poisonous potion in a witch's cauldron. I haven't entirely decided what I'm going to do when I get to the temple. I'm either going to beg that egotistical fucking god Zeus to remove his curse, or I'm going to do something worse.

One way or the other, my problem will be solved.

And, unlike earlier, now I don't give a shit that tomorrow is the start of the Crucible Mysteries and all the "rules" that come with the cryptic festival.

We mortals know only how the Mysteries begin, how they end, and how *we* celebrate in between. They begin with each of the pantheon gods and goddesses choosing a mortal during the rites at the beginning of the festival. They end when some of the people selected return. Some don't. The ones who do make it back don't remember a thing, or maybe they're too scared to talk about it.

Either way, mortals have been throwing this festival every hundred years since what feels like the dawn of time, everyone hoping they'll be chosen by their favored god. What can I say? Humans are foolish.

Zeus is probably in his heavenly city now, busy preparing for tomorrow, but I'm having it out with him tonight.

It can't wait.

Adrenaline pumps in my veins as I hurry through the woods. The temple is already cordoned off, just in case one of the gods needs it tomorrow during the Selecting ceremony. No one knows from where across the earth each deity will choose their mortal. But I retained enough of my thief training to be able to get around the barriers.

I approach the place from the back, where I'm less likely to be seen. The arcs of lightning overhead fill the air with charged electricity, masking the sounds of my footsteps as the hairs on my arms stand on end like toy soldiers.

I should take that as a warning.

I don't.

I keep going.

Staring at the pristine columns with the walled-off inner temple rooms in the center, I try to formulate a plan. Praying and begging first would be the smart move. But now that I'm standing before the temple, alone in the dark, with my hands clenching and unclenching at my sides, every unbearable, excruciating millisecond of misery caused by Zeus's curse flashes through my head.

I'm shaking so hard with a vile concoction of anger and heartache and mortification that I rock on my feet. But the worst part of all is that, maybe for the first time ever, I admit to myself how fucking *lonely* I am.

I've never known what it's like to whisper secrets to a friend, or hold someone's hand, or have someone to just sit with. We wouldn't even have to talk.

And I just…

In a haze, almost as if I'm watching myself from the outside, I search the ground around me and grab a rock. Cocking my arm back, I go to hurl it at the nearest column.

Only, a hand clamps around my wrist mid-throw, and I'm jerked back against a broad chest. Strong arms encircle me. "I don't think so," a deep voice says in my ear.

I forget every self-defense technique drilled into me and instead thrash against my captor's hold. "Let me go!"

"I'm not going to hurt you," he says and, for some reason, I believe him. Doesn't mean I don't want to be free, though. I have shit to deal with.

"I said" — I grit out each word — "let. Me. Go."

His grip tightens. "Not if you're going to hurl rocks at the temple. I don't feel like dealing with Zeus tonight."

"Well, *I* do!" I kick out, trying to twist away.

"He's an asshole, I get it. Trust me," my captor mutters, and I can hear an edge of bitterness in his low voice. "But if I thought throwing a tantrum would change that, I'd have brought that temple down with my bare hands years ago."

Something in his tone makes me still in his arms, almost as though the two of us were both sharing the same emotion. The same anger. The feeling steals my breath, and I find myself leaning back, reveling in the moment. And for the first time in my life, I don't feel alone.

"Now, if I let you go, do you promise not to attack a defenseless building again?"

"No," I admit, and I feel a sigh rumble in his chest. So I add, "That fuckhead doesn't deserve *any* prayers."

"Careful." His voice stills. "Talk like that could have dangerous consequences."

"Why?" I ask, a surprising grin spreading across my lips when only a few seconds ago, I was ready to throw down with a god. "You worried someone might want to hit me with a bolt of lightning—while I'm in your arms?"

"More like someone might fall in love with you." His voice is soft, his breath rustling the hair against my ear.

I go stiff in his arms, my chin falling to my chest.

"Good luck with that," I mutter at the ground. "Zeus made sure no one can *ever* love me."

A gaping hole of silence greets my bitterness. My interfering do-gooder drops his arms and takes a step back, probably worried curses are contagious. I immediately miss his warmth and shove my hands in my pockets.

"What do you mean?" he demands.

I'm so desperate to escape this entire scene, the change in his tone doesn't entirely penetrate as I round on him. "Listen, I'm fine now. You can move on…"

The rest of my words wither on my lips.

If I went dead still earlier, I might as well have looked Medusa in the eyes now. The only thing about me that moves at seeing his face is the blood pumping through me so hard and fast, my ears thrum. My mind races to make sense of what my eyes are telling me.

Oh no. This can't be happening.

Suddenly, it's as if all the emotions that drove me here like a banshee with a bone to pick blow themselves out, leaving me empty.

I finally felt a smidgeon of connection with someone and it's… I mean… I *did* come up here to have it out with a god. Just not *this* one.

Even in the dark, only illuminated by constant strobes of lightning, I can see the perfection of his sculpted face—with its hard jaw, a high brow, dark eyes, and lips almost too pretty for his otherwise harsh features—as a clue of *what* he is. Only the gods and goddesses boast that kind of beauty. But it's the pale lock that curls up off his forehead into the blackness of the rest of his hair that gives him away.

Every mortal knows the story of how his brother tried to kill him once by taking an axe to his head while he slept, but only succeeded in leaving a scar that changed his hair in that one spot. Unmistakable. Not to mention unforgettable—and extremely unfortunate for me.

Tangling with *this* god is so much worse.

Run. The instinct finally punches through me, urging me to make my legs move. But there's no point. The instinct to freeze in place is stronger.

"I'm afraid one of us shouldn't be here," I quip.

My tendency to say out loud every thought that pops into my head strikes again at the worst possible moment.

Not helping, Lyra.

I'm also not entirely wrong. What is *he* doing at this particular temple?

He says nothing, standing eerily still with his arms crossed, taking me in the same way I did him, only with a tension that fills the air with more electricity than Zeus's lightning.

I know what he sees—a slip of a woman with short raven hair, a smallish face, pointed chin, and catlike eyes. My one vanity. They are deep green with a darker outer ring and gold at the center, fringed by long black lashes. Maybe if I bat them at him? Except beguiling is also not in my list of skills, so I nix that thought.

He's still staring.

There's an intensity to him that sets me more on edge with every passing second, every part of me prickling.

Silence fills the gaps between us for so long that I reconsider running as an option.

"Do you know who I am?" he finally asks. His deep voice would be smooth except for the harsh growl at the bottom of it. Like a silky, still lake broken by ripples from something under the surface.

Is he serious with that question, though? *Everyone* knows who he is. "Should I?"

Holy hells, stop popping off, Lyra.

The god's eyes narrow slightly at my flippant response. Face taking on a hard cast, he takes two slow, long strides directly into my space. "Do you *know* who I am?"

Everything inside me shrivels like my body already knows I'm dead anyway and is just getting a head start. Fear has a taste I'm more than familiar with—metallic in the mouth, like blood. Or maybe I just bit my tongue.

The gods have punished mortals for much less than what I've done and said so far tonight.

My entire body quivers. *Merciful gods.*

"Hades." I swallow. "You are Hades."

The God of Death and King of the Underworld himself.

And he does not look happy.